TO BE A
NAVVY MAN

Building Victoria's Railways

Janet Goldfinch

DEDICATION

To those who slip beneath the
notice of history.

CONTENTS

ACKNOWLEDGMENTS

The book stems from scraps of family stories half-remembered, but intriguing enough to make me want to discover any truth behind the tales.

Once on the trail and unravelling the background, I owe a debt of gratitude to many genealogical websites, principally *ancestry.co.uk* and *findmypast.co.uk,* the latter incorporating a newspaper archive offering contemporary accounts of accidents, grand openings, board meetings, coach timetables etc. I am grateful to *genuki.org.uk* for its library of reference information, to *gro.gov.uk* and *nationalarchives.gov.uk* for their many resources. Among a multitude of books on Victorian life I would single out *The Railway Navvies*, Terry Coleman, Hutchinson, 1965; and *Thomas Brassey Railway Builder &Canada Works Birkenhead*, John Millar, John Millar (UK),1993. Information on the building of lines comes from the many web-sites set up by railway enthusiasts. My 'expertise' on tunnel-building derives largely from a splendid video at forgottenrelics.co.uk/tunnelvision. My use of Victorian Shropshire dialect comes from *archive.org/ details/ shropshirewordbook*, Georgina Frederica Jackson, Trübner and Co., 1879.

The major characters, John and his family, the much-honoured contractor Thomas Brassey, the engineer James Beatty, all existed. The minor ones, such as Scarface and Erc, exist only in my imagination.

The title of the book comes from a song *The Bold Navvy Man*, the first found mention of which comes in the book *Children of the Dead End*, Patrick McGill 1914, attributed by him to navvy Two-Shift Mulholland, though I have taken the liberty of supposing its creation to be earlier and added the odd verse of my own: I hope their shades will forgive me. My grateful thanks to Two-Shift and to all those nameless ones who die unsung. Any errors are my own.

Lines worked on by John Kirby 1846–1854

Crimea 1855

To Be a Navvy Man

1

Leaving Home

The boy loped along the street, with every so often a skip
or a twirl, kicking a stone as he went. His leather boots
were heavy on his feet, his father's old pair, the heels
recently mended. They were too big, so that his mother
had layered the inside soles with strong, brown card and
stuffed crumpled paper into the toes. The toes were
protected with curved, iron clinkers.

He kicked the stone again, raising sparks: a man's
boots and he was a man now, free at last from the stupid,
boring classroom where Owd Crow kept order with his
supple cane.

Not that he'd been made to go to school every single
day, with the pennies being short if his father was between
jobs. And sometimes he'd been needed to contribute to the
family coffers himself, bird-scaring or stone-picking on
local farms. He'd had enough, too much, of school: he
could write his name and more if he'd ever need to. And
he could read, if he'd ever need to do that either: a
broadsheet or a newspaper maybe.

The stone rolled into the road and under a passing
brewer's dray. He broke into a run. Work there was now
in plenty. Work on the best, the most modern thing of all,
the thing of the future, the railway. He began to sing:

'I've done it like a navvy, a bold navvy man,
A bold navvy man,
An old navvy man,

1

And I've done my graft and stuck it like a bold navvy man.'

He would go the long way round, see if he could sight his father. He walked through the town heading for the neck of land that bound the town to the body of England. It was a narrow neck, the only piece not looped by the River Severn that had been in olden times the town's defence against the marauding Welsh.

They were a little Welsh though, in Shrewsbury. You could tell from the names: Edward Evans, for instance, his own half-brother. Lots of Evans, there were in Shrewsbury. The same mother they had, he and Edward, but not the same father. He liked Edward, always up for an adventure but steady with it. Edward was already working with their father, must be six, seven years.

Tomorrow he'd join them, and his grandfather too. Still working was Grandad, a tall, strong, wiry man as they all were, but old now, getting on sixty. Sixty was a long way off. He felt pleased that it was such a long way ahead: years and years and years. He wanted most to be twelve. Come November and he would be. In the meantime there would be wages.

He came to the neck where the rails would one day run straight across like a collar. For now the only signs were markings-out with rope and wooden pegs. Some houses had been pulled down. There would be a stopping-place here before long, a station they were called, where the iron horse would puff and pant while it waited for its passengers or goods.

He looked north along the marked-out trail but no men were visible. He hadn't really expected that they would be. They'd be far up the line somewhere on the way towards Chester, an important place, thirty-five miles away. That was where the whole line was going to, his father had told him. Part of that line at the top end was already being built, coming near to completion. Another line was nearly finished too, joining it from the Welsh side, carrying coal and iron and bricks. It would soon be much quicker and easier to get all these things to other places in the country where they were needed.

There were canals of course - he'd been born in Canal Buildings, by the side of the Shropshire and Newport. Very useful they were too, but steam engines were so much faster than the horse-drawn barges, or so they said. How did they work, steam engines? He didn't know, though maybe he would one day. He'd never even seen one yet, though many were the tales. He would see lots when they'd built the line, he and Edward and his father and grandfather. And some other men of course. Maybe he'd see an engine tomorrow. Tomorrow he had to follow where the line was to be, going north until he met the gangs of navvies working there. His father had sent word last month by his grandfather that that was what he was to do and that he'd look out for him.

He cast one more glance into the distance but no-one was in sight. He'd better be getting off home. He needed to find and cut a stick to carry his possessions up the line. He needed to get all ready for an early start.

He followed the path along by the river, crossing by the English Bridge into the Foregate. The Abbey church, built of red sandstone, glowed in the late afternoon light. The colour was like that of the bricks that were his family's trade, though the sandstone blocks were larger. His younger brother and his three sisters had all been christened in that place, the baby, Mary, only last year, 1845. It was a huge place inside, echoing and cold. None of them went there very often: Christmas and Easter and the Harvest Thanksgiving. That last would be the next one coming up. His mother would take the younger ones; and the rest of them might go if they weren't working away from home. They'd said at school that the church was near a thousand years old and had been even more enormous once, much more than a church, a proper Abbey where monks lived, monks in long, black robes who prayed a great deal besides working in the fields to provide for themselves. They'd looked after the sick of Shrewsbury too and grown the herbs to cure people; and some of them, the ones who liked writing and painting, had written books on long rolls of parchment, animal skin. A king called Henry, the one who had had a lot of wives, had sent his men to take all the Abbey treasure and pull the place down - you could see the ragged ends of walls - and get rid of the monks. He wondered where they'd all gone to.

Would his little brother William miss him, he wondered, after he'd left tomorrow? He was never very well, William, and his mother worried about him. He didn't like it when his mother worried.

He came to his own house, black and white like many another in the town, but much smaller and more simple than most. Some houses rose tall and the black timbers were set in elaborate patterns and there were often intricate carvings in beam or wall. He rather liked those; but brick houses were better to live in, the sort his family had been building before the railway came along to offer better wages. Brick houses didn't catch fire easily and they could be built, for rich people anyway, with modern conveniences like water that came straight into the house. His father had worked on the brick-built Canal Buildings where they'd lived when he was born, across the river and in the next parish. That's where he'd been christened, not at the Abbey, but at the parish church of St. Mary; and on Christmas Day too, or so he'd been told, Christmas Day 1834: he couldn't remember living anywhere but the house they lived in now.

He opened the door and called, 'Mam?'

She was bending over the fire, stirring something in a kettle. 'Boilin' the pudding so a'll keep. Tell your Dad all 'e mun do is 'ot it up again and see it be 'ot all through. Should last a while, a's big as I could get in this 'ere pan. Now get them bits an' pieces together. And remember thee'll be carryin' 'em and it's a fair stretch, so dunna tek anythink thee'll not need. The blanket thee'll have to roll up tomorrow when thee gets up.'

' 'Ow's our William?'

'Worser.'

'Canna thee get the doctor?'

'Doctors cost money.'

'I'll get it for thee. Wait till I gi'es thee me wages.'

'There's a good lad. We s'll see. Esther, come 'elp wi' the tea.

His sister, the child below William, went over to the bucket, ladled out water into the kettle they kept for the purpose, hung it on the hook that swung out from the fire and pushed it back into position over the flames.

The smallest of them, little Mary, pulled herself upright by a stool before tottering towards a chair. Halfway, she plumped to the floor, her eyes widening in surprise, mouth opening to vent a yell of protest. Anne, the sister named after their mother, who was watching, helped her up, making soothing noises.

John went over to his brother lying in the corner, wrapped up in a blanket. He looked flushed and sweaty. John laid a hand on his forehead.

' 'E's got the fever again, Mam. Shall I give 'im a drop of anythink?'

'A spoonful. It's in that there jug.'

John poured a careful spoonful, raised his brother's head and the lad sipped it. It was his mother's special and most expensive remedy, used sparingly, made from currants, stoned raisins, tamarind and lemon peel, all boiled down, one of the recipes of the great John Wesley. It tasted better than his mother's usual Wesley remedy, the juice of ground ivy; and was more comforting than being

5

put into a bath of cold water.

At sunrise the following day John eased himself out of his bed, trying not to disturb his brother and sisters. He carefully pulled away his blanket, picked up his clothes and descended the wooden stairs to the living room. Early as he was, his mother was there before him, a hunk of bread and dripping on the table, water boiling over the fire and again and again the steam forcing the lid up before it dropped with a small plop. He tried to relate it to a giant steam engine, but failed.

He put a spare shirt and breeches, some oddments and his nightshirt into the centre of his blanket, along with a big cheese, a hunk of bacon and the boiled pudding wrapped in its cloth. Then he tied the ends to the stick.

'Eat now,' his mother said. And he did.

'Tek care now, John Kirby,' said his mother. 'God keep.' And she put her arms around him in an unaccustomed hug, then thrust a few Shrewsbury Cakes into his hand. 'To eat along the way,' she said. And then he was stuffing them into a sock which he pushed with its partner into the front of his jacket, slinging the stick with its unwieldy bundle over his shoulder and was off, out of the door, down the Foregate and away, following the wooden pegs that marked the future line.

The sun was above the horizon. The small signs that marked the way rolled out before him through the fields. A hidden robin announced its presence by a thin, high note, a herd of cows moved slowly in a line towards a nearby farmhouse to be milked. This was the life. No work with beasts or plough for him.

As he strode through the dewy grass, leaving dark footprints behind him, he whistled his navvy song, with a fanciful and vivid feeling that he was on the crest of a wave of time, whistling his way into an unknown future that was unrolling moment by moment to reveal itself to him.

Course, he wasn't quite a navvy: brickies were one step above your ordinary navvy. Navvies were fierce, rough men who'd built the canals and seemingly never gone home. If they had a home. They came from all over, Edward had said. Some from Ireland even, where home was a bog and they ate potatoes and not much else. They came across the sea to get any work they could. And some of them were finding work on the railways. He wondered whether he'd understand what they were saying, if they spoke in a foreign tongue, what they'd look like even. Could you tell if someone was an Irishman just by looking at them? Or a Scotsman?

When the sun got to its highest point, he began to look out for water and soon came upon a small stream that crossed his path. It was clear as it ran over the pebbles and he found a small patch of cropped grass that went down to the water, knelt down, cupped his hands and drank. Then he pulled out the sock of Shrewsbury Cakes and nibbled one. It was crisp and brittle. His mother must have baked these yesterday. Were his brother and sisters at home eating cakes, or were these made especially for him? He had an odd feeling in his chest and his eyes would almost have watered if he hadn't brushed them vigorously with his sleeve. Time to move on.

His bundle didn't feel as light as it had when he had begun his journey. His shoulder was sore where the stick had rested; he changed its position to the other side. And his boots were not as comfortable on his feet. He tramped on until the pain of stiff leather rubbing on flesh became acute. Then he sat down, took off his boots and socks, looked at the blisters on his heels, one of which had already burst to rawness and took out his second pair of socks, nibbling at another cake before transferring the rest to a pocket. But the air was cool on his feet and they felt light and free after the constriction of the boots. He wriggled his toes and waited until his heels stung a little less. Then he looked at the sun: early afternoon he judged. He'd best get there before dark, but there was plenty of time before that. He stretched out against a bank of cropped turf and fell asleep.

When he woke he saw that the sun had moved much further to the west. He waggled his feet experimentally, finding them less painful. So he put on both pairs of socks, hoping the boots would not flop so much, and stood up. He nibbled another cake to keep his spirits up. He'd walked long distances before of course. If you didn't have a horse, you walked. But he'd never walked this far. Twenty-five miles or thereabouts, they'd said. Should be six hours give or take, depending.

Six hours since he started, it certainly was by now, he thought. But he wouldn't walk as fast as Edward, say, who was much taller than he was. He'd struggle to keep up with Edward, especially if he was in a hurry. It would be good when he saw some navvies. So far he'd seen nobody but farm labourers spreading manure or little boys scaring crows in distant fields.

On he went, his legs wearying and his feet ablaze, slowing his steps. And then he saw them. Diggers first, with picks, gnawing and gouging the earth before them. Others with shovels, moving the loosened earth and stones into wheelbarrows, yet others hauling the wheelbarrows up and away to the sides of the track to empty them, a long serpent of raw earth stretching into the far distance. Every one of the workers was smeared and clotted with brown, from beard to boots.

'Boy!' the shout came from a man pacing the edge of the track. He was clean, dressed much like the other men in hat - though his was a topper - neckerchief, breeches and waistcoat, but clean.

John limped over, as fast as his blisters would allow.

The man did not smile. 'What's your name, boy?'

'John, sir, John Kirby sir.'

'Your father's back up the line, mebbe a mile. Get to it.'

'Yes sir.'

He was nearly there.

'And get off the track! Walk the top!'

'Yes sir. Sorry sir.' John scrambled through and across the earth of the track and climbed the mound of soil and stones at the edge in the direction the man pointed. He was on clean grass once more. He scraped his boots, even heavier now, clogged with the earth into which his feet had sunk.

A mile later he spotted his father and then his grandfather and then Edward. They were working as a team, one with pick, one with shovel and one with wheelbarrow. His father waved and John went over. His father was wielding the pick, deepening and levelling the track. 'Sit down boy. Keep out o' the way. We goes on till dark.'

John sat. John lay back and watched the sky. And fell asleep.

Someone shook him. 'Come on lad. Time to go 'ome.' The shift had finished. The sun had gone below the horizon. Men were cleaning up their tools, setting off, singing some of them. John followed his father. His grandfather joined them and then Edward. He could tell their weariness.

They walked by the track, away from the worst of the mud, until they came in sight of a sprawl of huts. He supposed they were huts, barely the height of a man, built all of planks with a plank roof. Inside the one that was theirs was a floor of beaten earth and four large sacks which nearly covered the space, stuffed with something which might have been straw or heather but which turned out to be bracken. Across the room was a rope on which several garments hung. Two tea-chests, one on top of the other, served as a cupboard.

A voice hailed them from outside, 'John?'

He looked up but it was his father who went to the doorway. 'The lad's brought cheese an' bacon an' a puddin'. Do the puddin' tomorrow an' we'll 'ave some then. What yo got for us now?'

The woman handed in a pot which steamed a little, four tin plates and four spoons. The pot was put onto an upturned barrel doing duty as a table. Food was spooned out. Meat there was, beef, more than John had ever seen at one meal, potatoes too and plenty of broth. John mashed his potatoes into it, clumsily, with the back of his spoon. His grandfather made slurping noises as he sucked it in.

' 'Er's Big Nell,' he said, nodding towards the doorway. 'Looks after us, she does.'

'Oh,' said John, in lieu of all the questions which came half to mind.

' 'Er man died,' said Edward. It did not seem to John that this explained things.

In a while the woman returned, collecting up the spoons and dishes. She was tall and shawled, with brawny arms and long, straggled hair. She wore men's leather boots.

'Goin' to mek the introductions, then?' she asked.

Edward said, 'This 'ere's John, me little brother.'

'John, eh? Another John? Well, John and 'ow goes it? Any use for a woman yet?' She grabbed his upper arm and felt the muscles. 'A fair way to go by 'eck, I'm a-thinkin'.' She laughed, a great guffaw and the others joined in. She put down a huge jug of beer on the plank. 'Get to it lads. An' yo, Nipper.'

2

Man's Work

The next morning dawned cloudy, though by the time they'd made a brew, outside over a small fire of sticks inside the circle of blackened stones, the sun was breaking through. While the others were sipping at the scalding liquid, Edward had cleaned off a shovel and rested it over the fire, melted a lump of fat, grated onto it several raw potatoes, stirred into the mixture some flour and kept it propped over the blaze until the potato softened when he scrambled in a couple of eggs.

'Ave a floddy,' Edward invited him, pushing a steaming hunk onto his tin plate. Each then sprinkled onto his portion salt from the tea-chest cupboard.

In the near future this was to be his job, John had been told, at breakfast both food and the brew. More tea-making would also be his lot. He would take the old tin with the wire handle down to where the men were working, hunt for kindling, light the fire, put the tin, half full of water, on to boil. Then he would collect from those who wanted a drink a screw of tea and sugar and empty it into the tin, which was called a drum; and what he would be doing was called 'drumming up'.

He would do this at the breaks. In between times he would begin to handle a pick, a shovel and a wheelbarrow. Last night he'd managed to ask Edward why they were labouring like this and not bricking. Edward had said that they would be bricking as soon as the opportunity came, which wouldn't be too long, but that in the meantime they were earning on the work available.

Had he seen the aqueduct? Edward had asked. 'No, yo wunna,' he said, answering himself. 'It's o'er there, towards Chester.' He pointed.

John picked out the top of a stone bridge on great stone stilts that crossed the valley to the north. A barge was sailing along it, high up in the air.

'Steam engines canna climb slopes,' said Edward. 'Rails, they mun be laid on the flat. To get the line o'er the valley, o'er the river, we mun build another bridge. If a's for a railway, a's called a viaduct. We'm agoin' to build the viaduct.'

'Out o' bricks?'

'Bricks an' stone, both.'

The aqueduct towered. Was it possible that he and Edward and his father and grandfather could build something like that, all by themselves?

Edward laughed. 'There'll be many to help besides,' he said. 'All the plans bin done. A man name o' Robertson, a Scotsman, an engineer, 'e's drawn 'em up. We get extra money, we brickies, 'cause we got the skill.'

John had had fat plastered onto his heels. They were sore, but better than yesterday. He hoped there'd not be too much walking.

They let him try out the pick. It was heavy in his hands. He attempted to gouge out a lump of soil but the pick head dropped into the ground and fell slowly sideways.

'Like this,' said his grandfather. 'That stone there. Stand back from 'er. See? Mind thee feet! Left 'and there on the shaft, right 'and further up. Like this. Yo do un.'

John took the pick and held it as directed.

'Feet apart. Bit more. That's it. 'Owd tight to the pick. Look at the stone as yo'm goin' for. Now, heft up that there pick and back o'er your shoulder. That's it. Now throw the weight o' the pick 'ead agen that stone. Arms right out straight as the 'ead goes down. Keep tight 'owd! That's it.

Now then, 'eft it up a bit to loose it out the soil. Give it 'ere. Watch.'

His grandfather began to swing the pick in an easy rhythm, over and over. John watched. He had a few goes and began to feel the right way of it. He'd have another go later. In the meantime he was provided with a shovel. When the wheelbarrow had been piled high he tried to move it, but he could barely lift the rear off the ground to wheel it more than a yard or two.

'It'll come,' Edward said, while some of the men looked over and laughed. John felt foolish and went back to shovelling.

'Thee'll not do thy twenty tons a day!' shouted the man they called Tweedle Beak, the one with the outsize nose.

How many shovelfuls was twenty tons? Suppose he picked up, what? Five pounds of earth on his shovel? Or would it be ten? Say ten, for easiness. How many pounds in a ton? In his head, Owd Crow with his chalk and his cane came to the rescue: 'Two thousand two hundred and forty, boy. Two thousand two hundred and forty, 2240. Write it one hundred times.'

So two hundred and twenty-four shovelfuls would make one ton. Twenty tons would be ... four thousand, four hundred and eighty shovelfuls. If he really was picking up ten pounds on each shovel. It seemed a mighty piece of work to have to do. He began to count each shovelful and very pleased he was when the ganger called time and Tweedle Beak shouted for a drumming up.

He put down his shovel and headed for a patch of woodland, realising as he went that he'd left this part of the operation far too late. It took him quite a while to collect enough dry tinder to start the fire and he cursed the others for not having warned him.

Other gatherers had been there before him, too, and fallen branches were more scarce than they should be. He would have to give more time to this aspect of his job. A sudden fear of mantraps beset him as he foraged in the undergrowth, though strictly speaking the law forbade them these days. Could take off a hand could a mantrap. Or a foot.

When he returned men were sitting around, munching cheese and onions and hunks of bread. They were drinking already, he was thankful to see, from their tea bottles, cold tea maybe, or more probably beer, but at least something. A ragged cheer arose as he set the sticks for a fire and he realised he'd been set up. He felt foolish.

'Let it be for now,' his father ordered, grinning nevertheless. 'Noon-spell we'll be needin' the 'ot stuff. 'Ave a lommack thyself.' He broke off a chunk of bread and handed it over, with a piece of the cheese and an onion. John gobbled, hoping to get something inside him: there was a sight more food here than he'd have eaten at home.

A whistle blew without his having done justice to and the men ambled back to their tasks. The agent walked by and activity sharpened up.

'Look lively, Nipper! You there!' he shouted. John tried to speed up his shovelling and missed the waiting barrow. Chagrin filled him.

' 'E'll learn, boss,' yelled Chester Red, a giant of a man with hair like a ginger tom cat, his face blotched with pale brown freckles.

'Better learn fast,' growled the agent. 'No room for shirkers.'

'Not to worry, Nipper,' John was told later. 'If we finish the job afore time, 'e gets more pay, the agent. If we runs behind, 'e loses money. So he drives us, see, Mr Tom. But 'e knows 'o's a shirker and 'o's new to the job. 'E's mostly fair, more or less.'

'An' yo knows what that's along on?' That was his grandfather. ' 'E's got Mr Brassey to answer to.'

There was a chorus of growling agreement. 'They say

14

'e'll be a-comin' to see the job, Mr Brassey, wi' Mr Robertson, the engineer, in a day or two. Bin in France, 'e 'as. They built a viaduct there, but it fell down.'

There was a general laugh, punctuated with ribald comments about weak and half-wit Frenchies and what they were incapable of doing and what would stand up and what would not. 'Rebuilt it at 'is own expense, Mr Brassey did, they say. There's not many as'd do that. Earlier this year, that bin. Expect 'e'll wanna see this un goes right. Lime bin the trouble, they said. Lime in the mortar. French lime o' course. Weren't right. An Mr Brassey, 'e'd told 'em it weren't right an' they wunna listen.'

'My dad fought the Frogs at Waterloo. Lost a leg, 'e did. Why Mr Brassey be wantin' ter 'elp them Frogs, only the devil knows,' one man said, the one called Punch, in his odd, drawling voice.

'British navvies 'e took with 'im, though, 'e did. An' yo know what? Mr Brassey roasted an ox and gave the 'ole lot a dinner after a bin all done! Six 'undred of 'em! An' them there Frogs bin so frit they'n 'ad a ring o' their cavalry right around the field where they bin eatin' their dinner. Thought as all them British navvies'd attack 'em.'

His grandfather stuffed tobacco carefully into his pipe and tamped it down with a whittled stick he took from his shirt pocket. It was a clay pipe, an outsize one. He looked around for a light. Edward passed over a wisp of stick, lit from his own gum-bucket. Grandad put the light to his tobacco and drew, nodding his thanks.

They were back by their cabin, if that was not too dignified a name. Big Nell had come again with food: his mother's pudding this time, one of her best: suet crust stuffed with meat, onions and potatoes. John felt suddenly protective of the pudding: it was his mother's, not Big Nell's. He thought of saying so aloud, but then looked around at the eaters and decided against it.

He roused himself to eat and felt some strength returning to him; he'd never eaten so well. He was given a tin mug of beer too, though his father told him sharply, 'Yo'll work tomorrow, badly or no. The ganger'll see to that. Or yo'll be out. And we mun 'ave as many bodies on our team as we can get. So that's your lot.'

Replete with food and mellowed by beer, they began to reminisce. They were outside, round the fire and men had drifted over to join them. Some brought firewood as an offering, others beer.

The accents were strange. Some were his native Shrewsbury or at least Shropshire. Others John could barely understand. Some of the navvies spoke little English at all, being Welshmen, for this line ran in and out of the border between England and Wales.

'Dost mind Limping Will, Big Nell's man?' someone asked.

'Eh, Ah does that. An' a fine man an' all. 'Cept 'e 'ad 'alf a foot.'

'Axe, it were, fellin' a tree, I were told. Afore my time. Only the one foot, though.'

'They say that's why 'e didna get out way quick enough when that wagon rolled down on 'im.'

'Smashed to pieces 'e were. Big Nell got left all on 'er own then. Wi' nowt an' no-one.'

'She'm all right, doin' all right though, with 'er cookin' an' that. An' 'er other bits, o' course.' There was a general laugh. ' 'O's payin' the rent this week, then?' There was a general turn of heads towards John's father.

'Little pitchers got big ears,' John heard. The talk turned to other things and he fell asleep.

Days passed in a blur of aching weariness. At times John felt as if he could never lift another shovelful, though he forced himself to do so. Occasionally he collapsed and lay inert from sheer fatigue until a few minutes rest and a kick or two restored him.

His father who, as the strongest, tended to take whichever part of the current job required the most effort, had by this time taken over the barrowing. They were cutting through a rise in the land so that the muck dug out by pick had to be shovelled into barrows which then had to be wheeled up the sloping sides to the top and dumped. As they cut further into the hill so that the sides rose higher above, planks had been laid up the sides of the cutting and his father had to walk up the steep slope of them while pushing his barrow. He was helped by a rope which, John saw, was attached both to the barrow and to his father's belt. The rope at the top was attached to a pulley; and the pulley was driven by a horse which walked in circles. John watched, as best he could while still shovelling, as his father wheeled the loaded barrow to the bottom of the incline. His father linked himself and his barrow to the rope and shouted to the horse driver at the top: the horse driver shouted back. The rope tightened, to on the muddy planks, trying to steady the loaded barrow in take the weight. His father began to push, his feet slipping front of him. Little by little the load rose up the slope until it reached the top. The barrow was emptied of its muck. His father turned round, the barrow behind him this time. The rope stayed taut as he walked down the planks again, trying not to skid on its greasy surface, being held from falling by the rope.

'It's fine when yo'n a good, steady gin-'orse,' someone told John, seeing him watching. 'If the 'orse slips or frolics or stumbles like, what do the man do then? 'E gets off them planks, fast as 'e can. 'Im one side, barrow t'other. If'n the barrow wi' all that muck in 'er falls on 'im, 'e's a goner see, like as not. Or 'e breaks a leg, what's as good as bein' a goner anyhow. Yo mun see some o' the slopes! Like mountains, they bin! 'E'll be a mighty strong man as can run a barrow up a slope like that.'

John felt a swelling of pride. His father, his own father, he knew, would be equal to that. And be not just a man, but a man among men.

As the line cut further into the hill the men were moving earth from the higher level to create the V-shape at an angle just shallow enough not to be prey to landslip. Temporary rails were being laid along the narrow gullet at the bottom of the V, just wide enough to accommodate the approaching train of empty wagons, four-wheeled, wooden wagons, pulled by horses. They came to a halt below the shovelling men. Whereupon the men shovelled the muck down into the waiting trucks. John wondered what they'd do with it.

A week later it rained in the night. The morning fire was slow to light and that was only possible because John, warned by Edward, had taken a bundle of kindling into the relative dryness of the hut. Even there, the rain had dripped onto him through the plank roof. He was still in his same clothes, the ones he had arrived in. It didn't seem worth putting on a nightshirt; and none of the others did.

The track, when they reached it, was a ribbon of slither and slide. Puddles lay in hollows, boots felt twice as heavy, shovelling was twice as weighty, the shaft of the tool slippery in his bare hands. He was pleased he was wearing breeches: a few men were wearing the newer, more fashionable trousers fastened with yorks below the knees in hope of holding the bottoms out of the mud, but they soon got splashed, sodden and mud-heavy and looked disagreeably uncomfortable.

A fire was out of the question, unless he could find some shelter for it. Otherwise cold tea from breakfast would be the order of the day: or beer. He trotted off, to see what he could scavenge.

He had slung an old flour sack over his shoulders to

help keep out the rain. It was heavy, didn't cover him very well and kept slipping off as he moved: he needed something to keep it together at the neck. He looked around to see what others were wearing. His father and Edward had flour sacks like himself, pinned together with a piece of wire. His grandfather, though, had a tattered, blackish-coloured coat, balding in places, of small, leathery pieces sewn together like patchwork.

'What's a made of, your coat?' he called, as they came close.

'This? This bin moles, lad. Skins o' moles. Mouldiwarps keeps dry along o' their skins. An' I'm dry too. Pretty well, leastways.'

'Where does a come from, then?'

'Come from my faither. Mun be 'undreds o' skins there. 'Ow 'e got it, I dunna know. 'Appen 'e bought the skins off a mole-catcher, an' your great-grandma Susanna stitched 'em together. Wore it all of 'is life, 'e did. Keeps the rain off a bit, anyhow. If yo wanna see as what all the gaffers is wearing nowadays though, 'ave a look at Tweedle Beak when we breaks for bait. Dunna thee go too near 'im though.' He laughed.

They had been moved to a different section of line. Here the digging, the dug-out scar with its temporary rails, was approaching the valley where the viaduct would go across, parallel to the aqueduct. Eventually ballast would be laid on the levelled base, then heavy wooden sleepers crosswise to the track, then the metal rails, riveted to the sleepers. That would make the permanent way. There would be two tracks, one for up-line, one for down-line traffic. The ballast, small chunks of stone, would be quarried from the vicinity: there was said to be material in plenty. John wished it could come by iron horse, so that he could see one at last. But there was little hope of that as yet. The canal, which here came so close, would likely be used for transporting materials, particularly those required for the viaduct.

Before the valley of the Ceiriog was reached, though, there was a concavity, a depression, in the ground. To make the line flat this would have to be filled. John watched as a line of loaded trucks came along the temporary rails, pulled by horses It stopped about fifty yards short of the depression. He realised then that the muck was probably coming from the cutting where they had been working before, or one like it, surplus muck that had been shovelled there into empty wagons.

Meanwhile a great baulk of wood had been lugged into place across the line just where the ground began to decline. He saw that the first wagon in the train was being uncoupled. Then a horse was led to the front of the lone wagon and hitched to it, though it stayed on the path that ran alongside. Its keeper, Gypsy Joe, clicked his tongue and the horse began to walk, then trot, then canter with the man now running by its side. Suddenly, the horse was unhitched, it and Gypsy Joe leaping aside. The wagon's momentum carried it on. Crashing into the baulk of timber it tipped forward, its load spilling ahead. Another man and his horse joined the empty wagon to a train of empty wagons waiting to return to the cutting to be filled again. Men with shovels removed any great heights from the spilled pile of muck to even it out; and the line had moved on a yard or so. Another full wagon was uncoupled from the waiting train, Gypsy Joe and his horse performed their ritual; and slowly the line unfurled.

There was a viaduct further up the line towards Chester, John had been told, in the Vale of Llangollen, where the River Dee ran. That had been started already, that April. It seemed to be becoming known generally as the Dee Viaduct: theirs, on their bit of the line, people were already calling the Chirk Viaduct, because it was near the village of Chirk John supposed, though the valley was the Ceiriog and so was the stream. It was a useful stream, providing clear, clean water for both men and horses. Punch, the man from Suffolk, had slipped out one dusk and got himself a couple of trout.

'He'd best take care,' John's grandfather had said. 'Poachin', that bin called. Doubt the Maister at the Castle'd take a kindly view of un. Strangers thereabouts aren't welcome. Mr Robertson even, when 'e bin surveyin' the line, 'e 'ad to go out by night, and sneak about in the dark, the Squire were so disobligin' and werrited 'im so. An' Mr Robertson were there *legal*. 'E mun be a magistrate, the Squire, all them sorts o' grand folk bin magistrates, an' God 'elp owd Punch if they catches 'im. 'Ard labour I'll be bound, an' a lot of it.'

John had seen the Castle: a fortress, squat, rectangular and grey, with rounded towers; and windows, some mullioned, others more menacing, mere slits. It crouched on an outcrop overseeing the distant meeting of the rivers Ceiriog and Dee. It bore no resemblance to the hut they now lived in, nor even to the cottage back in Shrewsbury. The man who owned that must be a man of power and best not get on his wrong side. Still, everyone did a bit of poaching given the chance: and why did God give the Squire all that and John's own family almost nothing? A man like that could surely spare a fish or two. He supposed it was God's will and he'd better not grumble. God, as Owd Crow had been fond of pointing out, had in His unquestionable wisdom put himself, Owd Crow, in total authority over dunces like John. That piece of pondering too gave him some disquiet: would he go to Hell for such thoughts, for daring to doubt that God knew best? Some might tell him so, but he felt rise in himself a stubborn resistance to thinking it true.

Hell was where criminals went. He could still feel, creeping through his bones and over his skin, the day, four years ago, when he and his father had walked along the Foregate towards the Castle and the gaol, just by where the station was soon to be built. A good day, a happy day, it seemed, and the crowds all laughing and joking. His father had hoisted him onto his shoulders so that he could see better; and he didn't really understand what he was going to see when the man on the platform new-built above the massive doors had a hood put over his head while the chaplain, all flowing in black, read sonorous words. Then a rope was put round the man's neck and noises came out of the muffle of the hood and the man struggled to get away and then he dropped and swung and his legs kicked and the mob roared and bayed and whistled in a euphoria of excitement. The man kicked for a long time before he went still.

'That there's what comes to bad uns,' his father said. 'And then they burns in 'Ell for ever an' ever. Yo be good now. Think on.'

His mother hadn't wanted him to go with his father that day, she'd pleaded for him not to go, but he'd been desperate to be taken, an expedition, just himself and his Dad, leaving his Mam and little sisters and William behind. He would remember all right.

He scouted the sides of the line for bits of cast-away rubbish. A piece of corrugated iron caught his eye, and he picked it up. If he could prop it above the flames ... There was another piece, a bit rusty but usable ... He could prop them together ... A piece of wire: that would do to pin his sack together round his shoulders.

On his way back and looking for anything small, dryish and combustible, he passed Tweedle Beak and recalled his grandfather saying something about how he kept the rain off. He looked. Tweedle Beak seemed, today at any rate, to be wearing a fairly ordinary-looking flour sack.

'Thought yo had a special sort o' coat, Mister,' he said. ' 'Gainst the rain.'

'And who told ye that, Nipper?' asked Tweedle Beak.

'It bin me Grandad.'

'Well, tell yer Grandad as I'll sell it 'im fer twenty shillin'. Special price fer an owd friend.' He guffawed.

John shrugged and went back to try out his shelter. He propped the two pieces together, brought the bundle of precious dry kindling out of the front of his coat, surrounded it with the driest of his twigs and lit a lucifer. Then he gently blew.

'Coming on at that, Nipper,' said a man, pushing past with his barrow. In a while the pan went over the flames. 'Drummin' up!' he shouted, and went round the men within earshot to collect their screws of tea and sugar.

Tweedle Beak came over as the first tea bottles were being drunk. Men rubbed their hands and held them in front of the flames.

'Grandad, forgot to tell 'ee. The Mister there says 'e'll sell you 'is special coat for twenty shillin'.'

'An where is it?' His grandfather held up his nose and sniffed the air. 'Reckon that there coat be o'er that way.' He pointed. The crowd all laughed.

Edward told him later. Tweedle Beak had been given, yes, *given*, a coat by a gentleman. It would protect him from the rain poor fellow, the gentleman had said. It was a new invention. Tweedle Beak said he should have known then that something wasn't right. But he thanked the man heartily and the next time he was wielding his pick in the rain he put it on. Lovely it was to be dry, even if the coat was a bit on the heavy side. But as he worked he noticed two things. First was, it kept the rain out alright but it kept the sweat in and plenty of it. Second thing was, water began to somehow trickle its way in through the stitching. Third thing was, the warmer they got, he and the coat, the more it smelt. It stank. It stank to high heaven.

And that night no-one wanted it in the hut either.

'Allus look a gift-'orse in the mouth,' said Tweedle Beak.

3

A Throng of Days

John was losing count of time. Had he been here a fortnight, a month, more? He couldn't remember: the days were becoming a blur. There were other boys, he'd caught sight of them, some younger than himself, but he'd not had time for more than the odd word to any as yet. The demands made on him were forever expanding, his days filled with carrying picks to the blacksmith for sharpening, greasing the axles and wheel-hubs of wagons, the drumming up and the breakfasts, shovelling. He hoped it was strengthening his body as they told him; but it was weary work: he was so tired at night that he barely gulped down his beef and potatoes before he fell asleep. One night Big Nell had brought chicken; and when he looked surprised he was told to ask no questions and be told no lies. He'd woken up once or twice in the night over the course of the days and noticed an empty bed where his father should have been: he asked no questions there either.

Visitors had come one morning at seven, an hour or so after the ganger had blown his whistle and shouted, 'Blow-up, blow-up!' as he always did to get them down to the line with pick and shovel at the ready.

They were well into their usual rhythms when out of the background on the far side of the valley appeared two figures, with others in attendance, revealing themselves as they drew nearer to be two well-built men with the air of authority. They were looking at the river-bed where the coffer dams had been constructed while the bed was prepared for the building of the piers to support the proposed viaduct: the area within the coffer dams had been pumped dry and the sand excavated. There was much talking and gesturing and scribbling on paper and glancing towards the nearby aqueduct whose own piers rose from that sandy bed.

After a long while, it seemed, the men left the river and climbed the near valley side to inspect the state of the line towards Shrewsbury. As they passed by, John got a close look at the two men.

One, the somewhat younger, had short hair under his hat and a face clean shaven save that from its underbelly, its underchin, sprouted a spreading and splendid mantle of beard, half covering his chest. His features were regular, his mouth firm and his keen eyes held a dreaminess, an aspiration, within.

The other man, older and in middle age, was clean-shaven entirely, with short, curly brown hair which looked as if, even though every morning restrictions were imposed upon it by a rigorous hairbrush, it were determined to escape and fly askew, corkscrewing into freedom. His features were rugged, overloading his face, with eyes wide-set under heavy brows; and his whole face had a cast of humour in it, as if he found life good-naturedly agreeable.

John noticed how the workmen they passed all doffed their caps and hats, headgear of every decrepit and battered description. That was usual as regarded the courtesy given to gentlemen, but there were ways and ways of doffing a hat. These doffings were almost all of respect.

The older man stopped by one of the working men. They spoke, the worker breaking into a smile and nodding. A hand was proffered from the gent, seized by the navvy, shaken vigorously and the gentlemen resumed their tour.

The two men stopped to look at the camp. A few words there, the agent nodding; and they passed on.

That evening he learned more. The man with the vast beard, it was confirmed, was Mr Henry Robertson the engineer. The other was the great Mr Thomas Brassey who had already built railways in Britain and France. Tales were told of working for Contractor Brassey on the Penkridge Viaduct on the Grand Junction, only the third railway ever to be built, the first being the Stockton and Darlington whose passenger carriages were at first pulled by horses until they decided on steam instead. Other stories there were about the conquering of wild Shap Fell on the Lancaster and Carlisle, while icy winds keened around bothies made of turf and heather. The navvy whose hand Mr Brassey had shaken told, several times, how Mr Brassey had remembered him from the Grand Junction, and had asked after him and his old mate Jack. 'Think on. A man like him rememberin' a man like me,' he kept repeating.

Mr Brassey had seen their camp. Mr Brassey had instructed the agent that at the extreme of the camp, away from the river valley, a trench should be dug with a superstructure of wooden privies above. Materials would be provided by the Company. Volunteers to construct this were to be asked for at no reduction in wages. Moreover, living conditions would be improved. Bricks were to be provided at Company expense for the foundations of huts and planking provided for flooring to raise huts out of the mud. Workers would build their own accommodation in their own time.

There was a grand toast to Mr Brassey. Followed by several more. And then a further few. John crawled into the hut and fell asleep on his sack as the tales became ever more scurrilous and the oaths more fearsome and the laughter ever more raucous.

On the following day he learned that he'd been volunteered to help with the building of the privies. The ganger indicated the area that had been decided upon, at the back of the camp, away from the shanties and walked off. John and another boy followed him to where lay piles of bricks and timber. Their job was to barrow or carry these to the bricklayers and carpenters and be on hand to help them as needed.

The other boy was also called Nipper, John noted. He appeared to be resident in the bender at the edge of the camp, inhabited by Gypsy Joe and his family. The bender had been pointed out to him before and was a larger structure than most of the shacks that the rest of the workforce were living in, about twenty feet long and half as wide. A man could easily stand up under the roof, which was made of some fabric, perhaps lengths of sailcloth, draped over a rounded framework. You could see the framework was of bent branches, holding up the sailcloth like ribs under the skin of the starving. At the moment, smoke was curling upwards through a hole in the roof about half way down its length. It looked spacious and homely in spite of the ribs, John thought, much more inviting than his own, slipshod cabin. There came a squealing and a small tangle-haired girl ran out, pursued round the bender by a somewhat bigger version of herself.

Two of the carpenters knew the gypsy lad. 'Surprised thee's not looking after the 'osses wi' thy Dad,' one said. 'Magic wi' them 'osses 'e is. Can mek 'em do anythink.'

'If there's one thing a Gypsy does know about, it's 'osses. 'An your Dad knows more'n most.'

Nipper's face moved not a muscle. He gave a brief nod and went to fetch more planks.

'Don't give much away, that lot,' said Chester Red, his

face scarlet with the effort of wielding the pick. They were now four feet down and still digging. Edward, who had also volunteered, was shovelling the last of the loosened earth over a slope some feet beyond the trench. John had begun to fetch bricks with the aid of a wheelbarrow. It was a job that made his legs and arms ache more with each trip along to the line and back.

'What bin these 'ere bricks for?' he asked.

'We mun 'ave a foundation. Summat for the plankin' to sit on. An' a mun sit above the ground so as floodwater canna get in an' fill up the trench.' That was Edward. 'An' stop pitherin' about, young John, an' get us another load o' them there bricks. Jakes dunna build theirselves.'

They worked all day. By the time they heard the distant voice of the ganger calling 'Yo-ho,' they still hadn't finished the job. But now there was a long timber framework standing on a brick foundation, its sides already boarded in, its roof covered with overlapping boards that projected beyond the front. 'An' the roof mun slope to the back so as the rain runs off that way,' one of the carpenters told them.

Inside ran a long raised box with a hole cut every three feet or so. 'An' walls between 'em so as each 'ole's your own un,' the carpenter had explained, which had alleviated a misgiving within John. Not having to find a place within wet bushes to squat, which might well have been found before by someone else, or even several others, he appreciated: but the idea of having to squat in a long line of other people, even maybe women like Big Nell, a woman devoid of any female modesty, who seized every opportunity to laugh at him, had been making him somewhat apprehensive.

'Lids o'er them 'oles, on 'inges,' added Edward, judiciously, standing back to assess the project. 'An' doors to the front,' he went on, looking at the blank spaces. 'Then a'll be a right nunty piece o' work.'

The ganger announced that the coming Saturday would be pay day.

'An' about time, too,' growled his grandfather. It was nearly six weeks since the men had last been paid and many were living on credit: John's father was one of them. A man, when he ran out of money, could ask the ganger for a sub and be given a ticket for, say, the value of his labour on that day. The ticket could be exchanged for food or drink at the contractor's shop. When he was eventually paid, the amount he'd had in the form of tickets was deducted from his pay.

John thought that sounded fair enough. 'And,' said his grandfather, 'so it would be if the food were al'ays good food an' the beer were al'ays good beer an' the prices were fair an' the weight was the true one. But that's all rare as hens' teeth. An' the ticket's on'y good for the tommy shop. A man canna use it anywhere else an' 'e mun take what 'e's gi'en, or go clemmed. Some bosses pays yo only in tickets. 'Ere it bin none too bad 'cause the contractor's a fair man an' we gets paid mostly in money an' the prices are high but none too out o' the way. Best not get into debt though. My Mary, er'll a summat to say if I sends 'er no money an' 'er's got a sharp tongue on 'er.'

It had been decided that John should walk back to Shrewsbury after the wages had been paid. The reason given was to take money to his mother and grandmother, though he sensed that his men-folk were keen to get him out of the way. He was warned in strong terms to speak of the money to no-one for fear of robbery; and he would carry as ostensible reason for his journey any clothing to be washed, though in fact Big Nell was doing the bulk of it. He knew now, sadly, that he'd be getting no wages this pay day: his work was not yet worth a wage. And drumming-up earned him no money. His labour just made the lives of the others easier so that they could complete the work the ganger required of them and earn full wages, out of which he was given food and beer.

Saturday arrived. John crawled out of the hut in the morning to find a scene of transformation. He stared. Men whose hair and beards had been wild and lush the day before were trimmed, even clean-shaven; and were trimming in their turn the hair and beards of other men. Men were kneeling by the river, washing bare chests, a few of the hardier splashing naked. Here and there someone had managed to warm a pail-full of water. Mudless clothes had appeared as if by magic: velveteen jackets, plush waistcoats of scarlet or blue or yellow, neckerchiefs to match or contrast, trousers of soft moleskin, which were not made up of dozens of skins like his grandfather's waistcoat but from a fabric with something of the same colour and softness. Tweedle Beak had mother-of-pearl buttons down the front of his scarlet waistcoat. Some men had cleaned the mud from their boots, others had best boots, special-occasion boots.

They were to receive their wages at the Inn in Chirk village and eager men were already on their way. John had no fancy clothes, but managed a shirt that was cleaner than the one he had first put on and wiped his boots on a clump of grass. That would have to do. He ran to catch up with the other three who had started off. Chirk he was anxious to see. It was odd to have no work to do, to just be walking into a village on a sunny day.

He looked around him as they walked. It was a daunting landscape for a railway builder: everywhere he gazed the land rose high and fell deep. He imagined tunnels and viaducts, embankments and cuttings in every direction. It was a green landscape and a fertile-seeming one for farming and he, seeing the Castle and some substantial houses, thought the place rich and rural. To catch sight of a spoil tip, a mine-head, surprised him, and over there were the rows of small, unkempt cottages where the men who toiled underground must live. Some of the navvies lodged in the village and, he thought, probably in those cottages, the householders eager for any addition to their incomes, even from the dreaded navvies: he was aware by now that his kind were far from welcomed by all and that outsiders lumped bricklayers along with the rest.

There was a wharf too, next to the canal: he'd already noticed barges laden with coal sailing across the aqueduct and the mine here was where they must come from.

The crowd of navvies was making for the centre of the village, where stood a handsome inn, *The Hand*, three-storey, built in brick, sash-windowed: a coaching inn too as the activity outside its portal displayed. Passengers were boarding in something of a hurry and the coachman flicked his whip just as the navvy vanguard crossed the forecourt to send off the departing passengers with a ragged cheer.

Not into the inn itself, but round the back they went, into a room where pay tables were set out. He had pieced together that Owd S'ewsb'ry, S'ewsb'ry and Young S'ewsb'ry, as his family was commonly called, were at present three of a butty gang of twelve, a system Mr Brassey favoured. Together, sometime in the preceding weeks, they had struck a bargain to complete an aspect of the line for a certain price: this would be equally divided between the dozen of them. John watched as arguing went on between the parties, words threatening to become blows. Eventually things were settled though he could see that his father was disgruntled as he took stock of the money in his hand.

' Nothin' there, good as,' he growled. 'Them blasted

tickets.'

' 'Appen a bit less o' the beer, son,' said his grandfather. 'An' Big Nell dunna come cheap. Nor that rainbow stuff yo'm wearin'.' He nodded disparagingly towards his son's canary-yellow waistcoat and scarlet neckerchief.

'An' I mun 'ave summat from yo an' Edward for the tommy we eats, what I pays Nell for.' His father was angry: John sensed a menace. He felt nervous.

' 'Owd thy crakin', lad. Dunna bist so knaggy. Now, we mun buy a pint or two afore they runs out.' His grandfather was ingratiating. His father's mood mellowed at the mention of drink.

A couple of barmen were serving from a hatch in the wall. Men were lining up and coming away with tots of whisky. John was bought half a pint of beer. His grandfather beckoned and they went outside to a secluded corner, away from the throng. 'Yo tek this to give to your Gran. In that pouch we gi'ed thee. An' remember, dunna say nothink to nobody.'

'What about me Mam?'

'I s'll do me best wi' your Dad, son, but dunna thee 'owd thy breath. Edward'll give 'ee a good bit shouldn't wonder. Stay 'ere awilde I 'an a word.'

He went back inside. John looked expectantly at the doorway and then, when he didn't reappear, up and down the village street. He could see the church, a stone building with a squat tower. There were a few buildings in black and white, similar to those he knew in Shrewsbury. Other buildings were brick. The ring of a hammer on metal drew his eyes to spot a forge in the distance. The street was quiet. On a Saturday more people should have been about. And they wouldn't be in the church, not on a Saturday. He wondered where they'd all gone. A shoemaker's shop across the way was shuttered. He found a low wall and sat, glad to be doing nothing, dreaming of the scarlet waistcoat he would have one day.

Or should he drive an engine? That would be something: he imagined himself in charge of something huge and strong, a person of immense importance. He'd have to find out how you got to drive an engine.

After a while he went back to the inn and peered through the doorway. His grandfather was dancing across the floor, whisky in hand. He looked around for his father and saw him at a table with his arm around Big Nell, who was holding forth in exaggerated manner to a tableful of peacock men. As he watched, she emptied a part-drunk tumbler of beer over one of them. Yells and curses erupted and he retreated.

After an endless while of waiting, Edward came out of the doorway, somewhat unsteadily, and gazed around. John went over to meet him.

'Tek this, our John. Afore I spends it all. Give un to our Mam.' He thrust some coins towards his brother.

'What about our Dad?'

' Yo'll not get nothin' from 'im.'

Reluctantly John moved off in the direction of the line. He went into the shack and picked up the bundle that had been put together, slung it over his shoulder and set off.

It was different, walking this way. The views were different and he had not the excitement in him that he had had on the outward journey. But he was anxious to see his mother again. And William. And even the girls.

It was dark by the time he reached the little house in the Foregate. He lifted the latch and went in, calling, 'It bin me, John,' as he went. They were all there, sitting candle-less near a very small fire. The girls jumped up and came to hug him, all three together, asking questions all at the same time. He disentangled their clutching hands and picked them up, one after the other and swung them round. His mother, after a gasp and exclamations of pleased surprise, bustled about, finding a hunk of bread and a very small piece of cheese. These she put on the table with a mug of her own ale.

John sat and ate: it was a very meagre meal compared to those he'd been having. He noticed his mother's hands as she served him. They were sore-red and dry and the skin was cracked across the knuckles. The room, he registered as he looked about him, was festooned with clothing not their own. His mother saw him looking: 'I'm tekkin' in washing. Meks a bit extra like.'

John fumbled in the pouch around his waist, extracting the smaller of the two cloth-wrapped bundles of coins. He put it on the table. His mother undid it and fell quiet. 'That bin all?' she said after a moment or two. John thought with shame of the much heavier bundle intended for his grandmother. He nodded. 'Edward's. I dinna get no wages,' he said. 'Not this month. 'Appen next. Yo sha'n a all on it, Mam,' he went on in a rush, 'When I gets it.'

'I'd 'oped to mebbe buy a mangle,' his mother said. 'Or at any rate put by for one. This'll not even feed us.'

It was strange, sleeping in his old bed with William: but it was good too, comforting. William seemed a bit more lively than when he'd left, though he coughed often, a dry, rasping sound.

Breakfast was a mug of almost colourless tea and a piece of bread. John noticed that his sisters got given even less than he did: his mother said that she was not hungry.

After breakfast she went back to the tub. She must have started long before the rest of them were up. It was a wooden tub like a half-barrel and hooped with metal. Linen had been soaking since the night before. As he watched, she turned a tap at the base of the tub, collecting the grimy water that ran out into a large metal pan which she emptied outside. Then she flaked slivers from a block of brown soap into the tub, pouring on warm water heating in another kettle over the fire. 'There's one good thing,' she said, 'Soap. My Mam 'ad to use ashes and fat and mek 'er own. 'Ard times then.'

'Got to tek Gran the wages,' said John. 'Come on, Will.'

As Esther, the eldest of the sisters, stepped into the tub and began to tread, the two boys stepped into the street and turned left along the Foregate. He felt light, a surge of joy rose in him: no work. They stopped by the start of the English Bridge and pitched stones into the water, trying to throw the farthest. They skipped across it, avoiding carts and carriages and peered into the windows of shops grand and small, before, half way up Pride Hill, they reached their grandparents' house, small and half-timbered and much like their own.

They waited for their welcome. Their grandmother's face cracked into smiles: two grandsons come to visit, moreover the sons of her precious only son. They went inside and John passed over the bundle of coins from his grandfather. Without counting she put them into the drawer, the drawer of a Welsh dresser of ancient black oak.

' 'Ow's your Dad, then?' she asked. John looked at her. There was a semblance of someone ... Big Nell? She was brawny and raw-boned, much more of a mangling woman than his slight mother.

'Gran,' he said, ' 'Ow much do a mangle cost?'

She guffawed. 'What would thee be wanting wi' a mangle, lad? A pick, or a shovel, aye; but mangles is woman's work.'

'For me Mam.'

'Ah, well, let's see. There bin mangles an' mangles. Cheapest sort, eight pund. Best sort, all mahogany an' brass, fifteen pund.'

John was trying to work it out in his head. The men were earning about five and twenty shillings a week, Edward less. Eight weeks then to buy even a cheap mangle, if you could make yourself live on the meagre bit you kept back for yourself. But that was on men's wages. It could be years before he earned that much. If they all helped, though ... He resolved to try persuasion. And maybe you could buy a mangle second-hand.

I've sumatt for thee, young John,' his grandmother was ferreting through a cupboard. ' 'Ere.' She held out a thick flannel shirt of a greyish colour. 'A bin your Dad's a power o' years ago but 'e grew out on it. There bin life in it yet.'

John inspected it: it was thick and would be warm. 'Thanks, Gran. Thank yo kindly. That bin grand.' William stroked the fabric.

'I turned the collar an' the cuffs.' She had her back to them, putting tea in the pot.

'It bin grand,' he repeated. 'Gran?'

'Yes?'

'That doctor, the big un ... Is 'e still mindin' people?'

'Dr Darwin? 'E's a tidy big un alright! Biggest man as ever I set eyes on! Upwards an' outwards. No, craitchy 'e be, they say, nowadays. Dwindered. Dunna do much doctorin' no more. Still lives in that big 'ouse o'er the river. Come 'ere once to see your Dad, that time 'e bin so poorly. Towd me 'e dinna want no money, God bless. Brought 'is son wi' 'im, Mr Charles. It were just afore Mr Charles went off to Edinburgh to be a doctor hissen, that summer 'e bin 'elpin' his faither, just left the School. Only a couple o' year older than your Dad, was Mr Charles. 'E went off somewhere, sailed round the world, they say. Away five year. But 'e never come back to live 'ere in S'ewsb'ry. An' 'e gied up the doctorin'.'

'I thought mebbe the Doctor could 'elp William. 'E's got a despert bad 'ask on 'im nights.' He didn't like to mention the blood that came with the cough; not in front of his brother.

'Well, 'e's better now, is William. Dunna thee werrit so. Now, drink up thy tea ... an' there's a bite o' summat for thee. An' I wants yo to gi'e this to your Dad.' She held out a small parcel. 'Rinder's Roughcut. Two ounces. Best there be. Four shillin' an' tuppence the pound.'

The boys left after a while. 'Sha'n we look for chumps for Mam?' said William. And they found a hefty branch lying by a ditch and carried it home in triumph, one at each end.

4

Pulling No Punches

John had been told to return on the Tuesday. On the way up the line, now becoming familiar, thoughts drifted in and out, half-formed.

When he had told his mother about the tobacco for his Dad, she had sniffed. 'Spoils 'im, 'er does. Al'ays 'as, al'ays will. Nine children an' four gone to the grave already and your Dad 'er only boy left.'

She paused, flat-iron in the air. 'An' two o' the rest no better than they should be.' John knew that that meant his Aunt Elizabeth, who had produced a small Elizabeth without the benefit of a husband; and his Aunt Rachel, a 'flighty wench', according to his mother, who needed to 'watch out'.

He spotted a useful stick and swished it through the grass, whipping off the heads of some oxeye daisies growing in his path. He hadn't mentioned Big Nell at all, not even to William.

He felt clean: it was a good feeling. He was wearing the shirt his grandmother had given him; and he had had a bath in the wooden tub, fetching the water from the rain barrel, heating it over the fire and sharing it one by one with the rest of them. He had gone last, as by far the dirtiest; and by that time the water was half cold again.

He was hungry: the food at home was meagre and he had got used to huge portions of meat and bread and potatoes. His mother had eaten almost nothing and seemed to live mostly on tea and the leaves used more than once at that: he wondered how she could. This time she had given him no provisions to take back to the line. He savoured in his thoughts the meal he would eat tonight.

He thought about the miles he had to travel and wished he could have afforded the coach. From Shrewsbury to Chirk the coach took only about three hours instead of the seven or so it would take him to walk the distance. But it cost 4s.6d. That was outside of course. The price nearly doubled if you sat inside and out of the weather. He'd asked Edward and his father and grandfather how fast a steam engine would go. None of them knew exactly, but Chester Red had said that a lot of them now went at twenty miles an hour! And the latest were reaching twice that speed! Engineers were dreaming of fifty miles an hour, or even sixty!

'Yer'd not be able to breathe, goin' that fast,' one of the men said, with authority.

'Yo might melt, wi' the friction o' the air,' put in another, 'Or likely yo'd shake to pieces.'

John thought that if he could board a train at Shrewsbury, going at sixty miles an hour, he'd be in Chirk at ... He worked it out ... In about twenty, twenty-five, minutes. If he survived the dangers, that is.

He thought of Mr Charles who had gone all round the world in a sailing ship. He'd been told about elephants and lions and things at school: it would be good to go to distant lands and see these things. He thought of Owd Crow reading them a few pieces from the newspaper about an expedition which had set off the previous year to explore the ice-bound north, to attempt to make its way through a Northwest Passage over the top of the American continent, a passage which might or might not exist. The names of the ships had appealed to him, *Erebus* and *Terror*, and after a moment or two he recalled the name of the leader, Sir John Franklin. There would be a proper map of those far-off lands one day, Owd Crow had promised, pointing out the unmarked areas at the top of his globe. John had heard nothing more and wondered where they were now. He supposed no-one had picked up any of the two hundred tin canisters Owd Crow had told them were carried by each ship, to throw overboard with details of their whereabouts and discoveries, so that people back home might learn of their progress. He supposed, with a certain wistfulness, that he might never now know. Perhaps school had not been as all-out bad as he had thought it at the time.

When he finally arrived at the camp, he found their hut as he'd left it: no-one had improved it in any way at all. His grandfather was asleep and snoring inside, his father was nowhere to be seen; and Edward was sitting on the grass outside with a tea-bottle full of beer in his hand. Food was absent.

They'd had a good randy, Edward said. After *The Hand* ran out of whisky and beer, or said they had; and after a few of the men hadn't believed this and had smashed the place up a bit - nothing too bad though - they'd gone, some to the *Bridge Inn* towards Chirk Bank, and some over to Chirk Green. When they'd drunk those dry they'd roamed further afield. They'd got a lot of black looks and the constables had been called out. But there were only a handful of them. Only fifty in the whole county, someone had said. Course the gaffer at the Castle was Lord Lieutenant of the County and his brother was a big army man, so it didn't pay to be too unruly: the militia could easily be summoned. Not that they were up to much, but they did have muskets. All in all they'd had a good few days: a man couldn't slave every day of his life.

There was a new excitement to come, though. Gypsy Joe had insulted another man, a man who went by the name of Fighting Jack. Insults hurled back had turned to fisticuffs which had become a general brawl as others took sides, until the parties at last had been overcome by exhaustion with only minor cuts and bruises to show. Next pay day, there was to be a proper prize fight to settle the matter.

The following morning drizzled from dull grey cloud. Men woke reluctantly and drifted down to the line. Some stayed in their huts nursing hangovers: they would not get paid and they could lose their jobs. John was relieved to see his three men all up and ready, if somewhat bedraggled. There was breakfast too, courtesy of Big Nell who appeared with potatoes and, surprisingly, trout. No-one asked, but they all ate: there had been no supper the night before. John, by this time, was ravenous and golloped down as much as he could grab.

Work was about to start on the building of Chirk station. His grandfather and Edward were already part of the force that would do the construction. John, they and the ganger agreed, could help as dogsbody. He would earn a third as much as the others. John accepted: there seemed little choice. At least he would be earning, though mangles, never mind coach rides, receded. His father had worked himself into a butty gang that would be raising the viaduct: he seemed to be relishing the danger and the glory.

John worked those first days as hard as ever in his life. It was of stone, this building, and there were masons as well as bricklayers at work. Already the ground had been levelled, the structure had been marked out from the plans and foundations had been dug by the pick and shovel brigade. John was still drumming up, which job did give him a rest of sorts, though in itself it paid nothing.

He was carrying bucketfuls of sand, lime - the local, Chirk Castle, commercial lime - and water to supply the men who were using their shovels to toss them together on boards. All had to be mixed together in certain proportions in a certain way. John took notice: you never knew when knowledge might come in handy.

As the building began to rise from the ground, so did the viaduct, in a way that was much more grand. Its central span of ten stone arches at intervals of forty-five feet, the stonework faces finely dressed by the masons, was beginning to take shape. Scaffolding would soon become necessary. ' 'Undred foot above the river she'll be, in the middle,' said his father. 'An' three more wooden arches at each end,' he went on. 'Why wood, I dunno. Wunna last as long, but 'appen it's quicker. Or cheaper.'

The weeks passed. There was a buzz of anticipation in the air: the coming prize fight. A few men had set themselves up as bookmakers, taking bets on the likely winner. ' 'O's to know?' said S'ewsb'ry, dismissively, when his father, ever cautious, said it was 'agin the law.'

Fighting Jack had a reputation. 'Used to spar wi' Ben Caunt,' John's father told him with awe. Then, seeing a lack of comprehension in his son's eyes, he added impatiently, 'Ben Caunt, as mighty a boxer as ever lived. Got beat, though, last year, by that there Bendigo. An' a despert soor job on a fight it bin too. Three an' ninety rounds. Jest think o' that. An' Bendigo ... one foul after t'other. But so many despert bad chaps wi' 'im as the ref was afeared for 'is life. Gi'ed Bendigo the match. 'Ad to. An' a downright shame too.'

Fighting Jack was tall and rangy. 'Bit like Caunt,' said his father, the connoisseur. 'Long reach, long-raught. Good solid muscle on 'im too.'

Gypsy Joe was shorter, but broader of shoulder. Folk said he'd come off worst in the scrap and the odds were building up in favour of his opponent. John's father favoured Fighting Jack and had placed his bet.

When Big Nell didn't appear one evening, John was

sent to 'see what the owd sprout's up to.'

'Tell 'er to look sharp!' his father shouted to his back as he left.

He walked over to the edge of the camp where Big Nell's shack stood. It was of the more primitive sort, mostly built of turves, though with an overhanging roof of planks covered in sailcloth and weighted down by stones. He peered in through the doorway. Nell was in the far corner presiding over a cauldron perched on a makeshift iron grid over a fire. The fire was small and smoky, most of it escaping through a short chimney above, the rest hanging below the roof. She turned, alerted by the blocking-out of the light as John stood in the doorway. A burst of swearing escaped her, becoming more good-natured as she saw who he was.

'Come in, Nipper. Damp sticks, consarnit. '

He moved over to see, curiosity overcoming trepidation. Across the cauldron lay a further stick, to which were tied several pieces of string. She pulled one up and at its end came a bag with a savoury smell to it. She felt the inside. 'Seems done, that. Better tek it, son.'

'What bin in t'others?'

'Them? That un's Chester's, that's Knobby's, that's Black Bob's. 'An I gets the broth. An' a bit o' the rest.' She winked, jerking a much smaller bag from the depths.

' 'Ow dun 'ee know one from t'other?'

'Ah well, see them notches?' She showed the main stick which was notched in series. 'Yer Dad's al'ays goes on the one notch, Chester's on the twosome, like that.'

He cast an eye round the cabin while she undid the string and put the food into a big tin bowl with a large dollop of broth. The cabin was unexpectedly warm. And it was quite neat: no haphazard litter as in his own hut. The floor was the same beaten earth: few camp residents had yet availed themselves of the offered flooring. A wooden bunk bed stood against a wall. An upturned barrel did duty as a table. A 'dresser' of rough planks stood against another. He saw, on the top shelf, gleaming in the dim light, a small, white, china cow.

A rumour circulated in the camp. Men who had bet on Gypsy Joe looked downcast. Some hedged their bets. Those who had backed Fighting Jack were cheerful. Gypsy Joe, it was said, had stepped awkwardly, stumbled, twisted a leg. A faint air of anxiety hung about him, and he walked, surely, with the slightest of limps. Someone saw him wince as he restrained a horse. He was watched.

A purse had already been collected, pennies and tanners produced from pockets. Fighting Jack insisted the fight must take place: Gypsy Joe shrugged. The brining of faces and especially the hands went on. 'Brine from a barrel o' pickled pork, as a starter,' his father explained, before muttering about secrets of the ring. 'Meks the skin tough. Tough as pigskin,' he added, impressed with his own wit.

The viaduct was rising. John saw his father perched small as a fly on the scaffolding. A man fell and broke an arm. 'I mun go 'ome,' he said, picking himself up; and started off for Shrewsbury. 'The Firmary'll tek 'im,' the ganger said.

His grandfather's face swelled on one side. He grew grumpy and short of temper and cut up his meat into very small pieces. One of the men had a small book of medical remedies. One evening he brought it round and passed it to John who read from it haltingly: "A cure for the toothache. - An eminent apothecary, in the vicinity of the metropolis, has lately recommended, as an effectual cure for the toothache, the following remedy, which he has been in the habit of using for many years, and out of the number of cases eight tenths have succeeded, viz.- to take three table-spoonsful of brandy, adding to it one drachm of camphor, with thirty or forty drops of laudanum, and then dropping a little on some lint, and apply it to the tooth affected, keeping the lint moistened for five minutes only to the tooth and gum."

The nearest apothecary for camphor and laudanum was in Shrewsbury, so that his grandfather decided to try the brandy alone. To swill it around and swallow it, he ruminated, might prevent waste and be equally effective; and though he became temporarily more cheerful, it failed to properly dispel the pain. He might, he thought, return to Shrewsbury in search of apothecary or dentist the following pay-day: though that would mean missing the fight. Then he heard from someone who had heard in his turn that one of the navvies was willing to pull teeth for a shilling or two and Owd S'ewsb'ry decided to trust to that, though at a later date maybe, in the future when the pain might become too bad to be borne. The man, Smithy, had once been a blacksmith and had kept with him a pair of pinchers.

Pay day arrived. A flat piece of sward had been chosen, and eight stakes knocked into the ground, ropes between them, to form the ring. Men went over to *The Hand* to get their pay and drifted back after a drink or two, carrying jugs of beer, bottles of whisky and the like. The contestants wore knee breeches and had stripped to the waist. The only other clothing was a neckerchief, each of a different colour. Each man had a second who carried a sponge and a bottle of water.

The seconds tossed. Fighting Jack won. He squinted towards the sun in a professional sort of way, put up a wetted finger to assess the wind; and picked his corner, his opponent taking the one opposite. Each contestant then ceremonially tied his neckerchief to the stake which marked his place.

Each second chose an umpire who between them

agreed on a referee: Chester Red. 'But 'e dunna know nothin' about boxing!' said John. 'Do 'e?'

'Well, 'e says 'e does,' said Edward.

'Look in 'is drawers!' The shout went up. The seconds duly examined both, then bent to examine shoes.

'What bin that for?' wondered John.

'Case they got summat as they shunna,' said Edward.

'Like what?'

'Spikes on the shoes.'

'In them there drawers.'

Edward shrugged. 'Dunno,' he said.

In the centre of the ring a groove had been scratched through the turf. Boxers and seconds came up to the scratch and solemnly shook hands over it. The seconds returned to their corners and the first round began.

Having watched Gypsy Joe during these proceedings, John had spotted the slight limp. The limp continued while the two opponents danced around, each sizing the other up. A sudden punch was parried; another punch hit only air.

Shouts of encouragement came from the watchers. ' 'It 'im on the smeller!' 'Tek 'is ears off!' 'Knock 'is peepers out!' The first blood came from Gypsy Joe's nose; and encouraged the crowd to frenzy. Blood was what they were after, blood and courage in the face of pain. But it was a slow round and disappointing in its lack of violence. It ended after sixteen minutes with a win for Fighting Jack and, as most had bet on Fighting Jack, there was felt some satisfaction.

The second round began and all of a sudden Joe was a whirl of fists. A blow caught Fighting Jack on the cheek on one side and then the other. Blood dripped from a split in a lip. Fists pummelled his ribs. Joe danced around his opponent, lissom as an eel, weaving through punches which, in spite of Jack's longer arms, never seemed to connect. Then Joe hurled himself at Fighting Jack and they crashed to the ground with Joe on top.

There came a few cries of 'Foul!' but the umpire gave Joe the round.

Thirty seconds later, Fighting Jack was back on his feet and the slaughter began again. Gypsy Joe was a lightning mover. Gone was the limp. The crowd, with their bets on Jack, shouted him on; but tall and rangy and muscular as he undoubtedly was, Fighting Jack began to seem the lesser man. Gypsy Joe pinned him against the ropes and rained blows into his large body.

The ninth round began and Jack was weakening, tiring, his moves slowing, his punches more wild and desperate. In spite of the pickling and hardening, blood ran from a cut above his eye, lips and cheeks were swollen. When his ribs were hit again and again he winced in pain. In desperation he hit out with all his remaining power. His fist contacted; but it landed, not on the face, but on the suddenly-lowered skull of his rival and it grew obvious to the watchers that the knuckles of that right hand had been shattered. Then he was moving more slowly, lumbering round the ring. Gamely, to rallying cheers, he fought on, using his left hand only, his right cradled to him. Another blow landed on Gypsy Joe's abruptly lowered skull and it seemed that Jack's left wrist was broken. He was wrestled to the floor with a crash. Blood flowed from his mouth and he lay quite still. The thirty seconds were counted and he did not rise. 'Time!' called the umpire. Fighting Jack failed to get to his feet. A further eight seconds ensued during which he struggled feebly but failed to come up to the scratch. Gypsy Joe, dripping far less blood, had won.

His second came to his side. Joe held up both arms in a gesture of triumph; though his face showed little expression. The crowd, most of whom had lost their money, growled. The growling grew louder.

'E's done that afore,' shouted a man near John.

'If we'd a known, we'd a bet different,' shouted another.

Gypsy Joe shrugged. Several men, sporting pick-handles, not particularly evident before as a group, moved in and escorted him from the ring. He had a slight limp.

John's father was in a fury. He'd bet two pounds on Fighting Jack and lost. 'Your Mam'll 'a to go short,' he growled at John.

John had some money in the pouch hidden at his waist. Edward's contribution was there along with his own; and his grandfather's was there separately. Keeping out of sight of his father he made his way to where one of the bookies stood. The queue was short. He produced a scrap of paper and the bookie counted out ten shillings. John had bet, just a little at long odds, on Gypsy Joe. And for no better reason than having worked on the privies with his taciturn son. With that and the wages he'd earned, his mother might fare a little better.

He set off on the long walk home to Shrewsbury.

It was harvest time. Reapers walked the length of fields leaving, behind their rhythmically curving scythes, neat swathes of fallen corn. In some fields stooks were already standing like cones and drying in the sun. The life of the labourers looked good on a day like this.

When he told his mother later she made a noise of derision. 'Looks good, mebbe, on a sunny day. But them wages is about what yo'm gettin'. An' that bin for a full-grown man, an' 'im wi' a missis an' childern mebbe. An' the cottage goes wi' the job. No job, no cottage.'

'Why did me Dad go on the line? Why couldna 'e stay brickin' in S'ewsb'ry? An' me Grandad an all.'

''Cause the work wunna there. Times be 'ard, lad. A man mun tek 'is chance where'er 'e can. An' the railways, they pays good money. Railways a-comin' all o'er these days. Mad, mind, folks wantin' to go faster an' faster. No good'll come on it. Yo mark my words.'

John returned to the line on the Tuesday, still snugly wrapped in the virtue of his gift to his mother and basking in her gratitude. What met him on arrival was an atmosphere of disgruntlement; and anger.

'Sloped, 'e did,' said Edward. 'All on 'em. Sloped.'

The place where the bender had been was an oblong of bare earth with a few discarded bits of rubbish around it.

They had left on that first night, it seemed, when most folk were too drunk to notice or to stop them if they had. Gypsy Joe had been given the purse. Gypsy Joe had bet heavily on himself, or rather his eldest son had, to his great advantage. A few men, perhaps those who had carried the pick-handles, men who had put very large bets on his winning, were also missing.

'Canna do nowt,' said his grandfather. 'The law wunna touch it. Towd yo.'

'We mun find un, one day,' John's father said grimly. 'An' when we dun find un ... '

John wasn't too sure. Gypsy Joe had the slither of an eel and had packed a frighteningly powerful punch.

5

The Fall of a Sparrow

Summer had slipped into autumn and autumn was falling in reds and golds towards winter. Days grew shorter and colder. The lengthening nights were colder still. No more did men splash themselves clean in the River Ceiriog on paydays. Clothes and blankets were never warm enough. Only when working did men feel comfortable: stop the physical effort and the flesh soon chilled. Meals, hot meals, and hot tea, were more necessary than ever.

John, on one of his journeys home, used three shillings of his precious wages to buy another blanket for himself, second-hand though still with plenty of substance in it; and on further thought, bought one for his father too, as a buffer against it being taken from him. His boots were wearing, the right one more than the left. Its sole had parted from the upper which itself was split. While he was buying the blanket he spotted a lone right-hand boot and tried it on. It fitted better than the worn out one, which had always been far too large, though there was still enough room in the new one to cater for growing feet. After carefully inspecting its sole and upper for genuine soundness, he bought that too. It was a different style and a different shade of brown from the other, but many a navvy or farmer's lad or labourer boasted the same oddity. Careful though he had been, the purchases meant that little money was passed on to his mother.

His grandfather's toothache came back worse than ever; and one evening after work Smithy was sent for.

Money was passed over. Shown the offending tooth he wasted no time. 'You,' he said to Owd S'ewsb'ry, 'Get down on't floor. On yer back. You,' he pointed at Edward, 'Get 'is 'ead between yer knees. You,' and he motioned to John's Dad, 'Lie on top er im. Don't let 'im move.'

'Now,' he said to Owd S'ewsb'ry, 'Oppen thy mouth.'

On one side of the jaws that obediently parted he thrust a block of wood. He produced the pinchers from his pocket, clamped them around the offending tooth and pulled. His grandfather made howling, animal noises from deep in his throat. He squirmed under the weight of his son.

'Keep still, yer varmint.' Smithy adjusted the pinchers and tried again. After a few abortive hefts, and the grandfather trying in vain to shout or to stop him, he fell back in triumph, a bloody tooth brandished in front of Owd S'ewsb'ry's face. 'You'm lucky, man. All in one piece. 'E won't trouble yer no more.'

The old man got to his feet, holding his jaw. 'Yo'n ruined me, yo butcher.'

'Gi'e 'im a noggin a whisky. 'E'll soon be isself agin.' and he departed, whistling.

Sundays were often work days, depending on the need to finish a stretch of line, or bridge a bye-road, or shore a cutting, or any of the other tasks which would push the railway onwards. Chirk station with its sharp-roofed gables and tall chimneys was finished now, for their gang anyway. The way was permanent as far as Presgwyn, the next station down the line towards Shrewsbury, being built in stone to resemble an ornate Tudor cottage; and temporary down to the second station, Gobowen, which soon would be begun in Florentine style with a small turret and its walls stuccoed white.

On the rare workless, payless Sundays men lounged about and drank and some set their dogs to fight. A local rat-catcher brought a sack of rats to a pit that had been dug in the ground, then planked above to waist-height, deep enough that the rats could not escape. Rats were tipped into the pit. The dogs had been paraded beforehand, their mouths inspected, muscles felt, temperaments assessed, bets laid. The crowd watched as the rats gathered themselves into a heaving mound: they stank abominably. 'Sewer rats, these are,' said the rat-catcher. 'Don't get bit. They's got bad teeth, they 'as.'

A dog was dropped into the pit at a signal from the timekeeper, timekeeper also for everyday labour, thus one of the few men on the works with a watch. The dog, a bull-terrier, rushed at the mound, nosing into it, bringing out rat after rat and killing them by breaking their necks. A rat caught at the dog's leg but the dog bit himself free. 'Time,' shouted the timekeeper.

The dog was removed, the dead rats picked up by their tails and counted; a fresh supply of rats was added to the pit. Another dog, a Manchester terrier this time, barking with excitement, struggling to get at the vermin, was dropped in. Rats were on his ears; he shook to free himself but the rats clung on. One bit into the dog's tail. 'Time!' again; dead rats were counted and a third challenger took the floor.

A good sport, thought John, his blood stirred by the daring of the dogs and their eagerness to kill. He preferred it to the fights of dog against dog, though their owners usually dragged the dogs apart before one was torn to pieces. Some dogs were loath to let go and their owners fluffed flour over them which blocked up their air passages and forced them to release their jaws. Sometimes very young, or elderly and failing dogs were used to spur on a promising, strong dog to increase its taste for blood and death. A patch of skin pinkly shaved on the victim improved the chances of the dog that was being groomed for victory to get an easy, early bite and rouse its blood-lust.

Plenty of coins changed hands at either sport.

One Sunday, a wagon appeared. It was pulled slowly by two horses, a wagon with sides and a roof, though one side was cut away to make an opening like a counter in a shop. There were white muslin curtains drawn together across the space above the counter and the wagon itself was decorated with a painted picture of a fragile-looking white man with long fair hair wearing a white robe and with a circle of yellow light around his head.

' 'E wouldna be much cop wi' a barrer,' said someone, gazing judiciously at the image, arms akimbo.

The man on the box descended and disappeared into the bowels of the vehicle. In a moment or two the curtains were swept back and those who were nearest found themselves being addressed by a clergyman flanked by ladies dressed all in white and closely bonnetted.

'Friends,' began the clergyman, leaning forward in an earnest manner, 'My good friends! When thou liest down to take thy rest, methinks the uncertainty of thy salvation should keep thee waking, or amaze thee in thy dreams and trouble thy sleep. Doth it not grieve thee to see the people of God so comfortable in their way to glory, when thou hast no good hope of enjoying it thyself? How canst thou think of thy dying hour? If thou shouldest die this day (and who knows what a day may bring forth?) thou art not certain whether thou shalt go to heaven or hell.'

Men had been drifting towards the newcomers during this speech. One of them now yawned loudly and long. Others took up the challenge.

'Canst thou be merry ...' The crowd hooted merrily. 'Canst thou be merry, till thou art got out of this dangerous state?' The clergyman persevered. He began to speak more loudly and his face reddened. 'What shift dost thou make to preserve thy heart from horror, when thou rememberest the great judgement day ...'

'Pay day!' shouted someone and the crowd laughed.

'The great judgement day and everlasting flames.'

'Everlasting beer, more like,' came a shout, followed by a roar of appreciation.

'Lovely wenches!' came another shout. 'Loose them buttons, Miss, you wi' the big uns, gi'e's a look!'

The bonnets bridled and drew closer to their protector.

'Gi'e's a kiss,' came a cry.

A burst of loud smacking noises followed and the bonnets began to twitter to their champion.

'Friends, my good friends...,' said the clergyman, holding up his hands in appeal to good nature; and persisted for a while, though his voice could hardly be heard above the interjections of the crowd which grew more obscene by the minute.

The curtains closed. The defeated missionary appeared on the outside. But before he could resume his seat on the box, a number of willing hands had uncoupled the horses and were drawing the wagon by their own strength off the premises. And as they did, someone struck up a tune and the rest joined in, a couple of score of male voices singing:

'I do not care for ladies grand who are of high degree,
A winsome wench and willin', she is just the one for me,
Drink and love are classed as sins, as mortal sins by some,
I'll drink and drink whene'er I can, the drouth is sure to
come -
And I will love till lusty life runs out its mortal span,
The end of which is in the ditch for many a navvy man.
The bold navvy man.
The old navvy man,
Safe in a ditch with heels cocked up, so dies the navvy
man.'

The incident provided many a happy reminiscence in the evenings that followed. No-one, at least openly, discovered a need to attend Sunday services at any of the nearby chapels or churches.

The viaduct was growing, the central piers beginning to curve into ten great rounded arches. One day, when it had reached its full height of a hundred feet, people crossing in trains would be able to look down upon people in barges sailing across the adjacent aqueduct. And the aqueduct, designed by the great engineer Thomas Telford, was impressive in its own right.

The face of the structure was being fashioned by the masons with stone blocks, presenting to the world a surface rough from quarrying. It was the cheapest way to build, though the total cost of the viaduct was said to be becoming worryingly expensive.

S'ewsb'ry was conscious of his eminence below what was curving to form the underside of the arch, standing on a flimsy scaffold at a dizzy height above the ground, taking the hard yellow engineering bricks brought up from below by a minion and using lime mortar to work them one by one to form a graceful curve. Those gazing from below saw that the bricks were being held up by a wooden form: what would happen when that was removed?

'There's the beauty o' the keystone,' said S'ewsb'ry, proudly. 'Locks it all in place, that does. Transfers the stress tension onter the pillars. Wood's tekken away then. Not no use no more, see. Then them masons mun cover up wi' stone.'

John hoped his father had it right. In the meantime he swaggered in reflected glory.

Another payday came and John was sent home on his usual mission. This time his father did send a little of his wages. John, when he had last been home had brought back a message from his mother which she had made John write down on paper, a message saying that William was not well, she feared for him and there was no money to buy medicines. John had seen his brother lying most of the day on a pallet near the fire. He was thin and his features were sharp in his face but he did not care for food. Sometimes he complained of being too hot, sometimes icy cold: at night he would break into wringing sweats. His cough came more often and seemed to pain him more.

This Saturday, five days after his longed-for, though largely unregarded, twelfth birthday, John was walking fast. Frost that at waking had glittered white on each leafless branch was melting into sparkles of droplets; and the sky, lit by a late, weak sun, was a pale blue: it was a beautiful day. In the fields folk went about their labours. A man who was rhythmically pulling turnips waved as he passed. Another man he saw with a cart piled high with dung, hauled by two horses, a black and a bay, with white-feathered fetlocks and great purposeful feet. There were more men pulling turnips. There was a man and boy turning up the stubble, their horse and plough weaving a tracery of deep dark furrows in harmony with the contours and inclines of a sloping field. He saw a cloud of husks as men winnowed in the draught between the two great open doors of a barn.

When he came into Shrewsbury he hesitated and turned right towards Pride Hill where the best shops were and where his grandmother lived. He remembered the last time, back in the late summer, that he and William had walked together up here, their faces pressed against the hard glass of shop windows, full of longings for what they could not have. There was one thing that William had lingered over. There it was again, in the window, slightly different but just as desirable. It had been William's birthday ten days before his own. He went in and asked the price.

'That there? That's fourpence, that is. Proper good quality. Yo wunna get one like that nowhere else.'

'Ah s'll tek it,' said John. He had already taken a few coins from the pouch in readiness, in the retreat of a niche where no-one could see. He handed his precious coins over.

When he reached the house in the Foregate his mother wrapped her arms around him. His sisters squealed with delight. He supposed they were alright, really, though they were only girls.

' 'Ow bist our William?' he asked. His mother gestured to the thin form on its pallet. 'Well, our William,' he said. 'Ow bist? Ah's brought yo summat. Summat for your birthday, now you'm ten. Look 'ere.' He held out the object that the shopman had wrapped in brown paper at his request.

William tried to sit up and John helped him. He hasked, the cough becoming violent. 'It hurts,' he said. His mother found his rag; and John saw that the rag was stained with blood.

'I've 'ad the doctor,' his mother said. She shut her lips in a hard line. ' 'E'll be better soon, come the warm weather.'

William pulled at the paper with feeble fingers. His eyes, already huge in his face, grew wider. 'We sha'n be playin' wi' un soon,' said John, 'Jest thee and me.'

William collapsed down again, the ball clasped to his chest. 'Thank yo, our John,' he said.

William died just over a month later, nine days before the Christmas of 1846. A letter, delivered by a nervous postboy, reached the camp on the seventeenth of December telling of his death the previous day. It bore a black, penny stamp, which meant that it had been paid for in advance; and it had been written by Susanna, John's aunt, his father's eldest sister. Neither John's mother nor his grandmother could write and Susanna seemed unsure of where the letters might fit into a word. Nevertheless the message could not be mistaken. William was dead and they were to come at once.

They downed tools, told the ganger who was not best pleased; and started out. Work was in progress so that they were able to get a lift in a horse-drawn wagon which took them as far as Rednal, almost half the way. The permanent way, making the whole track suitable for locomotives, still awaited completion: that grand moment was rumoured to be the Spring of 1848, sixteen months away.

The cottage, when they reached it, was quiet. The shutters were closed and the mirror turned to the wall. John's mother was restlessly taking things off shelves, wiping, replacing and beginning again but the girls were sitting in a huddle in the dim firelight.

' 'E'll be buried Saturday,' said his mother. 'St. Mary's.'

William was lying in a coffin stretched between two chairs in the corner furthest from the fire. His father raised the lid and gazed at his son. He said nothing.

The baby, Mary, toddled uncertainly over to the coffin and stretched out her hand to stroke his face. 'Wake up, William,' she said.

John's grandmother was sitting by the fire, rocking back and forth. She caught the little girl to her. 'Poor little lad. Yo shunna 'ave named 'im William. 'Is Uncle William went. 'Is Great-uncle William went.' She looked up at her husband. 'Three Williams, three generations. Unlucky name, William. I was wi' 'im, yo knows, along wi' Ann 'ere an' the girls. An' 'twas me went to the office and told 'em.' Her voice grew sharp and she stared at John's father. 'Where han yo bin, all them months an' the little lad so despert bad?'

His father looked uncomfortable. 'Workin',' he said shortly.

John stared. He had never seen his father so wrong-footed; and by Grandmother Mary too, who doted on him and all his doings.

'An' no money to feed 'im proper or gi'e 'im some 'appiness in 'is last darksome days. Dwindered away 'e did. Poor mite. An' no faither to bid 'im goodbye.' She hissed in anger and wiped her eyes on her apron.

'What bin done bin done,' said S'ewsb'ry flatly.

'An' we couldna buy no Godfrey's Cordial,' John's grandmother went on relentlessly. 'Not till yo sent that very last bit o' money. An' a wunna enough.' She glared at her son. 'Suffered, 'e did. Never seen such sufferin' an' 'im such a right brave little chap. 'E deserved better.'

A silence fell.   'I've paid for the coffin,' said the grandmother. 'An' I'll not be payin' for the funeral.'

Neighbours and family called. The women put their arms around John's mother and keened with her; and the men shook his father's hand with long, gripping handshakes, as if they didn't know when to let go. Pies were handed over and cakes and cheese and jugs of beer, all small offerings and more than the givers could afford. Some helped to sit through the nights of Thursday and Friday, keeping watch for signs: but the departed had truly left for ever. He began to smell.

John was too short to hold the fourth corner of the coffin, so Thomas Thomas, his Aunt Susanna's husband and a fellow bricklayer, helped carry William to the church, together with his father, grandfather and Edward. John walked behind.

Women did not go to funerals.

'Where dost 'ee think 'e bin now?' John had asked Edward, fearfully.

' 'Eaven, o' course,' said Edward, ruffling John's hair. 'Up there, in the sky, 'appy as a lark, wi' wings to match.'

John remembered the preacher who had come to the

line. Perhaps he should have listened a bit more carefully. He hoped if he said a prayer for his brother, it might keep him being always an angel.

There was shouting at night, after John should by rights have been asleep. In the morning his mother had a bruised and half-closed eye and a bleeding mouth. But his father was quiet, subdued.

'I s'll be payin' yo back for the coffin,' he told his mother, shortly. He produced some coins from his pocket and handed them out to the girls. Esther, the oldest, did not smile: she had a look on her, did Esther; but she took her coin just the same.

'Love an' cherish, yo said,' said John's grandmother, hands on hips, glaring at her son. 'Your promises bin like pie-crusses, made to be broken. Yo tek a good look at them girls, growin' girls the three on 'em. An' your Ann there an' all. Clemmed they bin. It's bin mortal long since they ate proper dinners. If thee dunna gi'e thy Missus more, 'appen thee'll be payin' for five coffins 'stead o' jest the one.'

.

6

An Awful Calamity

' 'O's them fellers?' said John's grandfather one morning as they rode a horse-drawn truck towards Gobowen, the second station down the line from Chirk. One storey of the station had grown into two, with slate, dug from the local quarries around Glyn Ceiriog, stacked ready for the roofing to begin. 'Them fellers' were all in a bunch, four of them, being talked at by Mr White, one of the sub-contractors. They were nodding their heads, agreeing to something. As the truck lumbered on and by craning back, they could see him gesturing the four towards a stretch of cutting that required further work.

Rumour, in the way of rumour, reached them later in the morning. The men were Irish. 'Bog trotters,' said Tweedle Beak. 'Steals our jobs, they does. Work fer starvation wages, they will. An us good honest Englishmen, they don't care nothin' fer us.'

A general murmur of agreement was heard. At the first break, a group of men trooped back down the line to where the Irishmen were working, still working though by rights it was bait time. 'What yer doin'?' A shout went up. 'Stealing our jobs, that's what.'

The Irishmen conferred briefly and downed tools. 'Sure and we want no trouble, lads,' said one.

'Well, yer'll get trouble,' retorted Tweedle Beak, 'Unless yer gets off of this line.'

The Irish stayed where they were. A clod of earth sailed towards them, but still they gave no ground. A hail of clods followed, but the call for the resumption of work meant the retreat of the Englishmen back down the track. The usual silence of the men when working was broken as grumbling punctuated the afternoon. Resentment festered.

As darkness fell the ganger called 'Yo-ho,' the signal to knock off. John, his grandfather, Edward and the others set off on foot back up the track, gathering more support as they went.

'Papists,' said one. 'Savages,' said another. 'Dunna even wear shoes,' said a third. 'Mostly,' he added, noting the Irishmen's footwear.

From time to time a man stooped to pick up a likely-looking stone. They reached the Irishmen as they were about to leave. The Irish saw the mob and quickened their pace. The first stone was thrown and then came a hail. The Irish ran; and the mob ran after them, flinging missiles and stooping to pick up more. One of the Irishmen was hit on the head and fell, stunned. The mob moved forward, ready to kick and punch. He crawled to his feet and somehow fear-injected adrenalin came to the aid of his legs. The mob pursued until the four were well away from the line.

'They shanna cheat us no more,' said Edward with satisfaction. John, who had thrown a fair few of his own stones, felt a glow of heroism: it was good to have driven off the savages. Back at the shanty he told his father of their daring: his father clapped him on the shoulder, pleased for once.

Mr White was seen heading towards them. He looked both angry and determined. 'What did you do that for?' he demanded. 'Do you not know that those men have left their homes, their country, because at home they cannot eat? They eat mostly potatoes for want of better fare and the potatoes, from one end of their country to the other, are a black, stinking mush: there is nothing else, nothing else to fill their bellies. They must leave their own land or die. Themselves, their wives and their little ones, die for lack of food.'

'An there bin a tall tale,' said John's father.

'It's a true one,' said Mr White.

'Then why hanna we 'eard on it? Not in *Eddowes's Journal* it wunna.'

Mr White pursed his lips. 'No,' he said. 'It has not been much reported in *Eddowes's*. Nevertheless, but for the wages of those poor fellows, their families back in Ireland, even here, die of hunger.'

'Why bin 'e so keen to 'elp them Irish?' said Owd S'ewsb'ry suspiciously when the man had gone.

'Most like 'e bin Irish 'imself. Leastways 'e's a rum way o' speakin'.'

'Nay, that's just nob talk,' said Edward, but it was more comfortable to think otherwise.

That incident happened in the April of 1847 when John had been on the line for seven months. He had noticeably grown though he could still do nothing like a man's work and earned nothing like a man's wages. One day, though ... He dreamed of running a full barrow up a slope, of bricking a graceful arch.

It must have been a Tuesday, or perhaps a Wednesday or a Thursday, and a month later, when they first heard. It was a man on the tramp who brought the news. He was given food and beer at knocking-off time, while men gathered round to listen to his news.

'Evenin', it were,' he began. 'But not yet dark. Chester train bound for Holyhead. Branch goes off to Wales, see, for the coal an' iron an' that. T'other line comes on 'ere. Can't get through 'ere though, to S'ewsb'ry like it ought, cos yo pitherin' lot 'anna finished that there bridge yet.' He gestured to the viaduct, its splendour only part materialised. 'Nor its brother o'er the Dee neither.'

'Geron wi' it,' someone shouted, 'Or we'll 'ave that beer back.'

The man grinned. 'A quarter past six, an' steam up. Train pulls out o' Chester station. All goin' well. Passengers, there bin this time. Not many, about forty they say. An' none o' them knowin' as they were goin' ter meet their Maker. 'Appen 'twere a blessing. Well, just out o' Chester, near the race course, doin' full twenty mile an hour ... Know the race course? No? Well, it were near the race course anyhow. There's the new bridge there, the flat-top bridge on two big piers where she goes o'er River Dee. Not the viaduct, t'other un. Well, engine gets o'er. Tender gets o'er. But rest of 'em, four carriages an' the van ...' He took a long swig from the jug ... ' Rest of 'em, they don't get o'er. Falls in the river, they does. Or on the bank. An' that there's a mighty despert drop.'

There were gasps, murmurs, whistles of dismay, from the circle of listeners. John tried to picture the scene. People in the water, trapped inside carriages. People crushed by jagged metal as a carriage hit the embankment.

'Five dead,' went on the story teller, relishing the reception given to his momentous news. 'Dead as doornails. Took 'em to the Work'ouse, they did. What was left on 'em. Anderson, the stoker, 'e got clear o' the bridge, but then the tender fell on its side, 'e fell out and a great lommock o' iron landed right atop on 'im. Squish. Finished 'im off. Power o' bad luck, that.'

A hat was passed round. Pence and farthings were parted with and given in thanks for the news and to help the traveller on his road: it was the custom to aid those on the tramp.

Over the next day or two, more stories reached them. A Mr Proud, at one moment enjoying the only first-class carriage, at the next found himself upside down in river water, glug-glugging inside to swallow him, upon which alarm he struggled through a window, and, being fortunately possessed of the ability to swim, was able to make his way to shore.

The crash was so thunderous that it was heard three quarters of a mile away in Chester Castle and barracks, where the 90th Light Infantry were turned out to march to the rescue.

The engine driver, Clayton, had felt the rails sinking under him as he crossed the bridge. He put on all steam, helped by the last living efforts of the unfortunate stoker, felt the severing of the carriages, which in falling had jerked the tender onto its side, but had himself got safely across. He then drove on to the nearest station, Saltney, where he raised the alarm. And, with what struck John as enormous heroism, the magnificent Clayton then changed lines and re-crossed the bridge in the opposite direction, passing on the up-line the so-recent tragedy, so that he could dutifully report the accident to his superiors in Chester.

On the Saturday John was sent into Chirk to buy a newspaper. Due to the accident having happened on the Monday evening, *Eddowes's Journal* had missed the glory of reporting on the story through the misfortune of coming out on a Wednesday, too soon for news to have travelled from Chester to Shrewsbury and reporters sent in the opposite direction to the scene. But Saturday was the day that the *Shrewsbury Chronicle* came out; and there was a full and satisfactory account.

'Now, our John,' his father had said, once an expectant gathering had assembled that evening: and John had stumbled through the report. Some parts were particularly enjoyed by the company and, having read the full article, he was enjoined to read sections of it again.

'Gi'e us the screams,' said Tweedle Beak.

'The screams of the slightly wounded,' he read, 'the groans of those whose limbs were broken, and the terror of all, was heartrending.'

' 'Ow does 'e know?' said Tweedle Beak. He was hushed while John read on. 'Few indeed except themselves heard those agonising shrieks, as there were not many persons near the spot at the time ...'

'See?' said Tweedle Beak triumphantly, but no-one answered.

'Tell us the bit about that driver again.'

'As another train was expected down in a few minutes,' John went on, 'the engineer gave information at Saltney of what had occurred. Having got the engine on the other line he then immediately returned, and with an amount of courage and intrepidity which can scarcely be credited, recrossed the bridge by the up line of rails which remained standing, and gave information of the disaster at the Flookersbrook station in Chester.'

Murmurs of approval were heard.

'That bit about the van ...'

'Mr Macgregor, a young pupil of the resident engineer, was one of four persons standing on the luggage van at the time of the accident. Seeing the sinking of the roadway he exclaimed 'Good Lord' and instantly leapt out on the other line of rails but, in doing so, fell, and his head coming in contact with the rails on the other roadway, he received a compound fracture of the skull.'

A shaking of sympathetic heads took place.

'The gent all spruced up for dinner ... '

'Major Robe, Royal Artillery, who was going out to dine, seeing the ruins instantly after the accident, rushed to the spot and instantly plunged into the water to assist the unfortunate passengers.'

The names of over a dozen injured were read again: they had been taken to Chester Royal Infirmary.

Glances were being cast towards their own viaduct. 'Nah,' said Chester Red. 'Different construction. The Dee Bridge - an' it's not the Dee Viaduct, that's much more grand - the Dee Bridge were just a girder bridge, flat iron beams, three on 'em on two piers. Ninety-eight foot long each one. This 'ere 'as plenty o' brick an' stone underneath it. An' a lot more piers.'

In the weeks that followed, more came to light. The design engineer had, rather disconcertingly, been the revered Mr Robert Stephenson, the son of the even-more-revered George who had built the Stockton and Darlington, the first passenger railway, a man who had floated his railway over the fearsome Chat Moss, a bog forty feet deep. Between them the two Stephensons had designed the Rocket, winner of the famed Rainhill Trials. Surely such a man as Mr Robert could not have made a mistake? Besides, the newspapers said that the bridge had been thoroughly tested before it opened by running thirty linked and loaded wagons over it, each weighing seven tons.

But the beams of the bridge were made of cast iron which was already being dropped from engineering favour in place of wrought iron which was more bendable, less brittle; though regrettably more expensive. There certainly were reinforcements to the girders, tie-bars of wrought iron, but they apparently served little purpose. Several people had noticed how much the bridge vibrated when in use but these observations had not reached the right quarters.

Tellingly, just prior to the accident the way had been covered in crushed-stone ballast, meant to prevent fire in the wooden sleepers, a well-meaning response to a recent fire in a similar structure elsewhere: the brittle cast iron girder bridge, it was concluded, had been overloaded.

As the *Shrewsbury Chronicle* had said, the accident was an 'awful calamity'. It was reported in newspapers all over the country. It was not unique: in the same week a railway bridge fell at Dudley. Engineers had more to learn.

In the wake of the Dee Bridge disaster, rumour about the safety of the Chirk Viaduct crept far and wide. It crept into the ears of common people who had vowed never to travel on such a dangerous form of transport and confirmed them in their worst fears. It crept into the ears of those who might have tried such transport but who now decided against the idea. And it crept into the ears of the Directors of the Shrewsbury and Chester Railway Company, who stood to lose a great deal of money if folk failed to travel on the transport they were providing. Mr Henry Robertson, Chief Engineer, was called to account before the Board.

'In consequence,' he began, 'of several reports which had been spread, to the effect that this work [the Chirk Viaduct] rested on a bad foundation ... ' And went on to explain that the celebrated Mr Telford, who had built the next-door aqueduct some fifty years before, had indeed, because of the existence of a strata of sand, built his piers upon piles driven into the rock below. It was true that the piers of his own Chirk Viaduct had no such piles, but they were built through and under the bed of sand and consequently rested on a secure foundation. He had, well before work began, satisfied himself by frequent borings that this design was safe.

The Directors were reassured. All was well for the future. The unfortunate accident could be swept into the past. Blame slipped smoothly from everyone's shoulders.

The Military were thanked for their assistance at the scene of the late accident. One hundred pounds was donated to Chester Royal Infirmary for their contribution to the victims, plus an annual donation of five guineas to both Chester and Shrewsbury Infirmaries. Dispensaries in Wrexham and Oswestry would each receive three guineas. Employees, though they were not mentioned, would no doubt continue to require medical services in time to come.

More paydays came and went. The navvies continued their drunken forays into the surrounding townships, ensuring the contempt and fear of the local population; and John continued with his missions to the house in the Abbey Foregate. It was solitary without William. The girls were there of course, though at school on weekdays: Shrewsbury had a number of Charity Schools and the girls had free education. Their mother had had no schooling but she wanted better for her daughters. Their father had no objection. He could perfectly well read and write himself, though he was happy to show off his son's ability to read a newspaper to the men; and was conscious that if John stumbled over a word it would be taken more or less in good part, whereas he doing the same might well face mockery.

John heard all about the doings of the family. Not that he particularly asked, but that his mother told him anyway as audience for her opinions.

His aunt Rachel had been dismissed from her position as servant to a brother and his two adult sisters, gentlefolk, living not far away in space from themselves in the Foregate, but in accommodation far superior. That had been last summer. She had proved his mother's oft description of 'a flighty chit' by being found very much in the family way. A baby had arrived, in the August in fact, soon after John had begun work on the railway, and been named Rachel.

'An' 'o bin the father? 'O knows?' said his mother, not for the first time. 'Bound to get inter trouble, 'er bin though, with them come-'ither looks an' aunty-praunty ways an' all.'

Miraculously the baby had survived. Babies in general were in peril and illegitimate ones in much greater peril than most: some viewed it as a blessing when the unwanted things succumbed, to laying-over, or too much Godfrey's Cordial with too little sustenance. Now it was June of 1847 and the baby, a whole ten months old, was about to be christened as Rachel Ann. 'Better late than never,' agreed everyone.

Susanna, the eldest of the aunts, had consented to care for little Rachel while her mother went off into service again, down London way this time: no girl could hope for any job while encumbered by a baby to restrict her movements and advertise her wickedness. Nor could a girl hope for a chance of marriage when sullied by another man's child, unless she were uncommonly lucky.

Susanna, on the other hand, had only one child. 'An' 'im already ten year old. Let 'er 'usband down, 'er 'as. But thank the good Lord 'e bin a boy, an' all. An' could be a blessin', little Rachel to fill the gap. Mebbe stop folks clattin' anyways.'

'An' that Elizabeth,' went on his mother, indignantly. 'There's a wench gone from bad to worser. Stayed at 'ome, 'er did, till 'er was twenty, lollockin' about, doin' nothin'. Canna do much, 'er, anyways. Simple, 'er is. Then 'er finds work at the factory. But 'er's not there long afore 'er 'as the babby, Elizabeth. An' now, 'er's gone an' got another 'un. Mary, your Gran, 'er says to me, "Never learns, that girl. Never 'as, never will." She wunna 'ave 'em in the 'ouse. An' proper right too. Two childern, out o' wedlock, and no-one knowin' the fathers! 'O'd 'ave 'er now?'

The two Elizabeths and baby Phoebe were living only a few hundred yards from home, John learned, squashed into a tiny, badly-built cottage in Coal Wharf Square which they shared with six other people: they were existing but barely on parish relief. Elizabeth, it was felt, had used a short spoon to sup with the devil and must take the consequences.

'An' your Granddad, too. Respectable man, 'e is. Got the right to vote an' all. Let 'im down, 'er 'as. Let the both on 'em down. 'Appen Ah dunna al'ays agree wi' your Gran, but 'er were real good to me when William went, God rest 'is sweet soul.'

Time passed. The whole line was scheduled to be opened in the spring of 1848. The station at Shrewsbury was to be built jointly between the Shrewsbury and Chester, the Shrewsbury and Hereford, the Shrewsbury and Birmingham and the Shropshire Union Companies. That way each Company would bear only a quarter of the cost.

But the line was not after all ready by the spring. The weather was unseasonably wet that year. Water poured its weight into soil. Mud clogged boots, sucked at boots as they were lifted, stuck to picks, made it impossible to wheel a loaded barrow up a slope where each footstep slid and slipped and could find no traction. Rain found its way through every roof and every coat and every boot-top. Morale slithered drearily downwards and men worked more slowly. And, on top of those afflictions, there came the case of Curly Dick.

It was April again, 1848, a year after the Dee Bridge accident. A gang of muckshifters were working on a cutting, near Newton Mere about three miles out of Shrewsbury. Time, of course, was money and it was a saving in time if a hill of earth and stone could be made to fall all by itself. One way to do this was to tunnel under the slope until it became an overhang and the overhang became no longer enough supported, so that of its own accord it fell. All the men had been warned of potential danger, or so it was said.

But it was midday and maybe Curly Dick was thinking of his bread and bacon to come and not enough of what he was doing and wanting the time to pass quicker. Besides, Curly Dick was a great strong fellow of twenty and felt as immortal as a big strong fellow might feel at that age. Only he dug a little too far into the hill. The rain-sodden mass fell down upon him, crushing him between itself and a wheelbarrow. Everyone liked Curly Dick and his gang rushed in to pull him out. They could see his legs, so they got him out in record time, put him on a wagon and when the line ran out they carried him between them all the way to Shrewsbury Infirmary. He lived till noon the next day. An inquest recorded a verdict of accidental death.

A collection was taken and he was buried decently under his real name which turned out to be Richard Bennet. Many went to his funeral, dressing themselves in a tidy way and taking off their hats in church.

'And I will love till lusty life runs out its mortal span,
The end of which is in the ditch for many a navvy man.'

The wetness of the weather was not the only cause of delay. There were strikes across the land that year of 1848 among working men, from railways to ironworks. But they were local strikes and the masters held all the cards. On the Shrewsbury and Chester Railway, masons the length of the line downed tools. Dissatisfaction with pay and conditions it was said. They held out for five weeks. Masons were skilled craftsmen: only they could dress the stone and carve the elaborations that beautified pediment and parapet, cornice and gothic window-frame: but there were always other, hungry and desperate, masons to take their places.

On the sixth of May three hundred masons were advertised for, from as far away as Scotland. 'Four an' ninepence a day,' mused S'ewsb'ry. 'That's three times as much as a lady gets as is a gov'ness. Near four times as much as a ploughman.' The strike broke.

7

Ends and Beginnings

While the masons were on strike in the spring of 1848, that year of rain, all work had stopped on the viaduct. Once a place of bustle and shouted orders, of the ring of iron against iron, iron against stone, now there was only the wind humming through deserted scaffolding, the moody slap of wet tarpaulin, to break the silence. Most of the sandstone blocks, blocks that had been shipped by canal from the quarries of Cefn Mawr on the north side of the Dee Valley, were in place, though not all; and plenty of skilled finishing work that could be done only by the hand of an experienced mason, remained forlornly undone. Rain dripped from the giant timber arches that rested at each end of the stone bridge as its link to land, lying as yet unconnected by the timbermen. Not only that but the masons had stopped work all down the rest of the line. Progress everywhere was disrupted or came to a standstill.

'An' what'll I do now?' S'ewsb'ry had asked. It was a rhetorical question. No possibility of solidarity with the masons in their strike: no work, no pay.

'There's the Hencott cutting,' he went on. 'Most like that's what it'll come to.' He sighed. The Hencott cutting was going to be heavy work. It was a couple of miles out of Shrewsbury, still unfinished and needing manpower.

He hired himself as a muckshifter, running-out his barrows up the slopes of Hencott cutting. The other three joined him, Edward and Owd S'ewsb'ry with pick and shovel, John leading the horses which pulled the full wagons along to build up the embankment to the north: there were 140,000 cubic yards of earth to be shifted. As the days lengthened so did the hours they worked and as pressure to finish built up, sometimes they worked all night.

All had not been plain digging and moving. Robertson, the engineer, had long spotted a problem: the line in one place needed to traverse a bog. It was a bog known locally as the Black Bog, a place reputed to be bottomless, a place in which, fireside tales told, stray animals or humans lured into following a will-o'-the-wisp might disappear leaving no trace. It was an ancient bog, having been, many thousands of years since, a meander of the great River Severn. Now it was filled with peaty mud. As fast as wagons tipped into it their loads of earth and stones, they slowly sank beneath the surface, releasing a miasma of rottenness. However, not for nothing had the great bog of Chat Moss on the Liverpool and Manchester line been conquered a score of years before. Mr Robertson had ordered brushwood to be gathered, branches to be cut; and from these hurdles were made, a whole line of them traversing the bog. Men working there strapped wide planks to their feet and waddled like ducks across the mud. Earth, sand and gravel were laid over all until a firm, though elastic, roadway was formed to carry the rails.

In the June of the previous year of 1847, advertisements had been placed in newspapers far and wide inviting tenders for the erection of the station at Shrewsbury. The *Shrewsbury Chronicle*, a newspaper with a pride in its ability to delight and enlighten its readers with illustration, drew attention to the advertisement by heading it with an engraving of a four-wheeled engine with neatly horizontal smoke and no apparent driver, pulling a tender with stoker visible and one closed carriage resembling three coach-bodies joined Siamese-style at the hip. The contract was won by Thomas Brassey, an event which had been welcomed with general satisfaction: he won the contract for Chester Station too.

At present the complex of lines, those lines of the four companies that would meet at Shrewsbury, was under construction; and its focus, the station building itself, was begun. It had been designed by Penson, employee of Mr Robertson the engineer, and a man almost local, being from Oswestry. The station was to be in architectural harmony with the ancient grammar school which it faced.

'Tudor Gothic, they calls it,' S'ewsb'ry told the others, 'Square tower in the middle an' 'er's got an oriel window, octagonal turrets, battlements all ornamental, pediments, carved 'eads and 'o knows what. Forty thousand pund for that un, athout the brick arch o'er Cross Street and a mighty great viaduct o'er the river. About an 'undred thousand all told. An' them there muckshifters, they'n moved fifty thousand ton of earth jest to flatten the site.' He pursed his lips and shook his head slowly. 'Not as big as the station at Chester: that bin the largest in the kingdom; but ... ' and here he put on a fancy voice, ' "on an hextensive scale".'

John's father was changing: he was a more sober man since William's death. John's grandmother might have exaggerated somewhat about the five coffins, but it had made S'ewsb'ry reflect. After the masons' strike ended and after the cutting at Hencott had been finished, S'ewsb'ry found a job at the now-rising station in his home town, with its additions such as platforms, signal-boxes and bridges, all requiring bricklayers. Owd S'ewsb'ry decided to join his son. That way they could each live at home: it would be far more comfortable than their leaking hut.

'Your Gran's Fidget Pie inna so bad,' said his grandfather, 'Nor 'er 'Tato Pie neither. 'Er used to make Owl Soup, but 'er's not done that this long while. Nice eatin', that bin, a fat young barn owl. 'Ave to catch one 'o course.' He pursed his lips reflectively.

John talked to Edward: neither felt ready to give up their independence and move back home. They would be even more free without the older men. So they stayed where they were for the moment, working mainly in the vicinity of the Chirk Viaduct, doing any jobs that came to hand and talking about what they should do next, for it was plain that the Shrewsbury and Chester was tailing to its end. Both felt the pull of adventure, of freedom, of seeing other places. For the moment Big Nell did their cooking along with that of others: John's father had been replaced with a live-in lodger. Drumming-up was John's job no longer, having passed from his growing hands to the smaller hands of a newer Nipper.

They were working one morning in early July, working in their usual rhythms, nice and steady, near the still uncompleted viaduct, when John heard, from far off, a whistle, a mechanical shriek that was at the same time both breathy and hoarse, and a clanking and a grinding of metal and a squeal of metal on metal, and then in the distance a hissing of steam. A silence followed.

John could not resist. No engine could yet cross the viaduct from the Chester side, but it was time, hearsay had told him, for steam to begin its operations between Chirk and Shrewsbury. Heavy parts had been arriving by canal over the last weeks. Men had been assembling a huge machine. Now the moment had come and the locomotive was on the move at last.

He skipped into the lee of the line of nearby wagons, edged further along the top of the valley into a cover of bushes until he came within sight of the monster itself. There it was: a creature made all of metal, with a round and somehow cheerful face surmounted by a tall, metal, upturned top hat. Behind was a long and rounded barrel of a belly, topped with shining copper bumps. And the wheels! Three pairs of them! Each wheel was spoked like the wheels of carts, and the middle pair was huge, as tall as his father. A man, a man to be envied as a god, was in charge of the monster, standing in an open cabin behind. As John edged around the creature, he saw that low down in the bulkhead in front of the man was an aperture, the maw of the beast, red-hot; and above were wondrous dials and levers.

Behind the engine was towed a four-wheeled truck, piled with coal, the manna he knew it fed on, the coal-slave in attendance. A group of important-looking men had just descended.

He stared for a while, which he knew was too long, before he left reluctantly to get back to his work.

The Board and Directors held a minor practice celebration of their line on the 5th of August after a meeting in Shrewsbury. Boarding the train just beyond the still-unfinished Shrewsbury station, they arrived just in advance of the almost-finished Chirk Viaduct.

John and others looked on as the welcoming party cheered and the visitors were regaled with champagne before continuing their journey to Chester by coach. Regarding with curiosity the train that had carried the illustrious personages, the spectators, being the muckshifters, bricklayers, miners, masons and various other folk, noticed that the coal had been camouflaged in special boxes and the seats covered delicately in green baize. Effort had been made to prevent smoke from the engine offending the fine-tuned sensibilities of the passengers.

An impromptu speech informed them that the distance had been covered in an hour and a quarter, without a single stoppage on account of defects in the rails.

'For which mercy may the good Lord be thanked,' said Tweedle Beak. 'For I doubt they'll thank us.'

By the end of the month the engineer, Mr Henry Robertson, was reporting to the Board and its Chairman Mr William Ormsby Gore, (Eton, Temple and Merton, former Dragoon Guards, MP for North Shropshire), that: 'The earthwork is completed throughout and there only remains the dressing up and finishing the slope of the heaviest cuttings ... Of the whole distance from Shrewsbury to Chester, the only portions of the permanent way not closed adjoin the Dee and Chirk viaducts, and in all do not amount to one mile.'

This report was given at another celebration, the dinner that honoured the laying of the keystone of the last of the arches of the Dee Viaduct which spanned the celebrated Vale of Llangollen, a ceremony performed by Mr Ormsby Gore using a silver trowel handed to him by the engineer. The Viaduct had been reached by train from Chester, the structure decorated with flags, banners, garlands and, a thoughtful touch, a long string of clean white masons' aprons.

It was the beginning of October when the brothers stared in awe at a two-headed monster dragging behind it a line of trucks piled high with stone. This must be the test they had heard tell of, the test which would decide whether the line and vitally the viaducts, were ready to bear at last their intended human and material cargo. Important men descended and were walking now across the viaduct, looking closely at its structure, talking amongst themselves.

The four Kirbys joined the celebrations on the day of the Grand Opening, one of those few days when work stopped; though so did pay.

On Thursday the 12th of October 1848, church bells woke them, as they'd woken everyone else in the town of Shrewsbury. The family assembled at a pre-arranged spot near the Castle, a large party of Kirbys, Evans and Thomases, all dressed in their best, the ladies in bonnet and shawl, the men in their fancy waistcoats and bright neckerchiefs over clean shirts, children in their clean Sunday best and warned to stay that way. They joined the other people who swarmed over the ruined castle walls, to look down on a good view of the proceedings.

John, looking across the sea of people, caught sight of his Aunt Elizabeth, in gaudy tatters, a man's arm around her waist, a small, thin child carrying a wailing bundle clutching at her skirts. He moved his eyes away.

Gigs, curricles, coaches, every type of vehicle, were joined by folk on foot, pouring in from miles around. Outside the Guildhall stood His Lordship the Mayor, be-chained and be-robed, surrounded by his Corporation, joined at 8.30am by the more distinguished citizens.

At 9.00am came a town band which arranged itself to play lustily at the front of a procession headed by the Marshal, the Sword-bearer, the Sergeants at Mace bearing the Regalia of the Corporation, the Mayor himself, various officials and a thousand invited gentlemen. Flags waved both from within and without the procession which proceeded under a triumphal arch, just one of many around the town, decorated with more flags. On reaching the door of the station building, which was flying from its unfinished heights extra flags portraying the Arms of Shrewsbury and Chester, the procession, all crinoline and top hat, halted for the solemnity of the National Anthem.

As it ended a train arrived from Chester crammed with ladies and gentlemen of that town. The band of the 46th Regiment of Foot descended to delight its audience which was growing ever more vast by the minute.

Slightly late, at 10.03am, doors (where doors were) slammed, the guard waved his flag, blew his whistle and the same train got up steam and chuffed back out of Shrewsbury, its thirty-eight carriages overloaded with more than a thousand people. As it majestically rode the rails, crowds leaned over bridges and packed the station platforms along the route, replete with their own triumphal arches and banners bearing such legends as "Success to the Shrewsbury and Chester Railway". There was much cheering and wild waving of flags.

The passengers, secure in the knowledge that the line had been thoroughly inspected the previous week by the Government Inspector of Railways and the engineers from the Company, were free to shiver in safety as they crossed the Black Bog, to marvel as they passed over still-flooded fields and to enjoy the engineering magnificence of the Chirk and the Dee Viaducts. Of these the Dee Viaduct with its nineteen arches and its cost of £76,000 was generally agreed to be the most splendid and the most picturesque in its crossing of the Vale of Llangollen. Gasps of admiration were heard for the beauty of churches such as that of Wrexham and for perspectives of romantic scenery, all viewed from a previously unseen angle.

Two hours and forty minutes, and forty-two and a quarter miles later, the train pulled into Chester. Some hours afterwards it returned once more, through scenery enhanced by the beauty of a clear autumn evening, having extended itself into fifty-eight carriages, pulled by three engines, pushed by another two and holding now some two thousand souls, none of whom that day paid a penny.

A triumph indeed; and one which was topped off by a dinner for three hundred persons of the greatest importance, followed by a ball for two hundred; after which came fireworks. The extended Kirby family much enjoyed the fireworks.

On the following day there was a rush to buy or to borrow that week's edition of the *Shrewsbury Chronicle*.

'See? Look at that,' said S'ewsb'ry, pointing to the engraving of Shrewsbury station as it would one day be, together with lengthy description, that graced the page of the *Chronicle*. 'That's what er'll look like. Not finished yet, but 'er shall be. An' by us.'

'What does a say about the goin's on?' asked his father. ' 'Ere, our John, yo read it for us.'

John read the whole article, followed, as usual, by the re-reading of particular pieces which had caught someone's fancy.

'The toasts. At the dinner. At least we'n bin toasted, yo knows,' said Edward, 'even if we dinna drink any of 'em. Count 'em, the toasts.'

John counted. ' Fourteen,' he said at last. 'That's athout the Loyal Toasts, as they started with. Dunna know 'ow many o' those. A power on 'em, most like.'

'I remembers the last un,' said Owd S'ewsb'ry. 'It were the good owd toast, "All friends around the Wrekin." '

'Where were we?'

John counted. 'Tenth: "The working men under Mr Brassey, men who have behaved themselves uniformly well, from the commencement of the railway till the present moment (Hear Hear). Those men might have had their little quarrels occasionally - where would they find a large body of men congregated together who would not? - but their personal conduct had been most excellent." '

'Mun 'ave 'ad 'is eyes shut paydays,' scoffed S'ewsb'ry.

' 'E dinna see the boxin' match neither,' added his father.

Nor the Irish, thought John, remembering. But nobody

spoke of that. There had been reports of the potato disease in Britain, he thought uneasily; and prices had risen. What Mr White had said could have been true.

'Eh well, what the eye dunna see ... '

'Wus Mr Brassey there?' asked Edward.

'Canna see 'is name,' said John, after scouring the account of the dinner and names of dignitaries.

'Likely 'e 'anna bin there,' said Owd S'ewsb'ry. 'They say 'e dunna like banquets an' such. What 'e likes is shrimps an' bread an' butter. An' 'e teks 'is Missis an' they sits outside by the sea an' that's what they likes best.'

'Or 'e wus somewhere more important at the time,' said his son, not being of a romantic turn of mind.

The following morning, Edward and John went out into the streets of Shrewsbury once more. The weather had held, sun shone on trees whose leaves still clung to their branches.

They walked along the Foregate and stood on the English Bridge, leaning on the parapet, watching the horse-drawn barges filled with coal and stone, timber, iron and salt. The masted, shallow-bottomed trows glided by, a fragile coracle or two skittered as on a skin from bank to bank. Boats could have come from Bristol or Liverpool or London. People were arriving, people were leaving, people were travelling, to far places perhaps.

'What dost thee want, Edward?' asked John, dropping a twig into the water and watching it bob down-river.

'Go. Somewhere. Look for another line. There'll be many a line goin' out of 'ere. Think on all the Companies buildin' the station. There's the S'ewsb'ry an' Chester, that's us. There's the S'ewsb'ry an' 'Ereford. There's the S'ewsb'ry an' Birmin'am. An' there's the Canal one, the Shropshire Union Railway an' Canal Company 'er's called, proper mouthful of a name, that. The on'y line that's started diggin' is the line that goes to Wellington an' that's the one that the S'ewsb'ry an' Birmin'am an' the Canal one are workin' on together.'

' 'O's the contractor?'

'Mr Brassey, they says. For the S'ewsb'ry an' Birmin'am anyway.'

'That's good enough for me. Mr Brassey it is. 'Ow does a get to Birmin'am?'

'Ah thinks a goes to Wellington, then one branch goes to Stafford, t'other one goes to Wolver'ampton. Mebbe it'll go on from there to Birmin'am.'

'An' from Birmin'am the line's already built ter London, the great London an' Brummagem Railway. Think on it, Edward, we could go to London. See the Queen, an' Albert an' all the childern.'

' 'Ave to wait till we'n built as far as Brummagem. The babbies may a bin all married by that time.'

'Best get started then.'

'Right. Tomorrow. Let's 'ave a walk around, then go 'ome, get packed up an' tomorrow we'll be off.'

They left their perch against the parapet, crossed the rest of the bridge into the Mardol and sauntered back via a roundabout way through the familiar streets, past the intricately half-timbered houses with projecting storeys and gables, past humble brick and red sandstone. In the principal places the streets were now paved; and in the centre and in the better parts the new gas-lighting had been installed. Shrewsbury was becoming a very modern town.

The next morning they woke early. It was still dark. Even so, their mother was already up and the small fire lit. They stepped out into a quiet, grey world with a hint of light in the east. And eastwards they travelled, following the line which was taking shape towards Wellington.

At the level crossing there were workers laying bricks.

'For a Lodge.' they were told. 'There bin work further down, stations they wants built.'

The two walked on, quiet, bundles on their backs, thoughts wandering. 'Dost 'ee remember thy faither?' John asked suddenly.

Edward shook his head. 'Dunna remember nothin',' he said. 'Died when I was on'y a babby. Mam towd me 'e bin a shoemaker. They'd on'y been married a year or two. I was their on'y child.' He was quiet for a while. 'Mam couldna manage, on 'er own like. 'Er tried washin' for other folks, like as er's bin doin', but it dinna work. 'Er 'ad to get married again: marry or starve, I reckon. Then your Dad come along. 'E moved into Canal Buildings where Mam and I lived. That's where yo were born.'

' 'Ow old han yo bin then?'

'Five, I s'pose. Dinna think much o' yo. S'pose yo'm not too bad now though.'

John punched him on the arm. 'I s'll be bigger'n yo one o' these days. Jest yo wait.'

Edward laughed. They walked on.

'Where shall we live, dost think? When we sha'n 'ave found the work?'

Edward shrugged. 'Where we can. Might be shacks, might be lodgin's. We mun find sommat.'

They came across a ganger overseeing a team of men. They were moving through a small landscape of piles of bricks, buckets of sand and lime and water. Trenches made an outline of rectangular shapes.

'Try 'ere,' said Edward. He spoke to the ganger who looked towards John, hesitation written on his face. 'Bin doin' this job two year, 'im,' said Edward. 'Other things beside: 'orses, wagons, turns 'is 'and to a power o' things, right good worker ...' They agreed a price.

' 'Ow dost want it?' asked John of the others, going over to the buckets and accepting the shovel thrown towards him. The ganger watched for a moment or two and walked off.

At bait time they talked to a man with a shapeless hat set over a frizz of dusty hair and a puckered scar that ran from mouth to hairline. 'If yer canna guess me name, lad, youm out o' 'ere,' he said to John.

John looked. In an environment where every third man had a finger missing or some other disfigurement, this man stood out. 'Scarface, Mister?' he said, tentatively.

The man shook his head in mock admiration. 'An' 'o would you be then?'

'I'm ...' He thought quickly ... He'd long wanted something other than Nipper. 'Black Jack,' he said. It had something big and menacing about it.

'Pleased ter mek yer acquaintance, Black Jack,' said the man. 'An' 'o's yer big friend?'

'Ed,' said Ed.

'Well, us'll see,' said the man. 'Got lodgin's 'ave yer?' They shook their heads. 'Two just moved out. Come wi' me at knock-off time.'

The shack was bigger than their old one. Fourteen bunks lined the walls. A stove warmed one end. Four men sat on the floor playing cards and smoking. One snored from a bunk. There was a smell of sweat and boiling beef and vomit and long-unwashed feet.

'This 'ere's Moll,' said Scarface. 'The one wot does fer us.' A woman trembled up from a bunk beside the stove, her face a shrivelled decrepitude, her mouth a toothless cave. She cackled. The two boys stared, then nodded in acknowledgement.

'Whatever yer wants, boys, Moll's yer man,' said Scarface.

'Just you gi'e us yer vittles an' I s'll cook 'em. Two shilluns a week. Washin's extra. An' other things is extra.'

She winked.

Time pressed. Everything should have been done yesterday. The shareholders were grumbling. The Company was in debt. More money was needed. And they, the workers, must work not hard but harder, not long but longer.

At night newspapers went the rounds. Accidents: the paper was full of them. A man aged seventeen was walking along the rails and the train overtook him from behind. The engine driver backed up the van and they loaded him in to get him to hospital. But he was already dead.

A stoker got down to grease the axletrees. His foot slipped and two carriages went over his ankle. They took off his lower leg in the Infirmary: under chloroform, it was important to state.

A guard on a coal train was unlinking the buffers when the front of the train stopped while the back section carried on. He was crushed between them.

All these things happened on the line they had just left.

And on the line they were now working, a hole, suddenly appearing in a road under which the railway had burrowed, was a second away from swallowing a carriage and horses and only minutes away from swallowing the mail coach itself and all its passengers.

Earlier in the year a half-built bridge had collapsed and a worker, one of themselves, leaning just at that moment on the parapet, had drowned.

Railway accidents were only part of the story. The roofs of mines fell on boys, a lad fell into a kiln and was suffocated together with his potential rescuer, a woman disappeared along with her kitchen floor into the depths of an old mine-working, a carrier fell under the wheels of his wagon. None survived.

The weather grew colder. Paydays were few and when they happened John now went on the randy with the rest of them. He drank more at work too. Some of the men in the shack owned to fourteen pints a day; but John and even Edward fell short of that. They were not admired.

That Christmas of 1848 for once was spent at home, though briefly: away from the job for long and your place would be filled. There was news from John's Aunt Rachel: she was married.

'Well, I never,' said his mother, sitting suddenly down on a chair. 'Well,' she said, 'Well ... I ne'er thought it'd 'appen.'

' 'O is 'e?' said her husband suspiciously.

John, who had been employed to read the letter brought down by his grandmother, scanned the few lines again. 'Says 'e's a sodger, in the 59th Foot. Comes from Dorset, she says.'

'Scum o' the earth, sodgers,' said S'ewsb'ry.

' 'O says?' said his father, indignantly.

'Duke o' Wellington.'

'Won the Battle o' Waterloo, though, didden they, the Scum? Where'd the Great Man a bin wi'out 'is Scum then?'

S'ewsb'ry shrugged.

'Well, 'e wunna know about babby then, will 'e? If 'es bin bein' a sodger?'

'What'll 'appen when 'e finds out?' S'ewsb'ry said ominously.

I 'opes er's towd 'im,' said his grandmother, folding her arms firmly. 'No good e'er came of 'iding things. If 'e dunna know, someone'll mek it their business to tell 'im. An' then there'll be trouble.'

'Is 'er comin' 'ome?' asked John's father.

'Says not,' the grandfather said. 'Er's got a job with a man as got 'is own business as a printer. Nurse to their little 'un. Then off to Ireland, they is. The both on 'em.'

'Where'll 'er live then? Canna live with 'im in barracks, can 'er, not athout 'e's an officer or summat?'

John's father shrugged. 'Live in lodgin's mebbe. That's 'er lookout. Mun be a weak sort o' feller to marry 'er.'

John's grandmother didn't say much, yet John felt the news had pleased her. She looked quite cheerful.

.

8

Moving On

John was fascinated by the scar that disfigured the big fellow that shared their hut; the big, lean fellow with pale blue eyes that crinkled at the corners. One night when they were eating Moll's beef and potatoes, one of the other men noticed his stare.

'Tell the young 'un, Scarface,' he said. 'Tell 'im as 'ow yo got that slash across your nob. Would a bin prettier athout it, mebbe. Mind yo,' he went on, 'wenches dunna seem frit. Flies round an 'oney-pot.'

Scarface grinned. Men drew near to listen.

'Wus a Waterloo?' asked John, his eyes wide.

'Nay lad. Ah'm not that old. It were Peterloo.'

'Peterloo?'

'That's what they called it. Afterward. Sarcastic like. Waterloo were a battle, a proper battle. Sodgers fightin' other sodgers. This were sodgers, sodgers on 'orses, cavalry, wi' gret big swords. But them there cavalry were fightin' men on foot wi' no sticks even. An' women an' children. I were one o' them children.

John stared, held in the tension of the story. The others listened intently.

'Why?' John asked.

'We was 'ungry. It were four year after Waterloo an't sodgers all come back 'ome an' no jobs fer them an' no jobs fer us. No call for uniforms ter be made now, see, nor boots nor guns nor bullets, nor food fer't troops. An't didna get no better. Too many folk lookin' fer work, too little work, wages rock-bottom. Price o' bread, we couldna afford it. Prices kept 'igh to please gentry, 't big farmers. An' me Dad, 'e said it wanna fair an' us should 'ave a say an' be able ter vote an' change things in Parliament. Manchester, a gret big place like Manchester, didn't 'ave one person in Parliament ter speak for 'em. Not one.

'There were a man called 'Unt, Orator 'Unt, a man as we trusted. 'E come to speak in Manchester, St. Peter's Fields. Beautiful summer's day it were. We all went to 'ear 'im. People come from miles around. We walked all't way from near Stockport, Dad, Mam, me an' me two big two sisters in us Sunday best, cos Mr 'Unt wanted us all to look respectable. I were six. Mr 'Unt'd said no weapons, no sticks even, 'cept for the very old 'uns as canna walk wi'out 'em. An' we 'adna got none. None on us 'ad. We all listened ter't speech, thousands an' thousands on us, forty, sixty thousand on us, listenin'. You'd 'ave 'eard a mouse squeak. Seems as them magistrates, the snug folk wi' their money-bags an' their game an' their fields o' wheat, decided we was agin the law. So, what does they do?'

He looked up. His audience were rapt. 'They sends in't cavalry. There's a pathway through ter't 'ustings and they gallop up that and arrest Mr 'Unt, 'o don't make no fuss. An' it's still all quiet like. But then ...' He paused. 'Then't cavalry shouts summat about flags - lots of us 'ad flags an' banners - an' then they starts slashin' away wi' their gret big swords. An' everyone screams and runs an' rushes ter try ter get away from them gret big swords an' them gret big gallopin' 'ooves. An' me Mam's cryin' an' me sisters is cryin' an' me Dad's covered in blood an' I'm down on't floor wi' me face shriekin' at me. An' that's 'ow ... He stopped speaking and turned his cheek with the great, ugly scar towards his audience.

'Fifteen souls as'd never see another day. Four 'undred, mebbe seven 'undred wounded, no-one counted. Riots, uprisin's all o'er. Didna do no good. Gov'ment cracked down. Orator 'Unt put in prison and't others as was wi' 'im that day. Anyone the Gov'ment thought was for 'elping poor people and getting some of us into Parliament were put in prison.'

'So tell the lads what you are now,' said one of the onlookers.

Scarface looked at his audience. 'A Chartist,' he said.

'An' what's that?' asked Edward.

'A Chartist. See ... A Chartist wants the vote, for every man over twenty-one, rich or poor. A Chartist wants the vote secret, so't landowners an't masters canna tek away 'is cottage or 'is job if 'e don't vote 'ow as they tells 'im to. A Chartist thinks a man shouldna 'ave ter own property afore 'e can be an M.P., 'cos that way a poor man never gets there. An' M.P.s, they should be paid, else 'ow could a poor man be one? Then we wants elections every year an we wants all the constituencies ter be't same size.'

The two boys considered. 'Sounds fair,' said Edward.

' 'Tis fair,' said Scarface. "But mind 'o yer talks to and mind as where yer talks. 'Tis dangerous stuff Ah'm tellin' yer, for you an' me both. An' *I* can't 'ide.'

The directors, the shareholders, were keen for the completion of the line. They pressed the engineer, Mr Robert Stephenson, who in turn pressed the contractors, who pressed the agents who pressed the subcontractors who pressed the gangers who pressed the navvies. The navvies worked on.

There was at the moment, a major sticking point: the tunnel at Oaken Gates. Its difficulties were constantly spoken of. It was less than five hundred yards long, a short tunnel as tunnels went, but first the canal had had to be diverted and then the men were burrowing through solid rock, working from either side and from two shafts driven down from above. More than the normal volume of rock had to be removed as it had been designed to take broad gauge: why was unknown, as there was no other broad gauge track for many miles, till down to the south-west, where Mr Isambard Kingdom Brunel held sway. The wet weather of the previous year had put the work behind and men were now working night as well as day to catch up.

From the tops of the two shafts horses had been lowered in slings. Men descended by way of great buckets, buckets which also brought to the surface the stone they shovelled away after the miners among them had detonated the fuses and blown more rock apart. A miner had to detonate the fuse and then climb into one of the buckets which was hauled up partway to be out of the blast. Sometimes buckets had failed to rise, sometimes they tipped and their occupants fell out. The walls of the excavations ran with water: the floor was awash with mud. The space resonated with the sound of explosions and the echoes of iron striking iron or iron hammering rock. The air was thick with the smoke of gunpowder and dust and tobacco smoke. Men and horses ate down there and defecated down there in the mud; and all by the light of candles. They used the nubs to brew their tea.

John and Edward had begun working on the station at Shiffnal, a little town further along the line from Oaken Gates, towards Wolverhampton. One day they noticed that a man had arrived with a number of flags and was erecting them along the two sides of the new bridge that spanned and darkened the centre of the little market town below.

'What's that for, then?' asked John.

Edward shrugged. 'Celebration, I s'pose,' he said. From time to time they looked up from their work but nothing seemed to be happening. Then, as the afternoon wore on, people began to drift towards the bridge, gathering in the market square, gloomily oppressed now by the massive iron structure above it. A strange wailing sound arose as a company of Scotsmen in kilts and bonnets marched in, manfully blowing their pipes.

'It mun be McLeod,' Edward said. 'The contractor, the Scot. Testin' out the bridge.'

Sure enough an engine appeared, 'Caledonian' emblazoned proudly on its side, laden with McLeod, Winstanley the engineer and several unknown and well-upholstered gentlemen of undoubted quality. After shunting back and forth up and down the line from Pains Lane several times it gathered its courage and, to cheers and banner-waving from the assembled company below, it glided smoothly over the just-finished bridge.

'An' what'll they do now?' asked Edward, cynically. 'They'll go an' stuff theirselves on the best dinner in the whole town.'

'An' there'll be a power o' toasts,' said John. 'Dost a think they'll heft a glass to us?'

'Did you ever 'ear tell o' the Battle?' asked Trapp one night after work had come to a close. Trapp was so called, he had divulged, more from the fact of his surname being Trapp than from his devotion to poaching. Trapp kept a lurcher and a shotgun which hung on the wall. He would come back with a hare maybe, or a pheasant or a rabbit and Moll would boil it up for him in her witch's pot. It was April now and the days were getting longer and warmer. Edward had found a girl in Oaken Gates, not far away from the shacks where they were living and had spruced himself up to go a-courting: John was on his own.

'No,' he said, avid for a story. Though the problem with anything that Trapp said was that his words, even more than those of most men, had to be picked out of a morass of expletives.

Trapp stuffed his pipe and tamped down the tobacco before applying a flame. He drew in the smoke with satisfaction.

'Over a year ago now it were, well afore them three boggers died.'

' 'Ow, died?' asked John.

'Oh, at the Oaken Gates tunnel just afore knockin' off time. Bloody great lump of earth fell on 'em. They got one out quick, but 'is 'ead were all in a bloody mess like. An' 'e said, "I am goin' to leave you" an' so 'e bloody did. T'other boggers, they was already dead as doornails.

'Anyways, the feckin' Battle was afore that. You'll 'ave noticed all the collieries an' ironworkings an' great pit-mounds an' such all around these parts?' John nodded. 'Well, them colliers, they don't like the bloody Irish any more'n we do.' John began to feel uncomfortable. He still felt a little guilt about the starving Irishmen. And he'd learnt that his grandfather's father had come to Shrewsbury, alarmingly, from somewhere else: he might have a bit of Irish in himself. God forbid.

'Mr Murray, the contractor, 'e'd taken on a lot of feckin' Irishmen on 'is stretch comin' out o' Shrewsbury towards Wellington. Most of 'em were livin' *in* Wellington. Them boggers works for less money, yer knows, so as we loses us jobs unless we lowers us wages. We went an' talked to some o' the colliers round about an' they agreed wi' us as the bloody Irish 'ad ter be feckin' damn well stopped. They'd got wind o' things in Wellington an' all the shops put up their shutters an' all the people barred their doors.

'Well, us lot an' some colliers walked into Oaken Gates an' collected some more men and then we all went on ter Shiffnal ter collect any others we could find. We'd all got pick 'andles an' sticks an' 'ammers an' such. Well, we gets ter Shiffnal but some bogger's told the bloody magistrate. 'E talked to us. We'd got no quarrel wi' Shiffnal, so we didn't do no damage, but we went back ter Oaken Gates. There's about two 'undred of us by now. On'y when we gets ter Oaken Gates, we finds the bloody Irish already there, come ter meet us, all armed ter the bloody teeth wi' sickles an' cleavers an' pokers an' old swords an' shoutin' an' comin' at us. We did get a few o' the boggers, beatin' 'em an' throwing 'em into the canal. But trouble is there's more'n twice as many o' them as there is of us. An' then what turns up but a great bloddy load o' constabulary from Wellington. We 'eld us ground, but next mornin' a fresh lot o' pillocks from Shrewsbury joins 'em. Then the bloddy infantry arrives from Wolver'ampton an' a party o' dragoons from Birmin'am. Brave lads we are, but they was a bit too damn much fer us. Everything quietened down after that. S'pose yer could say it were the battle as never was.' He grinned contentedly. 'We showed 'em though, showed the feckin' boggers we meant business. Yer can't 'ave them foreigners tekkin' advantage,' he said. John nodded. He had noticed that Trapp had considerably toned down his language during the telling, possibly out of regard for John's tender years.

'An', lad, what are ye payin' ole Moll?'

'Two shillin's.'

'Gi'e 'er one. Yous bein' robbed.'

Edward returned late that evening. John was already in his bed. When he first came to the hut he had listened at night with fascination to the sounds that came from Moll's bunk: now his curiosity had been largely appeased and he wrapped his coat around his ears to prevent his sleep being disturbed. He did not hear Edward's return.

Edward looked pleased with himself on the following day. He whistled as they rode the wagon away from Oaken Gates to Shiffnal.

They stood for a moment to admire the great iron bridge that spanned the centre of the town. The station that they were building was adjacent, high above the roadway atop the embankment: there were great arches, to be used, they were told, as warehouses, and much length and height of wall to build for support, for shoring up the earth that had been raised; and a tall, flat-fronted station master's house to build besides.

An old newspaper flapping among the unfinished buildings caught John's eye. He walked over and picked it up. A few other pages lay trapped in the mud further on. He put the pages together: some were missing. His eye caught another splotch of white and he walked over. It was the *Illustrated London News*, a relatively recent publication, highly prized because of its pictorial content. He folded it and pushed it into a pocket, to examine later.

When they stopped for their break John pulled out the pages. Taking up the whole of the front page was a picture: a lady and gentleman and their five children round a tall, cone-shaped tree. John had never seen such a tree though he had heard tell of one: it was called a Christmas Tree. The royal family had had one for the children for the past year or two. He looked at the picture again. There was a border to the picture, of fruit and game-birds with their necks wrung, of fish, rabbits and sheep, all lying dead and ready for the pot, symbols of plenty. Under the tree were what he supposed to be gifts for the children: a model of a steam engine, its tender following, a toy chariot with horse and rider, so many things. Dangling from the branches were what might be bowls of sweets and little packages of secrets. And each tier of the tree, far taller than the lady and gentleman, who must be the Queen and Prince Albert, was covered with lighted candles; and on the very top was an angel. His mother would love to look at this. He folded it carefully and returned it to a pocket. Before he handed it over he could read the paper himself, when time allowed: he enjoyed reading about the world; and pictures made things come alive.

That evening he took the paper out again. He looked at the date: the 23rd of December gone. His eyes turned to the children. They all had curls, but the girls' were longer, ringlets, was that the word? They all wore frocks but the elder boy had long pantaloons underneath: he couldn't make out the younger one. He thought he remembered William wearing a frock when he was small: he supposed he must have done so himself, though he couldn't remember one. He folded the paper up again. Prince Albert was a good-looking fellow and enviably dapper. You couldn't dress like that and work in the mud in all weathers as they did. He was supposed to be aristocratic and clever as well, though why she had to marry a foreigner, a German, he couldn't think. Scarface said that he spent £17,000 a year on his horses. Our money, Scarface said. He couldn't imagine having that sort of money. And knew he never would.

Edward was getting fussy about his clothes. Generally when they came in on a wet day they scraped the worst of the mud off and stood as near to the stove as they could get to dry the rest. If breeches, say, got really dry, you could beat them with a stick to get more dirt out in the form of dust. Sometimes they would give clothes to Moll to be pounded in a tub with a dolly.

The scraping and beating methods suited Edward on ordinary days, but for use on special occasions he had somehow acquired a fancy blue plush waistcoat with brass buttons and a newish pair of moleskin trousers and boots better than his working ones. He put a comb through his hair and trimmed stray whiskers from a satisfying growth of beard before he went out. John was full of envy: he frequently and surreptitiously felt his own chin, but it stayed disappointingly smooth. He knew any beard would be noticeable if it matched his hair and eyebrows: they were very dark. His chosen nickname of Black Jack had lasted less than an hour before being reduced to 'Blackie', a name which, he thought morosely, could as well be that of a dog or even a cat. His arm muscles though, he was pleased to feel, were coming on nicely. Come the summer he would be able to roll up his shirt sleeves as he worked; and be noticed. He dreamed of a girl with laughing rosy face and flaxen curls and tiny waist that he could encircle with his strong and manly arm.

This was an uncomfortable line, John thought, a bitty place. There were too many contractors, each concentrating on a small section; and a feeling of complications and tension, of quarrels on high. Mr Brassey seemed disappointingly absent and queries won John only a shrug or a shake of the head. Maybe they'd got it wrong and Mr Brassey was elsewhere. In the meantime he'd heard through the rumour-mill that tenders had been invited for the station at Wolverhampton. There'd be even more work there than at Shiffnal, he thought, with platforms, engine sheds, warehouses and carriage sheds besides the actual station building. That would no doubt be a grand construction, Wolverhampton becoming now such an important place. There would be new techniques to learn. His interest in his craft and its varied challenges was growing.

Part of the line, the stretch from Shrewsbury short of the tunnel at Oaken Gates and from there the line to Stafford, all thirty miles of it, was due to open in a month or two: the rest of it, the stem of the Y, from Wellington to Wolverhampton, their stretch, would have to wait until the finishing of tunnel and embankment made it possible.

The opening of the Shrewsbury-Stafford line took place on the Glorious First of June, so called, Scarface told him, because the English navy had beaten the Frenchies long ago on that day. But it *was* glorious, on that particular day of 1849, perfect weather for a triumphal opening. He, Edward and a few others, including Trapp, walked back down the line, past Oaken Gates tunnel to its far side. Trapp was an odd-looking man, thought John. He gazed, working out why. He was tall and thin, with a smallish head on a thick neck. His skin had a leathery look. John remembered a lizard he had once seen basking in the sun on a pile of stones. Lizards, though, didn't swear like Trapp did. Blasphemies and obscenities whirled thick as snowflakes through any hut or any social gathering of men, but where Trapp was the blizzard was at its most dense. Only when they were working were men quiet: the physical effort was too much and the focus too intense to waste energy on words. John was acquiring a fine vocabulary of his own.

The group looked expectantly in the direction of Wellington. Puffs of smoke and an echoing whistle told of the arrival of the iron horse. There it was. It had started its journey at Shrewsbury, they knew. Now it had come the three miles past Wellington as far as it could go before being stopped by the unfinished Oaken Gates tunnel.

They were no longer alone. Towards them had come a vast procession, headed by a band. Banners floated over two thousand or so men and boys, all neatly dressed and each with a strip of coloured paper round his hat, bearing such mottoes as 'Success to the Iron Trade' or 'Success to Snedshill Iron Works' or 'May good Masters have Faithful Servants': they were all colliers and ironworkers, their works having supplied the rails, beams and any other iron for the line.

'Come on, lads. Let's get to the bloddy beer.' That was Trapp. 'There's nowt 'ere fer us lot.'

They made their way to the new hotel in Oaken Gates, the Caledonian.

'Same as McLeod's engine,' commented Edward.

They drank a few glasses under disapproving eyes. It was evidently a place not designed for the likes of them. As they grew louder, the eyes became ever more disapproving. A couple of constables made an appearance.

'Dirty toads,' muttered Trapp. 'Not much joy 'ereabouts. Reckon us'll move on.' He led the way, turning to shower a few oaths upon the company; and the others followed.

'There's the George Inn at Pains Lane,' said Edward.

'Try that then.'

Half a mile and there it was, an ancient, half-timbered place slumbering by the village green. Though on the green, a marquee stood; and around the marquee was a crowd of workmen very far from slumber, standing about expectantly and gossiping loudly over mugs of beer.

Edward elbowed his way inside. John followed. A buxom woman was pulling beer behind the polished wooden counter. Younger girls assisted. Edward singled out one of them. 'Two pints o' your best, Mary Ann,' he said.

Mary Ann looked towards him and smiled, a knowing, impudent smile. Was this, John wondered, the lass he'd been seeing? Edward and she were close in conversation.

'Work to be done, Mary Ann,' said the older woman, sharply. Mary Ann drew away, turning to pull the pints. John looked at her. He wouldn't mind that himself: bosoms bursting, stays a-straining, black ringlets frothing past her shoulders. He felt a stab of envy and desire. Wait till he grew up.

They carried their drinks over to a bench. Edward gazed at the fair one, who gave him sidelong glances as she bustled about collecting glasses; and bent revealingly towards him as she wiped the table in front of them for longer than was at all necessary.

'I s'll see thee later?' Edward asked.

' 'Appen yo may an 'appen yo mayn't.' She bridled. 'If nothin' better comes my way. Now, drink up. We've dinner for three 'undred to get out there.' She pointed outside to the marquee.

'What's on then?' asked Edward.

"Tis the men from Snedshill's. Iron men, they are.' She tittered. 'An' the gentry, the ironmasters, they've just finished their own dinner an' they're to serve the workmen. Think o' that! If they can stand up, o' course. Too many toasts to the Wrekin, if you asks me. Now, be off wi' yo. Mebbe I s'll find meself a gentleman, Master Kirby."

'Not one as'd go down well wi' me Mam,' said John, when they'd struggled outside.

'An' all the better for that,' said his brother.

9

Small Happenings

It was the August of 1849 and John a few months short of fifteen. The trees at the side of the line were leafed in the dark, leathery green of maturity. The grass lay thin and bleached, the soil dusty. Some hold-up in supplies had caused work to be suspended and the brothers were seizing their chance to go home for a couple of days.

They had at first that day decided to join the others, going in force to the magistrate's court where one of the gangers was to appear, having been charged with using threats against the wife of the landlord of the Coach and Horses. The word was that a navvy, known as Rabbit, had got into an argument with the ganger there, that the publican's wife had tried to restore order and been subjected to a torrent of abuse for her pains. The ganger was not much liked, chiefly because he was a ganger; and men would lie through their teeth if they wanted to. The brothers had got as far as the venue at the Court in Shiffnal when they changed their minds: it would be good to visit home and perhaps it was better to keep away from the sharp eyes of authority.

Returning down the line they passed the spot where Poole had died. On the day of the Grand Opening of the Shrewsbury to Stafford in June he'd been one of their group, part of the festive scene near Oaken Gates. He'd had a bag of stripy humbugs which he'd offered to the brothers. They'd sucked them with pleasure, relishing the sweetness.

He had been coming down the track a few days later towards Shiffnal where Edward and John were working. They had seen him on previous occasions, jauntily riding the front wagon of a train loaded with huge stones, residue from the Oaken Gates tunnel and destined for the embankment. This time the stones had shifted, the wagon had tipped, throwing Poole forwards and out. Wheels had gone over his hands; a falling boulder had burst the fragility of his skull. Everyone agreed he must have died instantly.

The brief inquest had been held at the *Union Inn* in Shiffnal. Someone, to express regret or perhaps surprise that such a thing should have befallen such a one, had spoken of a young man of steady and sober habits. A verdict of accidental death was recorded.

The brothers doffed their hats as they passed the spot, half-seeing, half not wanting to see, splotches of dried blood, half-tasting again the peppermint in the sweetness.

'What dost 'ee reckon to our Dad, then?' asked John after a while.

' 'E's the on'y Dad as Ah know of,' said Edward. 'Canna remember me own Dad, tha knowst. 'E's al'ays treated me right. Like one of 'is own. Some dunna. Taught me a trade an' all.'

'If your Dad 'ad've lived, would you 'ave been a shoemaker?'

'S'pose as Ah would,' said Edward, considering. 'Dunna think it'd've suited me much, though, sittin' stitchin' all day. Like brickin' better. Proper good trade these days as well. Wi' all the railways. An' all the folks swarmin' into the towns to find work an' wantin' 'ouses an' all. We'll not go short o' work.'

'An' what do yo really reckon to that Mary Ann?'

' 'Er'll do,' said Edward shortly. 'An' dunna yo be goin' an' tellin' our Mam. Or there mun be trouble.'

'An' what do yo do, like, when yo's with 'er, like?'
'Never yo mind,' said Edward fiercely. 'Shut your trap.'

Home was much as they'd last seen it. Little Mary was no longer toddling everywhere, followed by whichever sister had been detailed to keep her from falling into the fire or climbing into the water-butt or whatever new adventure her curiosity inspired: instead she was employed in carrying from here to there, in shelling peas or scrubbing potatoes, whatever simple tasks were within the capabilities of a four-year-old.

John gave his mother the copy of the *Illustrated London News*. She took it from him with delight and smoothed it carefully out, her hands brushing off the now-dried smears of mud. The girls crowded about her and soon a finger was pointing at the beautiful lady in a dress so fine they had never seen the like; and Esther, usually quite sensible as girls go, was asking if she too could have ringlets; and Anne was wondering what was in the little packages dangling from the branches and imagining they contained all her most longed-for things ever seen in shop windows.

Aunt Susanna paid a visit, accompanied by her boy Edmund, now twelve, a schoolboy no longer and wondering whether to take up bricklaying like his father, or whether to try baking. 'Very 'andy, 'e is, at the bakin',' said his mother proudly. John looked at his cousin, for whom he had no particular affinity, saw again his newly-brushed and carefully parted hair, his clean clothes and his slender extremities and felt misgivings as to the bricklaying.

The small girl-child with Susanna was identified as Rachel Anne, the one born out of wedlock. She called Susanna 'Mammy'. 'Dunna know no different, see,' explained Susanna.

Susanna had a satisfied air about her. John noticed his

mother eying her up, and wondered. Susanna had had another letter from Rachel, her sister and the girl-child's mother.

'Says 'e 'ad the small-pox, 'er sodger. When 'e was a young 'un, like,' said Susanna.

S'ewsb'ry guffawed. 'Knew as there'd be summat amiss wi' 'im,' he said. 'Be one o' them despert bad cases, looks as rabbits been burrowin' all o'er 'im, shouldna wonder.'

'Says 'e's proper good to 'er,' Susanna said sharply. 'Which is more'n yo can say o' some folks.' She glared at her brother.

'An' 'e wunna get it never no more,' Owd S'ewsb'ry added belatedly, apropos the smallpox.

' 'Ow's work?' Edward asked of the two older men.

His father shrugged. 'A could be worse. Station's comin' on a bit fast. But there's wagon sheds an' engine sheds an' such. Al'ays rumours 'bout other bits o' building in S'ewsb'ry beside. We sha'n be busy as a dog in duff.'

'What bin the Openin' like this end?' asked John. 'Didden yo go an' watch?'

'Wunna a patch on t'other one,' said Owd S'ewsb'ry. 'Flags there were an' a brass band, but not a lot o' folks went to look. They said widders an' orphans along the line got an 'ole ox betwixt 'em, though. An' the schoolchildren got a grand dinner o' roast beef an' plum pudding.'

'That were at Pains Lane,' said Edward. And he told them about the ironworkers being served by the masters.

'Ah dunno,' said Owd S'ewsb'ry, shaking his head slowly. 'Ah canna fathom it out. Ah hanna noticed no widders nor little uns muckshiftin' at all. Nor the maisters neither. Ah wagers them maisters got a good dinner though.'

' 'Eard there bin dinner for eighty on 'em,' said Edward. 'At Wellington. They toasted whatever they could think on, same as al'ays. From the Queen to the ironworks to the Wrekin an' everythin' in between.'

'Edward knows someone as knows things like that,' said John helpfully; and earned a black look from his brother.

'Folks can get right to London easy now,' he went on brightly by way of diversion. 'Go from 'ere to Stafford, change to the London an' North Western line - big company, that - an' yo can be in London in five hours.'

Owd ShrewsS'ewsb'ry shook his head slowly from side to side. ' 'Appen we shall soon be comin' back afore we'm got there,' he said. 'It's enough to scramble a man's brains.' The older folk nodded in agreement.

'Then there's that electric telegraph,' he went on. 'Ship lands at Portsmouth, man from the newspapers jumps on, gets all the latest news, runs to the telegraph office an' suddenly it's o'er all the papers from Glasgow to wherever. Soon there'll be folk like us bein' able to send messages to each other, yo mark my words.'

John thought this an exciting idea, though he didn't say so as the older ones murmured in disparagement.

Owd S'ewsb'ry turned towards Edward. 'An 'ow's *your* line?' he asked.

The brothers looked at each other. 'It's alright when yo just workin',' said Edward, hesitantly. 'Cos then all yo's thinkin' on is work. But there's things goin' on.'

'What sort o' things?' asked his father suspiciously.

'Dunno, 'ard to say. Word is the London an' North Western wants to buy us up, the Shrewsbury an' Birmin'am, that is. They've already bought out the stretch from Shrewsbury to Stafford as used to belong to the Canal Company. Or leased it, anyway.'

'An' they wants to buy the old line beside, one as we worked on,' added John. 'The S'ewsb'ry an' Chester.'

'Gettin' too big for their boots, then,' said S'ewsb'ry. They all sagely agreed.

They travelled back the following morning by the early train, riding free with the guard as far as Oakengates, passing, to their right, the great hump of the Wrekin, centre of so many tribal toasts. In spite of having now ridden in a truck several times, John exulted in the sensation of speed and power. The puffs of smoke, the clatter of wheel on rail, steel on steel, the blink of hedges, trees, people and cottages flying past, all mesmerised his senses.

Asked how the ganger had fared, Trapp told them that he'd been bound over for six months to keep the peace. 'There was near another bloddy fight, though, wi' Rabbit. E'd got it into 'is rabbity 'ead that it were a good idea to celebrate 'is victory by dancing round the town with 'is feckin' friends, wearin' blue ribbons an' singin' "I 'ates bloddy gangers" or some such. Rabbit got off scot-free, cos 'e 'ad three witnesses, o' course.' He winked.

John was alone in the hut, except for the ever-present Moll, warming herself in front of the stove. He was wary of Moll. She had a tongue on her and a choice selection of oaths: he'd never heard a woman so prolific and it gave him a faint sense of shock every time she let forth: somehow it didn't seem right that a woman should swear so. It was rare to be alone there, but the other men were out drinking away their pay and Edward had gone to see his Mary Ann, she having a rare few hours off.

Moll looked round and saw him, saw that only he was in the room. He pretended to be reading a newspaper he'd borrowed from Scarface, the only man he knew who was regularly seen reading anything at all. She beckoned to him and reluctantly he went over.

'See this, Blackie?' She delved for something in the depths of her garments and held it out: it was a creased sheet, limp from folding and handling. He nodded.

'Couldst tha read it me?' He took the letter from her hand. 'I never learned, see.'

He opened it out and held it, trying to decipher the faded writing. 'Dear Sister,' he read, 'Hope this finds you as it leaves me. I am off to sea. When I get back I will come and see you. Your loving brother Christmas.'

'Don' that say no more?'

John looked at the paper again and at its back. 'That's all, Moll.'

'That be what it said last time.' Her voice was heavy with disappointment.

'When didden yo get this?'

'Oh, years agone now. 'E's never come though.'

'That's a' ... he considered ...'nice name, Christmas.'

'Norfolk, yer see. Lot o' lads as be called Christmas in them days. 'Spect they still be. Me Dad, 'e were called Christmas too. That were where 'e came from, me Mam said, Norfolk.'

John had never thought of Moll as having a mother or a father, never mind a brother who might still be alive: to him she was just Moll, as much part of the shanty as the walls or the floor.

'Me Dad were a navvy, see. Canals that were, not railways then. I were born by a canal. Dunno which one though, we kep' movin' on.' She sounded wistful. 'I were the littl'un. The others looked after me. Christmas, now, 'e were me big brother. Used ter carry me on his shoulders, 'e did. They all left though. Then there were just me and Mam. She died. I were fourteen. Went wi' a navvy. 'Ad to 'ave an 'ome, see. Or t'were the work'ouse, but didna fancy that. Christmas, he came ter see me the once. I were a-livin' wi' me man, on the railways by then. Later, 'e sends me this letter. It were a long time ago.' There was a silence. 'Better get yer teas then, or there'll be trouble.' She raised herself stiffly from the stool and ran a gnarled hand over John's hair. 'You'm a good lad, Blackie.'

John sat on the vacated stool. Moll busied herself in an aimless way. 'What 'appened to your man?' he asked after a while.

'Oh, 'e gone off lookin' fer work. Never come back. So I found another. I never 'ad no children, the good Lord knows why. P'raps it were fer the best.'

Scarface's paper had held some news that John found interesting. He resolved to ask Scarface about it when he had a chance. Scarface kept up with events in the wider world that were a mystery to John. He seemed to have a broader view of life than most of the men John knew.

'What's this about George 'Udson?' he asked, catching Scarface up a few days after and walking alongside.

' 'Udson? Railway King, they call 'im. Or did. 'E's been toppled from 'is throne, looks like. Were very rich, into railways all over't country. Now they've found 'e's been fiddlin't books, mekkin' 'isself rich by robbin't share'olders. It's all caught up with 'im. Owes 'undreds o' thousands.'

'Will 'e be transported?'

Scarface laughed. 'Not 'im. Not likes of 'im. When did you last 'ear of a gentleman bein' transported? Even if 'e is a self-made gentleman. Only poor souls as steals a few yards o' cloth or summat gets sent away from 'is family an' friends in a leaky ship ter be a slave t'other side't world. There was a chap lived near Stafford. Stole a pair o' clogs. Case come up this July. Transported fer ten year. 'Ad been in prison twice afore, mind, for stealin' things, but it's a lot less than 'Udson's stolen. One law fer't rich an' one fer't poor. An' don't never ferget that our Blackie.'

They walked in silence for a while. 'Someone said there ought to be what they call an independent auditor,' John said, stumbling a little over the words. 'To look o'er the accounts o' the railway companies. Make sure it's all honest.'

'That were proposed in Parliament, that were.' Scarface grinned. 'Companies weren't too keen by 'eck. An' what dost think? About forty M.P.s mek money from railways. Think o' the chairman o' this line, Ormsby-Gore, M.P.' He emphasised the 'M.P.'

'Chairman o' the S'ewsbury an' Chester besides,' said John thoughtfully.

'Been readin' about our S.&B. 'alf-yearly meetin',' said Scarface. 'Some weren't too 'appy wi't Secretary. Said 'e'd too much power and 'e 'adn't left enough time for firms to tender for contracts before 'e chose't one 'e liked best. Meanin' one as'd promised 'im a back'ander."

'A wrong 'un then,' said John.

'Mebbe.' Scarface rubbed his chin. 'Some folk'd wanted ter cancel't branch lines to Madeley an' Coalbrookdale as well ter save money. But they couldna do that 'cause Company'd already tekken't money for it from't share'olders. So they's mekkin' just the one line instead o' two. Cut costs, see. They got ter 'ave that line anyway, fer't money they meks from freight, from carryin' coal an' iron.'

'A's all too deep for me,' said John. 'Think I mun stick to doin' a job an' tekkin' the shillin's an' no worritin'.'

'Ah,' said Scarface, wagging a finger, 'Yer never knows. When't masters start quarrellin', somehow us lot gets drug in. An guess 'o gen'rally loses out? Guess 'o 'as to do their 'ard, dirty work an' their fightin' for 'em? While somehow they goes on 'avin' them big dinners an' them fancy toasts an' sleepin' in them soft feather beds.'

August turned to September. As the brothers walked towards Shiffnal one morning with the sunlight bestrewing bramble thickets with diamond-pointed lace, a man caught them up from behind. It was Harry the Egg, a man with a startlingly domed and hairless head.

' 'Ave you 'eard?' His tone was important.

' 'Eard what?'

' 'Bout that young Nipper.'

The brothers said nothing and waited.

'Inquest's this mornin'. *Dog Inn*, Shiffnal. Only 'appened last night. Late it was an' young John, the Nipper, 'e'd bin workin' since it got light. Must've fallen asleep 'cross the rails.'

'What job han 'e bin doin', then?' asked Edward.

'Oh, changin' the points. Easy job like, but a lot o' waitin', from one train to another. Anyway, it got dark an' 'e fell asleep. Must a done or 'e'd've 'eard the engine comin'. The Caledonian, it was, McLeod's pride an' joy. Cut 'im in 'alf. Well, better get on.' He hurried ahead and they saw him stop and speak to another group further up the line.

They heard about the inquest later. The jury returned 'accidental death' and recommended the Coroner to insist that Mr McLeod, the contractor, should not allow his boys to work so many hours together. It was a somewhat unusual and bold request.

It was a week or two on when Edward came in late one night and fell heavily into his bunk. John thought he caught a faint groan. In the morning Edward failed to rise. John punched lightly at his shoulder. 'Come on, Ed. Yo mun be up.'

A muffled voice from beneath the blanket seemed to express both intense irritation and a desire to be left alone. John yanked the blanket from his brother's face; and drew back in alarm. The side of the face which was uppermost was dark red and swollen. A cut could be seen near the jaw. As Edward turned his head John could see that the other eye was a similar colour. An ear and nearby hair were matted with dark and clotted blood.

'There's more,' said Edward painfully, gesturing

vaguely at his torso.

'What 'appened then?' asked John, trying not to sound alarmed.

'S'pose the iron men got me,' said Edward ruefully. 'One come first an' then a lot.'

'It bin that Mary Ann.' John spat.

Edward let out a stream of curses inveighing against all iron men and all Mary Anns so long and so loudly that a voice screeched into his words, 'Ladies present!'

John looked over and there was Moll, cackling with glee. 'Don't you be worriting, lad,' she said through her bursts of hooting, 'She'll not be worth it. You'll mend. An' you'll find a good lass, you wait an' see. In the meantime, come of a night-time an' Old Moll'll look after thee. For a price, mind.'

The Wellington to Wolverhampton section was surely to open in September. It would surely be open before October. Or surely during October. At last, Mr Stephenson the engineer and the Government Inspector together tested the line using, it was reported, wagons of the heaviest weights, inspected the Oaken Gates tunnel and pronounced it perfectly safe and substantial: preparations would be made for the Opening.

'There'll be six trains every day,' said Scarface, who had been keeping up with his information from the newspapers. 'Each way, that is an' all. They say they're't most comfortable an' stylish carriages yet. Even't second class are better than anythin' on't London an' North Western that's tryin' ter buy us all up.'

John had seen the famous carriages. They were red, crimson lake being the fancy name, with the panelling picked out by blue lines. Very elegant, he had thought.

' 'Ere, listen ter this,' Scarface crowed, waving a fist above his head in mock triumph. 'They've even thought about't guard. 'E's goin' to be protected from't rain an' wind by 'avin' a roof over 'is 'ead. It says: "Even with the guards' vans it has been rightly judged that efficient performance of duty is allied to personal comfort." Don't matter seemingly about third class passengers though. They don't get no roofs.'

He handed the paper over to John who scanned the columns. 'Three sorts o' carriages?' he queried. 'First, second an' third?'

'An' three sorts o' services,' said Scarface. 'Express, one hour from S'ewsb'ry to Wolver'ampton. Or'nary, an hour an' a half. An' Mixed, two hours. An' the faster yer goes, the more yer pays.'

'There's excursion trains so as folk can see the Wrekin an' such,' said John, reading further. 'There's special trains laid on for the fairs, cattle trains ... Seem to 'ave thought of everythink.'

'Still can't get ter Birmin'am, 'cept by 'orse an' carriage, though,' said Scarface. 'When's that bit o' line a-comin', I wants ter know?'

The Shrewsbury and Birmingham was at last set to open as far as Wolverhampton on the 12th of November that year of 1849. It was the day before John's fifteenth birthday; not that his birthdays were of much importance to anyone except himself. Even Edward had to be nudged into remembering. He supposed his mother might have remembered, though of course she was far away. A railway opening was as good a way to celebrate as any, he supposed. He had an idea.

'Edward,' he said tentatively, There'll be no work Monday. What about we buys a ticket an' joins the excursion train?'

Edward paused in pulling on his boots. 'We mun 'ave ter pay,' he said.

'It'll be cheap, third class,' said John. 'No, tell yo summat,' he said as an idea struck him, 'We needna pay at all. We could come up quiet-like, from t'other side an' climb into a carriage. No-one'd know. There'll be crowds an' crowds of folk. No-one'll notice us.'

'Right,' said Edward. 'Where sha'n we get on the train?'

'An where shan us get off?' said John.

They decided to board the train at Oaken Gates where it was supposed to stop for a while to take on more passengers. They would be able to view Shiffnal station from the point of view of the travelling public and see the hitherto unknown stretch as far as Wolverhampton. There would be a longish break at that important place and they could have a look round the town, get in a few beers and enjoy themselves before the ride back to Shiffnal.

Monday arrived. They woke to thick fog.

'It's early, though. Mebbe clear later,' said Edward hopefully.

They washed as best they could. Edward donned what John thought of as his courting outfit. He himself had acquired a red plush waistcoat in contrast to Edward's blue and had found, in a Shiffnal pawnbroker's, a pair of boots in sound condition: at least these were a matching pair, perhaps better able to make an impression on the fair sex.

After a pint mug of Moll's tea and a hunk of fried bread with fat bacon, they took themselves off to walk west towards Shrewsbury as far as Oaken Gates station, regarding its neat frontage with some satisfaction. One glance at the mass of bodies swathed in fog told them there was no need for subterfuge. They drifted in with the press and there they waited and still they waited, among the ever-gathering crowd, its murmurings gradually changing from an expectant twittering to a growlingly more sombre and ominous lack of patience.

At twenty-five minutes to ten the train heralded its very delayed arrival with a chorus of mighty whistles with musical accompaniment. It emerged through the fog, a monster of a train, headed by three locomotives, the Vulcan, the Salopian and the Wrekin. Behind these three smoking, steaming creatures came an open platform occupied by a band in full regalia, drumming and blowing for Queen and Country. This was followed by (and they had to count as the body of it passed and count the tail after the train had stopped) thirty-eight carriages already filled with excited people. In first class rode the dignitaries: the mayors and councillors, gentry and big business men. In second class rode the middle sort; and in third class rode people of their own ilk.

There was a tidal rush for seats, the brothers flotsam in the surge. Edward reached safety first and hauled John after him. They squeezed into a corner, standing. In contrast to expectation, this third class carriage not only had a roof, it had sides and doors and even glass in the windows. They could have been royalty, it seemed to John.

'Oh, look at them wenches, o'er there.' He pointed to the platform side where two girls were being elbowed to one side, crushed against the carriage. Edward forced his way to the open door, pushing away a clot of people and thus allowing the shorter girls to enter under the cover of his outstretched arms. John, who had held the corner, beckoned the girls to take their places, the brothers acting as bulwarks against the crush. The girls clung upright together, giggling in relief, blushing as they observed their rescuers.

'A deal o' thanks Sir,' said the elder, the first to recover herself. Neither she nor her sister was the flaxen-haired, tiny-waisted maiden of John's dreams, but they both looked good-natured girls.

'Think nothin' on it, Miss,' said Edward gallantly.

The girls stood silent. Edward and John looked out of the windows and at their fellow passengers. After a while there were hisses of escaping steam, a whistle and a jerk as the carriages began to move. The girls clung closer together and the younger one gave a little scream.

'Yo needna be frit, ladies,' said Edward kindly.

The younger girl looked at him with wide eyes. ' Ave yo ridden a train afore?'

'Many an' many a time,' Edward answered, with a reassuring smile.

John nodded in agreement. 'Nothink to be afraid of,' he said. 'An' when we gets to the tunnel, well, there's nothink to be afraid of there neither. Mr Stephenson, that's the engineer, says it's . . .' he remembered the newspaper. . . 'Perfectly safe an' substantial.'

The younger girl gazed at him with admiration.

'Yo'm proper safe wi' us,' Edward said, his tone fatherly.

Feminine shrieks and screams of apprehension coming from the carriages ahead portended the arrival of the dreaded tunnel, the train slowed to a crawl and suddenly their carriage was plunged into darkness. John took advantage of this to seize the hand of the younger girl and hold it, purely for purposes of reassurance and safety, until suddenly, and far too soon, they burst forth again into light amid manly shouts of 'Hurrah' and the hand was snatched back.

The train chugged on. John smiled again at the younger of the girls. 'Yo see?' he said. 'Tek no 'eed. Nowt to be frit on, while we'm 'ere.' She blushed and squeezed closer to her sister.

The brothers pointed out to each other, in tones loud enough to be clearly heard by the girls, the sights of the line; or what would have been the sights had they not been so indistinct in the dank obscurity. They reached Shiffnal where the train stopped at a station barely seen for flags and excited crowds, more of whom scrambled into carriages, the brothers sheltering the ladies as best they could from the crush of bodies.

'We built this station,' said John proudly and ill-advisedly.

The girls looked at him in shock. 'Yo built it?' said the elder one.

'Me an' me brother,' John said. 'Well, an' a few other folks,' he amended.

'But yo canna be ... ' said the elder, faintly ...'Yo canna be one o' them navvies?'

Edward managed a glare at John before answering, 'No, no, no, o' course not, Miss. Not navvies, no. We'm bricklayers. There's a power o' difference, Miss.'

She still looked suspicious but it was fading from her eyes.

'Eh dear yes.' John realised his mistake. ''Tis true, Miss. Bricklayers o' S'ewsb'ry. Al'ays 'ave been, al'ays will be.'

'But binna yo afeard, with all those despert men round about? They steals, yo knows, an' fights and drinks all their wages away. Folks all says to keep away. They care nothink for the law. There's nothink they wunna do. Nothink.'

Edward shook his head in sympathy. ''Tis true they bin a despert lot, Miss. But John an' me, we can 'andle 'em.'

At that moment the train drew into Albrighton and came to a stop. There was a delay while another half-dozen carriages were added. John craned his head out of the window to watch. A man came swinging down the platform, shoving others out of his way; a lizard-like fellow, letting a stream of filth leave his lips as he looked for the hint of a space. John pulled himself inside but it was too late.

'Blackie, man,' called the one on the platform. 'Let us in, yer bogger. Let owd Trapp in.' More oaths as he pulled open the door and tried to climb into the carriage. He was big and dirty and determined; and very drunk. 'Come on,

Ed, 'elp a fellow up.'

He clambered inside, jostling willy-nilly for room, tossed back the tail of a ragged nightcap and slapped a friendly arm around each of the brothers. 'Well, lads. Off to Wolver'ampton, bin we? Ketched some feckin' pretty ones a'ready, han we?' He leered at the two girls.

John looked towards the sisters. They clung together and their faces were stony. Any hopes, he realised, had been irretrievably lost.

10

Railway Wars

It was a week or two later, the year of 1849 entering its last dark, wet month, when a man walked into the camp near knocking-off time. From the bundle he carried and the relief with which he settled himself against a dripping hummock, pulled his hat low over his eyes and lapsed into slumber, it seemed that here was a man on the tramp, a likely bearer of news.

Later, the brothers joined the group of onlookers waiting to hear his story. He was first led into the largest of the huts to be regaled with beef and potatoes and a great jug of beer was placed next to him.

'Come on then, man,' someone shouted. 'What's the news?'

John nudged Edward. 'Lukka,' he said. 'Look a' that nose. Han 'ee seen a nose like that afore?'

'Tweedle Beak,' said Edward. They held up a hand to catch his eye and he grinned.

'If it ain't young S'ewsb'ry,' he said, 'An' Nipper.'

'Not so Nipper now,' said John. 'Blackie to yo, thank yo kindly.'

'Black Beard soon, more like,' was Tweedle Beak's response, eyeing John's upper lip with its dark down. John flushed and the men laughed tolerantly. At least his voice had settled to a satisfying low, he thought.

'Come on then. Earn yer vittles,' someone said.

'Well now ...' said Tweedle Beak thoughtfully. 'You'll 'ave 'eard o' the fuss at Chester station?'

There was a turning down of mouths and a shaking of heads.

'Belongs to sev'ral Companies, does Chester station. Includin' the S'ewsb'ry an' Chester. At least, that's what the S'ewsb'ry an' Chester thought. But the hoity-toity London an' North-Western thinks it belongs only to them, see. Blow any agreements in writin' or anythin' o' that sort.

'See, there's two ways now as can get yer from Birmin'am ter Liverpool. An' they're much of a muchness when it comes to miles. The L&NW wants folk to travel on their line. An' the S&C wants folk to travel on their un. Money, see?

'Trouble is, the L&NW goes all the way on their line, an' the other way's split in three, S'ewsb'ry to Birmin'am ... '

'That's this un,' interrupted John.

'... then S'ewsb'ry an' Chester, an' then Chester an' Birkenhead. S&C wants the other two to agree on a price that's the same as the L&NW charges.'

'So all's fair,' said someone.

'Ah,' said Tweedle Beak. 'But the Chester to Birkenhead won't agree. Bin got at, shouldn't wonder.'

'So they're stumped.'

'No. They 'ave a grand idea, the S&C an' your S&B to Birmingham.'

'Where it don't even go yet,' put in Scarface.

'They'll cut out the opposition by running omnibuses from Chester up to Birkenhead. Not use that bit o' line at all. An' they'll charge less than the L&NW an' all. So they gets the custom, see?'

'So?'

'So, they starts running omnibuses from Chester station up to Birkenhead an' they do it fer a few days an' then the L&NW gets wind o' the goin's on. An' the station manager, Jones, they tells 'im ter stop them there omnibuses. So Jones tells the omnibus drivers they can't use Chester station an' when one o' them teks no notice Jones 'as 'im took ter the police lock-up. An' poor Worthington, that's 'is name, finds 'isself up before the magistrates on a charge of wilfully destroying the business o' Chester station.'

There were murmurs of dissent. 'What did't magistrates 'ave ter say?' That was Scarface.

'They said they'd 'ave ter tek the matter to an 'igher court.' Mutterings of 'cowards' and noises of derision came from the listeners.

'What 'appened then?' asked someone.

'So Jones the station manager arranges a barricade outside the station. There's rails an' posts an' poles an' bolts, anythin' they can get an 'old of, an' all fastened together wi' chains an' there's just a gate in the middle an' no omnibuses allowed through it. Jones, 'e turns out the bookin' clerk that sells tickets for the S&C an' the S&B so the poor man ain't got no office no more. An' the L&NW gets a trainload o' their navvies wi' pick 'andles an' parks 'em nearby just in case.'

' 'As a bin a battle?' asked John eagerly.

Tweedle Beak glared, his story interrupted. 'Magistrates couldn't 'ave that. Decided the station were a public place an' told Jones ter tek 'is barricades down. That were on the 15th o' November. But Jones wouldna tek 'em down. So ... '

'Should a sent fer us!' someone shouted. 'We'd 'ave seen 'im off, that Jones an' 'is lot.'

'Irish, I'll wager,' someone else said. It was Trapp, grasping a pick with his scaly hands as if he were about to deal a blow.

'Anyhow,' went on Tweedle Beak, 'Magistrates, they told some o' the S&B men ter smash the padlock on the barricade gate wi' sledge'ammers an' when the L&NW engines started movin' into position they went at them an' all. An' the magistrates told the booking clerk 'e could sell 'is tickets an' they stood round 'im while 'e did it, too.'

'Good fer them after all,' said Scarface.

'That's as what the crowd thought,' said Tweedle Beak. ' 'Undreds of 'em by then an' they all cheered like the Queen 'ad come ter Chester.'

'An' what 'appened then?' asked Edward.

'Things quieted down after that. But that ain't the end of it all, you mark my words. There's no love lost between the L&NW and lots o' little companies. The North Staffordshire's been 'avin' trouble for years.'

After the November 1849 opening of the S&B line between Shrewsbury and Wolverhampton there were still jobs to finish at Shiffnal station and a few other spots, but the brothers knew that construction along that stretch of the line would soon be coming to an end. They talked to Tweedle Beak. There was the Shrewsbury to Hereford line supposed to be starting sometime soon, but Tweedle Beak said there were complications and ditherings and that nothing was happening.

Then they'd heard rumours of a wharf to be built near the temporary terminus of their own line where it reached Wolverhampton. Because the L&NW were holding up the last length of the S&B line between Wolverhampton and Birmingham, the S&B were thinking that if they could unload goods onto a wharf they could use the Birmingham canal, which ran nearby, to reach Eldorado. That was the name which Scarface had begun to give to Birmingham, that of the fabled, never-reached, golden city. There would have to be a proper station at Wolverhampton too.

There came a time when the brothers decided it was time for a trip to Wolverhampton, their first visit since last November and the Opening: John still felt aggrieved when he remembered Tripp's ruin of his romantic hopes.

'Mull things over,' said Edward, whose mind was on work prospects. 'Think on. 'Ave a look at what jobs is what.'

They walked towards Wolverhampton from Shiffnal on a white and icy morning in late February when all work had come to a standstill. When there was work, you worked, unless on a randy, of course; and when work stopped you had perforce to stop with it and hope not to starve. Many men were improvident, living only for the day, but the brothers always managed to save a little. They had enough in their pockets to pay for a night's lodging if they needed it.

Walking was a good time for thinking, John decided. Thoughts came unbidden and it was good to have a companion to share them with, one who would not mock. He thought about time. 'Edward,' he asked, 'Dost 'ee think it's agen God's will?'

'What's agen 'Is will?'

'Well, God made the world, thee knows. And 'e made midday to be when the sun's 'ighest over'ead. And if yo bin in London or' ... he thought of a town ... 'or Bristol on t'other side, it mun be midday when the sun's 'ighest an' that's different in London from in Bristol 'cause of the sun travellin' across the sky. But now it's midday when the *railway* says it is. And the railway says it mun be midday in Bristol at exactly the same time that they say it mun be midday in London. But it inna.'

'Thing is,' said Edward, 'folks catch trains nowadays, an' they mun know what time to catch 'em. An' if there's different times in all the different places, folks gets all in a scrobble an' a tather.'

'Scarface told me,' John said. ' 'Tis the electric telegraph. London sends a message to Liverpool sayin', 'It's twelve o' clock,' and the folk in Liverpool or Bristol, they sets their town clock to that same time, and everyone goes by that. But is a wrong, though?'

'Dunno,' said Edward. 'Dunna s'pose God minds o'er

much, really. Long as folks goes to Church on a Sunday. Which we'm mighty bad at,' he added. Then, after a long pause, 'Dunna call to mind anythink in the Bible. Nowt as I can remember, anyhow.' And after another long pause, 'Dunna s'pose sundials'll be much use no more.'

They tramped on, snow crunching beneath their feet. 'Edward,' said John after a while.

'Hmm?'

'About that there cholera. Dost 'ee think it's gone?'

Cholera was everywhere these days: any newspaper was sure to have an account of it hitting one town or another. Wolverhampton had suffered a particularly severe outbreak that last year of 1849 and the nearby town of Bilston had fared even worse. Owd S'ewsb'ry had said they'd never heard of it when he was a lad. 'Mun be foreign,' had said his son, darkly. 'Come from them foreign places.'

Edward shrugged. 'Teks our chances, dunna we? Our turn to go, we mun go.'

They walked on, ruminating.

The line brought them to the place where ran the canal, busy with barges, horses plodding the snowy towpaths. As they looked around they noticed two men in the distance with measuring chains and writing boards. They set off towards them. This barren stretch must be the site of something new in the planning: old buildings had been roughly cleared away but not much new building was yet in evidence.

'Any work Sir?' asked Edward, doffing his hat.

One surveyed him. 'Trade?' he asked.

'Bricklayers,' said Edward.

The man pursed his lips and shook his head. 'Not at present. Though if you'd be willing to do the hard work ...'

'Wages, Sir?'

'It's a piece job, goods station, carriage and wagon sheds, loco shed, repair shop for the Shrewsbury and Birmingham. I'm the contractor. You work with the team and the quicker you work, the sooner the job's done and the more you get paid. Maybe six, seven shillings the day.'

'When shall we start?'

'Be here in a se'ennight. Seven o' clock sharp.'

They gave him their names. As they went off, Edward said, 'We mun find lodgings: there'll be no camp 'ere. An' then look around the town.'

They took their way in the direction of the greater congestion of dwellings, shops and workshops. It was a noisy place, John thought, his ears assaulted with the clangour of metal on metal, from thin, high notes to great reverberations. It was a growing place too: houses, some looking recently built and more being under construction, stopping up gaps between the old. Smoke from house-chimneys and workshops thickened the air.

'Wusser'n S'ewsb'ry,' decided John.

' We canna be faddy an' there's a feel to 'er ...' said Edward.

'A feels busy,' John allowed. 'Folks all nippiting along. It's lively like.'

The place also stank. They paused by a deep ditch and looked down. John's eyes fell on a bloated dog, its legs and stomach stiffly piercing the iced surface below him. They knew the stink would be greater when the ice melted: they did not need to be told of the seething thickness of effluent below. There were many ditches.

'Well, we wunna lose ourselves,' said Edward, pointing to a sign. John had already spotted it and its like, placed at the entrances to streets, six-inch deep boards in black, with the name of the street picked out neatly in white. They agreed it was a good idea, helpful to strangers. They came to an open area, High Green its name, again proclaimed in white on black. Women and children filled buckets from a large water tank.

'Mun be the market place,' said Edward, and indeed even on this bleak day there were a few stalls selling butter and cheese and eggs, along with turnips and cabbages and leeks.

'We mun ask,' said John; and the pair began to visit the stalls, enquiring as to lodgings. But the stallholders were from the surrounding countryside and could only shake their heads so they made for an alehouse. Both the Angel and the Swan looked over High Green, but those they avoided as too grand for the likes of them. Eventually they came to a small establishment and ordered a pint of beer each before asking the landlady if she knew of available lodgings. She obligingly pointed out a street a few hundred yards away where lodgers were said to be wanted.

The houses of Russell Street were old and there were still open spaces between them. Next to the inn which called itself the *Prince of Wales*, but separated from it by a strip of land fronting the road and occupied by stables and outbuildings, were four cottages joined to each other. A door opened onto the street; and two small-paned windows, the lower bowing out over the cobbles of the road, belonged to each house. The mossy, uneven roofs were low.

They knocked at the door of 99 Russell Street and waited. A young woman came to the door with a baby girl in her arms. Edward asked, politely, about lodgings. They would have to come back later and see her husband, the woman said. He would be home about seven. A brewer, he was, she said. 'Fer the *Prince o' Wales*.'

'We'm bricklayers,' said John.

'There's a bricklayer lives next door,' she said. 'Thomas Roberts, 'is name is. Young chap, works on the railways betimes.'

'That's what we'n bin doing,' said John eagerly. 'Goin' to start on the goods station a few days from now.'

'Well,' said the woman, 'Come back in a bit, se'en o' clock like, an' see me man.'

'There's a rum un,' said John as they walked away. ' 'Er sounds like 'er's foreign.'

' 'Appen 'er's Black Country,' said Edward.

They walked around, though there was no river to look at and not many grand buildings. It was a higgledy-piggledy sort of a place, they thought, the new buildings thrown up with no thought for the old; and, to their practised eye, not very sound building either. They judged that Russell Street was not too far from the site of the new works, about a mile perhaps.

'Useful, that,' said John.

It was cold. The snow looked as if it would stay. Though they were well wrapped up against the weather, when they came to a forge open to the street they joined the others who drank in its warmth. They stamped their feet and held out their hands towards the glow and listened to the gossip: blacksmiths' shops were always good for that, natural spaces for the exchanging of news.

One man was talking about the Shrewsbury and Birmingham and the name alerted them. It seemed that the quarrels between the S&B and the L&NW were being talked over in the high courts of the land, the Court of the Vice Chancellor of England. In the meantime the S&B had reduced their fares again and the L&NW had reduced theirs in return.

'Wait a while an' we s'll all travel free,' said a big fellow in a dirty jacket. There was a general laugh.

The brothers waited until they got a sense of the feeling of the gathering. These men, it seemed, favoured the L&NW. The brothers stayed quiet: strong emotions were in the air.

As they wandered off, back towards the centre of the town, they saw a man, guardian of a large and highly polished can standing on four feet and betraying him as a seller of hot food. A tantalising odour wafted around him, of crusty potato mingled with that of burning charcoal. The brothers chose a large specimen apiece from the hot innards of the can. The seller split the tops with a knife, while extolling the virtues of the delicacy and filling the gash with a portion of the butter and salt which occupied a compartment outside the can proper.

The brothers walked on, contentedly munching, fingers upwardly stroking rivulets of butter back towards the mouth.

'We mun go back, I reckon,' said Edward. They looked about and caught sight of a church. The clock on its tower said ten minutes to seven.

'Look sharp then,' said John and they began to make their way along fast-becoming-familiar streets.

When they knocked again at the door of Number 99 it was opened by a dark-haired, unshaven fellow in a slop and heavy working trousers. He looked them over for a moment or two before holding out a hand which they shook in turn, measuring each other's grip. Seemingly the man was satisfied, for he said, 'Back chamber,' and motioned the brothers to enter before signalling to Edward to precede him on the narrow staircase that led upwards. They found themselves in a room with a low window looking out on a patch of sad, snow-covered fields with houses beyond. There was a bed, just wide enough for two, a planked floor and a chest with ewer and basin atop.

He named a price. The brothers looked at each other. 'All found?' asked Edward. They shook hands again on the deal and paid over the money for the night's lodging.

Over a meal of more potatoes, alongside dumplings

and faggots in broth, they exchanged details. Mr Mansell, George as they soon fell to calling him, was a man of few words.

'Dunny's o'er the yard,' he told them. 'Pump's round back, in the alley.'

'Share it wi' t'other three 'ouses. Bit o' luck, that,' put in his wife. 'Good water, an' all. An' never dries up. Never 'as, any'ow, long as we bin 'ere. An' George's father, too. 'E never 'ad no trouble neither. An' 'e were 'ere, oh, twenty year or more. Good fer the brewin',' she went on, gesturing towards the jug that the brothers would soon learn was a permanent fixture, courtesy of their landlord's occupation: they would never want for beer in that house.

She was a bright, merry little thing; and the baby that sat on her lap looked a bright and merry little thing besides.

'It'll come in 'andy, the money, towards the rent,' she said. 'Now as we've got the babby 'ere.' She bounced the child up and down on her knee, so that it gurgled and laughed and she stroked its hair lovingly. 'We s'll all eat better, fer a start, besides. My man 'ere, 'e likes 'is meat.'

The brothers agreed, being no mean eaters of meat themselves.

The next morning found them once again walking back to the Shiffnal hut to work a few days, collect payment due and pick up their belongings. Then it would be back to their new base in Wolverhampton.

When they arrived at their workplace on the morning appointed, that February morning of 1850, the space was slowly filling with the usual litter of men and horses, carts, road-wagons, timber, bricks, a pile-driving machine, a crane, scaffold poles, wheelbarrows, shovels, picks, ropes and all the paraphernalia of a great construction in progress. To begin with it would be work with pick and barrow and shovel. The site had been cleared of dwellings but it was uneven and foundations, yet to be marked out, had to be dug deep. By the end of the day John, hardened though he was with months of heavy bricklaying, felt himself tiring with the unrelieved activity. There was no time for talk: every ounce of strength had to be put into physical action. True, there'd been a break for bait, and a further break in each of which a Nipper had done the drumming-up, but never rest enough. John sized up the raw Nipper, feeling a satisfaction at his own status, so far ahead.

The ganger called 'Yo ho, yo ho,' signalling the end of the day and John went to down tools, keeping sight of Edward: he could see the tiredness in him, too. They quit the site amidst a group of others heading into town.

'Didst see Chester Red?' asked John. 'Leastways, 'e looked like Chester Red to me.'

'Workin' like a shire 'orse? Dunna seem to 'ave slowed down, do 'ee? 'Appen 'e's still around.' They looked but Chester Red was not in sight.

'Let's off to get a bite. 'Appen try the *Prince o' Wales* after.' And they began their short walk to Russell Street.

In early April there came a pay day and thus a chance for a brief visit home, providing they gave themselves only one day on the randy. Maybe they could afford to ride all the way from Wolverhampton to Wellington by their own line and then, using the just-again-reduced fares of the enemy, the L&NW, from Wellington to Shrewsbury.

The Vice Chancellor, common knowledge said, had ruled in favour of the S&B, who, in expectation of fair dealings, had put up their prices back to the just levels of former days. Now, it was said, the lawless L&NW was about to reduce theirs. The term 'price wars' was on everyone's lips, along with 'destruction' and 'war to the knife'. The brothers would test the prices.

'One penny, third class. As from today,' said the booking clerk at Wellington as they stood in front of his cubicle, fumes of the day's alcohol wafting around them. They looked at each other.

' 'Ow much first class, then?' asked Edward. And hiccupped.

'First class?' He looked at them: his face was not welcoming. 'First class, that's not fer the likes o' you.'

' 'Ow much?'

'Sixpence.' The answer came grudgingly.

John's face broke into a grin. 'Two first class tickets, my man. An' look sharp about it,' he added.

They reeled onto the platform in high good humour.

A distant whistle and in snaked the train, the driver leaning from his cab, the engine halting in a hiss of steam. They looked for the legend 'First Class' and mounted the steps. The comforts of gracious living surrounded them: padded seats in a rich fabric, rare polished wood, the whole so roomy. They flung themselves onto the cushions and sprawled, legs wide. A gentleman in dress coat and top hat drew his brows together and glowered, as only the rich and fastidious can glower. His wife, in silk bonnet and mantle, gave a little scream.

'I believe you have chosen the wrong carriage,' said the gentleman, frostily, puffing out his chest. 'Remove yourselves now and no more shall come of it.'

Edward, by reply, held out their tickets. The gentleman frowned darkly. 'Guard,' he called. But the train was already moving and no-one, not even a guard, could offer assistance until the next station was reached.

John noticed that the lady, to counteract any chill of the carriage, was in possession of a box of hot coals on which to rest her feet. She had neat little ankles. She noticed his stare and moved closer to her husband. At the next station it was not the brothers who alighted, but husband and wife. John, his head out of the window, saw the gentleman inspecting each of the other first class carriages before helping his wife inside a compartment presumably empty of common, vulgar people. They were left to luxuriate in pampered ease all the way to Shrewsbury whilst their imaginations roamed amongst a variety of furious letters aimed at the directors and shareholders of the L&NW.

Once in their home town, they and others spread the word of cheapness of fares, which rushed into the ears of still more, so that Shrewsbury, on a subsequent day, found itself thronged with over a thousand extra sightseers emptied onto its streets.

Work did not proceed smoothly on Wolverhampton's new station. Sometimes they were laid off. The L&NW were still delaying the completion of the Stour Valley Line and thus the S&B was still failing to deliver its passengers to Eldorado, except by packet boat along the canal, or by carriage. Both methods were demeaningly outdated forms of transport for a proud railway.

The non-transport of minerals was the most worrying for the S&B because potentially the most profitable. One Friday in July, about noon and while they were resting and eating their bait, a man appeared at a trot from the direction of Wednesfield Heath, the temporary station. 'Maisters wants yer,' he got out between gasps. 'Now, they says.'

Men looked at each other. 'What's the 'urry?' That was Chester Red.

'L&NW,' said the messenger. 'They're fed up wi' 'em. Maisters wants you lot ter mek a plank-way from line ter wharf so as ter get stuff on ter Birmin'am quicker. On'y S'ewsb'ry an' Birmin'am men, mind. Come quick as yer can.' He sat for a minute or two regaining breath while men finished their bread and bacon, drained their assorted containers of beer or tea and got up to leave.

'Look sharp,' said John. 'Mun be some action.'

They tramped down the line to the temporary station where they spotted Mr Darkin, gentleman and of some importance in the S&B, a few men already gathered around him. The brothers joined the group.

'Now men,' began Mr Darkin. 'Enough of this delay by the enemy! I will not hesitate to call them by that name for enemy they have been and are still! But we ourselves are honest men and by the strength of our arm and of our true English hearts, we shall prevail!'

There was a chorus of cheering. First to be done, explained Mr Darkin, was to make an opening in the fence - he pointed to its position - and then to put in a gate, thus making it easier to transfer goods from railway to canal.

A team had begun to work on this when there was an interruption. Another gentleman, by his clothes of equal elevation to Mr Darkin, came striding up and planted himself in the gap now opened up in the fence, shaking the remaining railings in his anger.

'I refuse to permit this ... this ... desecration to continue.'

An argument ensued, the outcome of which was Mr Darkins' ordering of two strapping fellows, one of whom happened to be Chester Red, to seize the interloper and take him into police custody. They being most eager to oblige he was led, protesting, away, Mr Darkins in attendance.

John and Edward stood for a while though, as no further action was forthcoming, they soon slipped off and back to their work. Later on they saw Chester Red returning. He told them that the magistrates had been alerted and that the dispute had been given a hearing in the Court. He'd tell them more later.

Later was when they were leaning on the bar of an alehouse, a pint on the bar before each, Chester Red's unpaid for by himself. From the numbers of faces a-gawp for news, he might not have to delve in his pockets over-often that night.

'Right, so they gets inter the Court an' Mr Darkin says, all proper like, that they'd been on their own land, S&B land. It were all S&B land up ter the fence. So Mr Moore - that were the gaffer as we nibbed - 'e says that Mr Baker, that's the engineer for the Stour Valley Line, 'ad give 'im orders, right tempersome-like, ter stop us mekkin' the 'ole in the fence. ' 'E kep' sayin' that, 'cause the engineer weren't there to say it fer 'isself.

'The magistrates asks 'ose were the bit o' line. "Oh", says Darkin, "It belongs to both companies." "Then what's the problem?" asks the magistrates. An' Darkin an' Moore, the one we nibbed, 'o it turns out is a contractor for the L&NW, they glowers at each other. An' our Darkin says that Moore were trespassing an' the magistrates can't see that.

'An' then the solicitor for the S&B arrives an' says that the line belongs to the S&B an' to no-one else an' the L&NW would 'ave to go all the way to the Vice-Chancellor to stop the S&B from connecting to the canal if that's what they wanted to do.

'Anyway, the magistrates dismissed the case. Too deep fer them, I reckons. Though Mr Moore was cautioned ter keep the peace, 'cos Darkin an' our engineer, Mr Robertson, thought there'd likely be a riot if they didna put a brake on things.'

There was a silence before questions began to surface. It seemed that blood had been stirred. By the time that men began to dribble unsteadily homeward, it had been decided: they would fight to the death, if necessary, for the S&B.

The Mansells had caught the spirit of righteous indignation from their lodgers and Mrs Mansell obliged with a hearty breakfast to set them up for whatever the day might bring.

When they reached the worksite they picked up whatever implements might prove intimidating: John favoured a shovel with its blade-edges well sharpened, Edward an iron bar. Then, with a motley of a dozen or so others, led by the giant Chester Red wielding a length of chain - 'Rip skin off 'is legs, see. Or pull 'is 'ead off' - they moved on towards the disputed ground.

They had been preceded: a group of maybe fifty other navvies, the enemy, similarly armed, had already taken up station on the far side of the fence, between it and the canal. Mr Parsons the S&B traffic manager and Mr Underhill the S&B solicitor listened to the first exchange of catcalls with growing unease. Chester Red whirled his chain around his head causing some slight alarm. 'Keep calm, men,' one of them advised. 'This situation calls for further measures. We need the Mayor.' And off they hurried.

The two groups had begun with insults, which raised some laughter, but tension rose as insults began to hit home. More armed navvies, inspired by group loyalty and alerted by the prospect of a good battle, arrived to swell numbers on both sides.

About half past eleven the Mayor arrived, his presence effecting a quietness whilst men watched warily to see what the outcome might be. He strolled around, asking questions of the masters, trying to assess the situation. Already the L&NW men numbered some three hundred, all armed like the outnumbered S&B with heavy and threatening objects. Arguments ensued between the Mayor and agents, engineers and contractors, on the conflicting sides, neither of which were willing to concede a jot to the other.

Then there sounded a distant whistle and a train of open wagons came lumbering down the line accompanied by the sounds of cheering. Two hundred S&B re-enforcements, each man distinguished by a red band around the upper arm, drew to a halt.

Mr Robertson the S&B engineer - and also, as the brothers knew, M.P. for Shrewsbury - gave instructions to the S&B men already there. Edward and John donned their red armbands as they were handed out. They were to carry on with what they had begun the day before, laying down planking to communicate with the canal. John picked up a plank. Edward, on the far side of the railings, took it from him. Others were doing the same. For a few minutes the L&NW men allowed this to continue, but just as the plank road was about to reach the embankment which sloped upwards to the railway line, a body of L&NW men swarmed in to throw the planks all awry. It was too much. Pick-handles were swung, John slashed out with his sharpened shovel, iron bars from both sides hit flesh and bone. One of the S&B men shrieked in pain, his leg useless. The opposition cheered.

Then, from the far end of Railway Street, came the sound of marching feet. A body of cutlass-wielding men appeared, headed by the Chief Constable himself; and in their rear, bayonets fixed at the ready, came a detachment of the 48th Regiment.

This proved too much for the crowd of casual onlookers who began to disperse in alarm. The navvies of both factions were made of sterner stuff and held their ground.

The Mayor, earning John's admiration for courage, climbed onto a pile of timber. 'Men,' he said, addressing the L&NW from his position of prominence, 'You are at this moment in peaceable possession of a portion of the embankment. And you men,' he turned to the S&B contingent, 'Are in peaceable possession of a further portion. Keep apart and I shall protect you both.' A few policemen were then ordered to protect the S&B men while they went on laying the planking. When a contingent of L&NW tried to push past the Mayor to stop them, the Mayor himself laid hands upon their leader and pushed him back. He then addressed the mob, his voice calm but his words resolute:

'I am called here, as Mayor of this Borough, to prevent a breach of the peace. I see before me several hundred workmen, evidently keeping the slope of this railway to prevent some other party using it, and I also see some hundreds of workmen brought here to take possession of it. I have nothing to do with the quarrel between the parties: it is nothing to me to whom the land belongs. But the law does not permit legal rights to be decided by violence and physical force.' One body of men, he observed, was now sitting peacefully. The other was peaceably working. Any man from either side, he went on, who attempted to interfere with the other side, would be immediately taken into custody. 'You now know my fixed determination.'

But one of the top L&NW brass objected with passion, 'This puts *them* in possession of *my* slope. It is *my* slope.'

'I know nothing of your slope or their slope, but they are working the railway -the station theirs - the servants at it theirs - the engines and carriages going over it are theirs. But, whether or no, they are in peaceable possession of that slope, and if you put a foot upon it I will commit you.'

The Mayor waited a little, during which time all remained peaceful, though there was a tension which signalled that as soon as he left, chaos would reign once more. He said as much and duly read the Riot Act. The L&NW navvies left, wandering over to a wagon newly arrived where they were supplied with dinner and ale. The S&B men also left except for about a dozen, which included Edward and John, working to complete the link from rail to canal.

They had been working for about twenty minutes when three angry gentlemen arrived. They, it turned out, were the L&NW. One was the engineer Mr Baker, the other two the contractors Hill and Moore. Sharp words were exchanged between the masters on both sides before Baker began to berate the Mayor for allowing the S&B men to 'break up' the railway: the S&B had, by this time, begun to dig a hole under the rails themselves through which goods could be tipped onto wagons and trundled down the temporary plank way onto barges.

Whatever disaster befell as a consequence would be entirely on the Mayor's shoulders, snapped the irate Baker. The S&B must be stopped. The Mayor reiterated that his only concern was to preserve the peace: legal rights were the province of the courts of law. More attempts were made to stop the S&B men. The Mayor ordered contractor Hill to be taken into custody. A kerfuffle took place between the police and L&NW men trying to stop the work of the S&B, in which the police, cutlasses drawn, proved the victors.

At about half past two, thirty or forty wagons arrived; the L&NW men piled aboard, their masters riding the engine.

'Gone, looks like,' said John.

'An' good riddance,' said Edward, wiping his forehead. 'Mebbe them poor passengers from S'ewsb'ry can get into the station at last. Mun be that tempersome an' crousty wi' waitin.'

They carried on working. But noise came to them, crashings and shoutings. The red-banded navvies of the S&B, it seemed, had been earlier withdrawn only as far as the train hoping to come in from Shrewsbury. And the navvies of the L&NW had come upon them at the head of the detained train. The L&NW men had leapt from their wagons on the orders of their masters and were tipping wagons over to block the line. The two sides fell to fighting. Stones were thrown as the police arrived and set about with their cutlasses once more, the military supporting them at their rear. The Mayor read the Riot Act again and eventually the two sides fell apart.

The S&B began to clear the line of tumbled wagons and the long-delayed passenger train from Shrewsbury moved towards the temporary station. The Mayor and the main agents assembled in the waiting room with the hope of compromise. To John and Edward, still working outside, catching the rise and fall of heated voices, it seemed to be long in coming.

At last the parties emerged. The brothers, along with all the other men apart from station officials and eight workers to make safe the rails and platform for the public, were dismissed.

Messrs Hill and Moore for the L&NW were, they found out later, bound in recognisances of £500 to keep the peace in the borough of Wolverhampton, the Mayor, in the face of their great reluctance to part with any money, threatening custody unless and until they complied.

By five o' clock, all was over. The brothers made an early end to what they fervently agreed had been 'a mortal good day's work' and, Edward expressing himself to be 'dry as a ragman's 'prentice', left with the crowd to enjoy a hearty and rousing celebration.

11

The Fairer Sex

Work there was, that year of the railway wars, from dawn to dusk; but other life there was too, creeping from under work's stifling edges.

When they had begun working on the goods complex at Wolverhampton that February of 1850, it was apparent that when men left in a body at the close of day, some would turn one way and some another. Some began in company with the brothers' homeward road, dropping off here and there to turn into different streets; but two men, sometimes three, regularly passed number 99 Russell Street only to turn into house 100.

The brothers remembered the words of Mrs Mansell concerning the bricklayer that lived next door and who sometimes worked on the railways. It must be he; and perhaps his brothers with him: they were all near Edward's age, older than John.

Onsite, they assessed the three men. Two were similar in looks, with broad foreheads and square jaws, one different: maybe a lodger, they thought. The older two were both bricklayers, the younger a smith, working on one of the portable forges that were part of any railway construction force.

Words began to be exchanged. Yes, two were brothers: Thomas was a bricklayer, young James a smith. Roberts was their surname. The other bricklayer was a lodger like themselves. One night they all went for a drink or two in the *Prince of Wales.* The Roberts parents came from Bridgnorth in Shropshire and all the Roberts children had been born there, while Edward and John hailed from its county town some twenty miles to the North West. The mighty Severn ran through both, a link in common. A glass was raised 'To all friends around the Wrekin' and another 'To the S'ewsb'ry and Birmin'am Railway and long may 'er prosper'.

The Roberts boys, it transpired, had a sister, born between the two of them, just Edward's age. The sister helped keep house along with their mother. With their father, a carpenter, in steady work and the two boys in good trades, she had no need to go out as a servant. They were all happy with things that way. No, she had no young man as yet.

In the April, John and his brother had returned to Shrewsbury on that memorable occasion of first class travel. They felt a certain loyalty and solidarity: to catch up on family events had an interest and besides they had a fondness for their Mam. They liked to contribute a little of their wages too, from time to time, even though they lived there no longer.

They had walked along the familiar Abbey Foregate and lifted the latch on the worn front door.

'Bad pennies, then?' was their Mam's comment as they came into the room. 'Chickens come home, han they?'

The chickens grinned.

' 'Tis late. There'll be a bite for yo this night, but termorrer yo mun buy summat. 'Appen bread an' bacon an' eggs'll do us. Eggs a-plenty an' cheap right now.'

They nodded eagerly and sat before the fire while their mother and the girls bustled about providing them with bread and cheese and home-brewed ale. John, alerted by signs of affluence, glanced at his mother's hands: rough-skinned they were but not now chapped and red-raw. He looked about him and saw, to his relief, that toppling piles of other people's washing no longer cluttered the room: his father must have reformed his spending.

Three excited little girls in pinafores asked questions. Had they come back for always? Where would they sleep? Had they brought anything with them? Were they rich now? It was good to be the object of so much female interest and enthusiasm.

The lads smiled and reached into their pockets. Mary found herself in possession of a small doll, its body, disguised under a blue dress and red mantle, a wooden clothes-peg. Ann unfolded a red satin hair-ribbon. Esther held out her hand to receive a comb which could hardly be told from tortoiseshell. Few presents ever came their way and they loved these brothers for the gifts.

Their father came in. The girls were sent off to bed. S'ewsb'ry looked over his two well-set-up sons with a pride he tried to disguise. The family fell to talking news.

'Aunt Susanna, er's got another babby,' their mother said, with some verve and an odd sort of admiration. 'Never would a believed it with 'er Edmund 'er on'y child an' 'im turned thirteen. Left school now, o' course. Doin' proper well in the bakin' trade. Sarah, er's called it, the babby. Susanna wanted 'Victoria' on account o' the dear Queen bein' so near 'er own time an' all. She was 'opin' the Queen's babby'd be born the same day but it ain't come yet. Anyways, 'er Thomas, 'e put 'is foot down an' said 'Sarah', so Sarah 'er is. 'Er's a pretty babby, but a teeny-tiny thing. Yo could put 'er in a quart jug. 'Cept for 'er lungs. 'Er lungs is mighty big an' that's a fact.'

Neither John nor Edward had much to say to this, being not over-interested in babbies.

'An' that Rachel, your Aunt Rachel, 'er's still in Lunnon. Your Gran, 'er still hanna seen 'er sin she were married to that sodger. An' your Aunt Mary Ann, she's got 'er two little uns o' course. An' a lodger.'

' 'Ow's the work?' asked Edward of his father, to

143

reprieve them from the flow of babies.

'Station's finished. Worked on ware'ouses an' such for a while. Doin' a bit round the town these days. Seems above a bit o' work about. More to come wi' the railways an' all. Anyways, I'm not fit for the chimley cornel yet. Nor's your Grandad. Sixty-three 'e'll be come May, or so 'e says. Still proper sharp, 'e be. 'Ow 'bout thee?'

John launched in with the troubles between the S&B and the L&NW.

His father nodded, ' 'Eard o' the broggil at Chester station. Mark me words, there'll be more trouble wi' that lot afore long.'

S'ewsb'ry chuckled with glee as the brothers described their ride in a first class carriage and the gentry brought unavoidably into close quarters with themselves.

'We bested 'em, though,' said John.

Aunt Elizabeth, the black ewe, was not mentioned.

The brothers left on the afternoon of the following day. The girls came a short way with them, Mary clinging to John's hand, Ann to Edward's. Esther, conscious of the weight of her nine years, walked sedately at their side. John, turning round well after they'd parted company, saw his sisters still waving.

It was a day in May. James Roberts was leafing through the *Wolverhampton Chronicle and Staffordshire Advertiser*, thoughtfully provided by the landlord of the Prince of Wales, Tom Blakemore, for his more literate clientele. Something caught his attention.

'Eh lads. 'Ark at this.' And he began to read: "Attractive excursions to Dudley Castle and illuminations of its celebrated caverns ... on Whitmonday, Tuesday and Wednesday ... the caverns which are nearly half a mile in length, and upwards of fifty feet high, will be illuminated by means of thousands of gas lights." What dost tha think?'

Murmurs of approbation were heard. 'What's the cost?' Edward asked.

James scanned the paper. 'We s'll go by packet boat from the S&B wharf. That'll see us to the caverns. 1s.6d, it says. That's the cheapest. But we don't 'ave to pay no more for the caves, nor to see the castle. An' there's a band: "The splendid band of the 4th Royal Irish Dragoons." Fireworks only on the Wednesday an' we 'as to pay a bit more for them.'

'Whitmonday we wunna be at work,' said John.

'Sounds like a good day then,' said Thomas. 'An' what about treatin' Ann?'

Edward, who had glimpsed Miss Roberts as she hung out or took in the washing in the back yard of a Monday or set off down the street with a basket on her arm, could think of no possible objection, and no-one else thought fit to raise one. And so the matter was decided, provided Ann herself agreed, of course.

John worked out the cost of supporting Ann: 'Thrupence 'a'penny each for the ticket leaves an 'a'penny o'er. If we gives Tommy Roberts sixpence apiece, there'd be enow to buy Ann a bite to eat, mebbe. We mun buy our own.'

'Says there bin a "limited amount of tickets",' said James, who had been scouring the advertisement.

'Best go tomorrer then,' said his brother. 'After work.'

In the end, and much due to the pleading of Ann, Wednesday was decided upon, largely because of the fireworks.

The day arrived, the 22nd of May. An anxious glance from the window on waking lightened their hearts: the day showed promise of growing ever more glorious with sun. Monday had been dull and gloomy and Tuesday not much better. It seemed a good omen.

Edward washed with the greatest care, imitated by

John: both went out to the pump and sluiced themselves, rather than make shift with the basin and ewer in their room. Scissors were borrowed from Mrs Mansell and hair and beards trimmed. It would be more accurate to say 'beard' as John's beard, discernable by his eyes only, did not as yet require much of a lop.

Both donned their best, Edward producing a velveteen square-tailed coat and a white felt hat, neither of which John had seen before. John had acquired a sealskin cap which he imagined gave him a jaunty air. His waistcoat of red plush contrasted as usual with Edward's blue. The brothers from next door, when they called, looked dowdy in comparison, though they each sported a large, bright neckerchief.

Ann looked lovely, John thought. He had few words to apply to the sort of garments women wore, but her frock was of pale blues and greens in a pattern of checks, half-covered by a green mantle. The sleeves of her frock were long and narrow, the skirt full which made her waist seem delightfully small. The dress had a round neckline, modest but revealing a modicum of smooth, pale skin. A wide-rimmed bonnet covered not all of her dark, glossy hair. 'A fine-looking woman,' he thought to himself. He had heard the phrase from others and it seemed apt.

In a body they approached the wharf from which the packet boats were to set off. The crowds were tremendous. The men stood around Ann to protect her from being hustled, Edward being especially on the alert.

A boat arrived and they piled aboard. A brother handed Ann in. Edward took off his new coat and spread it on the seat for her comfort. The boat filled with passengers. Encouraged by their driver, the horses before them on the towpath began first to strain and then to plod, and, as the boat acquired momentum, to trot. The leading steed was blinkered, the second bore the horseman with his whip. The craft picked up speed, its passengers pointing out landmarks and sights as they flew past, though, truth to tell, these were generally disfigured by cinder heaps and forges, blasted trees and ruined cottages, half-obscured in soot or smoke. From time to time they threaded a tunnel, their voices echoing off the brick walls. Narrowboats passed them laden with coal. Wharves appeared, patterned with piles of iron and timber, lead, slate and clay; and fringed with tied-up barges, empty and full, until, in less than an hour, they were landing at the Dudley wharf.

Above them rose the hill on which stood the grey ruins of the castle.

'Burnt down, it was, a castle afire on a burning hill. All the lead melted an' ran off the roofs in red-'ot streams. The town thought the cellars were full o' gunpowder an' they were that frit. But they wunna, thank the good Lord. A Dudley man told me the fire went on fer three days.' That was young James, the smith.

They climbed the slopes, now lush in verdant green, Edward offering Ann his arm, though blushingly she clung to her brother. Milling crowds were on every hand. They strolled for a while among them, noting booths for the provision of food and drink and assessing them for later use. Then they descended again to find the entrance to the abyss. There was both an entrance and an exit, an arrangement, they were told, to prevent the miseries of the last time the public had been allowed access, when hundreds trying to get in had conflicted with hundreds coming out.

Inside, pleasure at finding a dry surface underfoot turned to gasps as they viewed the scene. Brilliant light was around them, shining from innumerable sources, large lamps and small. These shone with not only the pale softness of ordinary gaslight, but colours of all the hues of the rainbow.

147

As they made their slow way through the hand-hewn vaults towards the radiant star half a mile distant that marked the end of their journey, rugged pillars of limestone threw strange shadows and hinted at secret places. Lamps shimmered against the dark waters in the depths and glittered from a great mirror positioned at the centre of the cavern. And there also, in patriotic splendour, were the initials V.R., highly illuminated; and above that the coat of arms of Lord Ward, by whose kind permission they were being allowed to view this spectacle. The visitors from Wolverhampton were most suitably impressed.

Miss Roberts was intrigued by the myriad of shapes in the stone, from large to small. 'They looks like shells an' worms; there's one coiled up round and round like a giant flat snail; an' look at that one - it's like a beetle but with three backs.' A nearby spectator, smiling at her enthusiasm, informed her that the shapes were the remains of sea-creatures from long ago. Trilobites was the name he gave to the beetle-like creatures and told her that there were so many hereabouts that the local people called them the Dudley Bug.

On emerging into the warmth of Whit sunshine, Ann returned the new coat, lent by Edward to protect her against the chill and they proceeded to one of the booths in search of refreshment. The men added mugs of beer to their purchase of pies.

The strains of the band wafted round them as they lay on the grass and wandered through the grey ruins. They ventured out into the streets of the town. A stall caught John's attention and he went to look. A man had three thimbles and a pea. Another man was trying to guess under which of the three thimbles lay the pea. John was sure he had the measure of it and made a bet. But the pea was not in that place but in another. He bet again. And lost again. Edward grabbed him from behind. 'Thee wunna win. 'E cheats, see. Keeps the pea under 'is nail. 'Tis an owd trick.'

At six o' clock the band, which had been playing in the courtyard, marched with military precision to the cavern while the crowds of onlookers rushed to hear what mighty and extraordinary sound would be the result. The Wolverhampton party listened as the music soared, echoing and re-echoing through that man-made space.

The day was only beginning to dim when the fireworks began, a further festival of light which had them gazing upwards in a chorus of approval. It had been a day of rare enjoyment and the glide of the return by twilight sealed the pleasure of the day.

The year was growing old, John noticed one morning in late September. The odd brown leaf was beginning to flutter among them as they worked. There was a faint chill when they woke. There was a mellow quality to the light. He exulted in time's passing: soon he would be sixteen. He was tall for his years, near as tall as Edward. Years of physical work had hardened his body and he was lithe as a willow. He craved a girl.

It was easier finding a girl now they were in lodgings. The brothers were not so readily identified as navvies and lumped in with the rest of them as lawless, reckless and dangerous to know. John had had one or two acquaintances with girls, but they had been fleeting. None had struck the spark in him that he saw in Edward and his Ann. For that relationship had bloomed, a respectful 'Miss Roberts' had become 'Ann'; and Edward, suitably cleaned up, was now welcome in the Roberts household to take a cup of tea or play a hand of cards in what was left of the evenings, and to accompany Ann and her mother to church on a Sunday. John thought it very dull. He still enjoyed, even more enjoyed, a randy on paydays. He could take his drink, he fancied, as well as any.

One Wednesday in the early evening he thought to take a walk through the streets. For some reason they had finished earlier than usual and he felt in need of companionship and an alehouse. Edward was otherwise occupied. He set off eastwards from Russell Street, and found himself in Cleveland Road where the cattle market was just coming to an end. It was a well-appointed market and big enough for thousands of sheep, cattle, pigs and horses: he'd been told that it was only a couple of years since its opening, built to relieve the terrible crush and filth of the old, separate markets which had far outgrown their original spaces. The townsfolk were proud of it.

'Where there's markets, there's alehouses,' he thought.

He wandered about, looking. The church caught his eye, St. George's, a plain, oblong structure of no great age. A disproportionately small tower, spire perched atop, looked as if set down by a giant-child on its flat roof. His eye was caught by a movement, someone going in by the gate into the churchyard. It was a slight girl, dressed all in black, a black shawl around her shoulders. The light from a gas lamp lit up her hair, a tumble of colour like that of a fresh-fallen horse chestnut. She looked young and walked with a certain grace. As he watched, she laid what might have been a posy on the grass; and stood, silent and still, head bowed. He tore his eyes away and went towards the pool of light spilling from the alehouse over the way. He got into rowdy conversation with a workmate that he recognised there. When he came out later and, remembering, looked towards the churchyard, the girl had gone.

John had several encounters with girls over the next few months. His birthday came and went. His brother was absorbed with Ann: and girls seemed drawn to John wandering on his own, into his seventeenth year now, broad-shouldered and flush with money. One of his short affairs was with a bold, ragged girl, who let him do to her things he had so far only daydreamed of, in return for which he offered all the food she could eat. Pieces of it she kept 'for later' in a pocket and he sometimes wondered if she had a child to feed. He lived for a while in a state of high excitement; and something less comfortable which, long after, he recognised as shame.

It was disquieting working for the Shrewsbury and Birmingham. Wolverhampton was full of men working for the arch-enemy, the L&NW, who seemed as determined as always to keep the S&B from connecting to Birmingham. The price wars were as active and malicious as ever. Edward, too, disliked the atmosphere, though he still mooned over his Ann.

On Christmas Eve it happened that they were both celebrating a payday with the Roberts boys at one of the alehouses in the town, Edward for once being separated from his beloved, when the latch rattled and a man walked in through the low doorway. As he came into the light, John called, 'Hey, Scarface.'

Scarface looked over and came towards the group. Hands were firmly shaken, introductions made. ''Ave one on me.' Pints were replenished and tales exchanged. Scarface, it seemed, had just begun working on a new line, the delayed Shrewsbury to Hereford: the first sod had been ceremonially cut earlier that month. The contractor was now Thomas Brassey. The oaken heart of the man had to be explained to the Roberts brothers. Scarface said he was finding conditions good. There was no Tommy-shop system. A shop there was, true, and one run by the contractor, but prices were fair and wages paid in money, not tickets only to be exchanged at the Tommy shop. Thomas, the eldest of the Roberts brothers, told them of working on such a line: 'The contractor got rich and be damned to all others. An' bad food it were, an' all. Tommy rot it were, true enough, weevils in the flour, eggs could near walk, milk made o' chalk an' water, "best steak" were 'orsemeat.' They sympathised.

'Brassey wouldna do owt like that,' said Scarface in his familiar northern brogue. 'Good master, Mr Brassey. Fair to 'is men, tha knows.'

'Tell 'em then,' said John, sensing the unspoken curiosity and proud besides of his friend, 'Tell 'em as 'ow yo got that scar,' and Scarface grinned and obliged. And the story of Peterloo was told once more, to keep within the hearts of men.

12

From Shrewsbury to Hereford

Scarface had entertained them that night of Christmas Eve
with a description of the Turning of the Sod. The citizens
of Hereford, it seemed, were almost drunk with the glory
and the blessings that would be theirs: this was the very
first railway to enter into their magnificent county of
Herefordshire and it would be inaugurated in a style never
before surpassed.

Plans had been made: a general holiday was declared,
a free ball would be held for which the Shire Hall, the
largest room in the town, was appropriated. Cake and
wine for the schoolchildren would be partaken of in the,
rather smaller, Town Hall after the grand ceremony. Free
gas lighting in both places was promised by an excited
and munificent gas company.

'On't day', said Scarface, 'thousands came. Just ter
watch a bit o' grass dug up. Fifteen thousand't paper said.
Banners, dozens of 'em, silk uns an' all wi' things on 'em
like "Prosperity ter't S'ewsb'ry an' 'Ereford Railway" an'
"Loyalty ter't Queen". An behind 'em every trade in't town
turned out wi' its own banner. Music, church bells a-
ringin', bands a-playin'. 'Uge procession there an'
Mayors an' maces, constables an' carriages. An't daftest
bit were a navvy, all in white, 'at an' all, carryin' a silver
spade. Lot o' good that'd be.'

'Get knapped soon enough, afore it 'ad time ter bend,'
someone put in.

'An', you'll never guess, six other navvies, an' them in
white an' all, carryin', *carryin'* mark you, a wheelbarrer.
Not yer usual mucky barrer what yer does a good day's

work with, but made o' mahogany, all shiny an' red, wi' "Prosperity ter't S'ewsb'ry an' 'Ereford" again, an' coats o' arms all o'er it. 'Ow them navvies could stand lookin' such daft boggers as that beats me. Mr Brassey were there though: that were one good thing. They all cheered 'im too. Said't railway'd do all right wi' Mr Brassey in charge.'

'An' 'oo cut the sod? Bin 'e any good?' That was Tom Roberts.

'Oh, that were Ormsby Gore. 'E managed, wi' 'is namby-pamby spade an' 'is silly barrer.'

'Bet 'e were mortal tired after,' said John. They all laughed.

'So, yo reckons it'll be a decent job?' asked Edward.

'I gi'es yer me word,' said Scarface.

'Good enough for me, then,' said Edward. He looked at the assembled company. 'What yo say, lads? I s'll be leavin' me fair one.' Here he looked at the Roberts boys, 'But a man mun work or all goes without.'

The Roberts boys nodded. They knew the imperatives of labour as much as anyone. 'We mun join thee.'

It was decided: though they would find themselves lingering in Wolverhampton for another three months. There were still jobs to do on the engine and goods sheds; they were reluctant to leave winter lodgings within four solid walls where food was cooked for them; and Edward was loath to leave Ann.

John, walking one early January day of 1851 along Merridale Street, a street which ran parallel to their own, found his eyes drawn to a figure walking ahead. It was a girl, dressed in heavy black; and something in her walk, some grace of carriage, drew his memory back to the girl he had seen in the churchyard. He quickened his pace. He saw rich brown hair. It was she. She was crying.

'Miss? Dost need 'elp?'

She rubbed her eyes on her sleeve, but the tears came

afresh.

'Let me see thee 'ome,' he said awkwardly.

'Don't 'ave no 'ome no more,' she replied. 'Goin' ter the master's.'

In bursts it came out. Her mother had died the previous year, of the cholera. John said he thought he'd seen her in a churchyard, St. George's.

'That's where they was buried, all the ones that died o' the cholera, all in St. George's.'

Now, it seemed, her father was dead too. He'd been buried that very day, the 5th of January, also in St. George's, which was after all the parish in which he had lived. He'd been a tinplate worker: Wolverhampton was full of them, rolling steel, plating it with tin to prevent rust, both operations apt to shorten lives if not to terminate them; and passing on the product as the basis for 'japanned' trays, boxes, teapots, furniture even, their elegant and colourful designs leaning towards the oriental and prominently featuring reds and golds. They were highly fashionable.

She had a brother aged twelve and a sister, only ten. Their father's brother, another tinplate worker, had said he'd take them in, but she, the oldest, had needed to find a place and had found it as a maid-of-all-work for a master mason in Merridale Street. Her brother and sister, the uncle had decided, were too young. For which she was thankful, she said, for many a child of these ages was a worker.

'And 'ow old bist thee?' asked John. He felt oddly tender towards this waif in black.

'Fifteen.'

She stopped by a forecourt where slabs of stone and marble leaned drunkenly together and a simulated funereal monument sat sombrely within its gravel bed.

'My Mam didn't 'ave no stone,' she said. 'Nor does me Dad.' The tears came again and she rushed up the path towards the house.

He realised afterwards that he had forgotten to ask her name.

Other girls, fly-by-nights, good for a cuddle and sometimes more, came and went. But the girl with the graceful walk lingered at the edges of his mind. One Sunday he went looking for her. He retraced his steps to Merridale Street and found again the workshop of the master mason. What to do? Servants were often forbidden to have 'followers' and he could hardly pretend to be a relation: he didn't even know her name. The place was quiet. He hung around for a while, trying not to look conspicuous; but the house was still. Maybe she was at church. Or chapel. Maybe she was visiting her uncle and brother and sister. Maybe she had returned to St. George's. He decided on the latter: better than doing nothing and he stood a chance of talking to her out in the street.

He was in luck. Just before he reached St. George's, he saw her coming away from the churchyard. He approached respectfully, so as not to alarm her, and spoke gently.

' 'Ello Miss, 'ow bist? Yo bin to see the graves, I reckons.'

She looked at him. ' 'Ow did thee know that?'

'I talked to thee. The day thy Dad were buried. Thee were in such a state, right tossicated, dunna s'pose thee'd remember.'

Recognition came to her eyes. 'I do that. Yo were kind. I do remember.'

'Can I walk wi' thee awhile?'

'Not right back ter me place. Mistress, er's got a temper on 'er.'

Somehow, he found it easy to talk to this girl. She was taller than he'd thought and, though still skinny, she looked less gaunt and strained than when he'd last seen her. The food wasn't bad, she said. But she missed her brother and sister.

'William, me brother,' she said.

John felt a leap of the heart. 'I'd a brother William once,' he said. 'But 'e died.'

She glanced towards him. ' 'Ave yer still got a Mam? An' a Dad?'

'Got both,' he said, 'S'pose I'm lucky, me.'

'Got any sisters?'

'Three sisters,' he said triumphantly, 'Esther, Ann and Mary.'

'Esther's a nice name,' she said. 'My sister's called Sarah. An' I'm Eliza.'

'That's a good name, Eliza. I'm John.'

'William wants ter go fer a sodger. When 'e's owd enough.'

'I got an aunt married to a sodger.'

Time passed happily enough until they suddenly, and far too quickly, found themselves in Merridale Street. They arranged to meet, out of sight of the mason's establishment, the following Sunday, Eliza's half-day holiday.

The girl became another reason for delaying their departure. John was forced eventually to confess her existence to Edward. A meeting was arranged, Ann, pretty, respectably-dressed, gentle Ann, was to introduce herself at the mason's house as Eliza's cousin. Then the four of them would spend an hour or two together.

The girls got on well, despite their difference in age. Eliza, little by little, revealed herself to be a practical girl with a quick wit that kept them laughing.

By the time April came, John knew he would like to keep on seeing this girl. She made him feel a larger, more important person: her presence inspired in him a sensation of manliness and protectiveness that was very pleasing. He liked the way she looked at him with adoring eyes and clung to his arm when they walked together. He liked to kiss her and was both irritated with and respectful of her when she resisted more pressing advances.

Eventually goodbyes were said, long and tearful in Eliza's case. But they could write, said John. Both of them were able to write, though neither of them were very practised at it. The post was so much better nowadays: often a letter could be posted in a town and reach its destination the very same day. If you really wanted to, and from certain places, you could write a letter in the morning and another in the afternoon and stand a good chance of both arriving.

'I s'll gi'e thee money for stamps,' said John, soothingly. Eliza smiled a watery smile. 'I s'll write first an' tell thee the address. 'Sides, Tom an' James'll be comin' an goin' an they can tek letters. An' I s'll come back an' see thee. Dunna cry so.'

Ann and Edward had decided on a different course. Ann was to accompany them as far as Shrewsbury, a town much easier to reach than Wolverhampton. There she would try to find a place. If a live-in place was unavailable, she would lodge with S'ewsb'ry and his wife and find day work. Edward was saving hard and so would she. They planned to marry as soon as possible.

The two sets of brothers and Ann set off for Shrewsbury a few days later, in early April, planning to spend the night, perforce a rather crowded one, at the parental house in the Foregate.

A little out of Wolverhampton they waited, by arrangement, near a high tank, used by the S&B for the taking-on of water. Just after 7.30pm railway-time, along came the last train, shedding sparks into the night, the driver and stoker both Wolverhampton men known to the Roberts brothers. Four of them clambered into the guard's van, a place both out of sight and more comfortable; but John rode the engine, shovelling, under the instruction of the stoker, quantities of coal into the red-hot maw of the iron beast. It was glorious. Once, when the engine had settled into its steady run between stations, the engine driver burnt the coal-dust from his shovel and replaced it with fat bacon. John drank in the glorious scent of it curling over the flames and saw the golden fat running out and the eggs, first of the season, flopped in to sizzle to perfection. Doorsteps of bread drank up the fat and held in the manna. It was, John thought, as he sat back and watched the trillions of stars flung out above him and the shapes of darkness flying past, perhaps the best meal he had ever had.

All were abed by the time they quietly lifted the latch. Palliasses of sacking stuffed with straw lay on the floor and on these they slept. The morning found them woken by the mother, up early as always to coax the fire into life once more, with breakfast to put together to feed her brood. Three shy faces peered around the edge of the door and were inveigled into the room. Mrs Kirby was curious to meet Ann and her brothers, having been informed of the intentions of her eldest son: and Ann and the boys were likewise curious to meet Edward's mother. As a starting point there was the amazing fact that the two women shared a Christian name. After that had been thoroughly talked over, conversation continued warm on either side.

The men soon left, feeling thankful that the two women were becoming increasingly more comfortable with one another, amid sighs from the little girls, who had quite taken to the Roberts boys, especially as they had come bearing paper cones of round, black Pomfret cakes complete with the curious stamp of a castle and a raven.

The line to Hereford was soon picked out, leading

almost due south from the station, its presence delineated by posts and ropes. It reminded John of that day, two and a half years ago, when he had followed another as-yet-unmade line northwards from Shrewsbury towards Chester. A tune came to his head and he sang:

'An I've navvied here in Salop and I've navvied in the south,
Wi'out a drink ter cheer me nor a crust ter cross me mouth.
I fed when I were workin', I were clemmed off on the tramp,
An' a stone 'as been me piller an' the moon above me lamp.'

And the others joined in the chorus:

'I'm a bold navvy man, an' an old navvy man,
An' I've done me graft an' stuck it like a bold navvy man.'

They went on for several verses, some extremely vulgar, extemporising from their own experiences as it took them, until they ran out of ideas and walked quietly for a while. It was a typical April day, its pattern one of sharp sunlight followed by bursts of cold grey rain. John noticed intermittent clumps of primroses by the hedgerows, pale yellow heads open to the sun.

'How far bin we agoin'?' asked James.

'Scarface said to just afore Hereford. That's the only piece started yet. Fifty mile, fifty-eight chains long, the new line is, so we mun walk most o' that.'

'We'll not get there this night,' said Edward. 'Nor termorrer, likely.' He patted the roll of palliass they each carried. 'Right good job we got these.'

'Wunna thee miss thee stone, then?' mocked John. 'For a piller?'

'I s'll miss me crust,' Edward replied.

'Good job me Mam gi'e we them lommacks o' bread

an' cheese, then.'

'Best keep those awhile till us be right clemmed.'

In the late afternoon of the second day they smelt wood-smoke on the air and heard the sound of axe and saw and the unmistakeable snappings and tearing, creak and crash as a tree toppled to ground. The woodsmen were felling; and late now, the sap already rising.

They stopped for a word. The woodsmen pointed south. Yes, shacks had been erected, built from the very stretch they had recently felled down the line. Maybe a hundred men there now, many more to come, it was said.

They walked on through a rolling country, feet, however horny, becoming sore within their unforgiving boots. More felled trees marked the way: it was a thickly treed country, they realised, with few signs of habitation thereabouts. Where the woodsmen had been, the different types of wood had been gathered together: bundles of hop-poles and bunches of black poles, each a product of the underwood, lay with their fellows. Some of the standards, maiden oaks all, lay with white-painted numbers on their sides. These were trees that had never been coppiced but left to stand, to grow tall and straight. All were due for auction, the maiden oaks to be sold by the tree, their trunks particularly suitable for Her Majesty's Navy.

On their left a rambling, impressive building came into view, a battlemented ancient pile set in immaculate parkland.

' 'E'll be payin' a fair bit in window-tax, I shunna wonder,' said John. 'Be pleased when they've stopped it, I dare say, like folks say they soon will.'

Just after they had passed a small village, the markings of the line turned to activity. A raw gullet, the narrow preliminary of a cutting, was being dug out by men with pick and shovel.

'When the sides gets ter about sixty feet,' said Tom, 'That's when they 'as ter think costs. Is it cheaper ter carry on cuttin', or ter start burrowin'?'

'Looks like they've started the burrowin',' said Edward. They had come to where a dark hole was being driven horizontally into the hill. Temporary rails were being laid for horse-drawn trucks to be filled with debris from both tunnel and cutting and hauled away.

They travelled the hill-top, passing two groups of navvies engaged in digging construction shafts; and descended part way to lower ground, just out of sight of the castle. There was the shanty town, a cluster of a dozen or so buildings, built of rough-hewn planking. A stream wriggled its way along the valley floor. The group of travellers eyed the huts judiciously: they had wooden floors which were a step up from the ground, so no seeping, icy damp. They had apertures, with shutters, so that light could be had at times and the worst of the cold kept out at others. Once inside they saw that the huts were fairly roomy, a double tier of bunks round three sides, with stove and lockers on the fourth. They dumped their baggage and went off to find a ganger. They were taken on, shaft-lining to be their immediate lot.

There was, open on some days, a shop. If more than bare necessities were wanted a walk to Hereford was necessary, about, oh, eight, nine mile or thereabouts. Or, and quicker, back along the line towards Leominster, four or five. Sometimes a man came with a packhorse and supplies along the road out of Leominster. He'd probably come more often as more customers arrived.

Scarface appeared. He had been shaft-digging all day. Mud clung to every part of him. 'At least, down't hole tha canst feel't wind,' he said. 'Sharp as a knife, that wind.' There were to be two shafts dug. Then there'd be break-ups. From them and the two entrances men would dig out in both directions to eventually form one long tunnel. Blasting was being done. 'It's rum ground though. Not too bad ter dig in parts, but that means there's no strength in it an' likely ter fall. Plenty o' clay, though. 'Clay's all bein' tekken up't line ter mek bricks fer't linin'. It goes out clay an' comes back bricks. Funny that.'

' 'Appen we'll be usin' them bricks,' said Edward.

They ate the last of the provisions brought with them. Scarface said he thought the pedlar would be there tomorrow. Someone gave a few potatoes, another a hunk of bread: they would do the same themselves for a man in need.

Palliasses were laid into bunks and they settled early to sleep. John pulled his blanket about his ears: the April wind keened its iced breath through the chinks in the planking. Tomorrow he must stuff up the cracks in the vicinity of his bunk with turf and clay. One pleasure: in a new hut the small creatures that delight in human blood had not as yet multiplied. He would have a restful night.

The first-comers to the railway had taken lodgings in the tiny village they had passed on the far side of the hill. It was called Hope, or to give its full name, Hope-under-Dinmore. Villagers, mostly low-paid agricultural workers, had been eager for the extra income afforded by their comparatively wealthy lodgers. All available space had now been filled.

Four shillings a day was the rate to be earned as experienced muckshifters, more for those with specialities, such as bricklayers. The Shrewsbury to Hereford line they were building would be single track only, though it would be created wide enough to take a second future track: except, that is, for the Dinmore tunnel. Because of the uncertain nature of the strata there, the friability of the ground, the engineer had decided to build a tunnel wide enough to take one track only.

The track, as with all tracks this far north, would be narrow gauge. The width was 4feet 8½inches. This width, John had heard tell and which was an idea which pleased him, was said to have been long predated by the ruts made in ancient roads by Roman chariot wheels. Brunel and his Great Western favoured a grand 7feet and ¼inch.

The tunnel under Dinmore Hill was to be 1056 yards long, It would be a great undertaking.

The following morning saw them ascending the hill, the country unrolling around them in wooded tracts and open farmland, a light scatter of farmsteads making the most of sun and shelter. There were lines of trees which must be orchards to judge from their hints of pink blossom and lines too of peculiar structures, bare poles and string.

There was much activity on the hill. They noticed a tall observatory for the surveying of the line of the tunnel: from it the positions of the shafts had been marked. They stopped by one of them. It was, John thought, about twelve feet in diameter: there would be just enough room to work within.

As he peered over the top, he saw that some twelve feet had already been dug out and lined with bricks. The timbermen had propped the lining from beneath, as they did after every six feet of bricking, by inserting a wooden curve supported on a timber frame. The next downward section had already been excavated.

'Not much muck-shiftin' for us,' said Edward. 'We s'll easy get brickin' rates here.'

Bricks there were, for the nearby brickworks had begun a line of supply as Scarface had told them and piles of them lay near.

At the top of their shaft stood the headgear. A wire rope descended from the headgear, from which dangled a huge skip or bucket, capable of carrying two tons of debris. The men from the previous shift, who were about to finish shovelling the last debris from the bottom, announced the bucket filled. Edward and John watched as it was wound to the surface by means of horse-power, the muckshifters riding atop the load. During a shift, and down at the bottom of the shaft, when a just-filled bucket slowly rose above you, it was sensible, though not always done, to stand to the side of the shaft: ropes, even of wire, had been known to break.

John and Edward were once more working their skill together. They descended in the now-empty, swaying bucket; themselves and a second team with their bricks, lime, sand, water and tools.

When their twelve-hour shift came to an end and another team took over, they left for the camp. The pedlar had arrived and they bought provisions, tea and flour and cheese. The farms roundabout might have what was in season, meat, potatoes, maybe vegetables if they wanted them, though there was little call for those. They would cook for themselves here: there was no Big Nell nor Old Moll, or not as yet.

Under Mr Brassey's rules, both alcohol and smoking were forbidden while working: they had early been informed of that when Edward tried to light up his gum-bucket. Sulky though they were, they reluctantly came to see some sense in it. Alcohol made men careless; and sparks and gunpowder made bad bedfellows. They were all the more grateful for the pull on a pipe and a pint of beer in the *Royal Oak* when they knocked off.

John struck up a conversation with the barmaid: the inhabitants were not yet too wary of navvy folk. He had a pleasant hour or two of flirtation before Edward dragged him away.

'That were just gettin' somewhere,' he said aggrievedly. 'Thee never knows what might 'ave come o' that. S'pose thee wants to write to Ann.'

'Thee cou'st write to thy maid. An' we mun cook our suppers,' said Edward grimly. 'An' there's gettin' up of a mornin'. Think on.'

Work went on, through rain and wind and sometimes sun. A pick was of little use when clay and pebble turned to solid rock. Then it was that the miners used their skills with gunpowder: tigers, they were known as, the gunpowder men. Some of them came from Derbyshire, where they'd dug for coal, some from Cornwall where they'd delved for tin. Explosions were frequent and disturbed the nights as well as the days of peaceable inhabitants for miles around.

There was another problem: springs were common in the area. Besides the hole of the shaft being a natural catch for rainwater, it might fill from the side or from underneath. The only solution was steam pumps, another area in which the miners were at home.

To relieve the pressures of labour, they drank. The shop on site sold no alcohol and they had to go elsewhere. The *Royal Oak* in Hope would serve them unless they became too unruly and there they sometimes talked to the locals. The ancient, sprawling building that dominated the landscape was Hampton Court Castle, very, very old, they were told, though it was no longer owned by a landowning family of equally ancient lineage. Times were changing and the Castle had been bought by one of the new men, the new rich, or at least the grandson of one, who had climbed from poverty like their own to make a fortune in cotton in the far-off north, Lancashire and Derbyshire. Mr John Arkwright was the present owner, Mr Richard, they thought, was the name of the grandfather, once called the Cotton King.

The lines of poles and wires all about were for hops, now clambering upwards and coating the structures in greenery. Hops, they knew, made the difference between ale and longer-keeping, more flavoursome beer.

One night they got into conversation with one of the miners.

' 'Ast seen me 'ouse?' He grinned. 'Tis a fine 'ouse. Went workin' down't line a bit, by Moreton, an' there weren't no lodgin's. An' what did us find?' He waited, but their faces stayed blank. 'A tree is what ah found. Right by't line. A gret big 'ollow tree. An' ah thinks ter mesen, "that'll do just fine." An' it's dry an' it's near big as a ballroom. Well, twelve foot across it is inside.'

John and Edward kept their faces without expression, fearful of being laughed at as gullible simpletons.

'True, is that,' someone affirmed, seeing their disbelief. 'Called Adam, that tree be, 'ereabouts. Got a wife called Eve, near as big, but Eve ain't 'oller. Adam blew down a year or two back, most o' the top, that is, but the pigs still fill theirselves up wi' acorns from it. Eve, she never 'as no acorns.'

'We s'll come an' see thee one day,' said Edward.

'Move in, most like,' threatened John.

13

A Rich Tapestry

April was coming to its close. The cuckoo had come to Dinmore Hill and so had Mr Thomas Brassey. He was lowered in the bucket they all used and stood in the shaft, inspecting its extent and workmanship. He seemed not unpleased, ran his eye over the workers and nodded.

'Never forgets a face,' said Tom. 'That's what they says. Never forgets a sum nor a debt neither. Dunna 'ave no office, thee knows. Everythink in 'is 'ead.'

'Got shares in't line, 'as Brassey' said Scarface. 'Don't get paid, see, as such. 'Is money'll come from 'is shares, so 'e's got ter do it right, see, or 'e'll mek no money outer't thing.'

Gossip said that Mr Brassey, who had spent a week inspecting progress, expected the line to be open from Shrewsbury as far as Ludlow by the end of December coming; and the rest of the line from Ludlow to Hereford, which included their tunnel and was the most difficult stretch, to be open by the end of the December following, 1852.

Then it was the last day of April. John and Edward collected their tools together at the finish of their shift and rose in their bucket into blinding rain. It poured all night. Half-asleep they could hear the drumming on the roof of the hut: water oozed and dripped through a hundred tiny cracks.

As they set out in still-damp clothes into the early morning air, they walked into works that had become a sea of cloying mud. Down in their shaft, now some hundreds of feet deep, lay a great pool of water, the steam engine pumping laboriously without seemingly making much headway.

'No good goin' down in this,' said Edward. The ganger shrugged in resignation.

'Not unless we wants ter drown,' said John. 'Come on, let's leave 'er awhile an' see 'ow the rest o' the line's agoin'.'

Leaving the engine to finish its work of making descent possible, Edward and John walked further to look down on the incipient cutting beginning to enter the hill from its northern side. Five men were standing on the top of the narrow gullet, its walls dangerously steep, almost perpendicular.

'Eh, look, Mr Field'ouse 'isself,' said John. Mr Fieldhouse was the subcontractor for the Dinmore part of the line. He'd taken a house nearby where he lived with his wife and children, a son usually with him on the works. Now, here he was, one of the five men who, with heads down, seemed to be inspecting the state of the land on which they stood.

Suddenly there was a shout of warning from Fieldhouse. They saw the ground break under his feet and he falling, tumbling in earth down the wall of the gullet. The other men, alerted, ran in retreat, but one ran straight into a wheelbarrow barring his escape. He too fell, this time a great torrent of earth and stones falling with him and completely submerging his body. The contractor, the first fallen, picked himself up unhurt, another man pointed to the spot where the second man had disappeared. Frantically they began to dig, using hands as shovels. A man's head appeared. But it was too late, they heard later. His jaw was broken, his collarbone and a leg; and worst of all his neck. He breathed, twice, and was gone.

The brothers stood for a moment or two, stunned. They

had known the dead man by sight though he was not someone close to their lives. There was nothing they could have done, nothing anybody could have done. Neither voiced the thought, but death was ever near. They would give a shilling so that he had at least a decent burial. Then they walked back to their shaft where the water was now mere shallow mud; and began the day's work.

More men were being taken on daily. One day two men with fearsome accents arrived, one Irish, one Scottish. They managed to finish a shift, but were driven off with clods of earth and stones before they could be paid.

'Gone bleatin' ter the masters,' someone sneered. 'Well, we threw the Irishman down the cuttin'. 'E'll know better than ter come back 'ere.'

After the rain came frosts, frosts in Maytime. Inside their hut, even with the chinks between the boards deemed well-wadded, the night wind whistled through. Frosts froze the rain that had seeped into fissures in the ground. The ice expanded, widening the cracks.

It was a Saturday, towards the end of the month. The brothers did not see this for themselves, but were told that evening by Tom Roberts who was working inside the entrance to the tunnel. He'd been near, though not at, the scene of the accident, and news travelled fast. Four men had been there, at the bottom of the cutting this time, when a huge mass of earth had fallen from above, burying them. Two were quite dead when their bodies were dug up. Another had fallen against a wheelbarrow which had acted as a shield against the major weight of the earth but more importantly had preserved an air-pocket, so that when dug out he was still alive, though now in hospital with severe injuries. One man had been to the side and so escaped the full impact of the slippage. There was grumbling, Tom said. Fieldhouse had been pre-warned, by some of the men and, more importantly, by Mr Brassey's Inspector of Works, that the gullet was dangerous. It was narrow, only seven and a half feet wide and the sides twenty-two feet high and almost vertical.

'What they been sayin',' said Tom, 'Is that the gullet should a bin dug wider an' the sides should a bin shuttered ter stop the muck a-fallin'. There's ter be an inquest on Monday at the *Royal Oak*. See what's said then.'

Rumour swirled around the works. Scarface arrived back at their hut on the Wednesday armed with that day's edition of the *Hereford Journal*. He read out the article .

'Read that again, what the Inspector said,' said John.

Scarface found the place: ' "On Thursday last ... I called Mr Fieldhouse to my side and said, 'For heaven's sake, Fieldhouse, put some stretchers across here, or you will have someone killed;' he said nothing; I thought then there was danger; on Friday I was at the spot again, and saw that no precaution had been taken to prevent danger; on Saturday morning I was at the cutting and saw Fieldhouse, and went to where the deceased men were at work; on the road going I said, 'Fieldhouse, why don't you alter this work ...' He said, 'They came to me yesterday and said the gullet would fall in.' " '

'And Fieldhouse was "severely reprimanded"?' queried Tom.

Scarface read again, ' "Unless immediate steps were taken to secure the works properly for the safety of the workmen," the Coroner said he'd write to Mr Brassey. "Two industrious and valuable labourers had been sacrificed," the Coroner says. Fieldhouse were gettin' paid by't yard o' course. So 'e'd likely not want ter waste time puttin' up shutterin'.'

'Mr Brassey mun 'ave trusted 'im though,' said John thoughtfully. 'Dunna it say 'e'd worked fer 'im eleven year?' The rest murmured assent.

'Let's 'ope 'e'll mend 'is ways,' said Edward piously.

Scarface, a few nights later, brought them a piece from the *Hereford Times.* The Great Exhibition, which had been in preparation and endlessly discussed for the last couple of years, had been open for a month at prices that were only for the upper classes. Now it had been thrown open to the public, ordinary people like themselves, at a price of one shilling. The article spoke of the most wonderful things, from the recently-acquired Mountain of Light diamond, the Koh-i-Noor, to a bed. The diamond, in spite of the gentry expressing fears of its theft by the lower orders, was still safe in its gilded cage. The bed was a curiosity. Scarface grinned and read the description: ' "The Early Rising Machine ... By means of a common alarum clock hung at the head of the bed, and adjusted in the usual way to go off at the desired hour, the front legs of the bedstead, immediately the alarum ceases ringing, are made to fold underneath, and the sleeper, without any jerk or any personal danger, is placed on his feet in the middle of the room, where, at the option of the possessor, a cold bath can be placed, if he is at all disposed to ensure being rendered rapidly wide awake." '

A further wonderful thing, not exactly part of the exhibition, was the innovative provision of plentiful closets for public need; and these the otherwise scarce water-closet. For a penny you could have the use of a clean seat, a towel, a comb and a shoeshine.

Talking one night, Edward declared his intention to wait for the imminent pay-day and, whilst others were drinking dry the nearby hostelries, to make his way back to Shrewsbury, home and Ann. He had saved money from the last pay-day and he could add money from this one, keeping a modicum for himself. It could be hidden for safe-keeping in the house on the Foregate. He could travel by the *Engineer*, the coach that ran from Hereford to Ludlow and from there by another coach to the *Lion Hotel* in Shrewsbury, though in the end he decided to walk as far as Ludlow and use the coach for the second but larger part of the journey. At three or four shillings, even travelling outside was expensive but he was desperate to see Ann. If he used the road there was the possibility of saving his feet for a few miles by a lift from a friendly wagoner, though that would gain him little if anything in speed.

John felt a sudden urge to go on a good randy. Many of the lads had begun a habit of descending on the village of Wellington, the Herefordshire Wellington that is, as opposed to the Shropshire one, which lay towards Hereford about three miles down the line to the south. It already had something of a reputation as a rough place, full of labourers from the farms, brickworks and quarries, so that the landlords were not over-scornful of railway labourers. After being paid the following day, he bid goodbye to his brother and joined the groups walking south to Wellington.

It was liberating, being on his own: neither Tom nor James had wanted to join him. He was Blackie here, anonymous to authority. He felt light-hearted and free as he walked the road. His companions were in a jolly mood. They could shout as much as they cared to, throw stones at birds or cats, mock passers-by, whistle after women, sing filthy songs; and who would say them nay? There was a power in numbers: they were strong, they were young, they were going to have a good time and there were many of them.

It was a Sunday, a day of glorious sunshine. The hedgerows blossomed a creamy-white with plump plates of elderflower, the roots deep in a pale froth of cow parsley and dog-daisy. Pink came from red-robin and red campion. A field of potatoes, John was pleased to note, showed the green tops of health. The meadow-grass was lush and tall, pricked with yellow buttercup. A black dot hung in the blue above, shrilling its perpetual song. Scents drifted thickly in the warmth of the air.

In Wellington they stopped at a beerhouse where the landlord doubled as a pig-farmer. He hadn't laid eyes on a constable all morning, he told them. 'Plenty sworn in,' he said. 'But they be layin' low.' He winked. His beerhouse was a plain dwelling, nothing valuable in it to worry over. The more beer he sold, the more profit he made. There was cider too, a local drink that John was beginning to appreciate for its strength; and plenty of less-good beer and plenty of less-good cider for later, when his customers would be so drunk they wouldn't notice the difference.

The mass of men moved on, to another beerhouse and then another. John found himself chatting to a brawny, buxom girl, and then they were out in the balmy half-light, wandering, lying close and doing much more than chatting. It was glorious. It was freedom. He was lord of the world. He was immortal.

He woke up next a grassy bank. His clothes were wet with dew. The girl had disappeared. Had she been there at all? Never mind, another day could be had, another liberating, dazzling day. He felt in his pocket: it was empty of money. He tried another: the same. And he realised, even before he tried to rise to his feet, that he did not feel well. A beer would no doubt set him right. But he had nought with which to buy it.

The depth the shaft needed to reach had been calculated by the engineer above. As the shaft grew deeper, a rod thirty feet long had been suspended from a spike driven into the tunnel lining. A second spike would measure off another thirty feet and so on. Now the bottom of their shaft had been reached.

At each end of the space directly below the shaft stood

174

a barrel of muddy water. In each barrel was a twenty pound weight suspended by a wire from the headgear at the top of the shaft, the thickened water keeping it steady. At the surface the two wires had been aligned to the exact direction the tunnel had to follow. Now that direction was being transferred underground. A cord that stretched between the two wires below was extended at each end until its line could be marked on the wall of the chamber. The men underground hammered and hand-drilled, blasted and shovelled in accordance with the direction the marks denoted.

The tunnel was a preliminary one, a pilot tunnel known as the heading, not yet full size, about eight feet in diameter, big enough to allow wagons on temporary rails to remove the spoil. Only later would they, bit by bit, enlarge the space above and to the side to achieve the full shape of the finished tunnel.

Timber supports must be put in by the timbermen to support the roof as the earth and rock was removed. Theirs was no easy job: heads protected by a cloth hat and eyes by its brim, working high up and close under an unsupported ceiling. Head trees crossed the roof, supported on side trees. Poling boards shuttered the walls. Sometimes the tunnel moved forward only a yard in a twelve-hour shift. Candles gave a little light.

They all complained about the air, calling it 'foul': and it was getting worse. Part of the problem was the smoke from the firing which, with as yet no through-draft, took a long time to clear; part of it was toxic gases released by their tunnelling; part of it was the effluvia of men and horses.

They were always wet, in spite of the efforts of the ever-pumping steam engines. Water dripped off the brims of their hats and ran off the pieces of sacking or tarpaulin or oiled cloth that they wrapped over their shoulders. Water dripped and ran everywhere: groundwater seeped through the earth above and the whole area was full of springs. The engineer, respected Henry Robinson, had judged it too dangerous, with too much risk of collapse, to try to drive the width of a double line. A narrower tunnel would be safer.

Under their feet the temporary rails began to be laid, to take at first man-pushed trucks of spoil. As more heading was bored and there was room enough, these rails were extended and horses lowered in to pull the trucks towards the shaft to be hauled to the surface. James, who had somehow become Wolf by the circumstance of coming from Wolverhampton, shoed these horses and others along with mending tools, riveting and a hundred and one other tasks of fire and metal.

If there were no bricking to be done the brothers turned their hand to other tasks: the best, the cream of navvies, like Scarface, could turn their hands to anything, learning by example and experience.

A connected train of empty wagons would arrive. Each wagon would be filled by two men working together. When the train was full it would be drawn away, to be replaced by a set of empty wagons. Fourteen times in a shift this should happen, said Mr Brassey. A pair of men filling that expected daily quota of fourteen sets, fourteen empty wagons, with each man using a shovel to lift nearly twenty tons of earth and rock over his head into a truck, was a source of pride; and of exhaustion. Edward, with his added years and strength, could just about manage this. John was improving as the months went by, but he still fell short of the target. There were men of legend who could do sixteen.

One afternoon in early July they all came up in the bucket leaving the tunnel clear so that Ilky, one of the tigers, could descend to pack the drilled hole with explosive, lay a charge and set his fuse to blast a further section. Ilky climbed into the bucket, got to the bottom. There was a pause. They could hear him whistling as he set the fuse. Then came the shout to raise him out of the way of the explosion. The horse strained, the bucket began to rise. A confusion of noise and crashings followed, amid which could be heard Ilky swearing profusely. The horse suddenly had nothing to pull: the wire rope had broken and the bucket, with Ilky inside, had plunged to the ground. Below, the swearing had stopped. Nothing happened. Edward and John and the other men, who had backed away from the shaft expecting an explosion, cautiously leaned their ears towards the void. They heard, 'Beat the bogger,' triumphantly from below.

Ilky, it turned out when finally he was rescued, had been well up from the ground when the rope broke. The bucket had remained miraculously upright, jolting him hard as it hit the bottom but leaving him conscious. With admirable presence of mind, he had pulled out his knife and severed the flaming fuse within a quarter-inch, so he said, of the charge. Bar a bruise or two he was unhurt. They, who had occupied the same bucket immediately prior to Ilky, plus the fortunate himself, all carried on working.

Edward, on his return from his end-of-May visit to home and Ann, had reported on the numbers of men now working on the line. When the four of them had made their journey from Shrewsbury to Dinmore Hill back in April, they had seen few navvies.

'Eh, there's thousands now,' Edward said. 'An' in S'ewsb'ry they bin startin' on a viaduct, near the English Bridge, where Rea Brook empties into the Severn. They's had to dig a new channel to tek the Rea first. Low land there. They's begun on the piers. Eleven arches. Dad an' Grandad, they's bin workin' on it. 'Appen I s'll go there meself. Nearer Ann an' I could live at 'ome.'

John heard this without replying. He did not want to live at home: life was considerably more free away from parental eyes.

'I've decided,' said Edward, 'Ann an' me, we s'll get wed in September.'

'What'll thee do then?' asked John.

'Find a job not too far away. Find lodgin's, or 'appen an 'ouse to rent like folks does, I s'pose. Till then I s'll get a bit put by.'

Ann, it transpired, had found a live-in place as a housemaid. They weren't bad employers, she'd said. Naturally she would rather be married and have a household of her own.

The conversation reminded John of Eliza and he went off to pen her a long-delayed letter. She wrote much more often than he, once or twice a week, letters full of longing to see him again, anecdotes about the children of the household. Her Uncle William had been to Court, she said. Something called Letters of Administration. Her father had left no will and any property had to be given into the hands of a suitable person. She and her sister and brother were not suitable because they were not of full age, not twenty-one. Uncle William, the person the Court thought *was* suitable, was supposed to use any property for the children's benefit until she, Eliza, was twenty-one, when it would go to her. She couldn't think there was much, she said, a locket that had been her mother's, some clothes, some tools, a stick or two of furniture, that was all.

John could think of little to write in return: life was mostly work; and what would she want to know about work, anyway? Work just happened: it wasn't something you wrote about. He couldn't tell her about his leisure time either: there were some things better left unsaid. Instead he told her that he'd missed her - partly true - that he was eating plenty of good beef and that the weather was much

178

warmer. As an afterthought he said he'd had a good wash in the River Lugg. He enclosed a few stamps and supposed he'd have to make a trip to Hope-under-Dinmore to post it. There was a barmaid there though, as consolation, whom he thought rather favoured him.

July, apart from Ilky's narrow escape, was quiet. Navvies working around Ludlow were, to everyone's surprise and some disbelief, commended by the *Hereford Times* for their restrained habits. There was talk of building a station at Birkenhead, to be constructed jointly by the Shrewsbury and Chester, the Shrewsbury and Birmingham and the Shrewsbury and Hereford. Birkenhead, said Scarface, who drank in information like beer, was on the Cheshire side of the Mersey, and was home to Mr and Mrs Brassey. The Brasseys, he informed John, had been yeomen of Cheshire for generations.

August was quiet too. Their tunnel was highly spoken of by all and sundry as progressing at a most satisfactory rate. Ann, the girl who had been so curious about the fossils in the cavern at Dudley, wrote in some excitement about a comet she had seen over Shrewsbury. It had been visible for several days to the north-west just after sundown. John's father and grandfather were working on the viaduct, which Mr Brassey had been to see and seemed pleased with, she said. It had been agreed with an anxious town council that the sides of the viaduct should, if necessary, be covered-in with sheet iron, so that horses would not shy at the sight of passing trains.

Nearer to Hereford the line was showing more activity. The cutting that had to be made to approach the tunnel at its southern end had at last been driven through the solid rock. The black hole which was the tunnel heading now extended some two hundred yards into the hill, which rose above it as a cliff of rock four hundred feet high. Much blasting was needed. The spoil went in horse-drawn wagons along the temporary rails to create an embankment towards Hereford and the crossing of the River Ludd.

The crossing was largely the province of the masons, who had been given access to quarries by the lord of Hampton Court Castle, that vast building that the travellers had been struck by as they had first approached Dinmore Hill. Large blocks of stone cut from the quarries and hauled to their destination by horse and cart were being used in the erection of bridges over the river.

Mr Arkwright, lord of Hampton Court Castle, was being paid £10 per day for the inconvenience of having a railway tunnelled through his hill.

The citizens of Hereford were full of excited anticipation of their railway. And when the first rails, those designed to be permanent, not temporary, were landed at a wharf, to transport coal for the tunnel's steam engines and to transport a ventilating machine to clear the tunnel's air, the enthusiasm of citizens led them to visit in droves to see for themselves and extol the marvels of this new age.

'What's up?' John looked skywards, where the circle of daylight had shrunk to saucer size. They were in almost complete darkness.

Edward peered over the edge of the bucket. 'Canna see a thing.'

They were part way down the shaft at the start of the morning shift and their bucket had come to a halt.

' 'Old the rope be best,' said Edward. John was already doing just that. If balanced centrally and secured to the rope they stood less chance of the bucket tipping and toppling them out. A buzzing, an alertness, seemed to be going through his body. They both shouted towards the tiny circle of light that was the surface and life. Nothing happened. They dangled, the bucket turning slowly.

There was a jerk. The bucket plunged downwards, swaying violently. A recollection of tales told, a confused series of pictures, seemed to have taken dizzying possession of John's brain. He could see splinters of bone piercing flesh. He could see legs broken in so many places that they folded in short lengths. He could see long bones that bored upwards through chests or came out through hips. He could feel the agony of his shattered spine. What if you jumped just as the bucket hit bottom ...?

There was another jerk. The bucket halted its violent descent, tipped, righted itself. And slowly, gently, continued downwards. John felt himself trembling. Neither of them spoke as they clung to the rope for a further thirty feet to the bottom of the shaft.

They were that evening the star turn in the centre of a small circle of sympathisers, happy to hear a good tale and ready with the free drinks.

'Should a seen 'im,' guffawed Edward, pointing a finger at his brother. 'White as snow, 'e were.'

'Tremblin' like a new-born lamb, 'im,' crowed John, bent half over with laughter. 'An' all it were were a bit of a tangle in a rope.'

A reporter from the *Hereford Journal* heard the story and their narrow escape made it into print, albeit without their names. It was a fortnight before the wedding.

14

Joinings and Dividings

The wedding had been fixed for September the 15th that year of 1851, a Monday. It would be in Shrewsbury, which made it convenient for bride and groom and the groom's parents but difficult for the bride's parents who were still living in Wolverhampton. The Roberts were determined to attend: it was after all the marriage of their only daughter. They would essay an adventure, their first journey by train. Fare wars were still being waged between the Shrewsbury and Birmingham and the domineering London and North Western which, to the satisfaction of the travelling public if not to the liking of the shareholders, kept down the prices: the forty-six miles from Wolverhampton to Shrewsbury cost 6d only.

Saturday the 6th was payday for the workers on the Dinmore tunnel. Instead of joining in the randy, the two pairs of brothers would trek back to Shrewsbury. The weather was dry and not yet cold. They could make a camp fire perhaps and sleep under the stars for the one night. It would be a good time of fellowship, a break from the drudgery of work.

The little house in the Foregate was reached in the small hours of Monday morning. There was exactly one week to go until the wedding.

A house had to be found for the newly-weds to rent; and one was duly decided on, near the ruins of the Abbey and not far from S'ewsb'ry and his wife. It was tall and thin as if built as an afterthought to fill a gap between two other houses. It was old, but so were the houses all, and it was crooked, like the rest. A heavy, carved beam jutted above the first floor and either side of the door was a post fashioned like a stick of barley sugar. Two worn stone steps led up to the front door and above the room into which the door led was a bedroom and above that another, tiny, low-ceilinged room under the roof. Ann was very happy and talked all the time of how comfortable and convenient it would be: there were pot-hangers over the fire for cooking and a pump not far away for water and even a tiny scullery behind for washing pots and clothes and themselves. Nor was it far from the market and shops.

Four strong and willing pairs of arms brushed flaking paint and cobwebs from every cranny. Four paintbrushes were borrowed and whitewash slapped on walls and ceilings to smooth all defects, kill all bugs and shed a bright glow through the rooms.

They bought a bed-frame for the mattress that Ann had made, a tick, stitched into a bag and stuffed with chopped straw. She had managed to buy a length of linen twill, prized for its close weave and its long-wearing qualities; and Edward's sisters and she had carried the straw home from a nearby farm, straw just cut and sweet-smelling. Sometime perhaps they would be able to afford a feather tick to put on top of it. The Kirby parents contributed a pan and some wooden spoons whittled by S'ewsb'ry. Owd S'ewsb'ry and his wife gave them a blanket. Aunt Susanna gave them a flat-iron. John had bought them a few plates and cups and spoons and forks, second-hand they were, but he'd got more for his money that way.

There were other things too, that Ann had long been saving in a bottom drawer, which her parents would bring with them along with their own grand contribution, a wash-tub with wooden dolly.

On the morning of the 15th the wedding party made

their way along the Foregate towards the Abbey church of Holy Cross that, folks said, had stood there for near a thousand years. You could see that it had changed at some time: old walling betokened a once-larger building. The groom's side approached with the comfort of familiarity, though as their small group passed through the doorway into the chill of ancient stone their confidence was dwarfed under the soaring roof and the height of the massive columns.

They were the only wedding party that day. Anne's brother James was a witness. John looked up at the ceiling far above and, with his own skills in his mind, felt a new respect for the monks of long ago.

Anne wore her best dress, the blue-green dress that she had worn for the visit to the Dudley caverns. Over it she wore a shawl, 'still fashionable,' twittered her proud mother, a paisley shawl in blues, a parting gift from her mistress, one that she herself had tired of. Anne's hair was parted in the centre as usual and hung in glossy, dark ringlets, product of being most unbecomingly tied up in 'rags' the previous night, but only the ladies were aware of that.

Edward wore his square-tailed velveteen coat and blue plush waistcoat. His trousers he had bought new. 'Needed 'em anyway. Last uns han already started work,' he said.

All the men wore their trousers free from the customary yorks, the straps that tied below the knees in the vain hope of restraining trouser-bottoms from dropping into ever-present mud.

Afterwards they all went back to the bright new house for the wedding- breakfast and gossiped. Mary, John's grandmother, had made one of her famous fidget pies with this year's early apples and cider and gammon. Later Thomas Thomas, Aunt Susanna's husband, brought out his fiddle and they drank home-made ale, sang songs and pounded the wooden boards late into the night.

One member of the family had not been there that day. Elizabeth, wayward daughter of Owd S'ewsb'ry and his wife Mary, had fulfilled everyone's gloomy prognostications and been driven to enter the workhouse, taking with her her two daughters, eight-year-old Elizabeth; and Phoebe, who would soon be five. The girls would be parted from their mother, of course: they might see her from a distance at mealtimes, but they would not be allowed to talk. They would all wear the cheap, drab workhouse uniform. However, said their grandmother, it was better than the rags they had been wearing. Besides, the girls would at least have a wash each morning and a comb of their hair and might even learn to read and write. And the food, provided that the present master was an honest man, was just enough to keep body and soul together, better than their feckless mother was giving them.

A momentary curiosity crossed John's mind as to why these two girl by-blows were to be left in the workhouse, while the other family bastard, their cousin Rachel Ann, had been given a home with Aunt Susanna, but he felt hesitant to stir what just might be very muddy family waters.

John left Shrewsbury with Tom and James Roberts the following day. It felt strange not to have Edward by his side, strange and lonely: they had lived together and latterly worked together almost all of John's life.

Edward, though, was reluctant to leave his bride; and there was work nearby, the viaduct and a wide bridge to finish over the Abbey Foregate, besides an embankment between the Abbey Foregate and the station. The materials for the embankment would have to be carried over the viaduct, so that must be built first. Mr Brassey had confirmed yet again that the line would be open by the end of the year, so all hands were needed. And for Mr Brassey, men would give their best.

Tom Roberts had a bricklaying partner at Dinmore with whom he was less than satisfied and would prefer to team up with John: it would be a new beginning.

John ruminated as they walked along the line back to the tunnel. There were hundreds of navvies along the route, two thousand now, someone had said. They toiled amid stone-pocked piles of muddy spoil, half-done bridges rising, rough-hewn cuttings striped through earth and rock, raw brown embankments raised across valleys. Men, like insects, swarmed everywhere; horses neighed, wagons rattled, iron clanged, explosions boomed.

He thought back over the wedding in snatches and half-thoughts, more feelings than organised words. Did he envy Edward and his new life? He supposed it would be pleasant to be cooked and cared for by a loving wife. And to bed a loving wife whenever he liked. But which wife, in his own case? He thought of Eliza: she was the only girl he'd met to whom he could think of attaching that epithet 'wife'. But settle down? With one girl for ever? Now? When there were so many others out there, so much in the way of newness and variety and excitement? Wild oats, didn't they call it? He had more to sow before he settled down. He wouldn't part from Eliza. Or not unless and until he found a better. It was a good feeling to have her love for him to fall back to; a comforting, safe sort of feeling. She did very well for the present. And there was something about her which he hadn't found with anyone else: he did care for her, wanted to protect her, his little waif.

A rhythm of blows caught John's ear: hammer ringing on steel. The sound grew louder as they approached: he guessed what he would see. Four men stood, each at a couple of arm's lengths, around another. That man in the centre, the holder, sat upon the ground, legs apart, hands gripping a five-foot bar of tempered steel known as the jumper, holding it firmly upright against the rock. One man from the circle, hammer-head pointing downwards, raised it behind him in an arc. It flew upwards in a semicircle, over his head and down, landing with precision and tremendous force on the rounded, inch-across, apex of the steel bar. As the hit came, a second man wielded his own hammer, then the third and the fourth; then the first again, on and on and on until the driven hole was deep enough to take the charge.

'Tried that for a while,' said Tom. 'When we was blasting all that rock up north somewhere. Twelve hours we done that at a stretch. Not no more. Nerves o' steel yo needs. The Irish'll do it. They could 'a been drinkin' all night, playin' cards all night, but they'll still do it. Not many injuries. Never is.'

John looked at him sharply; and understood.

The night they spent on that tramp back to Dinmore they bedded down on the floor of a hut, given shelter and food by its occupants in return for such stories as they could tell. The tale of the near-disastrous descent in the bucket provided some amusement, but made John think, with a pang of unwelcome homesickness, of his missing brother.

Then once more they were back at work. More and more men were working on the tunnel, nearly 500 feet below ground. The two entrances afforded work on two faces. The two shafts, 620 yards apart, each with men working both north and south, meant work on another four faces. They were still driving the heading.

Mr Brassey still adhered to his estimate that the Dinmore tunnel in this second, more difficult section of the line from Ludlow to Hereford, would be finished by the end of the year following, 1852.

Scarface told John about the randy at Wellington they'd missed by journeying to Shrewsbury for the wedding. He rarely saved a whole paper but tore out bits of his choice to keep in a pocket and bring out for any audience he felt might be appreciative. He read this one from the *Hereford Journal* verbatim, putting on a voice of gentlemanly indignation:

' "Notorious as the village was for fighting formerly, it has become much worse since the commencement of the works on the Shrewsbury and Hereford railway at Dinmore Hill and ... on Saturday the 6th, being the pay-day of the men employed at the tunnel and brickyards, when they had received their money they came to Wellington and for three nights and days, spent their time and money there in the most profligate manner, using profane and disgusting language and fighting like brutes more than human beings." An' a reet good time we 'ad an' all,' he ended, with satisfaction.

'This is a good bit, this,' he went on, unfolding another scrap. 'Ast thee ever 'eard't like o' this, lad?' He waved the paper in disgust, genuine this time, 'Women in trousers. Comes from America. A Mrs Bloomer, foreigner o' course, she started it by all accounts. Tryin' ter mek out as women in proper dresses an' stays gets consumption. Not 'ealthy, she says. There's women, an' not just in London neither, goin' on stages in tunic things an' trouser things underneath an' sayin' dresses get in't way an' dresses gives yer consumption. Daft boggers. They gets shouted at good an' proper.'

'O' course they'n be an' a good thing too,' said John, horrified.

There was another accident towards the end of

October. Neither John nor Tom knew the man, John Martin, but once again they were disconcertingly reminded of the fragility of life. He had been working with the trains of wagons, they said. He was uncoupling a line of empties when a train of full ones came charging down the gullet. A nail sticking out caught his waistcoat and spun him round. He fell, fracturing several ribs. They got him to the hospital in Shrewsbury but the ribs had lacerated his lungs, which collapsed. Accidental death was the verdict.

There was a letter from Edward in November giving scraps of news.

A Mr Finlay, contractor for the viaduct that he and S'ewsb'ry and Owd S'ewsb'ry were working on, had been so pleased with progress that he'd treated all the navvies to ale, as much as they could drink, 'Which were a lot,' wrote Edward.

They were still on schedule for finishing their Shrewsbury to Ludlow section by the end of the following month.

The bastard child, John's cousin, had died; the little one, Phoebe. They'd had her respectably buried in St. Mary's though, not in the unconsecrated burial ground of the workhouse.

Anne was a good cook, had a tasty way with beef, pies and puddings and such as well as stews.

The letter made John think of Eliza. It was months since he'd seen her and although her letters reached him regularly, he hadn't replied to the last two or three. Maybe he should make an effort and visit Wolverhampton over Christmas when the work might stop for a day or two. He discussed his plan with Tom and James: both were going home then. John could stay with them if he liked.

They were getting paid every Saturday now, at the

close of work for the day. Mr Brassey had, it was rumoured, come to the conclusion both that men wasted fewer days if paid more frequently and that it was better for the men in that they were inclined to spend less on a frolic of weekly occurrence and saved more.

This did not preclude many a good randy, however; and the local papers were full of the 'desperate and turbulent conduct of the navvies engaged at the works at Dinmore Hill', the 'terror' experienced by the local population, the fear and resentment of the local farm labourers with whom the navvies were accused of picking fights. Navvies had been blamed for breaking all the cups and jugs in one establishment, for rescuing wrongdoers from the custody of lawful constables and setting them at liberty, for mass fights of twenty or so navvies stripped to the waist, and for drink-crazed navvies offering vehemently to take on any man in the town.

The magistrates were indignant: something must be done. They resolved to make the railway liable for damages. A meeting was held, attended by Mr Brierley, Inspector of Works for the Shrewsbury and Hereford Railway, a meeting authorised by Mr Brassey himself. A special constable would be appointed, said Brierley soothingly, to operate where most of the unwelcome activity took place. He would receive eighteen shillings a week and be given a suit of clothes, all expenses to be paid by Mr Brassey. The chosen candidate was a late warder at the Hereford County Gaol, a Charles Hopton.

Hopton soon proved his worth by single-handedly capturing no less than three villains simultaneously, handcuffing them together and driving them by cart into the custody of Superintendent Gregory. Not a man to be trifled with, John thought.

In spite of confident official predictions it was becoming clear that the line from Shrewsbury to Ludlow would fail to be finished by the end of the year. When John, Tom and James stopped briefly at Shrewsbury that Christmas on their journey to Wolverhampton, they could see for themselves that the embankment between the station and the bridge over the Abbey Foregate was almost finished but not quite and that the permanent rails still had to be laid. It would not be long before the first engine used the track though, they decided, an opinion confirmed by Edward.

Edward was getting on well enough, thought John and it made him anxious to see Eliza.

Once in Wolverhampton they repaired to their old haunt, the *Prince of Wales*, greeting acquaintances they recognised from the months they'd spent in the town the previous year. Later they moved on to the beerhouses round the market place and looked about them. One of the customers, a man of large and loose frame and a shock of a nose, was unmistakeable.

'Tweedlebeak,' shouted John, laying a hand on the other's shoulder.

The man looked up without recognition. Then, 'Well, if it ain't our Nipper. 'Ow do?' and he grabbed John's hand and shook it with vigour.

'Blackie,' said John. 'Towd yo last time.'

'So yer did, Blackie, so yer did. Growed a bit sin' ah saw yer last, see. Well, where yer bin? What's new?'

John told tales of the Dinmore tunnel; and Tweedlebeak, delighted to find an audience to whom his own stale news was news of interest, settled down to give John, Tom and James an offering in return.

'Well now. Found me a job wi' the S'ewsb'ry an' Birmingham. Still ain't got ter Birmingham though. But there is a bit o' line joining Wolverhampton ter Birmingham. Stour Valley Line they calls it, though it doesna go through any Stour Valley. Anyway, it's finished now. And S&B's got shares in it. So it can run trains o'er it. So you'd a thought anyhow. Parliament said it could an' all.'

'An' I'll wager the owd L&NW comes into this,' said John.

Tweedlebeak nodded. 'You's right there. They've got the lease of it. Line's finished, L&NW fix a day to open. Then they cancels it. L&NW tells S&B it can't run its trains over that bit o' line 'cos it's gone an' got itself 'itched up wi' the Great Western. Deadly enemies, the L&NW an' the Great Western. S&B says, no it 'ain't, it's only *agreed* to 'itch up, 'ain't actually *done* it. Not the same thing. So L&NW polish up their 'earts o' gold an' come over all 'oity-toity about 'public safety'. Say it'd be *dangerous* to let the S&B use the line. Might be a collision.'

'Looks like trouble,' said Tom, his eyes on Tweedlebeak.

'Trouble it is. You'll know Mr 'Enry Robertson?'

'S&B engineer,' said John. 'S&H engineer an' all, come ter that.'

'Day Stour Valley Line's s'posed to open 'e comes on the train from S'ewsb'ry ter Wolverhampton, 'im and some important folks what's goin' on ter Birmingham. They 'opes! Start off from Wolverhampton on Stour Valley Line when what do the engine driver see but another engine right in front of 'im, on't same bit o' rails. Stopped. Steam up, brakes on, stopped.'

'Crash, do they? One o' them collisions as the L&NW bin so worried about?'

'Nah. S&B stops in time, buffers just touchin'. But L&NW driver ain't movin', even though Robertson tells 'im to. An' again.'

'So then what?'

'Well, that ain't the only thing. A bit further along the line the rails've been tekken up an' there's another engine an' it's off the line so as yer can't use the down line an' yer can't use the up line neither.

'Thing is, day before that, the Sunday, day before the line's due to open, L&NW put out placards everywhere saying it ain't openin' after all. Real sorry they says they are, real, real sorry fer the public: all my eye an' Betty Martin if yer asks me. An' the S'ewsb'ry an' Birmingham, they puts out more placards sayin' they's goin' ter use the line anyway. Mayor an' 'is lot knows there'll be trouble.

'So on the Monday morning Mayor goes down ter station wi' alot o' policemen an' some big army chaps. An' 50th Regiment were told ter be ready. An 'cos o' the 'andbills as 'ad bin put out, folks in Wolverhampton knew ter come along ter 'ave a look. Thousands, there were, all along the line, watchin'. Four, five thousand folks waitin' fer a battle. When Robertson arrives from S'ewsb'ry on 'is big engine, they all cheers. Anyway, there's argiments an' more argiments an' in the end the big bosses from the L&NW gets summoned by the big bosses from the S&B fer not lettin' 'em use the line an' they all troops along ter the Court. Four hours they carries on quarrellin', up before the magistrates, sayin' about sueings an' grand juries an' Courts o' Chancery an' such.'

'An' what now?' put in John.

'Nothin' much. No S&B trains though.'

'Pity there weren't no battle,' said John, thoughtfully.

When John managed to snatch an illicit half-hour with Eliza that Christmas Eve, she was so delighted to be in his company again that he felt most contented. Mrs Roberts, to whose house she was allowed to come in the afternoon of Boxing Day, pronounced her a good girl, a neat, tidy, modest, good-natured girl. John felt quite swollen with pride. And when he escorted her from and back to the mason's house, she kissed him in such a trusting, loving way; and when she quoted his opinions to others while gazing up at him adoringly, how could he not be flattered?

15

A Thing of Clay

On the last day of the old year an engine, pulling a load of twenty-five tons of materials, had passed successfully over the new bridge in the Abbey Foregate.

But from then heavy rain in the early months of 1852 slowed progress on the line. Much of the way ran through stretches of clay, and indeed, clay fine enough for manufacturing ware had been found and developed near the Dinmore Tunnel. Clay on the works prevented the water from draining away and the men worked deep in ooze where their feet and hands slithered and which splashed them into the appearance of pottery figurines themselves.

The shareholders combined with the rain to hold up progress by defaulting on their payments so that necessary equipment could not be bought. Still, by March, stations between Shrewsbury and Ludlow were mostly finished, waiting for the final furnishings of cranes, turn-tables, weighing machines and such; and though the opening of the first half of the line had overrun its date, it would not be by much.

A few Irishmen had 'sneaked theirsels in' as James put it. A group of them, walking back drunk in the small hours, had taken a fancy to a farmer's cabbages. Unfortunately for them they were spotted and though most got away, one was caught. When asked to explain before the magistrates, he said wistfully that they just seemed to be lying about, and he'd had a notion that they'd be nice cooked with a piece of bacon. His plaint cut no ice and he was fined 6d for the offence, 6d for the cabbages and 12s expenses. The choice was that or fourteen days imprisonment, which would lose him far more in wages. His companions in crime, who had meanwhile disposed of their share of the evidence with the help of a little bacon, helped him cover his costs though they called him 'Cabbage' for a while.

On the second half of the line, by March the heading had been driven through 864 yards of the 1,056-yard tunnel but no bricking of the interior had as yet begun. The work had proved much heavier than anticipated, the substance of the hill being a stratum of limestone shale, composed of fragments of hard limestone cemented by a clayey paste. This was so hard in situ that it could only be removed by blasting. Contrarily, when it was trundled away to be used for the embankments towards Hereford, and exposed to the elements, it dissolved into clay, which, when tipped from wagons, slid away and required repeated filling-in.

In the absence of bricklaying, and not knowing how soon they would be required in the tunnel again, John and Tom were working in the brick-yards set up on the slopes of Dinmore Hill. There were needed, it had been estimated, something over 3,000,000 bricks.

The material for the bricks came from the innards of the tunnel itself, brought to the surface in the great buckets, tipped into wagons, drawn by horses to the brickyard on the hill above. There it stood waiting in vast piles before being tumbled into troughs and pounded into a desired consistency.

Its next destination was wooden moulds, soaked in water to prevent the clay sticking; and able to contain a set of bricks. The clay was pressed by hand firmly into the moulds. Moulds removed, the bricks joined their fellows under cover for the drying out, a process which took a variable number of days according to the weather.

Next they were stacked, in such a way that the hot gases could surge between them. The whole kiln was faced with old bricks or fire-bricks and clayed all over. Tunnels were left at the bottom to hold the fire.

The heat of this was built up gradually over days, reaching over 1000 degrees centigrade and then slowly cooled, the whole taking from two to six weeks. Mine-owners would proudly advertise their coal as hot-burning, the most suitable coal to be had for making bricks.

That done, the bricks were ready, waiting to descend underground once more to their final resting place.

By the middle of April the iron bridge over Shrewsbury's Abbey Foregate was resplendent in a dark red paint, the colour chosen to harmonise with the venerable brick of the Abbey Church. Rails and bridges had been finally tested by two engines and forty wagons, a load of some 110 tons, carrying engineers and contractors as passengers together with the Government Inspector who passed the line between Shrewsbury and Ludlow as suitable for opening. Shrewsbury's iron bridge, under its enormous load, had deflected only 3/10 of an inch.

The heavy rains of the early year had ended and the weather, in its capricious way, had turned to exceeding dry so that the crops were now suffering from thirst. Thus the great day, Tuesday the 20th of April in the Year of Our Lord One Thousand Eight Hundred and Fifty-Two, dawned under a cloudless sky, the best possible weather for humans on a jaunt.

John, Tom, James and Scarface downed tools for the day and, accompanied by several hundreds of their fellows, set out for Ludlow. The town was wild with joy and expectation. Triumphal arches of evergreens spanned thoroughfares at every opportunity. Banners, inscribed as usual with the most feeling and patriotic messages, caught the eye, one reading, '1851 - London in 16 hours. 1852 - London in 6 hours.' Bells rang in a cacophony. Thousands in their Sunday best filled the station precincts and climbed onto the surrounding heights. About the gates of the castle were stands, selling cake and gingerbread and what you will.

A piercing whistle, puffs of thick smoke, cannon-fire booming from a truck at the rear of the approaching train, raised excitement to fever pitch. As the cavalcade drew nearer, figures riding in dignity in the tender of the first engine could be discerned: Esquires Ormsby-Gore (chairman), Brassey (contractor), Robertson (engineer) with his lady, Field (subcontractor), and Jeffries (locomotive superintendent). Mayors and fellow dignitaries flocked to greet them. There were cheers and a procession formed, accompanied by a band and more flags and more cheering as the exalted ones, 340 in all, proceeded to the Assembly Rooms for a champagne luncheon given by Mr Brassey.

Scarface would read parts of the menu later. The large boar's head, the eight dishes of potted lampreys, the eighteen dishes of lobsters, and the peacock, larded, its plumage re-attached, were much wondered over: most of his audience, like John, were more at home with the thirty-two couple of fowl, the various roast and braised gargantuan pieces of beef or the ten hams.

'A Frenchie for a chef,' said John. 'What's Charlotte à la Rousse, eh?'

'Dunno, but there's enough of it,' said James.

'Wouldn't mind a bit of one o' those fruit tarts,' said Tom, running a thoughtful tongue over his lips.

'An' after all that champagne they still goes on ter toasts,' observed Scarface.

'An' many of 'em,' said John. 'Last one, lukka, "All friends around the Wrekin", like they allus do, but they've got "All friends from neighbouring counties" an' all.'

Not having been invited to the luncheon, the four men wandered onto the castle green, buying their own eatables from the various stalls. John chose eel pie flanked by a baked potato and wondered whether he ought after all to have chosen the sheep's trotter. Tom pronounced his bread and beef dripping to be 'mighty good'..

Near one of the stalls, and engaged in buying boiled meat pudding, they spotted Edward with Ann.

'Dad an' the others bin 'ere somewheres,' they were informed.

Sports were being organised on the green, with the massive, ivy-covered ruins of the castle as backdrop. The Town Crier rang his bell and shouted for contestants for jumping in sacks.

'What's the prize?' asked Edward.

'Think 'e said a sovereign.'

'I'm on then,' said John and ran over to where a line of sacks was lying. James joined him. They were young and they were fit; but then so were many more and it was the first time they'd attempted the feat. Neither won.

They were inspired by the idea of a sovereign though; and when the town crier in his tricorn hat tolled his bell and shouted 'Jingling Match, Jingling Match, winner a sovereign', all five men rushed onto the pitch leaving Ann to watch from the sidelines. Ten were chosen, nine of whom submitted to being blindfolded. The tenth, hands tied behind his back, had small bells hung around his neck, which jangled as he moved. The game was played for about half an hour, during which time the belled man tried to escape his pursuers, who in turn tried to catch and hold him. Shrieks of hilarity came from the crowd as players crashed into each other or tripped headlong or came to blows. The jingler was eventually unable to wriggle out of the iron grasp of Scarface, who was awarded the sovereign. Pleasingly to the other nine, each was given a half-crown.

Tired by this game, they flung themselves onto the grass and watched while six boys tried to eat the greatest number of treacled loaves in a given time. This was followed by a race around the castle green for married women, the winner's prize a metal teapot, the second a pound of tea and the third a pound of coffee.

Then came the call for navvies. 'Navvies only,' thundered the town crier; and four rose to their feet, Ann pleading not to be left unguarded this time. She was expecting, Edward had told his brother in a half proud, half self-conscious way. Due in September.

'Tekkin' me good coat off,' said Scarface, suiting action to words. The others followed his example and, shirt sleeves rolled up to show off rippling muscles, they advanced towards the point of interest, a pole, thick-coated with animal fat, at the top of which was a bundle consisting, they were told, of a new slop and hat. The pole bore a strong resemblance to the poles holding the new electric telegraph, now in process of erection along the side of the Shrewsbury to Chester and Shrewsbury to Hereford railways. They watched, noticing the technique of those who got furthest, as contestant after contestant tried and failed to climb more than a few feet before sliding ignominiously down again.

'Right,' said Scarface of a sudden. 'Reckon it's time ter 'ave a go.' He got up, walked over to the pole and wrapped both arms and legs around it. He hoisted himself up with his arms, bringing his legs up to follow. He got over half-way.

'Not ready yet,' he told the group. 'Wants another 'alf-dozen up it first. Mebbe more. Case o' judging it right, see.'

They waited. The contestants were getting closer to the top now. Tom had a go. He got within the last six inches but as he reached for the bundle with one hand his grip relaxed and down he came.

'Me or thee?' James asked John.

'Go on, thee,' said John; and watched judiciously as James' hand reached upwards to touch the bundle but failed to dislodge it.

He found himself climbing, the pole still slippery, his feet and arms clinging with all the pressure he could muster. Little by little, with great caution, he inched nearer to the top. He would not repeat James' mistake. He waited until he was high to the top, a quick lunge and he was sliding down; but there was a bundle in one hand.

The watching crowd cheered. John walked back to his companions, holding aloft his prize, feeling, under so many eyes, a stiff self-consciousness mixed with pride. Reaching safety he looked around a little, his gaze falling on a pair of girls watching him.

'James, come an' bear me out. There's two wenches a-lookin'. O'er there.'

Nothing loath, James joined him and the pair sauntered nearer.

'Not S'ewsb'ry lasses, bin yo?' inquired John, pretending to half-recognise them.

It turned out they lived in the town, in Ludlow. Within half an hour they were strolling around the green together. Aunt Sallies were shied at, gingerbread was bought, they all laughed immoderately at the efforts of those seeking by mouth bullets hidden in tubs of flour, a feat eschewed by both men for themselves as being not conducive to courtship. Dancing began; and a highly satisfactory evening terminated with promises of further meetings.

The weather changed, mixing its sunshine with showers bountifully sprinkled over the parched landscape. Swallows swooped for insects, the nightingale was heard, on Dinmore Hill.

In the tunnel, the air grew ever more foul and there was talk of sinking another shaft. One of their fellows, in charge of transferring trucks of bricks from the brick kilns to the tunnel somehow fell under the wheels. A group of his muckers put him into a cart and two drove him to the infirmary in Hereford where his arm was amputated that same evening.

'Got a wife,' said Tom, ' an' little uns.'

What could they say? How could a man, with one arm missing, work to support a family? Penury and the workhouse was the likely outcome though it went unvoiced.

May Day was a holiday: it had always been so. This year it fell on a Saturday, which was also pay-day. John and James went southwards down the line to Marden, territory, as they warned each other, of the resolute Constable Hopton; but tales of cider-houses that kept open to all hours overcame caution. The *Navvies' Arms* welcomed them. So did the *Kite's Nest*. They drank all night. A musician played the fiddle and they danced, until the musician became so drunk he could play no longer and stumbled homeward, forgetting his fiddle. Whereupon it was seized by others, who thought it amusing to wander the woods the night through, screeching the instrument to annoy respectable citizens all abed. When they came upon a farmhouse they induced the farmer to give up his stock of cider and continued their music and annoyances all through the Sunday. The redoubtable Hopton managed one catch only, but was reported saying that through the one capture he would secure the lot.

It was a Friday, the 23rd of July. For some days now the parties driving the heading had been able to hear their fellows on the other side. Less and less rock was separating them. On the Friday, the breakthrough was made. The two halves of the tunnel were joined as one with only a few inches to smooth on either side. As the news spread over the next few days, many small parties came from the villages and towns around, to see the daylight end to end and to pass wonderingly under the hill for the very first time.

To their great surprise and pleasure, the men most concerned with construction of the tunnel so far were treated to a dinner at *England's Gate*, an inn some three and a half miles away at Bodenham. John and Tom were both invited with around seventy others. They enjoyed, for them, a very restrained evening, being most careful to be polite and respectful, discovering the joy of innumerable toasts; and responding most heartily, hoping for many more to come. It was a good, and unaccustomed, feeling, they agreed, for their work, for once, to be recognised.

Now there was a new enterprise to involve men's strength and skill. Though impatient as they were to begin, they had to wait. Mr Brassey's decision was needed; and Mr Brassey was away, no doubt having business with one of the many other railways for which he was contractor, though no-one knew where.

On the line towards Hereford there was another fatality. The side of a cutting was being dig out, using wedges to undermine the earth above, while below two muckshifters were shovelling the loose earth into wagons. It speeded up a job if the overhang fell under its own weight, but precise judgement was essential. Suddenly tons of earth fell together, catching one of the muckshifters and smashing his skull down onto the temporary iron rails. He died two minutes after they dug him out.

At last, in the middle of August, work resumed on the tunnel. At intervals along its 1,054 yards and outside the security of the narrow tube of the heading which had been put so laboriously into place, five-foot transverse slots were to be excavated upwards and sideways to form the full profile of the tunnel.

Roofed as fast as possible by intrepid timbermen, using scaffolding, levers and chains to wrestle with huge, unwieldy timbers up to twenty feet long and a foot square, each slot meant an additional pair of working faces. And that meant that work on the tunnel would proceed faster: time was money. Each slot was then extended another five feet each way, roofed with more heavy timbers which were supported by others below.

Tom and John, as bricklayers, had been joined by two others, thus four of them in all. There were also six other men, miners, timbermen and muckshifters, the whole team split into two groups to work on either side of the slot. Falling pieces of rock, from pebble to huge block, flurries of loose shale, oozings of liquid clay, were a constant hazard. Wholesale collapse was an ever-present possibility.

John and Tom as bricklayers worked behind the others. When a section had been excavated around the heading and temporarily shored up, bricklayers followed. They worked in lengths. Where there was rock the length might be twenty feet. If they were penetrating looser material the length might be only half that or less.

They were lining the tunnel, beginning by building the side walls up to the springing level, the point where the roof began to arch. According to the geological conditions and thus the amount of support needed, the lining could be a mere double-brick wall or a wall twelve bricks thick.

Near a shaft, due to the added load of its lining, the tunnel walls and ceiling had to have extra support. Such had been demonstrated in the Watford tunnel a few years back when there was a collapse at the base of one of the shafts. It had taken more than a month to extricate the ten corpses.

They were using thousands of bricks. Any space behind their bricks, caused by unevenness of the tunnel wall was in-filled with rubble.

Drainage had to be considered. Apertures, weep holes, at the foot of walls had to be left for water to drain into constructed channels running along the side walls.

Under Tom's experienced guidance John was acquiring new skills. It was a challenge. The footings for the side walls of the tunnel were used to support a sill. From the sill rose a scaffold floored at springing level, the level where the arch began. On that plank floor were propped wooden ribs or frames, often three of them in parallel, each a segment of a circle following the arched contour of the roof.

A plank, a lagging, was laid from the top of each sidewall against the curve of the wooden arch and a brick support built above: it might be six bricks thick, or more, depending on the stability of the roof. Another plank laid above, next to the side of the wooden arch with a further six-brick-thick course of bricks against it, followed the curve of the roof. As each course of bricks set, the timbers above had to be gently withdrawn to make way for more brickwork.

Gradually the two side curves of the arch grew closer together. When they were about eighteen inches apart, short, curved, wooden laggings were used to span the gap. This, the last stage, was called the key and was built forwards from the previous section of roof. The key, once the mortar had set, was truly the key, allowing the arch to bear weight, by transferring the load sideways and downwards to the walls.

Time was at a premium, so that while the bricklayers were lining the hole to the south which the miners had just enlarged, those same miners were excavating in the opposite direction and supporting the ground above and to the side with timbers. The process never stopped, twenty-four hours a day, six days a week, John and Tom working their twelve-hour shifts, trying to regain their strength in the two half-hour breaks for food, before another team took over. Sometimes they worked day-shifts, sometimes nights: in the darkness of the tunnel it made little difference.

Twenty-five of those twelve-hour shifts might follow one upon the other before one of those lengths of fifteen, twenty feet, succumbed to being both excavated and lined with bricks.

When Tom and John had accomplished the first piece of brick lining, the mortar had hardened in the keystone and the timbers had been gingerly withdrawn from above the new brick roof, they were told that the narrow, and curving, gap between that roof and the hundreds of tons of unstable rock and earth above must be filled in. Tom and John looked at each other. Tom was deservedly often referred to as 'Big Tom'. John, nearing eighteen, was no stripling. 'You'll need a Nipper,' the ganger said.

Among the ranks of the horse-workers they found a small boy who led them to his father. Both seemed pleased at the idea of a rise in wages. The next day the small boy descended the shaft with them, enjoying the long descent in the bucket as if it were a big adventure. He walked through the length of heading with them happily enough and was directed to climb the scaffolding and a short ladder to the top of the brick arch. This he did.

'Now, yo mun get inside,' said John. 'We sha'n be

throwin' bits o' brick up. Yo get back far as yo can. Push them bricks right back an' o'er to the sides. Fill 'er up, see?'

The boy disappeared, wriggling on his stomach into fifteen feet of darkness and John threw a shovelful of rubble into the aperture. There was a scrabbling. He threw another. Half an hour of shovelling and there was a noise of blubbering. The boy's head appeared over the brick arch.

'I dunna wanner do no more,' he shouted, coughing and wiping his rags of sleeves over his filthy face. His hands were bloody.

'Yo get back. Yo jus' get right back there.'

But the boy slithered down the ladder. Thumping and threats and jeers had no effect save to make him curl into a ball and howl the louder. Another boy had to be found, a voiceless, starved-looking creature who gobbled every morsel of food they fed him and who seemed mortally afraid of his father.

'By 'oly God!'
'Consam it!'
'Dear 'eart alive!'
'Bogger's come down!'

There had been a confused, rumbling crash, candles had suddenly been extinguished; then a silence. John found himself in a blackness thick as fur. He was swimming in dust, breathing dust, coughing, choking. But still alive.

Expletives ricocheted off the walls around, in which came:

'Get a light!'
'Tom?'
'I'm 'ere. 'Ell fire! What's to do? Scarface? Billy Bones? Jack?'

They were all there.

'Get a light! Find light!' The dust was settling. There

were fumblings in the impenetrable dark. A light was found, a candle nub, lucifers from a pocket. They stared at each other, taking in each other's live presence, eyes white in the grime.

'Look to the wagons. There's bin a fall.'

' 'O was drivin' 'em?'

'There's an 'and. Lukka. Careful now.'

They uncovered earth and stones from the body but there was no sign of life. They uncovered their heads, one by one.

'Body Bodenham,' said Jack. 'Local lad. Well, 'e's a body now alright.'

The wagon had somehow hit a support, the inquest concluded. A boulder had loosened in the roof. With it had rained down a great deal more. John Bodenham, seventeen, had died of a broken neck.

16

Time Passes

The top of Dinmore Hill, where Mr Wilmot's brickyard sprawled, was becoming a trampled morass. For those who noticed such niceties, only in secluded corners were the purple meadow orchis and the green twayblade still clinging to life.

From the top of that hill could be seen, looking either north towards Ludlow or south towards Hereford, the progression of the line, the ragged scar dividing fields of standing grain, orchards and hopyards.

Companies, about to converge on the county town each with its own railway, quibbled about whether they should, or not, share a common station and precisely where that should be. There was also a seemingly interminable and querulous dispute over the Red Lion Level Crossing. Simple in essence, for the Newport, Abergavenny and Hereford Railway was determined to create a level crossing at its entry into the town, while the citizens cried 'danger!' and had a passionate preference for a bridge, the complexities of argument and counter-argument were as easily unravelled as a Gordian knot.

The Shrewsbury and Hereford was prospering on its half-line of Shrewsbury to Ludlow. The August half-yearly report, held as usual at the *Lion Hotel* in Shrewsbury, proudly revealed that the Company was receiving £13 per mile per week between the two towns; and that the Company balance stood at a healthy £12,411.14s.5d. Timetables reminded travellers that 'The

Clocks are set to Greenwich time, and are faster by Eleven Minutes than those of the district ought to be.'

In a corner bunk in John's hut, Billy Bones, a thing of shrivelled skin, was coughing his life away. Sometimes he was fit enough to work, but more and more, and particularly it seemed since the choking dust of the roof-fall, he was not. The other men gave him bits of food and he tended their tins and pans simmering on the stove in return. Sometimes he went out to pick up lumps of coal fallen from wagons, or branches from the woods, though such finds were becoming more rare as foragings increased. Those who removed such items as fence-posts or shuttering were likely to find themselves before the magistrates and sentenced to fines or fourteen days as alternative.

Navvies were still being accused of stealing fowls or clothes hung over bushes to dry. At Wellington, it was said, as riposte, that numbers of men were lodging, dressed as navvies, but who rarely did a day's work. They kept dogs and the dogs hunted creatures they had no right to hunt. They were masqueraders, blackening the name of the true British navvy.

The magistrates, worrying about the 'depredations', queried whether the formidable Constable Hopton, recently re-appointed to cover the parishes of Marden, Bodenham and Hope, should not be appointed to cover Wellington as well. Constable Hopton demurred, saying that he doubted he could manage that amount of work. A compromise was reached: the parishes of Hope and Bodenham now being pretty quiet, he would consent to reside in Wellington for a month or two.

That Christmas of 1852 John spent at home in Shrewsbury. He longed for a few days rest from the constant labour, even though he would forfeit wages. Getting his job back was unlikely to be a problem, experienced in the work as he was; and known as reliable. Walking to Ludlow past stations built in part, bridges semi-erected, he managed to travel from there to Shrewsbury hidden from view in an empty wagon, thus saving himself a fare.

It was good to be welcomed by his mother, more grey than not in her dark hair now. She clasped her hands in appreciation at being offered the fowl he had already disembowelled and plucked while it was still warm, bought from one of his fellows with a wink and without questions into its provenance. The smaller feathers and the down he had saved to give her for future use in pillow and mattress. He was welcomed too by his sisters, though they were shy of their big brother after so long. He was a little disquieted by them, or at least the eldest, Esther, turned thirteen and now a hand at the cotton mill, though he would never have admitted it. His father slapped him on the shoulder but said little.

Something about his sisters put him in mind of Eliza, though he didn't trouble to ask himself what. Letters from Eliza, still in Wolverhampton, came at ever-lengthier intervals. John half knew that this was likely to be a response to his own letters, or rather the lack of them: he had never been an avid correspondent and his frequent adventures with other girls shrouded him in reluctance to communicate with Eliza. He did not like this feeling of discomfort and that too prevented him writing. There was time enough, he thought.

His mother was full of family gossip. Aunt Rachel was still working near London, though her husband, William Brown, had been sent to China somewhere with his regiment. She'd no children by him as yet: there was only little Rachel Ann the by-blow, ' 'Er as lives wi' Susanna.'

And Aunt Susanna's Edmund was doing well at the baking trade as he'd set his heart on. 'Such a minikin as 'e used to be, now e's gettin' a great big wros'lin' fellow.' And his sister Sarah Ann, the one that came after so many years as such a great surprise, was still small as an elf-child.

Aunt Elizabeth and her daughter of the same name were still in the workhouse, though it could not be long before little Elizabeth, now turned ten, would be given a set of clothes and discharged into the world to make of it what she could. Phoebe was in the churchyard, but they knew that. 'Poor mite.'

His father was full of reflected glory. ' 'Er Majesty, Prince Albert an' the Prince o' Wales an the little 'uns, all on 'em, came down from Wales an' all along the S'ewsb'ry an' Chester as we built. An' they was ordered to go slow when they got to the Vale o' Llangollen an' Chirk, the viaduct as what I built. 'Cause a was so beautiful like. Stopped at S'ewsb'ry for bait, then off again on the S'ewsb'ry an' Birmin'am as yo an' Edward built, lad.'

'We went to look. Saw 'em too,' added his mother proudly. 'An' that little lad, the Prince o' Wales, they says 'e walked right across the sea, atop of an 'uge bridge, along on 'is father an' Mr Stephenson. An' them right up in the sky, ever so high an' nothin' to 'old to.'

S'ewsb'ry nodded. 'That were the Brittania Bridge,' he said to his sons. 'O'er to Anglesey. Full-rigged man-o'-war can pass under.'

Edward and Ann's baby, born in September in Wolverhampton at her parent's house, had barely tasted of this world before being reclaimed by another. 'But that's often the way of it; an' there's good news.' Ann was in the family way again; and she wanted to go back to her parents in Wolverhampton for the birth as she had the last time. 'Right enough, and so she should.'

The couple also wanted, this time, to be together. The brothers conferred.

'Tom's 'eard there's a station to be built at Wolver'ampton,' said John. 'Was in the paper.'

'Thought there was one already,' said Edward. 'Seem to remember buildin' one meself, wi' thee an' a few others.'

'This bin another 'un,' said John. 'There's a line starts near Oxford, long line, about seventy mile, comes up through Worcester an' on ter Wolver'ampton. OW&WR it's called. Anyways, that OW&WR is goin' ter build a station in Wolver'ampton an' it's not the one as we built. Think the Great Western's got an 'and in it somehow as well.'

'They bin the broad gauge lot,' said Edward.

'That's right.'

'I s'll talk it o'er wi' Ann. 'Ow 'bout thee?'

'I s'll be alright long as I've a tunnel ter build. Don't look like it's finishin' as yet. Should a bin, this Christmas even, but it ain't.'

Edward nodded.

The few days John allowed himself in Shrewsbury passed all too quickly. He returned to the camp at Dinmore Hill rested, clean of body and clothes; and rather envious of Edward who had someone always to take care of such things, to cook him hearty meals and pamper him at the end of a hard day. Still, freedom was worth a deal and he was not yet ready to sacrifice it.

Wood was everywhere being felled and stacked, he noticed on his return journey. The auctioning of it would be in all the newspapers.

It was raining and he hoped for fewer deluges than there had been the previous year, but his wishes were not granted. There came a Sunday morning in the middle of January when he was woken by more noise than usual outside. His head was hammering as it often did on a

Sunday morning and he turned over, trying to shut out the racket, but it persisted until he heaved himself out of bed and went outside to discover the meaning of the disturbance. It was raining, heavily, as it had rained the day before and he knew that the Lugg was rising.

'It's the bridge,' shouted James, who was one of the group outside. 'They say it's goin'. Or soon will. Water's bringin' down timber, branches an' that. Trunks, some of 'em. They'm pilin' up agin the piers. 'Er can't 'old fer long.'

John got dressed: that is, he put on his outer layers of clothing over the ones in which he'd slept. He then remembered breakfast and decided that to be more important than a bridge succumbing to the forces of nature. He took some water from the can that simmered on the stove and made himself a brew. Then he fried himself a slab of fat bacon, dipping a thick slice or two of bread in the fat.

Ready to go, he draped a piece of tarpaulin round his shoulders, donned his hat and moved off southwards. He had not far to walk. A quarter of a mile from the southern entrance to the tunnel, towards Hereford, the line crossed the Lugg, a river of usually benign temperament. The bridge, a stone one of three arches, had been built to a rough but useable standard only a few months since, for it was essential for carrying waste earth and stone from the Dinmore Tunnel to form the half-mile of embankment beyond the crossing. So far there had been no problems. But today it was as Tom had told him. The waters were very high and the river running at far above its usual speed; and piled up against the arches were tangles of hefty log, trunk and tangled branch. Even as he watched, another mighty timber tumbled downstream to crunch into the weighty mass.

He watched for a while, one of an interested crowd, but the rain was running down his neck and he went back to the hut to dry out in front of the stove and to snooze in his bunk. In the evening he went out again. The arches had collapsed and the stonework lay wrecked with the waters piling up and around.

Next day the waters had receded somewhat and so they continued until the Lugg was gentle once again. Only the vegetation on its banks, its drowned aspect holding bleached wisps of foreign matter high above the present waters, told a tale. A temporary, wooden, bridge was constructed as fast as was possible and work went on. But that small disaster, together with others along the line, would hold back the finishing date: the end of August was now being mooted.

By the middle of February a third of the tunnel had been arched and finished. Now there was a through-draught the air was breathable again, but that came at a price: a whistling, icy knife of a wind, particularly when it came from the north and was accompanied by night frosts, as happened through March.

Down in the tunnel they missed the snow though, which those working the embankment and the cutting running into Hereford had to endure. John heard rumours that the station there was shortly to be started. The Hereford, Ross and Gloucester, one line that the station was to be shared with, was broad gauge as opposed to the Shrewsbury and Hereford narrow gauge, though like their own it was single-track. There was a great deal of discussion of the merits of broad versus narrow gauge. Some thought broad gauge might go all the way up to the banks of the Mersey instead of finishing in the Midlands as it did at present.

'Yo'd carry a lot more passengers,' said John, talking over the case with Scarface. 'Be more comfortable too, I s'd think. 'Er'd ride the rails easier.'

'Carry more goods as well, coal, iron an' that,' agreed Scarface. 'But she'd cost more ter build. More land to

214

build't line on, wider tunnels, bigger engines, bigger carriages.'

'Anyways,' said John, 'The S&H says it's not layin' down no broad gauge. 'Spect the station at 'Ereford mun manage both.'

'Like't one at Wolver'ampton,' said Scarface. 'There's broad gauge comin' in there too, wi', what's it? OW&WR?'

'That bin the station Edward's a-buildin',' said John. 'Might go there meself when this tunnel finishes. If Edward's not got it built by then.'

'Missin' that lass o' yourn?' Scarface grinned. 'Gather yer rosebuds while yer may, I say. An' marry in 'aste, thee knows. Dunna thee be in too much of an 'urry, lad, ter 'itch up.'

'Look ter yer powder, lads,' said the ganger one morning. It was May and the nights getting lighter. 'Orders ter keep it safe.'

'What's amiss, then?'

'Boys. Boys is amiss. Boys as works on the line in this case.'

'Boys'll be boys,' said Scarface. 'What they bin an' gone an' done now?'

'Near blinded theirsels,' said the ganger. 'One on 'em, anyways. Stole some powder, a group on 'em. Actin' big, see? Got a few little bangs from a few little bits, then tried a grand big bit. One on 'em lit a brand, put the end ter the powder an' waited fer explosion. Didna come, did it? So daft bogger bends right down an' blows the end o' the brand ter mek it flame up. Then it went off alright.'

'Dead?'

'Nah. In 'ospital. 'And all burnt, face all burnt. Like to lose an eye. Not as pretty as 'e used ter be. So, says bosses, keep yer powder safe.'

A letter came from Edward. The baby had been born, another girl. They'd named her Jemima as they'd done the first, after Ann's mother. He and Ann were still living with her parents. He was working on the second station at Wolverhampton and it seemed best to stay where the work was certain and Ann had her parents' support. Eliza was visiting on her afternoons off. Ann liked her and Eliza was fond of the baby, which this time was thriving: the two girls got on well together.

'Hoo hoo,' Scarface hollered in glee. He was sitting on the bank beside the Lugg, trouser legs rolled up, its waters washing up to his knees. 'Listen ter this, Blackie.'

John, who was lolling in the river, lazily letting his body stream out with the current, turned his head.

'Drunkenness an' fightin'! An' guess 'o? Constables! Constable 'Opton an' Constable Matthews, that's 'o.'

'There's a turn-up.' John's interest quickened. ' 'Opton's al'ays the one draggin' other folks to court. Gi'e us the story then.'

' 'Opton asks a chap in't *Racehorse Inn* if 'e'd give a lady friend of 'is a lift back ter Wellington.

'Old chap called Preece shouts up an' says 'Opton's not behavin' like a proper man. Said 'e were al'ays "pickin' up little dirty jobs". S'pose 'e means the wench. Anyways, that gets 'Opton in a right temper an' 'e says, 'Say that again yer bogger an' I'll 'it yer.

'So o' course Preece says it again an' 'e gets 'it good an' proper.

'Then Preece's son joins in ter 'elp 'is ole Dad an' there's a bit of a scuffle. 'Opton goes outside an' calls ter't son ter fight out there, but son wunna. 'Appen thinks 'e might end up in clink.

'Then 'e changes 'is mind along on all't insults 'Opton's chuckin'. Out 'e goes an' they 'ave a right shin-dig. Two rounds an' the son's winnin' an' 'Opton slinks off.

'So Ole Preece an' 'is son go off ter't *New Inn*, thinkin' all's done. But 'Opton turns up there too, wi' 'is mates this time. Then there's five on 'em, all mates wi' 'Opton, all fighting the son. 'Is Dad says, "Run!" but 'e don't.

'An' then Constable Matthews, 'o's at *New Inn* special ter keep't peace, 'cordin' ter't landlord Matthews, goes an sticks an 'ook in 'is mouth, son's mouth, an' tears 'is lip something cruel. They 'as ter call a surgeon, an' 'Opton an' Matthews ends up afore the beak.'

'Transported, then? I 'opes,' said John, raised to righteous indignation by this tale of low-dealing.

'Nah. 'Opton says it's all cos 'e summonsed Preece fer stealin' turnips an' Preece 'as bin callin' 'im names an insultin' 'im ever since. 'Opton an' Matthews keeps whinin' an' bowin' an' tellin' 'em, "great provocation me Lord". So all as 'appens is, they get "severely reprimanded", an' "the offenders thanked the Magistrates for their kindness, and assured them that nothing of that nature should occur again". Hah!'

They enjoyed reading the paper between the two of them, Scarface usually being the one who went to the expense of purchase. John often found bits that were of interest and Scarface usually knew details that John did not: he remembered things, did Scarface and had a rare curiosity about the world.

It was a Saturday evening at the end of July and together, and over a pint or two of cider, they were looking to see whether the *Hereford Times* had anything in it about the visit of several dignitaries to the tunnel the previous Tuesday. The group turned out to have been from various railway companies with an interest in Hereford, accompanied by the Mayor. Having been to see the marked-out station, they were viewing progress on the tunnel.

'After, they all went back ter't Mayor's fer a slap-up

dinner,' Scarface said. 'Well, 'course they did.'

He read further. 'Line'll be open October now, they says.'

John shrugged. ' 'Appen.' There was silence for a while. Then, 'Dost 'e ever go ter them meetin's nowadays? Political, like? About votes an' such?' he asked idly.

'Chartist meetin's, tha means? Nah, big nobs seem ter 'ave give up. Gone quiet like. Still believe in it all, though, me. Canna get there all on me own, though.'

John grunted and turned a page. 'Where's Circassia, then?'

'Now yer 'as me. What else do it say?'

'Somethin' about "unprovoked attack" on Circassia by Russia an' the Sultan o' Turkey "not retaliating".'

'The Russian Bear, that's what they calls 'em. Al'ays growlin' an' prowlin' an' very dangerous. S'pose Circassia belongs ter Turkey. Or did. S'pect they're frit, Turkey.'

Over the next month or two, the problems between Turkey and Russia escalated.

'We dunna like them Russians, dun we? Even though they bin Christian souls?' said John. And Scarface shook his head.

'An' it's the Turks, the Musselmans, as 'as the right of it?'

'Seems Parliament thinks that way,' said Scarface.

'An' we're friends wi' the Frenchies?'

'Seem ter be,' said Scarface. 'Weren't, when Boney were around, but we seems ter 'ave made up sin then.'

'Wish I'd a map,' said John. ' 'Ow many miles to all these places, dost 'ee s'pose? Al'ays wanted to go off travellin', me. Ever sin that son o' Doctor Darwin back in S'ewsb'ry went off around the world. Got back when I were two, but I remember folks talkin' 'bout it for years. Wrote a book about it 'e did.'

All through August there were political rumblings, worries roused then soothed, about the Russian military campaign and its gathering momentum; and the expressed English desire for peace balanced against its, also expressed, obligation to maintain the interests of Turkey.

September found the Russian Commander-in-Chief addressing his troops with the rousing words, 'Russia is called to annihilate Paganism', adding that the annihilation extended to those who would thwart Russia in her object. The *Hereford Times* complained, 'Prince Gortachakoff must know very well that the Musselman is no Pagan. If there is one thing the Koran insists more strongly than another, it is condemning Paganism and idolatry.'

The Russian army was reported to be marching on Bucharest; and to have 4,000 troops on the road from Focktchang to Jassy. None of these names had any meaning for Scarface and John, though they supposed they must be the faraway places being fought over.

The Turks for their part were 'arming on the Servian frontier', the people eager for war and accusing their leaders of lack of spirit.

'Somethin' might come of it,' said John hopefully. A good war would be something to hear about, he thought: all those rattling sabres and galloping horses and great cannons and shiny, spiked helmets; and glory.

More exciting, because at hand, was the finishing of the Dinmore Tunnel. They, the workmen, knew when they had finished: when the last brick but one was tamped into the keystone of the arch, when the scaffolding had been removed from the portals at either end to reveal them in clean-cut glory, when the permanent way ran from end to end over the new-laid ballast and the pristine sleepers.

But there was more. To celebrate such an endeavour, a tunnel sixteen feet wide, dug in two and a half years of labour and using three and a quarter million bricks, there must be a ceremony and that must be prepared for. That week, with the all-seeing eye of Owd Pollard, Superintendant of Tunnel Works, fixed keenly upon them, every extraneous stick, stone and drift of dust was removed from the tunnel. Ballast was coaxed so that no pebble dared run beyond its territory. Brooms were used, to John's disgust, to give an appearance of perfect cleanliness and symmetry.

A platform was erected in the centre of the tunnel, the height of a man below the roof; and at its centre, a small dais. Above the dais, brilliantly illuminated, was the site of the ultimate keystone.

A number of wagons were cleaned of mud and stones and spread with some heavy pink fabric which had arrived in bales.

On Friday the 16th of September 1853, John and his fellows dressed as if off to a randy and went down to take part in the proceedings.

At the blacksmith's shop near the north entrance, where James worked, a banner flew, proclaiming "Success to Mr Brassey". The mouth of the tunnel was hung with pointed scarlet flags, like the teeth of a dragon, while from the throat of the dragon came light in the form of innumerable candles and lanterns.

True, it was raining, but that was not going to spoil a glorious day. Coaches, brakes, and other conveyances converged from Shrewsbury and Ludlow and Leominster and Hereford. A band played - what joyous occasion would be complete without a band? The dignitaries climbed into the rich, pink wagons and, drawn by beautifully caparisoned horses, moved along the rails in musical procession towards the platform in the centre of the tunnel. Once there, they ascended a staircase to crowd onto its top, while Mrs Field, wife of the General

Superintendant of Works, was assisted by Mr Robertson, Chief Engineer, to climb upon the dais. A silver trowel with elaborate chasings was then handed to her; and Messrs Robertson and Pollard assisted the lady to cement into place the very last brick, distinguished from its fellows in that it was gilded and bore the lady's initials. A small and highly-polished wooden mallet was then handed to her and the vigorous thumps as she hammered the brick into place drew enormous cheers from the grinning navvies who lined the tunnel walls.

Three cheers were raised for Mr Arkwright, whose hill now held the perfect tunnel and there were speeches at the end of which Mr Field announced that a dinner for the men would be given by Mrs Field on the following day. The tunnel rang with enthusiasm.

The people of importance resumed their seats in the pink wagons and proceeded through the southern portal to the banks of the River Lugg where, in a marquee, they sat down to a splendid luncheon accompanied by the finest wines and ended by a countless number of the finest toasts.

17

Cry Havoc

At the beginning of October 1853 newspapers informed the public that the Sultan of Turkey, whose possessions of Moldavia and Wallachia had been taken over by the Russians, had insisted that if these were not returned to him within fourteen days, the two countries would be at war.

'It'd be good to 'ave a map,' complained John. But there were none. You could buy an atlas, a School Atlas of twenty-seven maps, for 2s, or a splendid affair bound in Moroccan leather and gold-tooled for £2.16s; but newspapers did not provide even a rudimentary map of the scene of conflict.

'Owd Crow 'ad a globe,' said John, remembering his schooldays. 'But I canna remember much 'cept there were lots o' shapes an' colours.'

Place-names which kept coming up, as if every reader should know them, were the Danube, often distinguished as a river, so that was helpful; the Black Sea, puzzling, as from what they had been told, seas were blue; the Caucasus, which they were pretty sure were mountains; the Dardanelles which might have been mountains or not. Where and how these fitted together, along with the Ottoman Empire, which was Turkey; and with Russia and its Emperor Nicholas, they could not know for sure. They assumed their betters knew all and would act, if action was called for, with the wisdom that was their birthright.

By the end of October, the Shrewsbury and Hereford

line had extended itself from its temporary resting place at Ludlow all the way to Hereford; though the station at Barr's Court was minimal, the electric telegraph incomplete and the line as yet uncertified by a Government Inspector as fit for passenger traffic.

All of which did not prevent, on the last day of the month, two powerful engines leaving Shrewsbury at 11.30am yoked to a train of fourteen carriages packed with worthies such as Messrs. Ormsby-Gore, Robertson, Brassey, the Directors, and gentry such as Lord Saye and Sele and Mr George Arkwright, seventeen-year-old scion of Hampton Court. A powerful and innovative salute of fog signals marked their departure from Shrewsbury station. Accompanied by banners and music they proceeded to a splendid luncheon for four hundred awaiting them in the Shire Hall in Hereford. That consumed, and upwards of a dozen hearty toasts and speeches later, extolling the benefits of communications, now or soon to be delivered, between Hereford and the Midlands, the North, the West, South Wales, Liverpool, Manchester, the Metropolis; and the prosperity therefrom to be derived, the party broke up, the Shrewsbury contingent being safely delivered back to their home town by 10pm.

A decision had to be made. Should he move to Hereford and get taken on to build the station there? Or should he rejoin Edward and work on the second station at Wolverhampton? John pondered. He would be nineteen in a month. He had the company of a lass in Wellington whenever he chose to make use of it, a lass who liked a pint of cider and a dance to a fiddle if such should be to hand, a lass who was happy to stroll with him into the fields and was greedy for the gifts he brought her. What more did he want? He suspected that Edward, straight-dealing Edward, would not approve.

He decided to walk south to Hereford and see if he could get taken on: Wellington, after all, was only six miles distant: he could still visit his girl. Tom was returning to Wolverhampton and so was James. To James, John entrusted a short letter to Eliza, wondering how long it was since his last. Scarface said he'd try Hereford station with John.

It was a mixed blessing working once again above ground. They were exposed to the elements and it was getting colder. But at least they were working in the daylight of the short, end-of-year days. Rain did fall, but that was preferable to muck or rock; and the first fortnight in November was unusually fine, fine enough that the sowing of the spring wheat was accomplished, for once, without hindrance. Billy Bones coughed his last cough and, Russia showing no inclination to remove herself from Moldavia and Wallachia, the Turks prepared for war. England and France, allies now, sent their fleets to Constantinople and thereabouts and hove to: orders precluded them from attacking Russian ships or entering the Black Sea.

As November advanced the newspapers were full of reports, little better than rumours. Letters had been received from somewhere telling of ... It was said that ... A returning traveller had given news of ... One of the few certainties seemed to be that there were movements of troops on either side.

'What's it s'posed ter be about, this war?' a puzzled John asked Scarface.

' 'Oly Land, Jerusalem an' that, wi' lots o' Christians in it, belongs to Turkey nowadays. Dunna ask me why, that's what they says. Russians say as Christians ain't bein' treated right an' they're up on their 'igh 'orses about it. But there's often excuses ter mek things sound 'igh an' 'oly. An' it might be that Russia just wants ter grab another

224

country or two,' Scarface told him. 'We don't want that. Them Russians is gettin' too big for their boots. So we're 'elpin' Turkey. Not very 'Christian', anyway, them Russians. Men an' women on big estates no better'n slaves. Serfs, they calls 'em. Knauts, they uses on 'em, leather whips wi' lots o' thongs an' wire.'

In England the price of grain was rising. Much of our grain, the papers said, came from the Danube region and Odessa, places within the scope of the conflict; and supplies were not coming and the future uncertain.

'So that's why the last loaf I bought cost 10d,' said John.

'Potato bread, folks eat in famine times. If they can get it,' said Scarface. 'That an' nettles. An' acorns. An' grass. An' bark. An' boots. An' cats. An' worse. If it goes on long enough.'

In the proud city of Hereford, any worries about hard times were put to one side: celebrations were afoot for which the October occasion had been but a preliminary. The Great Railway Fete would, on December 6th 1853, seal Hereford's entry into the Railway Age. Three lines: the Newport, Abergavenny and Hereford; the Hereford, Ross and Gloucester; and the Shrewsbury and Hereford would be formally opened.

One train would start from as far away as Euston, reaching Hereford by way of Birmingham and Shrewsbury. Another would start from Newport. The trains would call at all stations. Bells would herald the sunrise before continuing their ringing and pealing at every stage of the way. There would be cannons. There would be bands. There would be a procession. There would be two ballrooms, one of even greater splendour than the other, hosting banquets and dancing. There would be fireworks.

There would also be one or two surprising features, for was not Hereford a liberal and humane city? There would be free dinners, eaten in the schoolrooms of the Charity Schools by 2,000 children. There would be 800 tons of free coal for the poor. There would be a dinner within the workhouse of roast beef and plum pudding and even ale; and the boys of the workhouse would be allowed out, to watch the fireworks.

' 'Ark at this,' said Scarface, looking up from the handbill he was holding. 'We's gonna be in't procession. Eleven o' clock, we goes ter't Market Place, everything gets sorted. Band an' big nobs first, o' course. Then citizens. Then us wi't other navvies from t'other two lines, looks like. Then a Brass Band, then Odd Fellers from all o'er, Manchester even. Think they looks after each other, Odd Fellers, a Society like. Funeral expenses an' 'elp if they're out o' work an' that. An' a few good dinners, I 'spect.'

'Let's look,' said John, grabbing the sheet. 'Eh, an' we'm gettin' a dinner, by gad. Goin' ter an inn.'

'An' the subscription list,' said Scarface. 'Look 'o's at top. Mr Brassey, that's what. £20. More'n anyone else.'

Tuesday 6th of December dawned fine and fair, the first fine day for three weeks, mild and bright. John brushed his coat, donned a newly-washed pair of moleskin trousers and canvas shirt; a scarlet plush waistcoat with pearl buttons, his present pride and joy and one which reminded him vividly of Tweedlebeak from the old times; a dark blue neckerchief; his sealskin hat; and hobnailed boots specially cleaned for the occasion. Scarface looked correspondingly resplendent.

The city was transformed: 'Hurrah for Railways', 'Prosperity to Hereford', 'The Good Times Are Come', 'Success to Railways'. Banners hung over streets, festooned shop fronts, draped public buildings, floated from the cathedral tower. Everywhere rose triumphal arches of evergreens and the glory of - in December mostly artificial - flowers. Paintings of engines abounded, engines traversing lofty viaducts or ploughing through deep cuttings, heroic and proud. Models of engines were seen, one, of tin, contriving to have smoke puffing from its funnel. The Market Place was a bower of greenery and loud with bells and bands. Every concourse thronged with cheering sightseers. Eager people crammed the windows.

The procession was marshalled into position, headed by the Mayor, Councillors, guilds, bands and banners, then the navvies of the three railways that now converged on Hereford. A handbill was thrust into John's hand. He folded it away into a pocket and fell into step with the music, imagining himself a soldier, Scarface marching beside him.

To the station they went, to meet first the train from Newport, thirty-one carriages strong, pulled by three mighty engines; and then another from Shrewsbury. Cheers split the very welkin. Addresses were read, adulation in every word, followed by more mighty cheering. Lords, Viscounts, Ladies, Colonels, Lord Lieutenants, High Sheriffs, Captains, all joined the procession.

Returning by a different route, at the Shire Hall the great and the good in the procession peeled off. This was the venue for the most splendid banquet, designed for the most splendid people. John peered through the railings. He felt a hand on his collar, roughly jerking him out of the way, half-throttling him. He turned, in fighting stance, fists clenched, in a blind fury.

'Nay lad,' a voice interjected and a hand was laid on his arm. It was Scarface. 'Dunna fight today. Put it off till termorrer.'

A ripple of amusement came from those around. John chuckled in spite of himself and was content merely to shake a fist.

Back to the Market Place and the body of navvies was split up, John and Scarface finding themselves with forty of their fellows at the *Hop Pole Inn* in Bye Street, feasting on large joints of beef, pork and mutton, with vegetables on standby, a pound of bread at the side to fill in any cracks and a quart of ale to assist digestion. When they left the Inn it was already getting dark.

'Look up there,' Scarface pointed. A painted banner slung against the wall of a house had its colours lit up from behind, so that greens and reds and yellows shone brightly against the darkness. It was very cleverly done, they agreed. And then they saw more and more examples of the same effect, glowing through the dark. They were making for the Castle Green where, they'd heard, the fireworks were to be held. That was a grand sight, huge balloons rising into the air, a score or more, which then flared vivid bursts of coloured light and showers of rainbow stars.

It was not until a few days later that John came across the leaflet handed to him at the start of the procession. He read it with increasing irritation.

' 'Ark at this,' he said to Scarface who was absorbed in the *Hereford Times*. 'Says, "Show that English navvies can enjoy themselves without doing themselves harm by it, without losing their character for good behaviour, without rioting and drunkenness, without squandering their hard-earned pay in folly and wickedness ... Don't forget that you have a God, to whom you must give account for all you say as well as all you do." An' it goes on an' on like that.' He flung the paper away from him. 'What did *they* 'ave for bait, then, the parsons an' the 'igh an' mighty ones? What did *they* 'ave to drink? Bet they dinna squander any 'ard-earned pay on it neither. 'An' han *they* ever dug a tunnel an' seen a man die?'

'*They*,' said Scarface, sonorously, ' 'ad peacocks,

partridges, pheasants, ducks, geese, fowls, lobsters, crabs, prawns, meringues, cakes, jellies, blancmange an' mince pies. An' boars' 'eads an' a girt lot more. An' they 'ad more speeches than as ever been knowed an' drinks ter match. An' they danced well inter't next mornin'. Plain an' pure as driven snow, them Lords an' Reverends an' such.'

'Think mebbe some of 'em 'ad a bit too much ter drink though, afore they made their speeches,' he went on. 'Pin yer lugs back fer this, "See at Dinmore the mighty machine dashing into the bowels of the earth, hissing like some foul fiend, frighting the very elves from their recesses". Didna notice no elves mesen. Funny, that, considerin' Ah were there two year. But there's a bit 'ere abaht us, "Face-begrimed sons of toil who labour in the deep bowels of the earth." Wi' elves, Ah 'spects.'

John took the paper and leafed through it. 'Nearly the 'ole lot's about the Great Railway Fete,' he said. 'Eh, 'ark to this, we'm got "hardy iron frames, strength of limb, and bronzed countenances". I likes that bit. Let's 'ope a lot o' wenches likes it too.'

At the very end of that *Hereford Times* of the 10th of December, came a paragraph about the war. 'Latest News (By Electric Telegraph)' was announced, with pride at the speed of communication thus afforded. It described a Russian defeat where the baggage, the ammunition and the wounded were left in Turkish hands. Also, it said, there was in being an attempt at an honourable peace brokered by France, England, Austria and Prussia.

Turkey, comfortably, seemed to be the winning side until, later that December, the Turks suffered a naval disaster at Russian hands at a place they'd never heard of called Sinope. 'Carnage' and 'massacre', the *Hereford Times* called it, along with a few colourful and repellent examples of carnage. And a country called Persia threw its weight behind Russia and declared war on Turkey.

'Carpets,' thought John vaguely. 'Appen even magic carpets.'

The attempt at peace had failed; and France was so worried about the price of grain, when allied to the poor harvest of that year, that she began making quiet preparations for war.

John went back to Shrewsbury for Christmas. This time, a train went all the way, but he shunned passenger trains and rode an empty wagon.

His father and grandfather were still finding plenty of work: the Shrewsbury and Hereford had been empowered by Parliament to buy or lease land as they wished, both in their own parish of Holy Cross and St. Giles and in St. Julian's, to erect warehouses, engine sheds, depots and the like and there was plenty for a bricklayer to do. Both men seemed in good physical shape.

'It's mighty good to come 'ome, jest a short walk, at day's end,' said Owd S'ewsb'ry, 'An 'ave an 'ot meal awaitin', nice slab o' beef an' tatoes to go with un.' He smacked his lips. 'An' a sleep in me own bed.'

'Letter for 'ee from our Edward,' said his mother, presenting him with a folded paper. 'Come in one o' ourn.'

John took it, but pocketed it to be read in private. Later, stirring up a flame from the dim light of the fire, banked up to be revived next morning, he opened the letter. It was not long but, as he read, a frown gathered on his face. Eliza, it seemed, had had advances from a young man. She had confided this to Ann, who had told it to Edward, and between them they had thought it only right that John should be alerted.

The young man was a respectable person, a tin-worker like her father and in a fair way of trade. She and John were not betrothed, said Edward, and Eliza was receiving few letters from him and fewer as time went on. Was he still interested? Eliza had asked Ann if she felt it would be honest of her to accept the young man's intentions.

John, as he read this, felt himself growing in mighty grievance. Eliza was his. She had no call nor right to consider any other man. He sat for a long while seething in his anger and considering what he should do.

By morning he had made up his mind. He would not return to Hereford but would go to Wolverhampton and join Edward. The second station, Wolverhampton Joint, had not yet been started, wrote Edward, but he'd been finding plenty of work on the routes going out of the town and latterly in demolishing buildings and clearing ground in readiness. John wrote a note of his intentions to Scarface which later that day he entrusted to the care of a fellow-navvy who would be going back to Hereford.

Two days later, reaching Wolverhampton, he set off across the short distance between the old station, Wolverhampton General and the site of the new. He spotted a ganger and was taken on at once, keeping his eyes open for Edward as he worked. It was not long before he saw his brother wheeling a barrow full of bricks and rubbish across the uneven ground. John shouted, they exchanged acknowledgements. They would meet at bait time.

'Ow bist?'

'Thought as 'ow I'd better come an' keep me eye on thee,' said John.

'Where's thee stayin'?'

'Got nowhere as yet. Just come up from Shrewsbury. Thought mebbe the Mansell's again.'

'Still at same address, next to ourn.'

'I s'll try there then.'

That evening, after work, he walked the familiar ways to 99, Russell Street and knocked on the door. A flurried Mrs Mansell, wisps of hair escaping from her cap, opened it, looking over him to Edward.

' 'Tis thee. Come in, shall 'ee?'

' Dost not know this un?' Edward indicated his brother.

She looked hard at John and recognition dawned. 'Why, thee's grown so, I'd never've known. Come in, come in.' Three small girls peered from behind her skirts.

'Well,' said John, simulating great surprise, 'There bin on'y one o' yo last time.' And he was introduced to Ann Letitia, Sarah Jane and Elizabeth, who stared at him with large round eyes and said nothing.

' 'E's after a lodgin',' said Edward.

'Well, we've no-one just now, an' George knows thee, so do the back bedroom suit 'ee? 'E'll fix a price when 'e comes in. Same as last time, more'n likely.'

'That'd be proper fine,' said John.

Depositing his few belongings in his room and declining Mrs Mansell's offer of a bite to eat, John made his way across a couple of streets to the house of the master mason to whom Eliza was servant. Anger and resolve lent speed to his steps.

The door opened and someone stood there. But who was this? He was taken aback: Eliza yet not Eliza. Here was a girl no longer skinny but filled out, the skinniness turned to shapeliness. No longer did she seem ingenuously young, but poised. The grace which had first attracted him was still there and so was the chestnut hair, the glossy locks of which fell below her cap. Anger, vindictiveness, gave way to an awkwardness. He removed his cap and shuffled his feet. The realisation came to him that he had not seen her since the Christmas of 1851, two years since, when she had been fifteen. Now she was a young lady.

' 'Tis me, Eliza. John.'

She stared at him. 'What 'ast come for, then? Didna answer me letters. 'Aven't 'ad a letter from thee sin forever. 'Cept 'alf a dozen words two month back. Couldna even post it an' all. Dunna call that a letter, me. Anyway, got another young man now, a respectable man 'o'll not leave me waitin' wi' no word.' She turned to close the door.

'Eliza, please ... say thee'll see me. I bin ...' He could find no excuse.

The door closed with a firm snap. A key turned heavily in the lock. He heard an interrogative voice from within, followed by 'On'y a beggar-man, Ma'am,' from Eliza.

He stood on the step for a few moments, stunned. This was the world upside down. He had envisioned himself wielding power, exacting remorse. Now it was he who had been put into the position of supplicant.

He wandered off, his steps taking him without any conscious volition up to the market place and the alehouses, where he spent what remained of a miserable evening.

The new year of 1854 announced its arrival with extreme cold. On the night of Monday the 2nd of January the temperature dropped to ten degrees below freezing. On the Tuesday snow fell, whirling around them as they tried to carry on with a piece of bricklaying. The ganger called them together, 'No good in this, lads. The mortar wunna set proper: there'll be no strength in un. Best leave it fer now.' They mooched about for a while, grumbling, knowing 'no work, no pay'. Then they dispersed homewards. Afternoon came and the wind got up. The snow intensified, gusts of wind from different quarters whirling like dervishes, driving the snow, banking it into drifts, then picking it up again with a mighty thrust and hurling it elsewhere. That night the temperature dropped, to twenty degrees below, some said.

Wednesday came and still it snowed. Drifts blanked out houses up to the eaves, the few stray explorers in the streets appeared out of the spiralling snow-clouds swathed in shawls, puffed-up shapes of white.

Wagons stopped, coaches stopped, drays stopped, for horses could not get through. Trains stopped. And then came the call. They assembled at the station on the Thursday morning, with shovels. An engine took them down the line towards Shrewsbury. A train had been enveloped in drifts sixteen feet tall. Two engines had already been despatched to give assistance and neither had returned. Then they came, Edward and John and all the others, men with shovels, and dug them out.

On Friday, a train got through, slowly but without help. And then the worst was over, though perpetuated by travellers' tales, of spending long nights at freezing stations, of hunger and cold inside carriages deep in snow, of snow above the tops of the telegraph poles, of vital mail long-delayed, of the furnaces and ovens of the Black Country running out of coal.

John nursed his hurt. He was dour and silent at work; and Edward, failing to get answers, left him alone. Gradually he entered a time when he cursed himself for what he had lost. The memory of Eliza at the door and of what she had become, tormented him. What stung most was that she was an honourable girl, far more honourable than himself. She was a prize worth having, and he had carelessly thrown her away.

Ann still saw her from time to time when she had a half-day. Eliza was very fond of little Jemima, she said, and so kind and so ready to help. And little Jemima was truly a delight, sitting up now and smiling and joyfully throwing away anything that was given into her chubby, grasping hand.

John kept watch one Sunday and saw Eliza arrive next door. She was even more desirable in the light of day and carefully dressed in her Sunday best. And he noticed once more that grace in her which had first attracted him so long ago.

Her mistress had become very attached to Eliza, said Ann. She had risen from the skivvy, the maid-of-all-work, to being almost one of the family; and the children in particular were very fond of her.

When he was working, all other thoughts vanished from John's mind. It was in the after hours, before sleep overtook him, that remorse gnawed at him and he tried to combat it with a great deal of ale. He tried other girls but found he had little heart.

Time passed. What could he do?

18

The Dogs of War

Without Scarface, dejected and turned in on himself, John had little interest in external affairs. As if through a fog he heard others talking of the Eastern War, the reluctance of some parliamentarians to join in on the one hand, and the enthusiasm of others. The Queen, it was rumoured, was not inclined towards war and suspicion for her predilection fell on her husband. John had vaguely considered him quite a good chap, hero of the successful Great Exhibition, but now discovered him anew as a suspicious foreigner and one who might well have sympathies with Russia and fingers in foreign pies.

John's workmates seemed to be all for going to war. 'Put them Russians in their place,' 'Let 'em know 'o's boss,' were sentiments frequently expressed. He overheard someone reading a piece from the *Staffordshire Sentinel*, 'The English people are awake, standing in the light of justice and truth, ready to protect the weak against the strong, and to enter into the conflict with the ancient war-cry, 'God defend the Right.' And he joined in the cheers which followed.

Such feelings were heard constantly; and it was no real surprise when, late that March of 1854, he heard that England and her ally France had finally declared war on Russia.

He had made several more attempts to renew his friendship with Eliza but she refused to listen to his pleas. Once he saw her on the arm of her new love and rage rose within him. He looked at the man and considered what it would take to floor him and pound him into jelly. But then he thought that seeing him so cruelly used would probably make Eliza, being Eliza, love the vanquished one the more. He crept away. He did not know what to do. Briefly he considered going off to be a soldier, to return covered in glory and win back Eliza's hand. But common sense and a chance meeting with a legless and luckless survivor of one of Her Majesty's Regiments of Foot served to convince him that he was better off as he was.

After work he haunted the alehouses. Edward occasionally joined him but more often went home to Ann and Jemima: Ann was expecting another child, he told his brother.

John noticed an increase in the number of convivial men in red coats, sergeant's stripes prominent on the sleeves, often as not sitting in the alehouse, dashing in those red coats, white trousers, polished brass buttons, and shiny black boots. They were hearty men, telling many a tale of derring-do: narrow escapes, exotic women, feats of endurance or heroism under foreign suns. Gradually they would attract an audience, some of them as young as ten or twelve, mouths open and stars in their eyes. The drink flowed freely. John viewed the spectacle with cynicism.

He watched a young man, a fine specimen of about his own age, drink as far as the immortal stage and receive a silver shilling and a handshake amid the cheers of the surrounding crowd. He was so drunk that the Sergeant kindly took charge of him for the night. Tomorrow, John had been told, still half-drunk he would be brought before the magistrate to swear the oath, receive a bounty, a sum of near six months wages, a fortune as portrayed by the sergeant; and commit body and soul to the service of his country for at minimum the next ten years. That had been the situation in which his legless informant had found himself, to his everlasting regret.

For his part, one which gave him a strong incentive to capture as many ingénues as possible, the recruiting-sergeant would receive 11s, provided the man passed the medical examination, a procedure it was difficult to fail unless old flogging scars were detected, in which case a man could be rejected as unreliable.

Eliza was worried, Edward told him one day as the latest nipper was drumming up their brew. They were sitting on a couple of derelict kegs in the place that one day would be a bustling station. Already a fine structure of Staffordshire blue brick, fashioned, he was told, in the Italianate style, was, through the diligence and skill of himself, Edward and the many others, beginning to rise amid a landscape of hillocks and humps where machinery and men and horses strove amid chaos to impose order into a place which would see the meeting of broad and narrow gauge.

'That brother of 'ern, she'm worried. Says 'e wants to be a sodger. She dunna want 'im to be.'

'Why not?' asked John, though what was it to him?

'Dunno, says it be dangerous.'

'O' course it be dangerous. 'Ow old bin the lad, anyways?'

'Turned sixteen t'other day, she says.'

'Well, 'e be right old enough then. Army teks 'em at thirteen, so I've 'eard.'

' 'E's on'y young, she says. An' easy led. An 'e's got a good job learnin' the iron trade, she says. An' she dunna want 'im runnin' off an' gettin' killed, she says. An' what's more, that young man o' 'ern's eggin' 'im on.'

'Well, 'e be old enough to mek 'is own choices,' said John firmly. And it was left at that.

Troops began to leave, on sloops and frigates driven

by paddles, on sloops and frigates driven by iron screws, on ships propelled by coal and ships propelled by wind, ships with hulls of iron and ships with hulls of wood. Horses left too, over two thousand of them. The troops were enthusiastic to go. Twenty-five thousand of them were said to be needed and recruitment was going well. The public were most enthusiastic that they *should* go and there was much cheering of the heroes over the strains of bands urging them on with 'Cheer, boys, cheer'; and intertwining romance and glory with the old, old song 'The girl I left behind me'. They, with hearts of English oak, would show the Russians a thing or two. War fever grew.

John was aware that subscriptions were being asked for in Wolverhampton to help the wives and families of soldiers. A national association had been formed in March, even before war had been formally declared. The problem was that although few soldiers were officially allowed to marry, many more, because of the long duration of peace, thirty-nine years since Waterloo, had illicitly done so. His own Aunt Rachel and her husband Private William Brown came to mind.

Only a small number of soldiers would be allowed to take their wives with them; and a soldier, unlike a sailor, was not able to apportion part of his pay to a family left behind. Those families would thus be left destitute, thrown onto the parish, unless helped by private subscription. Some said that the soldiers had broken the rules, so their families had to take the consequences, but they were in a minority.

Aunt Rachel, thought John, was apparently still working, not living as yet with her husband, so should probably be able to manage. Though he could see that if there had been children and Rachel at home, the loss of the wage-earner would leave her penniless.

On that first night the Wolverhampton association had

raised as much as £170, 3d of which had been contributed by John. Offerings given at church services contributed more.

It was a week or two later, an evening in April after a day of sunshine and showers and John was in an alehouse as usual when a man came in together with a boy. The boy John felt he vaguely recognised and after watching him for a few minutes he felt sure this was Eliza's brother: the hair was brown, without the richness of that of his sister, but in the gestures and expressions he caught those of Eliza. The boy was referred to as William. John said nothing. Later a recruiting sergeant came in, sat himself down, made conversation with all and sundry and was free with his buying of the drinks. The boy crept nearer, his companion laughing heartily at some of the sergeant's tales and nodding in sage admiration at others. John thought he recognised him too: the creature to whose arm Eliza had been clinging that one time he had seen them together.

The boy had had more than was good for him. The sergeant ordered him another pint. The boy left the room, to answer a call of nature John supposed. But it was the opportunity for the sergeant. John saw him pass his hand over the full glass. He had no doubt that the boy's companion had seen the same, yet there was no reaction; rather, was that a wink that passed between them?

The boy, William, returned, somewhat unsteadily, picked up his pint and was about to drink when John jerked himself from his seat.

'I'll be tekkin' thee 'ome,' he said, wresting the glass out of the lad's hand. And as William half-turned, looking up with a face of blank surprise, John grabbed him and hoisted him to his feet.

'Yo can 'ave 'is glass,' he said, placing the pint in front of William's companion. 'An' much good may it do 'ee.'

The room went quiet for a moment before erupting into noisy hostility as he quitted the alehouse, dragging the protesting William along with him.

They marched thus until a low wall presented itself, on which John sat, forcing the boy, sobbing now with a mixture of frustration and rage, to sit beside him.

'Yo 'ark to this,' he said. 'There was a shillin' at the bottom o' that glass. I seen this done afore. 'Tis common knowledge. Termorrer yo'd be signin' your life away. An' they tells yo 'tis a big bounty you'm be gettin'. 'Tis an all. Till they've tekken money out for your uniform an' for this an' for that. An' then, they says, thee'd be gettin' an 'ole shillin' a day. An so thee would. Till they've tekken out the money for your bait an' for this an' for that. An' yo'm left wi' nearly nothin'. An' that's nearly nothin' for twenty-one years, ten if yo'm lucky. An' there's floggin' if yo tries to get away or 'its an officer or some such. Three 'undred lashes. Used to be two thousand till a few year ago. Not all fun for sodgers, thee knows. Now, I'm tekkin' yo 'ome.'

News reached him a few days later. Eliza and her young man had quarrelled, Edward told him, having heard of it through Ann. The young man had apparently encouraged Eliza's brother William in his desire to go and fight a war. Ann thought the young man was a jealous, possessive creature, said Edward, and didn't like him. The young man wanted Eliza all to himself, didn't like her spending time or thought on her brother, wanted her to himself absolutely, wanted to get William out of the way.

'Such wickedness,' said John, piously. 'Dunna deserve a good wench like Eliza be.'

' 'Er 'eard it were thee rescued the brother,' said Edward. 'Seems 'er's grateful. Might see 'ee if thee called.'

'I s'll think about it,' said John.

The following Sunday he presented himself at the

house of the master mason, as clean and as brilliantly dressed as he knew how; and was not turned away. He escorted Eliza to Ann's house, by a meandering route on the road there and an even more meandering route on the return journey.

' 'E were gettin' too jealous,' Eliza said. 'Dinna want me doin' nothin' without 'im. Dinna like me goin' ter visit Ann, me friend, even. Dinna like me seein' William or me sister Sarah, or me Uncle William neither. All as I've got in the world.'

'Yo be best sendin' 'im packin',' said John.

There was a silence, and then he said, 'I've not been mighty good at writin' letters, nor visitin' thee, I knows that. But I does truly love 'ee, Eliza. I knows that now.' And so he did, he thought, feeling only the smallest twinge of regret for his lost freedom. 'Can 'ee forgive me, dost think?'

Scarface turned up. 'Work runnin' out,' he said. 'Thought as 'ow might be more o'er 'ere.'

Together they resumed reading of the papers. Often there would be one in an alehouse and those who were literate would read to such as wanted to listen. 'Black Sea' came up often. That was where the fleets were, or some of them. 'Crimea' was another place. And 'Sevastopol'. It seemed that Crimea was a peninsular, almost an island, in the Black Sea, and Sevastopol (more often becoming 'Sebastopol' as if they couldn't make up their minds) was a port on the peninsula, very important to the Russians and where they had a great fleet of ships. 'The southern arsenal of Russia' said the *Staffordshire Sentinel*. There were still no maps.

Through May little happened. A port called Odessa was bombarded, a Russian port and in the Black Sea; so that was good, they supposed. Fourteen Russian merchant vessels were captured off Odessa. Were they the same as, or different from, twelve Russian transports carrying provisions and munitions, captured in the same place at probably the same time? News was vague. Public and papers grew restive. The *Staffordshire Advertiser* complained that army and navy 'had not yet had an opportunity of performing any great exploits or displaying their gallantry' though 'when the time arrived ... no doubt [they] would evince the courage and skill which had always distinguished the British forces.'

The month of June proved rather more interesting, as the Russians took their forces out of the places called Wallachia and Moldavia and retreated to their own territory behind the River Pruth, where they waited. This action appeared to be prompted by a siege, by the Russians, of a Turkish town named Silustria, in which the Russians were defeated and suffered heavy losses, twenty-five thousand men, one report said. This was much more exciting than a few dozen here and there on either side bayoneted to death as prisoners, or shot, or dying of wounds or of cholera, a disease often mentioned.

'Well, we'm back to where we were afore the war started,' said John. 'Back ter peace, then.'

But he was shouted down. 'Them Russians is up ter something.' 'They's only pretendin'.' 'Trickery, I calls it.' 'Now's the time ter stamp on 'em so's they don't go meddlin' in other people's business no more.' 'Show 'em what's what.'

The war did not stop. A fleet of British and French ships blockaded a Russian fleet in the ports of the Baltic Sea. Another allied fleet blockaded the Russian Black Sea Fleet at Sebastopol. To take Sebastopol was spoken of as a logical step.

But, 'In the Black Sea and in the Baltic,' fulminated the *Wolverhampton Chronicle* in the middle of July, 'Nothing of any account has taken place ... The nation is certainly fast getting tired of this inactivity.' More English troops embarked, however; and many French troops, though largely in English transports.

Edward, a more regular correspondent than John, received a letter from home written by their sister Esther, to whom writing seemed not greatly arduous. Aunt Elizabeth had died she said and, in what seemed an echo of the words of her elders, 'Er got to sup sorrow by spoontles, poor lass.' John could see them in his mind, the wise old heads shaken in mournful commiseration. The funeral had just been held, on the first of July. She'd been buried in St. Michael's churchyard in her parent's parish of St. Mary.

After little Phoebe had died in the workhouse nearly three years ago, Elizabeth had remained there, never well. Then she died. Whereupon her parents had been informed that if they did not reclaim the body within seven days and pay for a coffin and a churchyard burial her body would be sent to a teaching institution for purposes of dissection. The idea threw her mother in particular into transports of horror. Dissection was linked in the minds of many to the fate of executed criminals and to body-snatching. They sprang into action.

Now she was 'laid to rest' wrote Esther, 'at peace at last'. John supposed it must be so: that was what they were always told, anyway. He hoped she would henceforth tread a smoother road than the hard and stony one that had hitherto been her lot on Earth. He wondered if she had ever been happy and nothing came to mind. When she was a child, perhaps? He hoped so.

Ann's baby was born on the 9th of August, another girl and given the name of Ann after both its own mother and Edward's mother. It was a healthy baby. Ann could not help worrying, said Edward, after the loss of that first child and, in his opinion, fussed too much. Eliza adored the baby; adored both the little girls.

'She'm a born mother,' said Ann. 'Dunna keep 'er waitin' too long, young John.'

It seemed that the Russians had not totally evacuated Wallachia and Moldavia, as in August more reports gave the same news as before, having the Russian forces again forced back behind the River Pruth. Sebastopol kept being mentioned. A siege, perhaps. Troops could land at Balaklava, a place on the coast only twelve or fourteen miles down the coast from Sebastopol. True, the landing could be difficult, due to the 'steep and precipitous' nature of the shoreline; and the terrain between Balaklava and Sebastopol, over which would have to be dragged the heavy guns and horse-drawn wagons of supplies, was 'exceedingly mountainous, rugged and without proper roads for the purpose', but no doubt the forces of right would prevail. In the meantime, there might still be peace.

There was a victory to celebrate that month: a place called Bomarsund, a fort, was bombarded by troops both French and English and the Russians had the worst of it. The fort was blown up and totally destroyed. 'The effect was most magnificent,' said the account. Some Russians, taken prisoner, were brought back to England, to Sheerness. Bomarsund was in the Baltic Sea, not the Black Sea.

'Bin they near each other?' a puzzled John asked Scarface. But Scarface only shrugged.

Strange place-names came thick and fast. It was impossible to keep up. But then came the news that an expeditionary force was to sail from a place called Varna on the Black Sea, where the Allies seemed to have been gathering. Numbers varied, but, 'Big, this is,' said Scarface. Some 25,000 English, 26,000 French and 15,000 - or was it 30,000? - Turks were to be transported 80 leagues eastward across the Black Sea from Varna to the Crimea. They would go in two divisions and would land ...

' 'Ark at this,' said John, excited, reading from the *Staffordshire Advertiser* of 16th September - ' "To land three leagues to the north of Sebastopol, on a flat beach, 1,500 yards in length, between two rivers, a most eligible point, for the rest of the shore offers a succession of cliffs." Sebastopol, that's where the Russians got that great fleet. 'Appen they bin there now, this very minute.' He scanned the columns, 'Says they sailed 2nd o' September, a fortnight ago, the first lot thee knows. Most like they'n fightin' now, by jings.'

'Fifteen 'undred 'osses with 'em an' all,' said Scarface, who had come round to peer over John's shoulder. 'Light Brigade, that is. Under Lord Cardigan. An' 'Eavy Brigade ter foller in't second lot. 100 field guns they got, an' 10,000 gabions, whatever gabions is.'

'They's like baskets,' said a voice, 'cages, an' yer fills 'em wi' stones or earth an' such. Yer puts 'em where yer wants 'em, round yer big gun, like. Or yer can mek a wall of 'em an' sleep be'ind 'em. Stops yer gettin' shot yersen.' They looked over towards the speaker, a shrunken, wizened man with a peg leg and a pair of crutches laid by.

'Last lot,' he said, waving at his leg by way of explanation. 'Thirty-nine year ago last June. Lost it at Waterloo, as yer may 'ave 'eard of. Twenty, I were then. Don't know nothin', these 'ere Generals an' such. Never bin in a proper battle. Rarin' ter go, aye. But they don't know nothin', they don't. No proper battles sin' Waterloo. Wellington, now 'e were the man. Done a lot o' battlin', 'ad Wellington, afore 'e won at Waterloo. Dead now.' He hawked and spat voluminously before relapsing into silence. They bought him a half-pint, at which he nodded his thanks, but volunteered no more, except to repeat, with dismal relish, 'This lot, they don't know nothin'.'

Six hundred ships carried the troops. How could they not be successful, such huge numbers of men? Cholera had attacked some at Varna, but then, cholera was everywhere in the world, even here in Wolverhampton from time to time. When John read that cholera victims, buried near Varna, had been dug up by the natives for the sake of the blankets in which the corpses had been wrapped and those corpses left on top for the vultures, he grimaced but felt a grisly satisfaction, as distant from it as if it were a play.

And the 'health of the men was excellent,' said the official report carried by the newspaper, not at all mentioning cholera. Their 'excitement was intense.' When informed of departure, 'officers and men were beside themselves with joy.' They 'were in the greatest possible spirits.' 'They will not bear to be told they are going to make an attempt on Sebastopol; they say they are going to take it.'

John thought for a moment that it might be good to be on one of those ships, seeing strange lands and people and places, before recollecting that he had lost the slightest desire to be a soldier.

The fleet had arrived, a 'telegraphic message' from the commander, Lord Raglan, informed the public. It was marvellous, everyone said, how quickly news travelled nowadays. The message had been sent on the 16th of September and was in the columns of the *Staffordshire Advertiser* on the 30th. Infantry, artillery, baggage and horses had been disembarked in three days. A storm had delayed things a little. The locals, Tartars, 'do not conceal sympathy for our cause' and the 'troops were confident of victory'. They would be marching south towards Sebastopol, while the Russians were marching north to meet them.

Then the newspaper boys were shouting the headline,

'Fall of Sebastopol' and people, in a surge of excitement, were rushing to buy. John felt a minor surge of disappointment. Surely the thing could not be over already? Though even in the paper as he read on there was a creeping sense of disbelief and the figures of dead, wounded and captured on each side differed so much from one account to another that scepticism edged into play.

Over the days it was admitted that the Fall was a rumour and that somehow Sebastopol had become confused with another, less crucial, battle, which had been fought on the 20th of September around a wooded gorge through which ran the little River Alma and was soon being referred to as the Battle of the Alma. Still, it appeared that the Allies had been triumphant. The English lost 1,800 men. Or 2,000. The French lost 'less'. The Russians lost 6,000 or 8,000 or 10,000 or even 28,000. It was a great victory; or perhaps, as time went on and lists of casualties were printed, not quite so great.

The local papers were full of news of the War: the public were intensely interested in its progress. Local papers borrowed news from other papers, as they did all the time; and some major papers sent out their own correspondents.

So much first-hand information was a modern development, and the electric telegraph, that wondrous up-to-date means of communication, facilitated swift dispatch, though that was possible for only part of the route from the Crimea to London. The journey of a message was, however, being speeded up. Every other day now a steamer would carry intelligence from the Crimea across the Black Sea to Varna, from whence it would be transported by a corps of mounted couriers overland to Kronstadt in Transylvania. From there it would go by electric telegraph to Vienna and thence to London: a cable had been laid across the Channel three years before.

There was an account written by a 'Special Correspondent of *The Times*' from which newspaper it had been reprinted, a long account in the form of a journal, which caught their attention. It was not in the usual mode of newspaper writing, but more poetic perhaps and began with that initial landing of the troops. 'Towards night the sky looked very black and lowering; the wind rose and the rain fell. The showers increased in violence about midnight, and early in the morning the water fell in drenching sheets, which pierced through the blankets and greatcoats of the houseless and tentless soldiers. It was their first bivouac.' John recognised within the description Lord Raglan's inconvenient storm, shook his head in sympathy and felt glad of his lodgings with the Mansells. Food was being supplied by the local people, and cheaply. But 'the want of water was very great . . . None can be had within four miles, and even then it is insufficient in quantity, and such as no-one would willingly drink.' Why, John wondered, had the transports not provided the men with water? They must have been pleased, those soldiers, to get to the River Alma.

There were letters home which the recipients made public, one from the Hon. Hugh Annesley of the Fusilier Guards: 'Dear Mother . . .A most summary dentist the ball was, to take out all my teeth at one smash, except for four grinders (there was a decayed one, which I hope has gone with its brethren, but I can't make out yet if it has or not). There is a good bit of tongue gone also, but the doctors say that will not signify, and that I shall speak as plain as ever, or, at most, only with a becoming lisp.' No doubt his mother was pleased at his being alive: his brother was already dead of cholera at Varna.

Something of the reality of war came from those Correspondents, things that official accounts never mentioned: the acre of dead and dying left after the Battle of Alma, for whom little could be done; the one British surgeon left to do what he could among the Russian wounded.

The Allies did not immediately attack Sebastopol, for while its main strength faced seawards, its strongest land defences lay towards them. Instead they skirted round it to the south-east, thinking to attack where defences were weaker. As they marched, the British met a body of Russian Infantry who fled, abandoning Hussar jackets, champagne, boots, a money chest, rich fur-lined cloaks and jewellery as they went, morale-boosting booty for the troops.

The British force entered Balaklava down the coast where 'the inhabitants came out to meet him [Lord Raglan] bearing trays laden with fruit and flowers.' From that direction they hoped to attack Sebastopol on its weakest front. The French took up one position on the heights overlooking Sebastopol and the Turks another. Together they formed a semi-circle. Supply ships used the harbour.

The Allies omitted though, as the Correspondent of the *Morning Herald* pointed out, to cut off the Russian line of supply which connected that strongly-defended northern side to their own hinterland. He also drew attention to the cholera which, he said, was killing some twenty-five men a day while many more lay sick. Surgeons did their best.

On the 17th of October that year of 1854 the bombardment of Sebastopol began in earnest by both land and sea, the land forces pounding from their positions on land, ships sending cannonades from the splendid harbour, though as the Russians had sunk a line of their own ships as defence, the Allied fleet could not get in very close. Powder magazines exploded on all sides.

Accounts were everywhere read aloud, thrilling the listeners, who could feel themselves deafened by the gunshot: 'the scream of shot and shell was enough to make one's hair stand on end', wrote the Correspondent of the *Morning Chronicle*, reproduced for the readers of the *Staffordshire Advertiser*. Or they could imagine being half-blinded by the smoke, 'a thick, lurid smoke which seemed to suffocate'; and cheered or groaned as appropriate. As at Alma, lists of dead and wounded followed: names were given; and sometimes more - 'SHIP, NIGER. Killed: Edward Palmer, boy, cut in two by round shot.'

Sebastopol must surely fall in a day or two; though one correspondent wondered why the Allies had not attacked at once, straight after the victory at Alma, instead of leaving time for the Russians to strengthen their defences.

An officer said he had not washed even his hands for a week. He was still wearing his full-dress coat in which he had marched and fought and slept for the last three weeks, for the troops had landed with no baggage but what they could carry. On his back was a filthy haversack with some rations of biscuit in it and whatever - eggs, honey, bread - he was able to buy from the inhabitants. The artillery had tents, but the line regiments none, he said.

Small battles and skirmishes were happening constantly, as the Allied forces dug themselves in around the city and struggled against Russian might. Then, a fortnight after it had actually happened, the papers carried an account of a bigger operation.

On the morning of the 25th of October, the Russians, with a superior force of some 20,000 to 30,000 infantry, cavalry and artillery, had stolen out of their granite-walled fortress of Sebastopol and attacked Balaklava. It was so early in the morning that the Allied troops had neither watered their horses nor eaten. Things had gone badly for them: you could tell that even from the account of Lord Raglan, who always liked to put the best face on things. The heights above Balaklava, beyond which, to the north, lay Sebastopol, were taken. Numerous actions followed, praised for their gallantry by Lord Raglan. Then the Russians reformed with artillery at the front and upon both flanks.

There was an order, which Lord Raglan admitted 'from some mis-conception' caused the Light Cavalry, under Major-General Lord Cardigan, to advance. Raglan's words were, 'Lord Cardigan charged with the utmost vigour, attacked a battery which was firing upon the advancing squadrons, and then, having passed beyond it, engaged the Russian cavalry in its rear; but there his troops were assailed by artillery and infantry, as well as cavalry, and therefore necessarily retired, after having committed much havoc upon the enemy . . . the loss they have sustained has, I deeply lament, been very severe'.

The French perception was, ' The English Light Cavalry, 700 strong, led away by too much ardour, charged vigorously the whole mass of the Russian army'.

Prince Menschikoff, Commander of the Russians, mentioned 'extraordinary impetuosity'. Others called it 'madness'.

A Correspondent spoke of the Light Brigade 'riding through the guns' with 'the most brilliant valour' in an 'excess of courage' and 'daring'. 605 sabres went into action 'strong', he said. 198 returned.

Lists of casualties followed. And, said a Correspondent, 'We make very little way. The men are worn out. We must have more men and that speedily.'

In England, ideas for more combatants were multiplying. Recruitment of civilians was continuing. The

Militia too were being called upon for volunteers, who would receive an augmented bounty of £7 in place of the usual £6. Irishmen were appealed to for their services.

Night attacks by the Russians continued. The troops slept uneasily, if at all, turning out if the cannonade grew insistent. They grew increasingly weary. The weather turned. The night of the 28th October brought hail and sleet. Tents, if such there were, were torn or blown away. It was so cold that men got up to run around in an effort to keep themselves from being frozen. And this was only autumn: what might winter bring? Reinforcements were needed: growing numbers were falling from sickness or war. Ammunition was running low: guns were ordered to fire only once every half-hour or twenty rounds per day. The mountainous terrain and lack of roads combined with the vicious weather were making it increasingly arduous to transport heavy guns and supplies between the harbour at Balaklava and the troops around Sebastopol.

The plight of the wounded had not gone un-noticed in England. John noticed a few lines in the *Staffordshire Advertiser*, saying briefly that a 'Miss Nightingale who is to conduct the nurses to attend the sick at Gallipoli, left England on Saturday,' the 21st of October. She was taking thirty to forty nurses with her. He wondered where Gallipoli was. A Patriotic Fund had been set up to collect for widows and orphans.

On November 11th, the *Illustrated London News* brought out a 'Grand Treble Number'. As advertised, the supplement contained a 'Grand Series of Scenes and Incidents from the Siege of Sebastopol' together with a 'Large Pictorial Map of the Seat of War'. Scarface and John contributed sixpence each and bought a copy. At last they had a map. Together they pored over it, working out positions. The map showed Varna, Sebastopol and Balaklava. The wounded from the Crimea would have to cross the Black Sea to westwards, sail through a channel into a further sea, the Sea of Marmora, and cross that to arrive at Gallipoli in Turkey to be helped by Miss Nightingale. It looked a long way.

Sketches of the action, they were both pleased and puzzled to see, showed many tents and clean, healthy-looking, relaxed troops: this did not fit at all with the accounts of correspondents.

Ideas for more combatants continued. A reader pointed out that men who were languishing in prisons might contribute their services. And the country was full of men just lazing about. Our sporting country gentlemen for instance, assisted by their gamekeepers, might form a regiment of crack shots. Our military should be recalled from distant parts of the globe.

And someone, in early November, recollected all the effort which had gone into the country's new railway system, thought of the determination and the physical strength of the workforce that had engineered all those heavy miles. Someone remembered the navvies.

19

Into the Breach

' 'Ark at this,' said Edward. It was a Sunday morning in late November of that same year of 1854 and the three of them were sitting in the *Prince of Wales*, the brothers relishing the prospect of a good dinner ahead of them, Scarface saying he had plans of his own. Edward had the paper.

There had been another battle, another attempt by the Russians to raise the siege of their city. On the 5th of November had come a second dawn attack, this time at a place called Inkerman, a place not named on their bought map, but evidently near Sebastopol. As the *Times* Correspondent had it: 'The morning of the 5th of November dawned darkly through a drizzling mist upon the heights of Inkerman.'

The gist had been that 8,000 British troops were, at dawn, taken by surprise by some 40,000 Russians. The outnumbered British held them off until at 10 o'clock 6,000 Frenchmen arrived to assist. One could almost see the puffing-out of British chests as the account continued with the information that even with a further 20,000 reinforcements of their own, the Russians could make no headway against the troops and 'withdrew in retreat', 'hotly pursued to the very walls of Sebastopol', leaving behind 15,000 men of whom 5,000 were dead, the rest wounded or taken prisoner. British casualties totalled 2,612 of whom 635 were dead.

' 'Ark at this,' Edward said again. 'It says, "Let us send every man that can be secured at once to Sebastopol." And, "We have enough men idling about the world to take Sebastopol and Sebastopol must be taken." Plain as the nose on yer face, it is. Them Russians 'as the numbers. One of our lads is worth ten o' them, but there's still too few on 'em. An' the Russians is well set up in that fortress an' for gettin' in supplies an' that. Our lads fight like lions but they'm ill an' they'm cold an' they'm tired.'

'Dunna play fair, them Russians. They kills our lads if they'm wounded, specially them Cossacks - barbarians they are, them Cossacks - whiles we 'elps their wounded,' John said. 'I think,' he added.

'That Miss Nightingale, 'er be askin' for lint an' linen rags. There's a nob in Wolver'ampton says 'e'll send 'em on if yer gives 'em to 'im, said Scarface.'

'Women mun 'ave some,' said Edward.

The door was pushed open and a group of men came noisily and excitedly through.

' 'Ow bist?' said Edward.

'Eh up lads,' said Scarface.

' 'Ast 'eard?' asked one.

' 'Eard what?' said John.

'Peto, Brassey an' Betts.'

'An' what about 'em?'

'They be goin' ter build a railway.'

'Oh ah?' said Scarface. 'Thought as they did that all o't time.'

'Not in't Crimea, they don't.' He was triumphant, the fellow with the shaggy hair. 'Told government they'll build a railway, from Bala, Bala ...'

'Balaklava,' supplied John.

'Aye, from Balaklava ter Sebastopol. An' best of it is, we'm goin' ter mek it.'

There was a silence while the three took in this news.

'Mr Brassey, 'e wants volunteers. Gotter be in London at them offices as they've got down there, 2nd o' December. First come, first served. Mind, yer's got ter 'ave a ...' he turned to one of the others.

'Sustificate o' good conduct. Yer gets it from yer boss.'

Scarface, protesting half-heartedly, was taken back with them to 100, Russell Street, redolent with the scent of roasting beef and crisping, golden-brown potatoes. The women did no more than blink before finding another plate and squeezing in an extra seat.

Ann gazed at her husband open-mouthed. 'But the babby's not even bin christened yet,' she protested.

'Do it when we gets back,' said Edward, unmoved, reaching for another potato.

'Yo means IF yo gets back,' cried Eliza. 'What yo want to go there for? Cholera an' great big guns as'll blow your 'ead off afore yo've gone two paces. An' what dost 'ee know about fightin' an' such?' This last directed, like a dagger, at John.

'Eh, 'old thee 'osses, missus,' said Scarface, comfortably. 'We won't be doin' no fightin'. We be goin' ter do what we does best, mekkin' a railway. We be goin' ter save our lads whiles they gets on wi' tekkin' Sebastopol. An' about time.'

'Our line'll carry the guns, see,' said John, 'An provisions an extra troops an' such, right from that 'arbour at Balaklava right up to the walls o' Sebastopol.'

'Yo'll need warm clothes,' put in Mrs Roberts. 'Better start knittin', our Ann, like as the good Queen's doin'. I 'eard as 'er were knittin' a comforter fer 'er cousin, Duke o' Cambridge, what's out there. An' she'm got all 'er ladies knittin' an' all, socks an' mittens an' woolly 'elmets an' that. All knittin', they are, in the palace, knit, knit, knit, busy like. Cold, it is, I 'eard, out there. Right cold.'

'Them generals ain't a patch on Mr Brassey,' said Edward. 'Mr Brassey'll do things proper and 'e'll do 'em quick, you mark my words. We sha'n be safe as the Tower o' London wi' Mr Brassey in charge.'

On Friday the 1st of December, early just in case, the three men were on the train to Birmingham. They stopped there for a while, Edward having a fancy to see the place. Half a dozen engines spumed smoke and steam into the echoing space of the station. They were awed by the vast, fretted-iron, glass-paned roof soaring above them. 'Single span,' said Scarface and the others nodded in respect.

As they went out and looked back, the front of the New Street station impressed them: 'Yo'd strain your neck lookin' up there for long,' said John, gazing roofwards past serried rows of windows above a line of colonnades.

From there they wandered towards the centre to have a look around. It was a bustling, noisy, dirty, vivacious sort of a town.

They found a grand market hall and going inside found themselves once more straining their necks to look upwards at a ceiling some sixty feet above them.

'Canna see no bulls,' said Edward, gazing downwards again and across at hundreds of stalls looking smaller and smaller as they faded into the distance.

' 'Appen that bin long ago,' said John. They'd seen a sign saying 'Bull Ring'.

'Good bit o' work 'ere, I shouldna wonder,' said Edward, looking round him as they pushed their way through the crowds. 'Folks floodin' in. Oncommon lot o' 'ouses they mun be wantin'.'

They filed this away for future reference.

The London train was headed by an engine in green livery lined with black. They admired the pair of huge driving wheels, the four leading wheels ahead - 'two- axle bogie,' pointed out Scarface - and the two trailing wheels behind. 'Dunna see this sort often,' he added.

They settled themselves into a third class carriage.

'Leastways we han a roof,' said John as the train steamed out into a sudden rain-storm.

The journey found them pointing out pieces of navvy-work.

'Kilsby Tunnel. Longest tunnel in the world. When 'er were built, anyway. Five mile, more'n twice as long as Dinmore,' said John.

'Quicksand, they 'ad ter deal with an all,' added Scarface. 'Six an' twenty men died buildin' this tunnel. An' do 'ee know what 'appened ter three on 'em?'

'Go on, tell us then,' said John, as they rattled through the darkness.

'Laid bets they could jump o'er't top o't ventilation shafts, didn't they? On'y shafts were specially wide. One jumped and fell, next follered 'im. Third one knew 'e were't best jumper in't world; but 'e weren't.'

'Few cobs o' sweat lost there,' John commented as they sped through a couple or more miles of steep cutting, the vegetation still revealing the chalk that had reluctantly given way to pickaxe and shovel, before they stopped at the next station, signboarded Tring.

A few lines of song followed:

'A bold navvy man,
An old navvy man,
An' I've done me graft an' stuck it like a bold navvy man.'

'Sixteen million bricks, tha knows,' said Scarface as five hours and fifteen minutes after leaving Birmingham they were passing through the massive curved walls of the gloomy, almost-tunnel of yet another cutting before pulling into Euston.

And Euston was a station that the glories of New Street sat pale against.

'Even owd Samson 'isself'd 'ave 'ad a right job there,' said John, as they left the concourse and turned to look behind them at the mighty Doric pillars of the facade.

'Mun find out where we'm goin',' he said. 'Better ask.'

'Bet they knows,' said Scarface, nodding towards a row of cabbies, their horses' heads half-hidden in nosebags.

'They'll see we'm from the country an' tek we 'alf way round the town an' charge us a week's wages to do it an' all,' said Edward.

He fumbled in a pocket and brought out a scrap of paper. 'Says, "Walk straight ahead till yo gets to the Euston Road. Cross it. Go a bit to your left. Straight ahead again down a broad road till yo gets to the river. Cross it over Waterloo Bridge. Then that's Waterloo Road an' the offices is down there, next to the York Hotel."

'Sounds clear enough,' said John.

They began to walk.

'Robert Stephenson planned that railway, tha knows. Chief engineer,' said Scarface. 'They say 'e walked that route, London to Birmingham, twenty times, all 'undred an' twelve mile of it. Big landowners, they made a right fuss, they did. Didna want no nasty railways goin' near them. Had ter keep changing 'is plans, did Stephenson.'

'Did it in the end, though,' said Edward.

They looked about them as they walked, feeling somewhat awed at being in proximity to Queen and Parliament, grandees and wealth.

'Paved wi' gold, they says,' said Scarface, looking down at cobblestones deep in horse-dung. 'Must be round't corner.'

At the bridge they negotiated the turnstile, paying the toll-keeper his half-penny; and stepped out on the wide footway over the waters. The dusk was coming fast now, but they could just make out the spires of innumerable churches punctuating the skyline, while upriver an impressive tower or towers seemed to be rising. Horses clopped past them, pulling vehicles of all sorts. Leaning over the parapet they could see a multitude of craft, boats using oars or sail or steam. The river spread out to wide mud banks on either side. There was a stench that made them pull their neckerchiefs over their faces and hurry across: miasma, they knew, carried disease.

They spotted the crowd, a goodly bunch of men dressed much like themselves forming a rough queue, chatting, laughing, singing or silent; some standing, some sitting, some leaning against the wall of the building; some holding the implements of their trade. As they drew nearer they were welcomed, loudly. They joined the tail end of the queue.

'Russians won't know what's 'it 'em,' someone shouted. There was a laugh from the crowd, evidently in exuberant mood.

'Office doors open termorrer,' someone told them. 'Fust thing.'

'Goin' to be a long night,' said Edward.

'I bin clemmed,' said John. ' 'Appen I'll go an' look for a bit o' bait. Mun be summat somewhere.'

He turned to a man leaning on the wall. The man pointed down the road and gave a few directions. John disappeared, returning after a while to draw three sheep's trotters from his pocket. 'An' these 'ere bin called 'am sandwiches, wi' mustard an' cabbage, so 'e said. Al'ays a first time.' They tried them cautiously and nodded approbation.

'Good job we bin all mobled up,' Edward said. 'Be cold tonight, most like.'

They had indeed had the forethought to be well-clad.

John and Edward were both wearing newly-knitted comforters and mittens. Scarface, who wore a sort of cape of broadcloth, pulled low his hat and stuck his hands in his pockets.

Through the night the queue grew longer, extending rapidly as Saturday dawned. Eventually a man with a large key unlocked the office door and shut it firmly behind him. Several others of authority were admitted. Feet along the queue were shuffled as a mild protest but no-one risked losing his place for disorderly conduct.

At last doors were latched open, a doorkeeper kept the queue, and the first men entered, to be interviewed from behind four stalwart desks.

It was John's turn. He was nervous. The man behind the desk did not smile.

'Certificate of good conduct.'

John handed it over and the man perused it briefly.

'Age?'

'Twenty-one next birthday, Sir.' He forbore to mention that the next birthday would be in three hundred and forty-six days time.

The man looked him over, assessing his physical strength and fitness.

'Experience?'

'S'ewsb'ry an' Chester, S'ewsb'ry an' Birmingham, S'ewsb'ry an' Hereford. Wolver'ampton Station just now, Sir.'

More questions followed, John trying to remember all the skills he had acquired and used over the last eight years.

Scarface was being asked the same questions. John heard, 'Age?' followed by Scarface's satin-smooth reply, 'Thirty-two, Sir.'

All three of them were accepted.

They walked back over Waterloo Bridge in a state of euphoria. They had signed an agreement to serve engineer James Beatty, for 'Six Months at the least', to 'promptly and faithfully execute [his] orders to the best of [their] skill and ability' and to 'conduct themselves soberly and steadily'. In their pockets they held railway passes. They were to say goodbye to their families and proceed to Birkenhead and the Canada Works, the model engineering works only recently built - and in a miraculous five months - by Brassey. From there they would steam or set sail for Balaklava. They would be the Civil Engineering Corps, Mr Brassey having refused to have his men put under martial law, as the Army had wanted.

Peto, Brassey and Betts would provide men, materials and transport and take no profit.

Five hundred of them were to go. Their passage would be paid for, their clothing, food, tools and tobacco provided. They would receive £2.16s a week. Unlike the army, whose masters had only just conceived the idea for the troops without yet having managed to instigate it, they would live from the start in wooden barracks, portable and weatherproof, each holding forty men. Each hut would have a stove, for which quantities of coke, coal and firewood were being sent out.

 Mr Beatty, together with his staff, had already arrived from Canada where he had been engaged under Mr Brassey in building the Grand Trunk Railway, 540 miles of it, across the arctic Canadian wastes. Mr Beatty knew about cold.

They were told they would build enough miles of railway from Balaklava to serve all parts of the front. Comprehensive lists of all materials required had already been made. Orders for those materials were even now going out, to manufacturers of rails and sleepers, of wheelbarrows, capstans, forges, cranes, horses and of each and every thing needed in the construction of a railway.

Ships were being bought or chartered. And, to save time, they were being procured, as far as was possible, from the closest point to the materials they would carry.

Leave-taking was delicious, John thought, as he held a warm and tender Eliza ever closer, stroking her hair, drying her tears, soothing her with long kisses and finding more leeway than she'd ever previously afforded him. Perhaps it was too much leeway, he would later reflect with a pang of anxiety; but reassured himself that they would be married on his return and that would be no longer than a few months.

The public mood had changed. No longer were navvies drunken rioters and insolent thieves, abhorrent to decent citizens. They had metamorphosed into being 'proverbially powerful and hardy', 'fine stalwart men', the 'very elite of England', 'broad, muscular, massive fellows, scarcely to be matched in Europe'. In the raising of earthworks one of them was equal to three soldiers (who themselves stood unmatched by any foreigner). There was at least one poem penned to praise 'Our Brave Navvies'.

In Birkenhead they were accommodated at the *Sun Inn*. The first ship, the *Wildfire,* a clipper sailing ship of 457 tons, had been delayed by a heavy gale, but they were in time to see her set off, on the morning of Saturday the 23rd of December, under tow, speeded on her way by a cheering and hat-throwing crowd. John was relieved to see that the water was perfectly calm.

Their ship was to be the *Mohawk*, a clipper too, but nearly twice the size at 800 tons. She would leave on Christmas Eve, which they realised, with the shock of time passing, was tomorrow. They were directed to a company store and issued with more clothes than any of them had ever owned at one time. But first they were given a waterproof bag to hold all.

First they might don a pair of linsey, i.e. wool and linen, drawers. For the torso there was a selection of shirts: a red flannel and a white, three of coloured cotton and one 'fearnought' slop, a loose-fitting top made from thick wool. Over that they could wear the moleskin vest lined with serge. A choice upon rising could be made between the blue worsted cravat or the cooler one, also blue.

Below the waist and over the drawers came a pair of moleskin trousers held up with flannel belt and secured at the knee by strap-and-buckle yorks.

A single pair of grey stockings lined a choice, according to the day's conditions, between ordinary boots, strong nailed boots, long waterproof boots or fisherman's boots. A pair of leggings added extra protection to the legs and a pair of mitts to the hands.

A woollen coat could cover the whole, and/or a waterproof suit.

Night-time was honoured with a pallet and pillow, a pair of blankets and a rug and blanket.

Besides this wondrous stock of comforts they were each given two pounds of tobacco 'for the present'. And for every ten men there was a portable stove which, they were assured, would boil, bake or fry outdoors.

'Sling the bag o'er your shoulder an' let's find the *Mohawk* afore we goes back to the Inn,' John said.

They walked back towards the area from which the *Wildfire* had departed. She was a long, sleek ship, the *Mohawk*: like all clippers she was built for speed. Masts the brothers knew of, from vessels on the Severn, and spars, and shrouds, and sheets. But this creature, bare as yet of sail, bedazzled with its superfluity of all those things.

265

'Never stops, a clipper. Might be 'eelin' ter't gunnels in a force ten, but never stops,' said a lounger, leaning on a rail, chewing tobacco while watching the bustle before him. 'Loadin', that lot are, though they don't carry too much, them clippers. Speed, they's made fer mainly.'

'We sha'n be sailin' in 'ere termorrow,' said Edward.

'Oh aye?'

'Out to the Crimea,' put in John.

'Seen 'em comin' back,' said the lounger. 'Some on 'em. Them that's still alive. Quiet like. Thin, white critturs wi' bandages, can't 'ardly walk. Or bein' carried wi' no legs. Or's got no fingers 'cos o' frostbite. 'Alf starved, they looks. An' all in rags.'

'We'm goin' wi' Mr Brassey,' said John. 'We'm goin' to 'elp them sodgers an' build a railway.'

''Eard o' that,' said the lounger, brightening up. 'Thee'll be alright then, wi' Mr Brassey.'

Tomorrow came: Christmas Eve. They all had signed a paper gifting a pound of their weekly wages to their families. Edward had named Ann, John had named Eliza. Scarface had named someone, but who the someone was remained unknown.

The innkeeper, Mr Pear, had provided an excellent breakfast accompanied by ale. They felt content as they made their way down Bridge Street towards the docks. This was the beginning of his travels, thought John, and thought too of how often he had longed to travel. Already there was a foreignness, for the inhabitants of Liverpool were more varied of physiognomy than any he had seen before. His eyes were drawn to people with skin of bronze, of ivory or black, with startling hair or eyes or noses; and all going about their own concerns much like himself.

They walked up the gangplank past scurrying crew and coils of rope thick as a man's thigh; and were told to keep out of the way below in their berths. Their bunks smelt of freshly sawn wood, the ship having been re-fitted at speed in the last few days by Brassey employees. Beds were laid out, packs stowed away. They sat on their pallets, hearing orders shouted, bumpings and creakings. A steam-tug started up. Were they away?

Other men began to get up and climb the ladder. They followed to find the ship moving slowly and gently down the centre of the waterway.

'This is proper good.' John was excited: he would see the ocean for the first time in his life.

'Wait a while,' said Edward.

They entered a larger channel and swung to the right. The 'West Float,' someone called it, a curving channel thickly bounded by quays and docks swarming with activity. Road bridges swung aside to let them pass. Then there was a mighty lock and they were in open water.

John could see that there was still a far side. 'This 'ere's the River Mersey.' said a sailor. They stared after him as he turned away, a man of wonder with his dark skin and close-cut, minutely-curled, black hair.

They turned left in the wake of the tug, two now of innumerable vessels, heading, they supposed, towards the open sea. The river began to widen out. The water grew more choppy. Land dropped away to their left and then their right and receded until there was nothing but sea. It was disconcerting to be alone on vast waters with only the friendly tug still pulling them along.

'She'll drop us round Holyhead,' said the friendly sailor. 'In the Irish Sea we are now. Pick up a good nor' westerly there, I shouldn't wonder.'

John began to feel that he should not have had that magnificent breakfast. It was a feeling he resisted as long as he could, before the breakfast left him altogether over the side. He was so long engulfed in misery that he hardly took in the laying to, the shouted orders, the hoisting of the great white sails. He managed at length to struggle down to his bunk and wish he were dead, before sleep at last overtook him.

Christmas Day passed in a blur of misery; and Boxing Day too and the next, before he felt some glimmer of life returning. He went up and sat on the deck, near the heads, in case. 'Heads' and 'bowsprit' were two of his first sea-words.

Up at the front of the ship, the 'bows', was the bowsprit, pointing gracefully forward over the waves. And on each side of the bowsprit was a wooden box, covered by a grating. It was not called a dunny, but 'the heads'. If you glanced through the grating which topped the box you could see the salt water sluicing through underneath and thus clearing and cleansing what might be below. Sometimes the water came too close and icily cleansed you too.

'Officers an' men. They all use it. Only Cap'n Barclay's got 'is own,' he was told. The Captain's word was that of God.

The sailors were friendly, though without much time for conversation. They had a language all their own and obeyed in an instant orders quite incomprehensible. They would scurry and squirrel to let out a 'stuns'l' or haul in a 'main moonraker' or reef a 'top gallant'. They climbed to dizzying heights and walked out on footropes slung under the yards and sometimes sang in unison.

By listening and exchanging ideas between themselves, Edward, John and Scarface and their fellows began to understand at least a little. Starboard and port, fore and aft, bows and stern, galley and scuppers and the time-pattern of the bells became, after a while, familiar.

It was icy on deck. December gave way to January and the new year of 1855. They had passed what they were told was France, then Spain and Portugal. The sails underwent even more quantities of re-arrangement than usual and then they were calling at one of the Pillars of Hercules before passing through into the Mediterranean and there was Spain again on the port bow. At Malta they docked for a short while before sailing on under the toe of Italy; and the weather grew warmer. A ship hailed them when they were off Cape Matapan at the foot of Greece. It was the 25th of January and they had changed course and were now sailing in long zig-zags against the wind. At each turn sails flapped and cracked, the ship heeled violently to its other side, sailors dashed purposefully hither and thither; and for a while there came smoothness again and a gurgle under the keel. They were sailing 'close to the wind', they were told, 'beating up' under 'double-reefed tops'ls'. Topsails they'd worked out: the largest sails, second up from the deck; and reefing meant tying up the sail so that less of it was exposed to the wind. Double reefing meant that only a third of the sail still caught the breeze. For the wind was wild and roaring strong and inspired a mighty respect.

They were sailing through a maze of islands: it grew warmer and calmer. They were rested and well-fed, for provisions were ample, watched over by a clerk. They were healthy; and a surgeon was there if needed. They were disciplined, for they had to answer to the foreman and his assistant: all was the provision of Peto, Brassey and Betts.

It was a holiday. It was undreamt-of luxury; and they made the most of it.

Then they were in a channel where they could see land on each side, 'The Dardanelles', a sailor told them. So that's what it is, thought John, not mountains but a stretch of water. Turkey, the country they were saving from the Russians, lay to both port and starboard.

The Sea of Marmora followed and the temperature

was dropping. Then the ship entered another narrow channel with the fabled city of Constantinople to port, where they briefly stopped; and Scutari to starboard, where they waved in homage to the wounded soldiers in the care of the odd Miss Nightingale whose family were wealthy so that she, and a woman too, had no rational need to do this thing.

Came the end of the channel called the Bosphorus; and land was once more out of sight and there were icicles on the rigging and it was the Black Sea at last, though not black but grey and sometimes green or blue with great rollers, which their ship climbed and breasted and down-swooped.

'Balaklava tomorrow,' they were one day told. It was the 11th of February in the Year of Our Lord 1855.

20

The Slough of Despond

The harbour, when they nosed quietly into it through a narrow entrance flanked by hills, was thick with craft. The sails of the *Mohawk* had been reduced to the barest minimum. Slowly she was manoeuvred towards land. Heaving lines were thrown to expectant hands ashore. Attached heavier hawsers followed them and were secured. The *Mohawk* came to rest.

Wind was howling, carrying sheets of blinding, piercing rain. John was glad of the thickness of clothes beneath his waterproof coat; and glad of his long boots.

Hand over eyes, he did his best to survey the scene around him: the mile-long, sheltered harbour, with its sea-entrance through which they had passed made narrow and almost invisible by a projecting point, was hemmed in by a jumble of steep-sided, limestone hills, rugged and rocky where they could be seen through the mist and rain. Through a temporary thinning of cloud cover, John caught sight of what looked to be a fort. Such ground as could be seen was almost bare of vegetation. He looked at the strip of muddy beach on the eastern side littered with piles of supplies left open to the elements, chaotic heaps of broken timber, parts of ships, stones, anchors and rubbish, all tumbled into the mud. He saw houses both one and two-storeyed, some roofless. He saw men wearing turbans and voluminous trousers drawn in about the knee.

Carried on the wind, or perhaps between its flurries, came the most overpowering stench.

They knew by now that cargo had been split between the different ships of the Civil Engineering Corps, all nine of them. The first ship to arrive could thus begin work without delay. And if one ship were lost, the total venture would not fail. They soon learnt that the first ship to reach Balaklava had been the *Lady Alice Lambton* from Blackwall, 90hp screw-steamer of 511 tons, a whole fortnight before. The *Wildfire*, the only other sailing ship besides their own and the first craft to set off, had not yet arrived.

Unloading began. Provisions, timbers for huts, a pile-driver, a couple of sawing machines and portable forges, rails and sleepers, carefully packed into order of possible need, began to be manhandled from the hold with the help of a ship's crane and swung over the deck onto the new, raw wharf jutting out from the beach. John felt his muscles in use again and was filled with the joy of it. A spirit of willingness and comradeship pervaded them all. They were filled with glorious energy. They had come as saviours.

John walked on land and felt it sway beneath his feet. He saw men, navvies like himself, some with the familiar, pointed shovels, some with wheelbarrows. He saw the vestiges of something else familiar, a line of rails that began from the beach itself, a line already carrying trucks; one with sides, stationary and empty, one flat truck carrying rails and timbers and being pulled by a horse.

It was slow work, the unloading. Why were there so few proper wharves or jetties, no apparent organisation? The army had been here for nearly six months.

When headway had been made in unloading the *Mohawk*, the crew were left to carry on, stowing the supplies in a long railway shed as new and raw as the wharf in front of it.

Alongside the projected line, just out of town and running north and placed on a long and level platform precisely cut from the hillside, was positioned a line of neat huts. From each rose a stovepipe emitting a thin column of smoke. They, the navvies from the *Mohawk*, were ordered to take the elements of the huts brought with them, transport them on horse-drawn wagons along the line as far as they could, to ground already levelled beyond the existing huts and erect their own.

'Get an eyeful o' that,' said Scarface as they drew level with the first hut. A board hung by the door, proclaiming it to be 'Blackwall'. The next was 'Victoria'.

'What shall us call our'n?' someone said.

' 'Ow about Birken'ead? Sin' that's where us sailed from.'

'Or *Mohawk*?'

'Brassey Terrace,' proposed Edward.

There was a murmur of agreement.

'Brassey Terrace it is,' said Scarface. 'Find a piece o' wood, 'eat a bit of iron and, abracadabra!' He flung up his hands.

By dark the structure was up and the stove installed. Trips were made to find kindling, to the goods off-loaded from the *Mohawk* for coal, to the Commissariat for provisions: from now on they would be receiving soldiers' rations. The stove began to roar and a red glow to diffuse its warmth. Drenched clothes began to steam. A savoury smell curled and spread. Bedding was laid down - bunks would have to wait for the morrow.

They were sipping their first mugs of tea when the door opened and a dripping crowd arrived.

'Shut that bloddy door!' came from a dozen voices as a gust of rain whirled in.

'Welcome ter Balaklava,' said a fellow with long crinkled hair the nondescript colour of walnut shells.

'Eh up,' said Scarface, staring hard. 'It's Curly. Or I'm a Dutchman.'

'An' no mistakin' thee neither. What's thee been up to, me old mucker?'

'Later, lad, later. Fill us in on this 'ere place, will yer?'

Curly accepted a mug of tea. 'Mr Campbell's surveyed the line, mostly. Done afore we even got 'ere. 'Fore M. Beatty even. Not too bad this end. First mile an' an 'alf pretty level, one in sixty. We done some o' that bit already. Was given a couple o' 'undred sodgers from 39th ter 'elp out at start. Too starved an' tired ter do much, but better'n nowt. On'y loaned fer ten days, mind. Just as they's gettin' ter know't ropes, they's needed back at front. Too many sick an' they's short o' men.

'Railway's ter go on up to Kadikoi. That's near where't big battle were fought, where't Light Brigade lost all them men. More fools them. Not that they 'ad a choice, like. Lord Cardigan, chap in charge o' that, gone back ter England, tha knows. Cannon balls all o'er. Valley o' death, they calls it.

'Next 'alf-mile, steep, one in fifteen. That'll be't worst bit. Then not so bad - one in twenty-five - fer another mile an' an 'alf. Then pretty level again till yer gets near ter where Lord Raglan's 'eadquarters is.'

'What about road?' asked Scarface.

'Ain't no road, not so as yer'd notice,' said Curly. 'Just mud. An't devil's own job ter get through it.'

'What about 'osses?'

'Trouble is, there's not 'osses enough.'

'Thought army 'ad a power o' 'orses,' said Edward.

'Ah,' said another man. 'That's what yer'd think, but yer'd be wrong. Most on 'em dead, or as good as.'

They looked at him, disbelieving.

'Smell anything?' asked the chap next to Curly, a fellow with impressive breadth of shoulder.

'Good bit o' salt pork a-boilin'?' said John.

'Nah. The right stink outside. Well, that's 'osses, that is. An' mules an' oxen an' anythin' on four legs. In't

274

'arbour, there's a great raft of 'em floatin' in't water, all blown up like bladders. An' there's dead uns all o'er, 'undreds of 'em, all't road up ter Sebastopol, if yer can call it a road. Mud ter yer knees, it is, an' more, most places.'

'Why dead?' asked Edward, shocked.

' 'Ad 'em pullin' stores up from 'ere, didn't they? Through't snow - three foot on it sometimes - an't rain an't mud. But does they feed 'em proper? No. Does they shoe em? No. So they dies, don't they? An't dogs eats bits on 'em. Packs o' wild wolf-dogs they 'as round these parts. An' vultures an' ravens an' such. An' rats,' he added after a pause. 'By gum, them rats is big uns.'

'So 'o gets stuff up now?'

'Well, men, o' course, wadin' in mud, dressed in rags an' mud, wi' a piece o' sack round't legs fer gaiters.'

A silence fell, the new arrivals trying to picture this scene of desolation.

'We saw some tents,' John said.

'Oh aye, tents. Up at Camp, that's them sodgers round Sebastopol, they's mostly got tents now. But weather comes an' weather goes. An' they comes back ter them tents full o' snow an' mud and they 'as ter shovel it out afore they lies down ter sleep. An' then it snows in't night an't snow comes in an' there they am wi' one wet blanket.'

'Used ter bury men decent-like,' put in Curly. 'Set o' clothes an' wrapped in a blanket. Not no more. Livin' wants them blankets. Livin' wants them clothes an' all. Weren't allowed ter 'ave more'n their uniform at start. An' rushed on shore when they come over from Varna, wi'out 'aversacks even. Went back ter Varna, them 'aversacks did an' ain't never been seen no more.'

'An' they's not got no music neither,' said the fellow with the massive shoulders. 'Drums, cymbals, flutes, saxes, the lot. Left on board. Nowt left ter cheer them sodgers up. Poor sods.'

Someone beat a tattoo on the side of the hut. 'Grub's

up,' he shouted.

There was a rush for the door.

Morning dawned, dark with storm-cloud. The wind still blew, carrying both rain and snow.

The men of the Brassey, replete with hot floddies which, while rich in potato, were lacking in egg, left their hut to the familiar cry of 'Blow up' and joined the others at the beginning of the Grand Crimean Central Railway.

A line of wagons came slowly along the tracks, wagons piled with men from the night shift. They clambered out, while the new men looked to see if they recognised a face. There was an occasional triumphant shout of welcome.

The new gang loaded up the trucks with sleepers and lines while the prized horses of the Railway Corps were unyoked and led off to be fed and watered. Their replacements arrived, fresh beasts from the carefully-tended Corps pool of thirty-seven horses and twenty Commissariat mules. The cavalcade began to move, five horses pulling each load, some men atop the loads, two sitting on the rear buffers, some walking beside.

John chose to walk, at the rear of the train, and gazed around him. The line was being laid along the main street of the town though the navvies had been able to start work on the line itself only four days ago. The ten days prior to that had been spent clearing ground, building their own huts, pulling down buildings, constructing the railway wharf and the like, while the loaned soldiers had been set to work collecting stone from walls and buildings between Balaklava and Kadikoi and laying it for the rail bed. Someone pointed out the old Post Office which was now occupied by Mr Beatty, master of all things railway. What had once been its garden gave onto the landing place and was piled high with railway stores.

A rat ran across in front of him. Rats were, they had

already realised, everywhere.

'Eh, Blackie, get an eyeful o' that.' Scarface pointed out a couple of shaggy beasts, tall, long-necked and splay-footed, each surmounted by a man in strange costume. It was John's first sight of a camel.

After a while they reached the limit of the line,

A man of some authority was talking to the gangers.

'That be Mr Beatty,' someone said. 'Was with 'im in Canada, building the Grand Trunk Railway. Good sort o' chap. Fair, like. 'Elp yer out if yer was in a spot.'

John studied the man. Average height, still young, strong-built, his hair was fair and he was clean-shaven. He smiled.

'An' a grand day, me brave boys, for building a railway. Isn't it a fine bit of shovelling we have for you today.'

He was Irish. Still, he was in charge and he'd just been recommended. They went to work with a will,

Edward rubbed his aching muscles. 'No good for a man, all that eatin' an' tekkin' things easy what we did on the ship,' he said.

They were taking their midday break. Tea was being brewed on one of the portable stoves they'd been issued with. Fine things they were too, thought John. Evidently he was not alone. A pair of soldiers were approaching, using the laid track in lieu of a road. A pair of poles rested on their shoulders with a huge canvas bag slung between.

'Could do wi' summat like that mesen,' said one, nodding towards the stove.

' 'Ow dost cook then?' asked Scarface.

'Wood where wood is. Mostly gone now. Roots as we digs up. Meks us own fires, on't ground.'

'French don't,' said his friend. 'Proper camp kitchens they 'as.'

'An' proper rations.'

277

'What dost eat, then?' asked Scarface.

'Coffee.' The soldier dug into his pocket and brought out a handful of green beans.

'That bin coffee?' asked Edward, doubtfully.

' 'As ter be roasted, o' course. Over't fire. When us 'as found enough fuel an' fire don't go out fer bein' drownded. Then us gets an old shell-case, bit o' round-shot or a couple o' pebbles, grinds it till it come like powder. Pour on boilin' water an' there yer goes. Nothink like a good cup o' coffee.'

'Rather han me tea,' said John.

'Well, we ain't got no tea. Tea ran out, they says. We got coffee - an' word is, it's goin' ter come roasted afore long - we got salt pork, we got biscuit, we gorra bit o' rum. Sometimes we gets potatoes. Onions we 'as ter buy extra.'

' 'Ow much pork?'

'Pound, should be. Raw o' course. Filthy stuff when yer 'as ter eat it raw 'cos yer can't get no fuel or yer's too tired ter bother. An' a pound o' biscuit. Afore Christmas were worst. On quarter rations we was. Sometimes none at all. Couldn't get 'em up from Balaklava, see. Be better soon wi' the railway an all. Got ter carry this lot the rest o't way, though. Twelve, fourteen mile, all told, there an' back.' He pulled open the top of the bag he was carrying, to show it packed with ammunition.

'Us pulls up big guns an' all,' said his companion.

'Boots came, t'other day,' said the first, looking at the navvies' thigh-high specimens. 'Good uns, we were told, called ammunition boots. Most of 'em turned out too small. An' them as fitted, soles come off after a day or two.'

The two moved off, climbing slowly upwards, thin, tattered uniforms sodden, boots bound together, soles to uppers, with rags.

John's eyes followed their course into the murk, wondering a little that their own rations so far seemed to be better than those of ordinary soldiers.

Little of the surrounding terrain was visible through the wet but what there was was largely mud. A great swathe of ground, on either side of what had been the road as it approached bleak hills, was torn and trodden into mud. Only the line they were building was in any way fit to walk on. On either side he could see what had been described the evening before, corpses of animals poking through. There must be many more, he thought, in various stages of disintegration and in deeper pockets, which remained unseen.

'Best get on then,' said Edward.

Late in the day they were following the markers to where they disappeared into a courtyard. The near walls and outbuildings were pulled down to facilitate the track. Then they were through into the yard itself; and the walls opposite followed in destruction and with them a tree, a poplar. It landed, not by design, on a roof, smashing the tiles, breaking two windows and carrying away part of a balcony. A head appeared looking startled, saw what they were doing. Mr Beatty looked at it, shouted something about omelettes. A hand was raised in acknowledgement. The head withdrew and they carried on. They learnt later that the house was the lodging of one of the newspaper men, the Special Correspondent of the Times, William Russell.

Knocking-off time found them weary. 'I'm tired till I can't 'ardly lug a leg,' John told his brother. But he thought of the soldiers they had seen earlier and, in contrast, of the dry, sheltered hut they would return to, the stove soon coaxed into giving out its heat, the ample provisions to soothe the hunger of a tired man, the warmth and comfort of the bedding to insulate against the biting cold; and was thankful.

A second day passed. Mr Beatty seemed to be everywhere, encouraging, advising, raising a smile. The weather appeared to be improving, the mud becoming less liquid.

Those first two days had been spent digging ditches in the swampy ground for drainage, barrowing the dug-out earth and rock up on top of the rough bed already laid. Sometimes they were digging or blasting through hillocks, barrowing the muck and shifting it up the line to fill in the hollows and firm the boggy ground. The ganger checked the levels, then came the laying down of sleepers, timber sleepers, shipped in by Peto, Brassey and Betts from England. There was the sound of explosive, of hammer striking metal and pick striking rock. Speed was of the essence: the gangers had been told that their priority was to provide a workable line in the least possible time and that the standard of precision expected at home might here be relaxed, if only by a little. Their line thus avoided the more immutable obstacles wherever possible and, as it lengthened, began to resemble the trajectory of a worm rather than that of a crow.

All the time there was the intermittent boom of far-off heavy guns accompanied sometimes by bursts of much nearer rifle fire.

As John and the others turned out of Brassey Terrace on their third morning, they were met by Mr Beatty. Volunteers was what he was after having, he explained.

'You'll have noticed a wee whiff of unpleasantness in the air,' he began. The men laughed and held their noses. 'Quicklime is the answer,' he went on. 'The limestone's all around us.' He gestured widely at the hills. 'My proposal - and Lord Raglan has given his permission - is to build a kiln to produce the quicklime which will rid us of the noxious miasma which spreads its evil over us and brings disease. There's no doubt but that the warming of the weather has brought the typhus which you will have heard spoken of. I'm after men who are masons, bricklayers or familiar with the operation of a kiln. Yes?' John had raised his hand.

'Fashioned and operated brick kilns, Sir. So's me brother.'

'Good man. Anyone further?'

Half a dozen volunteers came forward, giving their levels of skill. One was Erc, the chap with the massive shoulders. 'Short fer 'Ercules,' Curly had volunteered, with an awe that was reciprocated by his listeners, 'On account of 'im bein' a sixteen-set-a-day-man, like.' Beside being a demon shoveller, Erc, it transpired, had once built and operated lime kilns in his native Derbyshire. He was most welcome, said Mr Beatty.

The site had already been chosen, an old and dilapidated kiln which they could repair and rebuild. It was on the far side of the harbour away from the town, the fumes, as Mr Beatty explained, being nauseating and sometimes deadly. It lay though, not far from the railway, which would make transport easier.

They set to work. Some, using picks, retrieved rough lumps of limestone lying on the surface, rough-trimming them if necessary; or split them from larger rocks with hammer and chisel. A day, and they had rebuilt a hollow structure perhaps twice the height of a man with, at the bottom, a low frontal arch, the drawhole. This, as its name suggested, allowed air to be drawn in to create a high temperature. Erc told them it must heat to 1,650 degrees Fahrenheit. Building the arch, its strength coming from the central keystone, put John in mind of the Dinmore Tunnel and days which seemed so very long ago.

'Yer needs small chunks o't limestone now,' said Erc. 'Not too small, though. Got to get air through. 'Tween three an' six inches.'

One of the forges had hammered out a metal grid and

that was placed over the top of the drawhole. Over the grid and inside the hollow chamber, limestone cobbles and coal were set in layers, the coal supplied by Messrs Peto, Brassey and Betts, by arrangement with the authorities and taken from the steamships in the harbour. The whole was fired. As the temperature rose, acrid fumes rose from the open top of the kiln and quicklime in the form of ash began to drop through the bars of the grating. It was shovelled into barrows and wagons and taken off to cover the nearest piles of ordure and animal and human decay in the town. Later that would extend, first to its immediate environs and later further away still. Coal or coke chutes had been built into the sides of the kiln and fuel was fed down these into the heart of the furnace. The small pieces of limestone were fed in from the top. It was a twenty-four-hour-a-day enterprise.

On the Thursday the temperature rose to 60 degrees. Coats were discarded, then waistcoats, then a shirt or two. On the Friday it became colder again and when the occupants of Brassey Terrace poked their heads out of the door to sniff the morning air, they found the ground white with a hard frost. Later it began to snow.

'Got a mind of its own,' said Scarface.

As the line progressed out of town that day it met an obstacle, a ravine bordered by swampy ground. Where there were ravines, bridges were built. The lads of the Railway Corps were long apt to retell newcomers a particular tale.

'Goin' all out,' John would say. 'Come edge-o'-night an we've got through town, an' then there's a stream comin' down from the 'ills, in a ravine like, an' marshy bog round it an all.'

'An us were a-scratchin' of us 'eads,' Erc would follow, 'An' Mr Beatty comes up an' says, "Come on boys," 'e says. "Back ter't railway stores. Ah knows it's late," 'e says, "an' you lot be wantin' yer suppers, but there's a pile-driver just landing. If us gets it out 'ere tonight, us can get bridge done termorrer." '

'It were't *Wildfire* what'd docked. At last. An't lads all mucked in,' Curly would continue. 'An' that there pile-driver come out an' by't end o' next day lads 'ad piles driven an' a bridge made o' wood yer could a drove an 'erd o' elephants over.'

When they came back to the hut late that evening they found that another hut had spawned to sit like a mushroom alongside their own and there were fifty-four navvies in peak condition clamouring for answers to their questions.

Then it was Sunday, a day of rest, the end of their first week. It was the 18th of February. Their line had now, and in ten days from the laying of the first rail, reached the small village of Kadikoi with its domed Russian church.

They decided to visit a place close to it which they passed each day, an ill-assorted arrangement of shacks where things were being bought and sold.

They walked up the railway track from Balaklava for some three quarters of a mile. Before the armies had churned the valley to mud, they had been told, this place had had deep, fertile soil, feeding rich vineyards and planted with rows of poplar trees. Trees, vines and all had been used for firewood. A few skeletal poplar roots remained, too tough for the limited tools of the soldiery.

On their left was a mound surmounted by a battery, its guns sweeping the plain beyond. On the near side of the mound a new bazaar had sprouted, some hundred and fifty shacks and tents thrown together. The three made their way towards them.

Between the shacks the raw ground had already been churned up. The three stared curiously at men whose aspect they had never before seen, garments they had not thought existed. A gabble of unknown languages filled the air.

'Behold Sutler's Town,' said an English voice. 'All the scoundrels of the Levant who can get across the Black Sea. All making little fortunes by the sale, at the most enormous prices, of the vilest articles of consumption. Beware, my friends.'

They looked at him: not a soldier, not one of themselves. The man gave a half-bow and walked away.

' 'O dost 'ee reckon that bin?' asked Edward.

'Appen one o' they correspondents, shouldna wonder,' said John.

'Gift o' the gab, anyways,' said Scarface.

They walked through the booths. One shopkeeper was selling cooked ham.

'Looks proper good that,' said John. ' 'Ow much?' he asked.

'Five shilling.' The man pointed to a pile of about a pound.

They turned away, grinning.

'Two weeks' wages,' John said.

A fowl, rather scraggy, was seven shillings and sixpence. A bedraggled goose was fourteen shillings.

'Officers only,' said Scarface. 'An' rich uns at that.'

'Thought as all officers bin rich,' said John. 'They mun be rich, an' above a bit, to buy commissions an' that.'

They would be working nights for the next week and knew they needed a few hours rest, so turned and walked back towards the town and Brassey Terrace. They overtook a party of soldiers on foot, some bloody, some roughly bandaged, one sitting on a plank between two of his comrades, head hanging, one prone on a litter carried by four men. When they reached the beach they saw them being lifted or helped into boats and watched while the boats were rowed off out to the hospital ship amid the all-powerful stench. They supposed that the hospital ship would sail when it eventually filled with cargo. Judging by the numbers, some forty a day, whom they had seen coming down during the week, the day of sailing would not be long: then in three to five days they would be in the care of Miss Nightingale. Fewer men losing fingers, ears and legs to frostbite now, they had been told. Exposure, lying in wet clothes all night, was still a problem; so was cholera, and dysentery and, less frequently, wounds.

They turned back to Brassey Terrace, its nameplate nailed over the door, the letters burnt blackly into the wood. A few games of cards, thought John; and a noggin of the army rum, which took a little getting used to. The place was beginning to feel like home. He whistled a few bars and the others joined in, Erc in booming bass, singing:

'I've navvied in the Old Country ter lay the Perm'nent Way,
An' I've braved the Seven Seas ter get ter where I am today,
I'm a-servin' of me Country an' I'm doin' it like a man,
An' I'm doin' it with all me strength as only navvies can.
A bold navvy man an' an old navvy man.
There's few as is as loyal as a bold navvy man.'

21

Knights of the Railroad

Their second week and they were working nights. They were now back on the ever-extending line, communicating in dumb-show with some phlegmatic Croats, who had been loaned to the Railway Corps over the past fortnight. Few of them were proving much use with pick, shovel and barrow, so they had been put to gathering stone for the rail-track bed. Those who had not taken to navvying were about to be transferred to unloading ships for which they were said to be better qualified. They were an odd lot, if what was said was true, preferring biscuit to salt pork and potato and even to rum.

The Corps worked by the light of braziers, always hoping for a moon. Rails were laid and secured over the sleepers, trucks filled up with ballast of well-broken stone and the top-ballast shovelled between the rails, flush with the surface of the sleepers to hold them in place. Planks were laid over the sleepers parallel to the rails to enable the horses to walk unhindered.

The next day's shift would clear the way onwards, levelling up the lows and cutting down through the highs to make the track level; and at night their own shift would fill in and firm up behind.

News had been seeping through of another major battle. It had taken place in the previous week on the 17th of February, up the coast though, fifty miles away to the north, where the Allies had first landed from Varna in September and well beyond Sebastopol. As far as they could gather, the place, Eupatoria, which had been strongly fortified, was mostly occupied by Turkish forces. They'd been attacked before dawn by a superior force of 40,000 Russian cavalry and infantry.

'Them Russians,' said Scarface, 'Never seems ter move 'cept 40,000 strong.'

The Turks, under their commander, Omar Pasha, had prevailed, helped by British men o' war firing at both Russian flanks. It was an Allied, Turkish victory.

A few Turks celebrated, said the rumours, with Russian heads spiked on bayonets. Local Tartars stripped the Russian dead. Numbers of dead and wounded on both sides, as always, varied.

The weather of that second week changed again, giving way to drying winds, welcome in that the mud was firming up, making the trek between coast and the soldiers' camps more easy for both men and horses. Where trenches were the soldiers' protection, they had at last become less wet, shelters instead of ponds. But, as Mr Beatty had told them, warmer winds and higher temperatures had brought a new peril: typhus fever. Several regiments had had outbreaks that week.

Since the line had reached Kadikoi, at least the sick and injured had had a more smooth and solid track to follow. It was only about three miles long, but already making a difference. Movement of provisions had improved, though apart from the Highland Brigade who had embraced the idea with enthusiasm, the railway was as yet not being used for this, permission having been unaccountably refused; and soldiers were still sent on foot in parties all the way to Balaklava to fetch them.

Months ago, when the campaign was in its first infancy, Commissary-General Filder was said to have expressed a desire that out-depots should be established, but had apparently been over-ruled by Lord Raglan. The hurricane with its loss of shipping and destruction; the mud which could not be struggled through; the reduction in numbers, through sickness, of already overworked soldiers who could not be spared from the trenches; the death of thousands of horses from wounds, starvation, overwork and disease, had postponed thought of depots. Now, the making of the railway was turning ideas into reality: or endeavouring to.

Someone overheard an irate Mr Beatty talking to one of the officers, and the story spread through the camp. Commissary-General Filder believed that there was no need for the railway to transport provisions. He had served in the Peninsula War in 1809; and the routine there had served well enough. There were more than twenty wagons which the Commissariat could use, fumed Mr Beatty. He'd offered to provide the skilled men to manage them if Filder would see to the loading and unloading. The wagons could make two journeys a day, each laden with three tons of provisions. But no, said Filder. According to Filder, men should be sent down to Balaklava to collect their own provisions, as had always been the custom, as had been the custom under the Great Duke. Moreover, two sets of rail journeys would result in overwork for his department: no member of the Commissariat should begin work before eight in the morning, nor work after five in the evening. Mr Beatty was said to have spluttered some very bad words at this point.

Still, some fresh vegetables had begun to reach the camps as much as twice a week in an attempt to check the scurvy, a disease now beginning to show itself in an increasing number of cases. Scurvy is a drawn-out disease of intense fatigue, bone and muscle pain, blackened bleeding gums, loss of teeth, fever, open suppurating wounds, diarrhoea and eventually death. Its cause, lack of fresh fruit and vegetables, was well-known, but those items had been earlier not at all and even now were only intermittently being included in the diet of the soldiers.

Nor was bread. Ovens, supposedly sent out from England for the purpose, had never arrived.

Beyond Kadikoi, at the head of the valley, the line had turned to the west along the side of a hill topped by a gun-battery. The gradient was becoming steeper, one in fifteen, and progress slower as they worked upwards for a third of a mile to the French Camp on the Col. The Col was the lowest point of the ridge which surrounded the plateau on which the army was camped. The line followed the existing road.

Beyond Kadikoi there was no ballast except for what came out of the cuttings which were driven through sandstone rock, soft at the top, but hard and compact at about six feet down. A few excavations were necessary between the French Camp and the point known as the Flagstaff, a length of about a mile with a gradient of one in twenty-five; and the stone from these was used as ballast.

On the top of the plateau and about half a mile onward from the Flagstaff, were the headquarters of Lord Raglan, a long, whitewashed, one-storey farmhouse. It may have been less grand than the great houses he was used to, but it was infinitely superior to a trench or even a tent.

They never caught sight of the man himself - he was reputed to show himself abroad but little - but Scarface told them that he was an old man, veteran of the Napoleonic Wars, and was missing his right arm, amputated at Waterloo.

From Kadikoi to that plateau above was the most difficult part of the line, a rise of some six hundred and sixty feet. The one in fifteen section up to the French

Camp was going to be too much for horses dragging loaded wagons and Peto, Brassey and Betts had already foreseen this. With their usual diligence and caution they had sent out two stationary engines where someone else might have deemed one to be sufficient, if indeed they had thought at all. Already these had been assembled and trialled successfully. The first of them was due to be put finally in place on French Hill, the spot where the steepest gradient of one in fifteen ended. It had been ascertained that the water supply there was sufficient to run the engine.

On the Wednesday when they assembled for the night shift, there was an overlay to the smell in the air. It differed from the usual stench, but was unpleasant all the same. Noses traced it to the beach, where they could just make out an enormous spreading heap of darkness.

'Vegetables, rotting. Wasn't it a mix-up with the paperwork? Too long, they were, debating and arguing about who should sign and who signs what for the unloading of the cargo. Would have helped fine against the scurvy.' Mr Beatty was already there, engaging their attention. Some gangs were sent off to extend the line. He indicated John's group.

'Now, lads. It's a grand piece of work you'll be doing tonight. Here's this engine, all in pieces as you see. It's to go to the top of French Hill. Pulling shot and shell up that hill is more than any horse can stand, but this engine can.'

By the end of the night they had most of the engine up. They had used a crane to load pieces onto a flat truck which was then hauled up the line towards French Hill. Several trips were necessary, carrying as much as the horses could take at a time. The day shift would take over, levelling a platform, blasting if necessary. Then would come the pile-driving to hold the engine firmly in place.

John wondered if and when he would get a letter. On

the voyage here they had been told that if they had letters ready they could be posted home from Gibraltar where the *Mohawk* would pause to take on board fresh water and provisions.

A sailor had pointed out a speck in the distance, which had grown into a rock, rising from the water like a monstrous fin and bristling with batteries of cannon. They had been allowed ashore, having been assured that this place, as did Britain, belonged to Her Majesty Queen Victoria. They had been informed about the apes and even caught a glimpse; and had spent a few hours drinking, egging one another on to do ever more daring feats of scrambling on the cliffs.

John had put his letter to Eliza in the bag with all the others and imagined it making its way back to England and on to Wolverhampton. On to Shrewsbury too, for he and Edward had written a letter between them to their parents and sisters. He imagined Owd S'ewsb'ry and his son reading it out to their drinking companions in their favourite watering holes of the *Waggon and Horses* or the *Market Tavern* on Pride Hill; or the *Dunn Cow* and the *Barley Mow* on the Foregate, while doing their best to pretend themselves unaffected by their closeness to renown. With a twinge of some odd, hollow, twisting feeling, he wished they'd asked for a newspaper from home. Some of their fellows had, he knew, though there had not been time for anyone to have received one yet.

On the second Sunday, the 25th of February, they walked around Balaklava; not that there was much to see. The railway went down the main street, already familiar from the twice-a-day journey. The people who used to live there, the Turks and Tartars, had been removed on the orders of Lord Raglan when the Allies first took over the town, in spite of the placatory offerings of flowers and fruit.

Turned out to fend for themselves, their houses had been ransacked, windows smashed, doors used for firewood, possessions stolen or burnt. Habitable buildings had since been taken over by officers. The most substantial had Lord Raglan's name on the door, though it appeared deserted.

'One 'ouse in town, one in the country,' said Edward.

Wooden shanties had been thrown up by others on any spare piece of ground. The place was a tangle of stinking hovels and decrepitude and many of the thoroughfares were almost impassable for mud, though the main street on either side of the track had been recently surfaced with broken stone by the ancillaries of the Railway Corps; and spreading outwards was evidence of the efforts of the quicklime workers: cesspits, rotting animals, ruins, all covered in white. It still stank.

Traffic not destined for the harbour had been diverted to a back road, similarly recently surfaced.

One small part of the town was organised, the land surrounding the old post office, headquarters of Mr Beatty, the railway jetty and yard and the railway workshops for the smiths and engineers.

'Eh up, lads,' someone shouted. It was Curly and a group from the *Lady Alice*, first ship to arrive. Scarface signalled recognition and they walked over.

'Anythin' worth lookin' at in this apology fer a town?'

'There's't 'arbour. If thee canst call it an 'arbour. Frenchies've got a much bigger place at Kamiesh, up the coast. Nearer Sevastopol too, so don't 'ave't same problem o' gettin' supplies up ter't troops. Anyway, come an' 'ave a gander. Mostly somethink ter look at there.'

The harbour was crammed with craft, large and small, the large tight-packed into a modest area where there was a greater depth of water.

'They comes in an' there's nowhere ter land stuff. 'Ave ter wait days afore they can land cargo, even if it's sheep or cows an' such an' no fodder fer 'em left on't ship.'

'Lord Cardigan, 'im o' the Light Brigade, 'ad a grand yacht moored 'ere. The *Dryad*, it were called. Went back to it after't battle an' 'ad a bath an' drank a bottle o' champagne. So they says. Wouldna send 'is precious 'osses ter 'elp fetch provisions fer't troops neither. An' 'e missed Inkerman! 'Avin' breakfast on 'is yacht.' It was Erc.

'Then there were't Great Storm,' Erc went on. 'Afore us got 'ere, but yer can see't wreck o't *Prince* from't 'eadland. Screw steamer, she were, anchored outside't 'arbour. Carryin' winter clothing, more's the pity. Middle o' November, it were. Wind like a banshee. Roofs torn off, rows o' poplar trees torn down. Sea boilin'. Thirty ships wrecked. *Prince* went down in ten minutes, dragged 'er anchors an' dashed on't rocks. Crew an 'undred an' fifty. Six saved.'

'Don't mind 'im,' put in Curly. 'Gorra brain like a giant, 'as Erc.'

Along the beach as they walked, they came across a huge and twisted metal wheel reminiscent of a wheel from a watermill, identified by Scarface as the paddle from a paddle steamer, assorted pieces of broken masts, a damaged rudder, animal corpses, scattered piles of a disintegrating something that might once have been biscuit, rafts of decaying hay, as yet unassembled pieces of hut and scattered, sodden clothing. Gulls screeched and fought over the redolent, rotting pile of vegetables.

'Course, lots o' useful bits gone now. Made into shelters or burnt fer firewood,' Curly said.

'What about Sebastopol, the sodgers there? In the storm?' asked John.

'Lost their tents, didn't they?' said Curly. 'Blew away, tents, clothes, blankets an' all. Were a Roman chaplain 'o 'ad ter dress like a sodger after, 'cause 'is cassock went off wi' the wind like. Keep well away from them sodgers, by the by,' he went on. 'Full o' lice, they are.'

While they had been wandering along the beach and
talking, a troopship had begun to discharge its human
cargo.

'New recruits,' said Curly. 'Just you watch, now.'

The recruits, many of them boys, as John saw, were
descending the gangplank onto the beach. Each carried an
enormous load on his back.

' 'Eavy clothin', 'eavy supplies,' said Erc. 'Everythink a
man could want they gives 'em now. All ninety pounds of
it. Got ter get that lot up ter't camp outside Sebastopol.'

The boys reached the ground and staggered off.

'Some of 'em doesna mek it more'n a mile or two,' said
Erc. 'Raw recruits, no trainin' ter speak of. Can't 'andle't
weight, see. Collapses, they does. Worn out an' they ain't
even 'andled a gun yet.'

'As't seen't teashop?' said Curly.

'Yo's jokin',' said Edward.

'Nay. Come an' look.'

They were shown a wooden hut adjacent to the
harbour. They peered through the door to see wooden
benches occupied by soldiers in various states of misery.
Many cradled a large mug.

'Now, see, if they's ter wait fer't 'ospital ship fer a day
or two, they comes in 'ere, sits theirsens down an' 'as a
cuppa.'

It was now their third week. They were back on the
day-shift: a 6.30am start, finish at 6pm with a three-
quarter hour break for breakfast and an hour for dinner.

A Colonel Harding seemed to have taken over the
lime-kiln operations and had his squad of soldiers busy
pulling down the buildings of Balaklava and liming
everything and everywhere. This was just as well because
for a few days the weather grew warm, almost too warm,

and the snow on the peaks began to disappear.

A story was going round about the stinking corpse of a horse near Lord Raglan's headquarters, When queries were raised as to why the abomination had not even been buried, the answer came that the horse was a French horse and thus was not the business of any British soldier.

The warmth, which became suddenly oppressive, was not to last. On the Wednesday evening came heavy rain succeeded on Thursday by snowy sleet, an ice-cold blast driven by a great wind.

As they battled through the elements, swathed once more in waterproof coats and thankful for their long boots, John looked over to what Edward was indicating with a jerk of the head. The number of sick seemed to have increased. A long train of them were coming down the track towards the harbour, some carried piggy-back, many on the backs of ambulance mules, most of them these days French animals lent by their always helpful allies. John grimaced.

That night came bright moonlight, a boon to the night-shift. They could never guess in advance: some nights they were enveloped in mist, a Black Sea mist that smothered all outlines in a thick, soft whiteness.

Then it was their third Sunday, the 4th of March. A late breakfast was being cooked on the stove. A bang on the side of the hut and someone shouting about post.

Edward went to the door. John stood to listen. A bundle was thrust into Edward's hands. He scanned the names. 'John?'

John took the letter. Eliza's neat script.

He sat on his bunk, his mug beside him, a plate of floddy half-eaten, and tore the letter open.

'Dear John,' it began. It was quite a long letter and he read it slowly to savour it. Then read it again. Edward was similarly engrossed. Scarface was whistling, arranging a damp shirt near the stove to dry.

Edward finished and looked over. 'What's 'er say?'

'Says all's not well between 'er master an' 'is missis. 'E's not getting the work an' it looks as they'n be goin' north, missis an' the babbies, back to 'er Mam an' Dad. Says she'll move in wi' your Ann if it 'appens an' wait for me to come 'ome. 'Er's gettin' the pound a week. An' savin' it so far. Wants me 'ome, 'er says.'

'When were it wrote?'

John looked at the letter and then at the envelope. 'About when we got 'ere. Says 'er's just got the letter I sent from Gibraltar. What about yours? 'Ows your Ann?'

' 'Er bin very well. An' the babbies. Reads about the war an' Sebastopol an' all that in the paper, she says. Bit behind, like. Says we ain't got there yet.'

They went into Balaklava again, Edward wanting to have a look at the newly-set-up bakery, the venture of a French entrepreneur. It had a queue and a crowd of loungers drawing in the scent of fresh-baked bread. They bought a loaf, at the vast expense of two shillings, and pulled it apart between them while watching comings and goings from the shelter of a rocky alcove high above the harbour.

A vehicle hove into sight.

'That mun be Electric Telegraph,' said John. 'As we've bin 'earing of.'

'Let's 'ave a closer look,' said Edward. They scrambled downwards towards it. It was a large enclosed wagon with a pair of large wheels behind and a pair of smaller to the fore, at which end were harnessed three pairs of horses. On its top was an object not immediately identifiable.

The sapper in charge of the horses was happy to rest for a few minutes to describe the glories of his machine.

'Line planned from 'Eadquarters all the way down to

Balaklava. Should be open in a week or two. Then we'll be gettin' lines out to the Divisions. An' if a Division moves, well, us can get a new cable in quick as anything. Got a plough, see.' He showed them. 'Digs a trench. Cable laid into the trench. Runs off this drum, see.' He pointed out an un-missable horizontal drum, as wide as the wagon. 'Twenty-four miles o' copper wire, we got. Insulated. Gutta percha. 'Gainst the wet, o' course. Come to a river, got a mortar, small cannon. Shoots the line across.'

The brothers made appreciative and admiring noises, peered into the back at the shelved batteries, benches, and table. The strange object on the roof was explained as a lightweight, folding boat complete with oars. No, said the sapper, it had not yet been used.

'Tell you summat,' said the sapper, on a note of triumph. ' 'Lectric Telegraph Company, they be goin' ter lay a cable all the way from Varna 'cross ter Balaklava. Bottom o't Black Sea.' He waited for their response. They stared at him in disbelief before shaking hands and silently watching the wagon as it lumbered into the distance.

'News'll speed up,' said John. 'Soon be gettin' news at 'ome quick as we are.'

'An' Lord Raglan, 'e won't 'ave to wait for messengers no more, gallopin' from one bit o' the battlefield to another. 'E can talk to 'is officers right then an' there, any time, day or night an' what's more, they'll get the right message. That Light Brigade charge, couldna 'appen now.'

' 'E wunna be 'is own boss, neither,' said John. 'Gov'ment in London, they'll be tellin' 'im what to do, changin' their minds every minute.'

They shook their heads in wonder at modern communications, the pace of change and man's ingenuity.

They chatted to a soldier who bemoaned the lack of

fresh meat. 'One day,' he said, 'December it were, we was on quarter rations. Steamer, *Pride o' the Ocean,* comes in from Varna. 'Undred an' ninety bullocks on board an' run out o' fodder. Commissariat refuses to allow 'er to enter 'arbour for five days. Only eighty still alive, an' them livin' skeletons.' He spat.

When they returned to Brassey Terrace, there was some desultory gossip about a Mrs Seacole, a person, moreover a black person, from Jamaica. She had come, it was said, and at her own expense, to build a hotel. Or it might be a hospital, or something of the sort, for the succour of invalid officers. She was going to build it at Spring Hill, up beyond Kadikoi, out of whatever she could find. It sounded a strange idea. But then, there was much that was strange in this Crimea.

Scarface was not back, having decided to go up to Sutler's Town. Edward settled down to a game of cards while John looked through the shelf of books that had been provided by the ever-thoughtful Peto, Brassey and Betts. There were several Bibles, prayer and hymn books; and the men said that those would be the gift of Mr Peto, who was an M.P. and a religious man and a man who cared deeply for the spiritual welfare of his workmen. Mr Peto had insisted on two railway missionaries accompanying the Railway Corps.

John took down one of the Bibles and tried to find the story of Hercules, though without success. He did, however, find the Ten Commandments, and returned the book to its shelf feeling an altogether better man.

Scarface came in later with a bunch of others, singing, lurching, fighting amongst themselves.

'Local rotgut. Got it in Vanity Fair. Not cheap, mind.'

Vanity Fair was yet another name for the squalid Sutler's Town.

'Better watch out,' said John, half asleep. 'Or thee'll be

up before the Provost Marshall. Flogged, thee'll be, like that other chap.'

Their day of rest was over.

22

Duty Done

They were pulling on boots at the end of their third Sunday the 4th of March, after too little sleep, getting ready for the night shift. Scarface woke groaning, opened an eye, and curled up again under the blankets. He lay there for a moment or two before swinging himself, with mighty effort, out of his bunk.

Tonight, in the light of many braziers, they were working on the far side of the harbour, in pursuance of the long-conceived plan that the Railway Corps should construct or strengthen wharves and jetties there and lay a railway line to convey goods from that side of the harbour as well as from the beach and thus facilitate the movement of supplies.

On the western side of the harbour, opposite the beach and the town, the rock came down steeply to the water's edge, but at the north-west end there was a landing-place known as Diamond Wharf, adopted as a terminus for heavy siege guns and mortars, some even now waiting their turn aboard a vessel moored alongside. The line, the first hundred yards of which they were tonight ballasting and planking, began on the wharf itself so that equipment could be loaded directly onto trucks. They worked steadily, with rhythm, economy in every movement, never tiring. They were conscious of being the target of quiet admiration.

Scarface, at the beginning, winced with every

swing of the pick. 'Never learn,' he growled.

By the time they had stopped for bait he had recovered somewhat and began to tell them of his adventures that morning.

'Met a bunch o' sodgers. Tellin' us stories, they were. Ship carryin' boots, in't winter when they was so short o' boots, went from Varna ter Balaklava, Balaklava ter Varna, four times afore the Commissariat'd let it land. Another un, carryin' two thousand greatcoats, taken back to Constantinople three times. An' then they wasn't issued cos some bit o' paper says they can't be issued more'n once in three years an' they was s'posed to 'ave 'ad 'em once already. Daft.

'An then there were't sheepskin coats. Just afore us got 'ere, that were. Several 'undred of 'em. Wonderful fer sodgers in fear o' frostbite. But dear me no! No invoice! Can't accept goods without an invoice! Military rules, old boy. An guess name o't ship?' Nobody volunteered. *'Golden Fleece,'* he said triumphantly; and raised a groan.

'Still,' he went on, cheerfully. 'Doin' summat about them wild dogs, they are. Officers, they's organisin' wild dog 'unts, just like they does wi' foxes at 'ome. 'Mostly they's even got red coats but 'ere they shoots the quarry 'stead o' tearin' it ter pieces. Sodger said 'good thing' cos dogs digs up 'is friends what've been buried an' it makes 'im feel upset like. Other lad said no, dogs've got plenty o' food eatin' all them 'osses an' camels an' mules, just lyin' on't top. It's the sodgers or't locals what digs up the corpses, fer the blankets, 'e says. 'Eard that afore, anyways. Run 'orse races as well, them officers. Like Newmarket. 'Ad a grand time on St. Patrick's Day, sweepstakes an' all. Russians could see 'em from Sebastopol an' kept firing. Didna stop 'em though.

'They said that right from't start French bought up any provisions that traders brought in. Then sold 'em ter their sodgers at cost price. Our lot let traders charge't earth. Two shillin' fer a two-pound loaf o' black bread! Three shillin' fer a pound o' butter or a pound o' cheese! Wickedness!

'Camps fer't French are in good order, they said. Clean, plenty o' food, good sheepskin coats fer't men, good boots, bands playin' ter cheer 'em up. Why can't our sodgers get the same? Least they get their coffee beans roasted now though they say it's poor stuff. Boggers can laugh an all, can yer credit it? Cheerful lot, gi'e 'em that, lice an' all.'

'Leastways we'n bin gettin' decent rations,' said John. 'We bein' on the doorstep like.'

'An' Mr Beatty bein' particular,' said Edward.

Through their shift they could hear, as they often did, the grumble and echo of heavy firing and saw the sky to the north lit up over the hills. Balaklava to beyond Kadikoi was defended by Turkish forces which gave the inhabitants security; and Kadikoi itself was the site of a substantial French battery. The Russians had never yet attacked the line, by which omission the Railway Corps were slightly puzzled but for which they were also truly thankful.

Such soldiers as they met continued to be cheerful. The line had already made an enormous difference to their labours, they said.

The engine was now in place on top of French Hill, firmly secured to its platform. The drum and its cable which had been hauled up there had also been fixed into position. Henceforth loaded trucks at the foot of the incline would be detached from the horses which had brought them thus far and attached to the cable, the steam engines winding the cable round the drum to haul them up. At the summit they would be under horse-power again. The line ascending the hill had been made double-track.

On Tuesday night they were told that Lord Raglan and some of his generals had been down to visit Balaklava that day, expressing satisfaction at the order being imposed by the Railway Corps and now being furthered by the army.

'We can do it, boys,' said Mr Beatty.

John thought that if Mr Brassey came top of the respect stakes, Mr Beatty came a likely second; even though he was Irish.

The nobs had also visited the building site of a rising hospital, at last being established at Balaklava, designed to take four hundred patients. It was up on the eastern heights above the town for good clean air; and close to a spring of fresh water.

The weather improved, fine, clear and bright. Optimism was in the air.

On Saturday the weather broke. All day they were swathed in dense, white, wet mist. Then something happened. By the time John's gang went on shift, the news was flying from man to man. There had been men hurt, a death, maybe more.

'Mr Beatty, come as quick as 'e could, 'e did. They told 'im it was Raimondo Martinez as 'ad died. One o' the muleteers. Run over 'e were. Wheel went right over 'im when 'e got tossed out. Right across 'is thighs, it went. 'Ead smashed too. An' chest.'

'Good man, good driver,' John said to Edward, 'Even if 'e bin a Spaniard like.' Edward nodded his head in agreement and sympathy.

'T'other muleteer, injured. Gone to 'ospital, e 'as, they think. An' the brakesman.'

There had been four wagons involved, it transpired, coming down the one-in-fifteen incline from the top of

French Hill. Each of them had a brakesman in charge. One of the brakesmen, John Giles, he in command of the fourth wagon, in which was also one of the Spanish muleteers, had somehow lost control of the brake. The third and fourth wagons had then picked up speed, crashing into the first two. The fourth wagon had mounted the third, on the buffers of which Raimindo, the dead muleteer, had been riding, throwing him off. The fourth wagon then went off the rails, a wheel going over and killing instantly the thrown muleteer, and injuring the navvy brakesman of that errant fourth wagon, who was also now in hospital.

The Spanish contingent began to murmur and gesticulate amongst themselves, staring at the gathering crowd. One of them interpreted for Mr Beatty. It appeared that Raimondo had always worn a leather money-belt. In it was as much as a hundred pounds, some in Spanish gold. It was not on the body. Suspicion began to fall on the navvies who had rushed to the scene. The second muleteer, he of the fourth wagon, was sought as witness. But the second muleteer had never reached the hospital and could no longer be found.

The injured navvy was taken into the care of the surgeon and nurses, another thoughtful part of Railway Corps provision, based in the *Prince of Wales*, now become a Corps hospital ship and anchored in the harbour.

The day following the accident, their fourth Sunday, March 11th, was another day of swirling, dense white. They passed it quietly.

Then they were again on the day-shift. Tuesday was enlivened by the impressive, and unexplained, sight of two thousand French cavalry and infantry massing on the heights, and though they heard heavy firing in the evening, it was from a distance, and nothing befell them.

Although something had befallen John Giles, the injured brakesman. He was at first thought like to live. He spoke to friends who visited. But he too had been terribly gashed, from the splintered bone of the left knee, to inner thigh. In spite of opiates and stimuli he died on that Tuesday before dawn.

John, Edward, and Scarface were on the day-shift and not able to attend the service for the dead navvy, performed by the Reverend Fayers, one of the thoughtful provisions of Peto, Brassey and Betts. John Giles was buried by his comrades, his grave dug as deep as they could in the rocky cemetery overlooking Balaklava, his body well-limed.

The branch line serving the far side of the harbour was finished. John and Edward were re-deployed, to live elsewhere for a while, using their brick-building skills in the construction of a depot to incorporate sheds, platforms and sidings at Kadikoi. If stores were regularly hauled to this point, went the military reasoning, they could be distributed in a shorter time to the front when needed. Scarface, in rich language of his own, expressed the opinion that the military mind worked a little slowly.

The track was now four miles long, creeping beyond Kadikoi, beyond the site of the stationary engine and had reached the French Camp. From there it would go towards their next goal, of headquarters and Lord Raglan's residence on the plateau. Two more lime kilns were being built near the Camp before Sebastopol: the weather was showing signs of warming again and the stench at the front was intensifying.

Scarface was with a gang engaged in blasting limestone to feed the kilns. He came back one day with an air of having a story to tell.

'Blastin' we was, just gettin' on wi't work, when all on a sudden there were this great whistle an' bang. Not one o' our bangs neither. Well, we looks up an' around, an' then Bill, 'e says, "By gum," 'e says. "Gerra look at that," 'e says. An us all looked an' there were't General's tent wi' a big piece tore clean out on it. An' then there's another bang an' this time there's a cloud of earth flung all o'er, an' an almighty cluckin' an' crowin' an' bleatin' an' that, an't shell 'as fell right in't middle o' them animals as General keeps around fer food like.'

A group had been attracted during this speech. 'Frit, was yo?' Edward grinned.

'Went straight ter't nearest officer. Asked fer guns. Cos us knowed 'oo dunnit, see? Us knowed it were them there Russians. Two mile away they were too. Seen our kiln-smoke, like as not. Mistook it fer summat as we might be up to, mebbe. We asked fer a cannon ter let 'em know what's what. Wouldna let us 'ave none though.'

He undid the buttons on his jacket, revealing the source of a bulge that had been drawing John's eye. ' 'Ere y'are, Blackie. Get this inter't pot sharpish. 'Ad ter put it out of its misery, like.' It was a hen. Or most of it.

The Naval Brigade had run short of water. Gangs of navvies were deployed to the rescue using the well-sinking machinery they had brought with them - more contingency thinking on the part of Messrs. Peto, Brassey and Betts - and their hard-honed expertise: the process was little different to that of sinking shafts for tunnels. John and Edward, being two of the only twenty rough-masons/bricklayers of the expedition, were in demand.

A wash-house was being built next to the new military hospital on the heights, making more use of the clear spring-water.

Then it was another day of rest, March the 18th. John had a feeling of satisfaction. They, the once-despised navvies, were truly making a difference. The atmosphere had changed since their arrival. Men, soldiers, were more purposeful, more optimistic. He decided to write to Eliza. He found himself a sheet of paper and an envelope, sat on his bunk, balanced the paper on a book taken from the shelf, eschewing the Bible for something called *A Christmas Carol*, and prepared to begin. What did a person say in a letter? He wrote, *'Dear Eliza,'* and stopped. He chewed the end of his pen. Inspiration seized him. *'I hope you are well. I am very well.'* After a moment or two he got up and went to the door. Outside, and shading his eyes from a brilliance of sunlight, he saw one of the lumbering country wagons that folk called arabas, pulled by a black buffalo.

He wandered around, searching for a suitable twig to fray at the end and use as a toothbrush, thinking the while.

He'd seen oxen and camels and dromedaries. He thought that Eliza might like to know about strange things like that. And maybe about the whitewashed, two-storeyed houses, those which still stood, where the animals lived underneath and the family climbed by an outside stair to a verandah which ran the length of one large room with a small bedroom at each end. They did their cooking at a corner of the verandah, which was protected by a roof, overhanging to four or five feet. There were raw-necked vultures, kites and ravens soaring and swooping above; and wild flowers in untrodden parts and the odd flowering shrub on the hillside which had escaped being dug up for fuel. He would put a few late snowdrops or crocuses into the letter, if he could find any, and violets. He'd do it circumspectly though, so that nobody saw. And he would not write about the corpses, nor the rats.

They were back on nights and capriciously whirled away was the warmth of yesterday. It meant a return to thick waistcoats and waterproofs, at least until the heat of activity caused them to shed garments again.

At bait time they lit up their pipes and settled to their biscuit, cooked salt pork and onions. One man began on a story, a somewhat rambling one, which told of a ship's captain being told to fetch oats for the cavalry horses. 'Vital, it were, vital. So the captain sets off an' comes back with oats. But is 'e allowed to land 'em? No. Waits ten days, then 'e's told to fetch hay. No argument. So off 'e goes to Constantinople again an' brings back hay. Waits another ten days. Can't land. Told to go an' get oats. No argument. Orders, it is. Look, on paper. So goes to Constantinople to get oats which 'e's already got. Constantinople thanks 'im for bringin' in the oats. Cos they needs 'em at Balaklava, urgent.'

They all laughed, though Scarface looked unconvinced.

By the 26th of March, six weeks since the *Mohawk's* arrival, the line had reached the depot at Lord Raglan's headquarters on the plateau, four and a half miles from Balaklava and about midway between Balaklava and the troops at the front. With that and the Diamond Wharf branch and the line now made double between Balaklava and Kadikoi with the second stationary engine in place, it meant that the Railway Corps had completed over seven miles of railway in seven weeks. A haulage task which had once absorbed the energies of 17,000 soldiers was being effected by 500 navvies with a railway.

That railway was now transporting weaponry, ammunition, hutting and, essential for life, provisions. Lord Raglan had spoken. Commissariat-General Filder had been forced to change the order of things as sanctified by Wellington. Salt meat, biscuit and groceries for the frontline troops were at last being moved by rail.

There was, these last few days, almost a superfluity of some things. Items once all but unobtainable: books, stationary, clothing, their dire need written of by the special correspondents or in soldiers' letters made public, had touched the hearts of the British people and had been responded to with overwhelming generosity.

Gangs of navvies were extending the line even beyond headquarters, turning from west to north-east, away from the coast and in the direction of Inkerman, towards where, about seven miles from Balaklava, the line would finish as it came to be crossed by the Woronzov Road. That road ran south from Sebastopol and, by reason of Sebastopol being at the head of a long inlet, ran inland and roughly parallel with the coast.

On the top of the plateau the line had to bridge a series of ravines draining water northwards from the heights towards Sebastopol: the skilled men of the Railway Corps took this in their stride and pushed ever onwards.

As John and the others travelled up and down the line to their work of the day, they passed an iron storehouse and a number of wooden sheds, erected next to the railway, halfway between Balaklava and the Col.

It was a sort of hospital and dispensary and the abode of the strange Mrs Seacole. She treated everyone who needed her, not only officers but ordinary soldiers and navvies too. What was more, she did not charge for her powders and potions, recipes learnt, it was said, in the course of her travels in the Americas. Even more laudable than Mr. Seacole's refusal to accept payment was that her remedies, particularly against cholera and diarrhoea, actually met with success. The camps were being encouraged in cleanliness: even so cholera was about again, though there had been few deaths so far, due partly perhaps to Mrs Seacole.

She was often seen in or after any skirmish, riding out to the battlefield with her basket of remedies, to help and comfort the wounded. Men she'd treated spoke of her care for her fellow-creatures; and blessed her.

Although the French had long had a very serviceable road from their harbour at Kamiesh, it was being noised abroad that their commander General Canrobert was so impressed by the railway, saying that it could take up twenty guns in less time and at less cost than he could take up one, that he wanted a railway of his own, built moreover by the firm of Peto, Brassey and Betts. The navvies, on hearing this, transferred restrained pride into extra effort. They were making good progress; and the weather had managed one of its stage effects and for a few days was magnificent, hot as a hot July day in England.

On the Thursday and Friday there was an increase of gunfire, the Russians making sorties, they were told. But nothing decisive was taking place. It was war, yes, but on a very small scale. Nothing of much note had happened since Eupatoria in the first week of their arrival, and that had been up-country.

All Fools' Day was a Sunday, the end of their seventh week. They went into the still-redolent though newly white-walled Balaklava after spending a while scraping mud from clothes and boots, cleaning and mending, washing themselves. Something was up. They could hear shouts and screeches of mock fear. A bull had somehow landed alive on shore: usually the cattle were killed aboard and their carcasses put into wagons on the quay before being transported up to the camp before Sebastopol. This bull was not dead but very much alive and was making desperate efforts to stay so. Off-duty soldiers, navvies, sightseers, were trying to corral it and running off as it hurled itself at them. It was a bull without horns, but it was fighting for its life. Men hurled stones from the safety of walls, tried to drive it with sticks. John, Edward and Scarface joined in. Over an hour back and forth through the streets of Balaklava it took before the bull wearied and the men tired of their game. John imagined himself writing to Eliza, telling her of his exploits as a bullfighter. It was an animal of courage though, he thought, and the shooting of it somehow less than it deserved, though he'd never say as much for fear of ridicule.

That week also saw the railway transporting its first human cargo apart from themselves. Four wagons of sick and wounded soldiers, loaded at headquarters, propped against knapsacks in lieu of pillows - an effort was belatedly being made to keep a soldier and his knapsack together - came comfortably down to Balaklava in less than half an hour. What a difference from dangling askew across the saddle of a stumbling, half-starved mule. They would go to the hospital on the heights above the old Genoese castle.

On the Thursday they were meeting up for the night shift when they were met by a series of rumours from the gang returning: 'Accident on the incline.' 'Men dead.' 'Soldier dead.' 'Mr Beatty hurt.' 'Mr Beatty thrown out of a wagon.'

Curly came from the rear of the crowd. 'Bad news,' he said grimly. 'Mr Beatty, 'e won't be with yer tonight.'

' 'Ow bad?'

'Bruised bad. 'E can walk though. Day or two's rest should see 'im right.'

'Whereabouts did it 'appen?' John asked, though he almost knew the answer.

Curly nodded. 'Same place as last time.'

Over the course of a couple of days the story was pieced together. Three hundred men of the 71st Regiment of Foot had been sent up, on mule-back, to work on the trenches before Sebastopol. Returning in the evening, they convened at Lord Raglan's headquarters, where the

General himself inspected them, and where the men were handed cups of hot coffee. Most graciously, when one of the men fell sick, Lord Raglan helped him onto a mule with his own hand.

Wishing to spare the men marching all the way back to their quarters, Lord Raglan suggested they return by rail. The group of infantry then marched the few hundred yards to the railway terminus and climbed into the wagons. Going down the incline towards Kadikoi from French Hill the loaded wagons gathered speed. Brakes were applied, but the brakes would not hold: there may have been dew on the rails. At twenty miles an hour or more, a wagon left the track, men were pitched out. One died on the spot, one was like to lose a leg, many others suffered injuries, some severe. Two officers were bruised. Mr Beatty was with the train and 'has sustained a slight shaking, but is now quite well.'

Mr Beatty took very little time off duty, but when he returned, zealous as ever, he looked very drawn and he winced at times.

April the 9th was a Monday. There had been intimations that something momentous was about to happen.

Thirty-three wagons a day had been employed the previous week transporting immense quantities of armaments from Balaklava to as near as the railway had got to the siege lines. Eighteen hundred barrels of gunpowder had gone up the line. Ten thirteen-inch mortars with six hundred thirteen-inch shells to match had travelled: and each of those shells had weighed one hundred and ninety pounds. A ten-ton crane had been taken up the line to headquarters to help with the off-loading. There was now a station there.

Six hundred stretchers and two hundred extra tents had gone, by wagon, up to the heights.

Lord Raglan had inspected the trenches and surveyed the battle lines.

The Electric Telegraph had now lumbered and ploughed and completed its magic wires from Lord Raglan's headquarters on the top of the plateau clear to Kadikoi and from there down to Balaklava. Cable had been laid into the siege lines. Communications, ordnance and ammunition supplies were ripe for battle.

Before daybreak on that Monday, in a wind blowing enough to whip away the tents of the unfortunate and half-drown them in furies of rain, a bombardment began. The brothers and Scarface were on the day-shift, but were woken early by the sudden intense din. This was different from anything John had yet heard. The others in the hut sat upright, listening to a wind-blown roar which seemed to shake heaven and earth, overlaid with heavier dull booms of bomb and mortar. One occasional sound stood out. It was identified as the sound of the great Lancaster muzzle-loader which could fire a sixty-eight-pound shell. Each shell cost a fabulous thirty-five pounds and, fired from the Lancaster, was nicknamed the 'express train', because after the sharp crack of the initial explosion, that was the sound the mighty shell most resembled as it flew with a whistling roar towards its target over three and a half miles away.

The bombardment, over the sixteen-mile length of the front, lasted all day, diminishing somewhat through the night and resurging the next day, through dense fog and rain and gale. The sea lashed itself into foam.

There was a third day and a fourth and a fifth and then a sixth, all the Allied artillery firing upon the besieged fortress of Sebastopol from ravine, from ridge, from plain, from land and from sea. Surely nothing made by man could withstand such an onslaught. Occasionally the weather cleared but mostly it continued wild and wet.

The wounded were arriving constantly by rail from headquarters, having been first picked up from the field by horse or mule ambulance. Amputees, their operation performed in the field, and those with severe wounds were taken to the Balaklava hospital, the rest put on board ship for Scutari or elsewhere.

The Railway Corps under the indefatigable Mr Beatty lent themselves with a will to loading and driving the wagons. More ammunition was required, more mortars, more guns. The supplies were there and the Railway Corps could move them.

Over days the intensity of the battle continued. By the 16th it was diminishing slightly, though trucks were still groaning under the weight of the ammunition they were transporting up to the plateau. On the 17th and just as their night-shift was coming to an end and a dense night fog clearing, Edward pointed upwards. Silhouetted against the lightening sky was a horseman, swiftly joined by more. They stood looking down upon the town; and then suddenly they had gone. Later they learnt that the strangers had been Russian cavalry estimated at several hundred and accompanied by a body of the feared Cossacks. Probably on reconnaissance, it was said.

By the 20th of April the fighting had fallen to skirmishes again. And still the fortress of Sebastopol held. Men and provisions and armaments could be continually supplied from its rear; and as fast as one bastion was demolished it was again reinforced, making particular use of the night hours when the Allied fire was less heavy. Russian engineers had created a spider-work of defences: stakes, deep ditches and the like, outside the walls, between the fortress and the Allied lines, so that the town could not be stormed on foot. Sebastopol seemed impregnable.

By Sunday 22nd there was scarcely a gunshot. The weather in its unpredictable way had turned hot. They went out into Balaklava.

'Bit of a whiff,' said Curly, sniffing the wind.

'Well, gone 'ot, aint it?' said Scarface, joining him.

'Be the cemeteries, likely,' said Erc. 'Need more lime, I reckons.'

'I bin worryin' about the water,' said John. 'Only one spring bin left, an' one little stream, that's still got sweet water in it. All the rest got rubbish chucked into 'em or got filled in wi' rubble. Not much water this morning, there wunna.'

'Funny, aint it?' said Erc. 'First too much water by a long chalk. Now too little.'

A van lumbered past. Erc waved and the man on the box behind the single horse waved back. There was a sign affixed to the side of the vehicle: *Photographic Van*. 'Mr Fenton,' explained Erc, though everyone knew that already. The van was about at all hours, taking photographs of all and sundry. Mr Fenton had taken photographs of the harbour, the railway sheds off the beach and of their huts and of themselves at work. They stared at the flimsy-looking vehicle with its tiny window and large wheels and its rear doors which could open. Someone said it had once belonged to a wine-merchant.

They had observed Fenton at work before: people had to be arranged by Mr Fenton in front of his wooden box on legs; and then stand very still while he dashed into his van and out with his covered glass plate. This he would then slot into the front of the box to catch the likeness. A few seconds later Mr Fenton would disappear back into the darkness of the van, where he worked more magic using the mysterious photographic apparatus within. In something like fifteen minutes you could view an oddity where dark and light were reversed: those glass-plate

315

'negatives' had to be sent back to England to be transformed into true likenesses on paper. It was the latest thing in photography and very fast. 'Everything's getting very fast,' said John, to nobody in particular.

The railway was being commended by everyone for the speed of its progress. They were now almost up to the Woronzov Road, about seven miles from Balaklava and had begun a spur round Cathcart's Hill, last resting place of officers, including General George Cathcart, veteran of Waterloo, killed at the Battle of Inkerman. The spur of about a mile took the line to the 3rd and 4th Divisions and the left siege train. The railway would thus be supplying depots at both the right and the left of the siege lines. It would have reached its zenith.

Personages from Britain were occasionally to be seen in Balaklava. On the 26th of April, a Thursday, an unfamiliar ship, a paddle-driven gunboat, the *Caradoc*, nosed its way round Castle Point into the harbour. It was early: the men of hut Brassey were pulling on their moleskin trousers and looking for their hats. From the flurries of activity outside, the sharp military shouts, the sounds of pipe and drum, of voices redolent with respect, it was deduced that this was no ordinary visitor; and indeed, gossip soon gave the newcomer a name. This was Lord Stratford de Redcliffe, more familiarly known to his peers as Canning, Britain's ambassador to, and friend of, Turkey, enemy of all things Russian.

'What bin 'e 'ere for, then?' asked John, of no-one in particular.

'Picked a grand day for it, whatever it bin,' said Edward. The weather had made its decision to stay hot and Balaklava was looking, though far from smelling, at its best.

He had come accompanied by wife, daughters, other

ladies and gentlemen, all so elegant and beautiful as to be beings from another universe. Men starved of female company nudged each other and muttered obscenities. An officer was heard to observe that the ladies had 'produced a most lively impression on the troops'. Hopefully the ladies were spared the exact and intimate details of the 'impression'; and were also spared the news of a resurgence of typhus.

Hearsay abounded over the next few days.

The noble Lord had come to see Lord Raglan, to clear up matters raised by the Commission of Enquiry into the conduct of the War, taking place in London.

He had come to confer with General Canrobert.

He had come to advise on the course of the siege.

He had come to be shown a marvel of the modern age. At the beginning of the war, communications between the Crimea and London had taken some twenty days. In the last two weeks, over three hundred miles of submarine telegraphic cable had been laid across the Black Sea. It began its sea-travels near Varna. It ended them at the monastery of St. George near Balaklava on the coast of the Crimea. A short land-connection on either side enabled Lord Raglan, from the time of Lord Stratford's visit onwards, to communicate with his masters in London - 1,600 miles away - almost within the hour.

Firing had diminished since the 25th, on which day the noble Lord had been expected, though had not arrived on time. For three days the guns fell silent, until the night of the 27th when Lord Stratford's gunboat slipped away amid a renewed ferocity of artillery and small arms fire. The railway had used those three days to send up ammunition enough to satisfy any future hunger of the guns.

But the work of its makers was almost finished.

23

Home is the Hero

It was the 3rd of May. They were leaning on the stern rail, gazing back at the retreating land.

'Yo canna see an 'arbour nowhere,' said John, with mild surprise. 'From the sea yo wunna know 'twas there.'

The hills between which lay the little town of Balaklava, centre of their lives for so long, were growing smaller, whilst the stretch of coast to either side spread wider, and lowered itself until it became a smudged line on the horizon. And then there was only sea.

' 'Ow long did we tek to get 'ere?' asked Edward.

'Fifty,' said John after some thought. 'Fifty days. Started December 24th 1854. Got to Balaklava February 12th 1855. Should be quicker goin' 'ome on this 'ere fine ship.'

They were on the *Prince of Wales*, iron-built screw steamer. They turned with one accord and surveyed their vessel. A large funnel amidships belched smoke above their heads. Three short masts held only rigging.

'S'pose they'n got sails for if the engine breaks down,' said Edward tentatively.

'Mun go down an' look at that there engine,' said John. 'Sometime, like, when we'n got the lie o' the land. Or the ship,' he added, after a pause.

'Wonder what owd Scarface bin doin' now? While we'm 'ere eatin' an' drinkin' an' sleepin' an' all paid for, like Lords o' the Land?'

318

For the contract made by Peto, Brassey and Betts had come to an end. Mr Beatty had said he could manage without some of his workforce, masons and bricklayers for example, but others, such as miners and drivers, he needed, at least for a while. Scarface, a miner among his many talents, had remained behind, moving into a hut with Erc. The two had ideas in common.

The government had been impressed by the Railway Corps, so impressed that they were forming an entirely new Army department, an Army Work Corps to make their debut in the running of the railway where they would be trained initially by Mr Beatty and such of the Railway Corps who were staying on. The new Corps was even now being organised by Mr Joseph Paxton who, as everyone was aware, had been the architect of the Crystal Palace.

Mr Beatty the brothers had, emboldened by their near departure, bid goodbye with a hearty handshake and wishes of goodwill. Each had noticed independently that he looked far from well, though he seemed to be driving himself as hard as ever.

'Ne'er been right sin' that there accident,' said John. 'Dwindered, 'e looks.'

The two of them had decided that enough was, after all, enough. Edward was eager to get back to Ann and the two little girls, Jemima and Ann. His wife would have used much of the weekly pound sent back home, he thought, for her upkeep, though he still had the most of what he had been paid in the Crimea.

John, with twelve pounds to his name and, if Eliza had, as agreed except in the case of dire want, saved the whole pound a week sent to her, was now the master of twenty-three pounds ten shillings and ninepence-ha'penny, more money than he'd ever had at one time. Enough, well, enough to rent a house for at least a year.

'I'd want a mighty good 'ouse for that,' said Edward.

'Six rooms at the least. An' a water closet. An' all in good order.'

'Get more'n that in S'ewsb'ry. Six rooms, cellar, garden, brew'ouse an' stables, I reckons.'

'Dost still think Birmingham?' he asked after a pause.

'Like to be our best bet,' said Edward. 'Be building a-plenty in a town like that. Folks comin' in from all parts lookin' for work, settin' up in trade. An all needin' 'ouses an' that.'

'An' workshops an' churches an' shops an' schools an' better grand buildings,' said John.

Neither brother had looked forward with enthusiasm to resuming the uncertainties of a roaming life. Each had confessed to a desire to settle in one place as paterfamilias. 'I'm lookin' forward to a clutch o' lads,' said John. 'Set up a business. Evans, Kirby an' Sons.'

'An' beer,' he continued longingly, as they made their way towards the mess. 'A pint o' good English beer, that's what I'm a-waitin' for. Ne'er got used to rum, meself, though there were plenty of it. Or porter.' They had been able to buy a pint of porter at cost price three times a week.

Their vessel was moving out into deeper waters. 'Ten knots, they says she does,' said Edward. 'Not so steady as she was neither,' he added. The wind was stronger and the waves were beginning to heap up alarmingly.

' 'Appen I s'll put off breakfast a while,' said John, as the deck dropped from under his feet.

Their next landfall would be Constantinople, on the further side of the Black Sea, three hundred and fifty or so miles away. It took them two days, during which the good ship *Prince of Wales* rolled alarmingly, a fault, they were told, of many screw steamers. The vessel steadied as it entered the Bosphorus, that narrow and crowded strait with Constantinople at its end: though neither brother felt desirous of exploration ashore while the vessel coaled up, even had they been allowed.

There were forty returning navvies aboard and a handful of army officers, all in the charge of Captain Raymond, a familiar figure as it was he who had supervised the ships of the Railway Corps in Balaklava harbour. There were two men on board sick. Only one man of the whole Railway Corps had died of sickness, of typhus fever, a foreman carpenter. Apart from that, two men had died in the two accidents on the steep incline down from French Hill. The rest of the workforce were both said to be, and felt, healthy, happy and contented.

'Them doctors an' nurses had summat to do wi' it,' said Edward. 'Jest 'em bein' there's bin a right good thing. An' a deal o' fine food.'

'An' we 'ad plenty o' rest. An' Sundays off, like,' added John. 'An' no sleepin' on wet ground neither. An' plenty o' good clothes. Bet Granddad would a give 'is arm for one o' them painted coats as kept out the rain. 'Stead of 'is owd mou'dywarp-skin, dost remember?'

'Them boots'll last us a while,' said Edward. Then, as a thought struck him, 'Dost think as they'll want 'em all back?'

'Nah, not Peto, Brassey an' Betts. Not out for they pound o' flesh, bin they? Remember them three men as stole their shipmates' clothes on the way out in January an' got court-martialled? Then got drunk soon as they landed an' got put in clink? They'n bin sent back passage paid. An' they'n bin paid for the voyage out, 'cause that were the agreement. Bin very generous to us, have Peto, Brassey an' Betts. Fancy payin' us to do nothin' an' nowt aboard this 'ere ship.'

Mr Peto as good as owned the ship, they were told. It belonged to the fleet of the North of Europe Steam Navigation Company, of which Mr Peto was head and had been lent to the Railway Corps from the outset.

After Constantinople the brothers began to get their sea-legs. Crossing the Sea of Marmara saw the wind calm, the sun shine and the rain become infrequent. The Corps lay on deck, played cards, smoked their pipes, swapped stories of derring-do and hard times, and spoke of what they might do next. Lines of song were picked up and improved upon.

'I've built a workin' railway in god-forsaken lands,
Kept the Army of Old England from disgrace at foreign hands.
I rallied to my country's call, faced danger o'er the sea
An' now I'm sailin' home again, I'm sailin' back to thee.
An' I've done it like a navvy, a bold navvy man.
Oh, I've done me graft an' stuck it like a bold navvy man.'

Some thought the great days of the railways back home were largely over. Some were gripped by a spirit of adventure and thought they'd try their luck in far-off countries. Some dreamed of mighty bridges still to be built, mountains to tunnel through, desolate wastes to cross.

Seven days after leaving Constantinople they had passed through the Dardanelles, entered the Aegean Sea and were heading into the sun. The sky was a cloudless blue. The wind was hardly enough to puff out a sail. They shed even waistcoats, then shirts. So many islands.

A thought of the *Erebus* and the *Terror* flitted unbidden into John's mind; and he tried to picture the ships and their crew on their own very different sea-journey in that grim, snow-swirling, white-frozen north. Another explorer, one of the many seekers of their fate, had returned at the end of last year with news long-awaited, garnered from the Esquimaux; but odious news, of ships crushed in ice, of starvation and death: news most shockingly of cannibalism, though almost everyone agreed that John Rae should have refused to believe the savage Esquimaux. It was much more likely that the savages themselves had murdered and eaten those fine British explorers than that such flowers of British manhood could ever have sunk to that pit of moral degradation.

John gazed out over the warm blue water and thought how small were the chances of retrieving one of those tin canisters; and how much the explorers would have appreciated the new electric telegraph.

'Know something as I dunna miss about the Crimea?' asked Edward reminiscently, pouring a bucket of water over his naked torso.

John grunted.

'Flies,' said Edward. ' 'Undreds o' thousands o' flies.'

Then they were heading west again. On the 12th of May they reached Malta. They were making good time, they were told.

'I'm a-comin' to like this 'ere lollockin'.' said John. Day after day they had spent lazing. They had been down to the boiler room where stokers, stripped to the waist, sweat running down their backs leaving paler streaks in the black dust, spent hour upon hour shovelling coal into the insatiable maw of the engine. It was dangerous work: boilers had been known to burst, steam peeling the skin from a man's body, leaving him a bloody, dying fruit.

They viewed the island, or such of it as they could see. The sea was a magnificent turquoise, the water clear. There were flat-topped cliffs of white limestone. The land was green, but curiously bare. 'No trees,' said John. It was most gloriously warm.

The harbour, thick with craft, was fortress-like, sun-bleached, buildings rising like stone cliffs, barren.

They went ashore. 'Not the weather for workin' in,' said John.

They spotted a dome and made towards it through

narrow streets, a clamour of sellers and buyers, fabrics and pottery and silverware. They had a sense of the innumerable intricacies of the world and their own tiny sphere in it.

Then it was Gibraltar, remembered affectionately from their trip out. That mighty rock they left on the 20th of May.

'Home stretch now, boys,' said a sailor. 'Look out fer a puff or two.'

They came round the bottom of Portugal and headed north for the feared Bay of Biscay. The weather cooled. A wind sprang up, waves rose in disarray and spat across the decks, but the ship steamed steadily northwards.

'Good time, we made,' said the sailor. 'Thirty hours Finisterre to Ushant, three 'undred an' fifty mile to you, near enough. Be 'ome in no time.'

The shores of England grew from a distant line into a flat green canvas which wrapped its arms about them and sucked them in as bay became estuary and then wide tidal river. They anchored on the south bank of the Thames at Gravesend at 2pm on Saturday the 26th of May in the year of our Lord 1855. Home at last.

'Canna wait,' said Edward.

They were in the train within a few minutes of Wolverhampton, looking out of the window, pointing out familiar landmarks.

John nodded. He wanted to see Eliza. Particularly he was curious. Would she have a belly on her, or not? He thought it would be good if she had, the first of that tribe of sons he was hoping for. But she'd said nothing in her letters. On the other hand, he supposed it would be more easy to find a place to set up home and look for a job when unencumbered by a baby. He was determined to marry her, become respectable, the both of them. Just get settled first, he thought.

'We'll go 'ome for starters,' said Edward. 'Tell 'em the plan. Then termorrer or next day, we two'll go back to Brummagem, find lodgin's an' the women can come an' join us.'

They walked in through the door of 100, Russell Street and were met with first, cries of surprise, followed by callings shouted to others, who came running amid a flurry of hugs and kisses mingled with exclamations at the growth and precocity of the two little girls, Jemima remembering and clinging to Edward's legs, Ann hiding her face in her mother's skirts, not recognising the stranger.

Someone ran round to next door and out rushed Mrs Mansell in her apron, her cap awry, followed by Ann Laetitia, Sarah Jane, Elizabeth, George Edward and Amelia, all of whom goggled at the heroes who had come home from a war far, far away over the sea.

'Dear 'eart alive. Yo'm back. Yo'm back. We reads everythink, we reads all about yo,' said Mrs Mansell, the words tumbling over themselves. 'Ev'ry week George were readin' it all out ter us, out o' the paper. 'Ow 'ard yo was a-workin' an' 'ow the railway was a-growin' an' that. 'Eroes, yo are. They all say it, everyone's sayin' it. Savin' them poor sodgers.'

'Thomas an' James'll be back soon,' said Mrs Roberts, wobbling hot water onto a plentiful heap of her best tea. 'An' Mr Roberts.'

'An' Mr Mansell,' put in her neighbour, who was as merry and chatty as they remembered, if somewhat wider in girth. 'An' yo'll be goin' round to the *Prince o' Wales* for a drink, I shunna wonder.'

'I mun go get Eliza,' said John.

'Oh, my stars yes,' said Mrs Roberts. 'Surely they'll

spare 'er on a day like this. You'm 'eroes yo knows.'

Amid more cries of welcome, hearty handshakes and hugs and promises from Elisa's stonemason employer to join them all later in the *Prince of Wales*, Eliza was indeed spared for the evening.

John put his arm round her small, firm waist and kissed her hair, nuzzling his face into its softness. His hands strayed.

'Now, John Kirby,' she said. 'Jest 'cos thee's an 'ero dunna entitle thee to everythin' thee wants.'

'But dunna thee love me? Jest a little?'

'When we'm married, thee can love me 'owever thee likes.'

'See thee inna wi' child.'

'An' best not. Not till we'n bin wed.'

However, she didn't move his arm from her waist but snuggled closer while they wove their way, drunk with desire, as close as a limpet and its rock, to the *Prince of Wales.*

The tavern, whose name John thought most appropriate in view of their recent transport, was full. As they entered, men rose to their feet and cheered. Even the taciturn Mansell managed a smile. Edward was already surrounded by a crowd, a troupe of pints standing on the table before him. He caught sight of them and waved them over. Ann, sitting at his side, was pink with pride. Eliza was offered a chair with a flourish. The crowd were greedy for their stories, which, as the evening wore on, began to acquire more than a sheen of varnish. It was a wonderful evening.

Morning dawned. John groaned. Evenings like that of last night had to be paid for. But there were decisions to be made, things to be done. He crawled out of bed.

In the kitchen Mrs Roberts was already up, the fire lit, the kettle on the hob.

'Shall yo go an' see your fam'ly back in S'ewsb'ry?'

'Best get work first, an' lodgin's. Brummagem today.'

But Edward disagreed. 'Mam'll be wantin' to see us, after all this time. Best go there first thing, tell 'em our plans, like. Sleep there tonight. Birmin'am can wait another day.'

So it was decided. And their reception as they progressed through the taverns of the Abbey Foregate and up Castle Hill, toasting innumerable 'Friends around the Wrekin', was little different from the previous evening. Their father and grandfather basked in reflected glory and John was filled with a feeling of contentment in himself, a feeling of wholeness and rightness. He could, he thought, turn his hand to anything. Not only his own folk, but others too, believed in him. He was not just a navvy, a disregarded serf from the bottom of the heap: he was a person of account at last. 'Respected I am. Respected.'

Two nights were spent in Shrewsbury instead of one, catching up on old friends and family news. Their time abroad seemed like a chasm, an age, to the brothers but, when calculated, proved to be a mere five months. In the land they'd left behind nothing much had changed. No-one of interest had married or died during their absence, though Aunt Rachel, married to her soldier William Brown, had written to say that she'd given birth to a son in Londonderry and named him for his father.

'Corp'ral, 'e is now,' said John's grandmother, proud that at least one errant daughter had retrieved her standing. 'Six-footer an' all.'

'An' blind,' put in her son. He sniffed. 'Knew 'e'd not be a proper feller,' he said disparagingly. ' 'Ow can 'e be a sodger when 'e's blind, anyhow?'

' 'Appened when 'e bin abroad. Fightin' for Queen an'

Country an' all,' said Owd S'ewsb'ry. ' 'E bin on sentry duty, see. In China, 'Ong Kong they calls it.'

'Mighty rum name, that.' S'ewsb'ry spat neatly into the fire.

'Consarn it, man, it were a foreign place,' shouted Owd S'ewsb'ry, having remembered just in time that he was in the presence of ladies. 'That's where they goes to, sodgers. Foreign places. Anyhow, 'e's on sentry duty, an' doin' 'is duty above an' beyond, an' the cold gets in 'is eyes an' blinds 'im. An' 'e's bin in 'ospital six times an' they canna do nothink for 'im. But now 'e's bin discharged. Wi' a pension, a Corp'ral's pension. So put that in your pipe an' smoke it yo knaggy owd man.'

John's father snorted and relapsed into silence.

'An' then they'll be comin' back 'ere,' said Susanna as a final word. 'To S'ewsb'ry. Wi' that grand pension. An' a fine son an' all.'

Then they were on their way. In Birmingham they tramped the streets looking for lodgings. Hockley Hill lay to the north of the centre, past what they were told was the jewellery quarter. Fields, where cows had for centuries sheltered under oak trees, were turning to raw earth, raw earth turning to red brick. The area was full of new housing, thin three-storey terraces and courts of cheap back-to-backs interspersed with more substantial properties. There were workshops full of the noise of metal being ground, hammered or cut; workshops spilling goods, boxes, barrels onto the pavement; smoke from chimneys; the shouting of orders; the clatter of horses' hooves; the rumble of drays. All around them was a most satisfactory landscape of brick, John noted with the eye of his trade.

Ann and the girls would come as soon as Edward had found work. Power, the master stonemason, had confirmed what Eliza had told John: his business was failing. He himself was not well. Their only recourse was to return to his wife's parents in West Derby. It would be a squeeze fitting them all in to the little house in Back Lane, but they were good people and would take them in. In the meantime they would be glad of Eliza's help until they made the final move: it would not be long, he said.

They found a house to rent in Hockley Hill. Both men found building work: there was plenty of it. Ann soon arrived by train with the two little girls and made their lives comfortable.

They had been following the progress of the war in the papers. It was wondrous to read of events in the Crimea, over 1,600 miles away, within a day or so of their happening: it was as if time itself had changed in the few months since they had left for the war. News from Australia on the other hand arrived three months out of date. John wondered if people who had been transported or gone to settle there would ever in the future be able to send news of some triumph or tragedy almost instantly, instead of it as now being received long after the event.

There had been more onslaughts on Sebastopol, but the war went on. The Commission which had been investigating the conduct of the war came, after putting 21,000 questions, to its conclusion. The summary of the Report in the *Birmingham Journal* picked out words such as such as 'unsatisfactory', 'neglect and incompetence', 'dreadful consequences', 'suffering', 'mismanagement', 'an inadequate force', 'fraud and corruption' among contractors. It apportioned blame to, among others, Lord Stratford, who had made that short visit with his women-folk. He, they said, as long-term ambassador to Turkey, ought to have been aware of Russian policy and strength but left the Government in ignorance. Lord Raglan too was censured.

The 18th of June saw one further abortive attempt on

Sebastopol by the Allies. Lord Raglan had made yet another wrong decision, was the consensus. The totals of those dead from wounds and sickness, the numbers of the merely wounded and the merely ill, were depressing.

Lord Raglan himself fell ill with some complaint said to be akin to cholera: newspapers carried the story. The illness was brief. On the morning of the 28th of June he seemed improved. But shortness of breath overcame him. He fell into a coma and died about nine o' clock that evening.

In one of those odd courtesies of war the Russian guns fell silent, to be replaced by the Dead March echoing from the Crimean hills, as his corpse was escorted in solemn procession to *HMS Caradoc* and from there shipped back in state to be entombed among his illustrious forbears. The Queen's message, extolling his 'great and brilliant services' was read out in the Lords. Newspapers talked of 'among the bravest of the brave'. Any mention of misdoings was lost.

'What dost think?' John asked Edward.

'All them men dead,' said Edward. 'An 'e's bin in charge, 'annad 'e? Wunna fit for the job, I thinks.'

'I agrees wi' thee,' said John.

In September Eliza arrived at the house on Hockley Hill with a large amount of luggage, her 'bottom drawer' as she informed John.

'Bin collectin' it up for years, sin' I first met thee, John Kirby,' she said.

The *Birmingham Gazette* of the 1st of October carried a description of the fall of Sebastopol so frightful in its descriptions of the scenes that met the victors when at last they penetrated within its walls, that John hid his newspaper. Eliza found it and read with tears in her eyes. The Russians, after all, were human like ourselves, she said.

In the window of one of the shops in town, they spotted a map and John tried to trace, for Eliza's benefit, the journey he had made and the land he had been to. He was shocked.

'Crimea, 'er's so small,' he repeated for the third time. 'An' look, there's Balaklava an' there's Sebastopol an' they're only on a teeny-weeny corner of a teeny little place.'

His eyes were drawn beyond the small peninsula of the Crimea to the vast, spreading landmass to its north. He jabbed his finger at it. 'Look, look at that. 'Er's Russia. 'Er's like a mortal great crinoline wi' Crimea small as the toe on a slipper comin' from under.'

'Look o'er there, at Ireland. Yo mun get three Crimeas into that. An' all them men died, or they'll ne'er be the same no more. An' all for a town an' a few snippets o' land.' He shook his head and drew his lips tight.

The newspapers, though they would never quite agree, told them that about 25,000 British soldiers had died and that for every soldier dying in battle, over six times as many had died of disease.

'An' the French lost four times as many as that,' said Edward.

'An' think o' them Russians,' put in Eliza.

'More'n all the Allies put together,' said John, gloomily.

John took Eliza into the jewellery quarter to choose a ring. They were to marry on the 15th, a Monday, at St. George in the Fields, a modern edifice from the environs of which the 'fields' were fast disappearing.

'It's beautiful,' was Eliza's comment, as she viewed its square and battlemented tower and its dozens of slender pinnacles, its great arched windows of coloured glass, the traceries of ironwork in window frame and gallery.

331

'We'll not fill it,' she added when they went into its vast space to hear the banns read.

John, when asked, had declared himself to be of full age. Which he surely was, bar a month of course, but what was that? Eliza, they decided, should also declare herself to be of full age. This was stretching the truth rather much, as Eliza was only eighteen. However, she was an orphan; and there was nobody to object.

Edward was one of the witnesses on that October day in 1855, the sunlight soft, the trees thinning of their autumn-scented leaves as they walked the half-mile to the church.

John wore an elderly jacket with wide lapels, well-brushed for the occasion, with a pair of not-too-old trousers. His shirt, though, was white and new and of the fashion, with a high, upstanding collar and a large bow-tie at its neck. He had, at his bride's pleading, cultivated, au Albert, a neatly trimmed moustache and long sideburns which almost joined beneath the chin; and felt somewhat conspicuous and uncomfortable.

The bride in question had found a second-hand heavy-cotton dress with a pointed waist and bell-shaped skirt, made magnificently full with the help of all the petticoats she could muster. It had the tint of autumn leaves, which meant that it not only echoed the season and would be of service for many a coming year, but also showed off the glistening chestnut hair, gathered, for today, into a heavy bun under a set-back bonnet.

Aided by that natural grace of movement which delighted the eye, she felt, and looked, beautiful.

It was a quiet ceremony, officiated by the curate.

'We'd need be grand folk to get the Vicar,' said John.

He signed his name 'Kirbey' as his family often did, embellishing the 'K' with as many curlicues as it would bear. Eliza signed beneath in her usual neat, no-nonsense script.

Ann came, disguising her expanding belly as best she could beneath a shawl.

'Be a boy this time,' said Edward confidently.

'An' mek sure as we christen our Ann wi' 'im an' all,' said his wife severely. 'What if 'er died an' couldna go to 'Eaven? Worritin' me to death, it is.' But she smiled and linked her arm into that of her husband all the same.

And John squeezed his bride to him to intimate the joy they would have in producing a tribe of their own.

'We s'll mek a Firm,' he said. 'John Kirby an' Sons, Builders.' And he hummed a line of a song, the words silent.

> 'Oh, a winsome wench an' willin',
> She is just the one for me.'

Eliza who, if she had heard the words, would not have been displeased, smiled with contentment. The world lay at their feet.

Printed in Great Britain
by Amazon